NO OTHER WOMAN

NO OTHER WOMAN

NO OTHER

BOOK TWO

HEATHER GRAHAM

No Other Woman
Paperback Edition

Wolfpack Publishing
1707 E. Diana Street
Tampa, FL 33609

www.wolfpackpublishing.com

No Other Woman was originally published in 1996 by Heather Graham writing as Shannon Drake.

Paperback ISBN 979-8-89567-705-6
Ebook ISBN 979-8-89567-704-9

To Jody Cabot with many thanks and to all the folks at Crow Haven Corner

THE DOUGLASES OF CRAIG ROCK

- David Douglas (1799-1875)
  - m. Mary, Lady Argyle (1810-1850)
  - m. Flying Sparrow (1827-1856) "Kathryn"

- David Douglas
  - b. 1837, presumed dead buried 1870

- Andrew "Hawk" Douglas b. 1840
  - m. Sea of Star (1847-1872)
  - m. Skylar Connor, b. 1853
  - Little Hawk died in infancy 1872

NO OTHER WOMAN

PROLOGUE

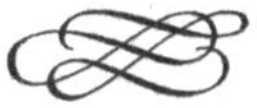

TO DEAL WITH THE DEVIL

Grayfriar Castle, commonly known as Castle Rock, The Highlands— Fall, 1870

David awoke instantly at the faint scratching sound at the ancient stone window leading from the master's chamber to the fortress balcony beyond. The years of warfare in America—not to mention the lessons he had learned among his brother's people, the Sioux—had left him with the ability to awaken instantly at even the slightest shift in the breeze.

He half opened his eyes and saw her there before he heard her sultry whisper, a siren's call, on the air.

"David?"

She was framed in the window, caught by starlight and the faint glimmer of firelight now lying low within the hearth, a slender, perfect young form hugged by the wind and the silky garment she wore, clinging to the wondrous dips and curves of her body. Her long hair, as black as India ink, flowed in the night breeze as well, sweeping around her.

Instinct had awakened him.

And instinct aroused him.

Yet he was ever cautious of the lady, for they had certainly clashed on many an occasion over the years. Most often, he had enjoyed taunting her. One day, he thought, he would challenge her airs and independence, and the arrogance with which she had come to greet him more and more with the passing of time. They lived in the modem world, of course. But by the old standards that continued to mean so much in the Highlands, he was the overlord here, and she seemed to resent it. No matter. Both of their clans and family septs had lived in and near Craig Rock for hundreds of years. He was the heir to all the Douglas of Castle Rock holdings while she had inherited the MacGinnis title and properties at her father's death, three years ago.

She took it all very seriously.

But then, he'd had the opportunity to know a different life as well, to travel over much of the world, even fight other men's battles with them. She knew their Highland world and little more. He'd known ladies, maids, countesses, and whores. She'd been protected by the MacGinnises and all their septs, for it was most important that their heiress marry well. He'd done his honorable best to remember her position each time she had regally taunted him, but she was certainly not a child anymore, and he was quite sure she knew full well just what effect she was capable of having upon a man. He had threatened often enough to teach her a few lessons if she did not take care, and he was not sure himself just how far he would take his threats.

And now...

She tiptoed softly down the stone steps, nearing his bed to watch him sleep. Yet, as she paused, staring down upon him, he reached suddenly for her wrist, startling her so that she nearly cried out.

Yet she composed herself.

"David!" She whispered his name fervently, her Highland burr soft and sweet, tempered by hours with stem tutors, yet still there, for it seemed that no amount of study of what was deemed as "proper" elocution could ever truly hide away a Highlander's burr.

"Aye, lass, whom might you be expecting in my bed? And if you haven't come planning on joining me here, I would suggest that you leave quickly and not visit your overlaird in the dead of night while he lies sleeping naked in his bed."

She snatched her hand free, indignant and regal in the firelight that burned softly from the hearth.

"David, I need to speak with you."

"What interesting apparel you have chosen for a conversation!" he told her, rising upon his elbows to better survey her. Her gown might have been chosen for a trousseau, for a wedding night, in fact. The fabric seemed to shimmer. Even the soft firelight passed cleanly through it. "And what an intriguing time and place you have chosen for a talk."

"I do not choose to talk here!" she informed him. "It is just so difficult to reach you at times. Come with me now to the stables. You must do as I ask."

He arched a brow. "Must I? Come to my office tomorrow, Shawna MacGinnis."

He started to roll away from her, angry, realizing that he really shouldn't be terribly surprised to see her here tonight. He had received documented proof that day of criminal activity by her kin. He had threatened earlier in the day to bring charges against her foolhardy young cousin, Alistair, for siphoning Douglas funds into his own bank account. He'd no intention of doing it—a sound discussion with young Alistair would surely suffice. But still, Alistair's crimes might well bring about a heavy sentence before the law, and for once, her ladyship was truly in a position where she needed Douglas mercy.

He should have been forewarned then.

Right then and there.

But he had no reason to suspect any truly evil intention from the lady.

She was here, swallowing her pride, because she was "The MacGinnis of Craig Rock." Titular head of her family. Alistair would never have met him face-to-face to argue or to fight. He knew he would have lost. Exposure to the lawless American West had taught David Douglas what fencing lessons given by the finest French swordsmen might have overlooked, and he was an expert in any battle of weapons or fists. At times Alistair was reckless, but he was no fool.

Had he put Shawna up to this?

And just what exactly did the lady intend?

Her fingers touched David's naked shoulder. "David, you arrogant aristocrat! I must talk with you. I am begging you, please!"

He paused, rolling back to her, not so much struck with sympathy for her plight as he was intrigued with just how much she was willing to risk in the name of family honor.

"Please!" she whispered again.

He sighed. "Get out, girl. I'll be along."

"You'll tell no one?"

"I know of no other fool awake at this hour."

She spun around, her grace, youth, and beauty highlighted by the crimson firelight. She hurried silently back to the window. He watched her, wondering how many times through the years his ancestors had welcomed their lovers so, for to those who knew the way, an enclosure along the balcony wall led to a secret stairway that ran below the rock and the wall to the forest that lay southward of the castle. It was said the Bonnie Prince Charlie once escaped his would-be captors by way of Castle Rock. Shawna knew of it, he realized, because he had once teasingly invited her to his chambers by way of it.

Well, she had come now.

He rose and found his velvet robe hanging on the hook by the door and wrapped himself in it and nothing more. If she'd come half-naked to his room, he wasn't going to dress formally for an assignation out in the stables. Did she mean to beg and plead and seduce his mercy? She'd have done better, he determined somewhat angrily, to come to him honestly and ask that he drop the charges against her cousin. But then, if she was convinced that she was so powerful—let her have her way. When she was done, he'd tell her that he'd never intended to bring the law against young Alistair.

The stables to which she had referred lay beyond the castle walls. The structure was large and long with a roof made of thatch. At one end was a room where the stable master had slept in ancient times. A wooden bunk remained at the right rear corner of the room, hay was stored to the left, and a desk with ledgers took up most of the space.

The light of a small lantern created a ghostly dance along the walls, ceiling, and floor as he entered, and even against the silky fabric of her all-but-sheer nightdress. She awaited him by the desk. He could see she'd planned the tryst. A silver tray with two goblets of wine sat by her side. She offered him one. He took it, then waited, not offering her a word of encouragement.

"It's very good wine," she said. He thought she seemed angry yet also determined not to betray her true feelings—or her cause.

He nodded. "Get to it, girl. What is it you want? Why have you awakened me in the middle of the night?"

"You know why. You mustn't prosecute Alistair."

"Why not? He's a thieving young rascal who needs a good lesson."

She swallowed a large mouthful of wine. He was touched by the inner struggle she seemed to be experiencing. If he weren't so irritated with this pretense of hers, he'd be tempted to take her tenderly in his arms and whisper assurances to her.

Because she was an extremely beautiful woman. Shawna was pure fire, inside and outside, a fascinating tempest. As reckless as young Alistair, but fiercely proud of being a MacGinnis, loyal to her family—softening only in her love of children and helpless little animals. It was dangerous to give to Shawna. She saw too clearly her own power in all that she might hold.

She set her wineglass down upon the desk and pressed his glass to his lips, urging him to drink. He swallowed several sips of the wine. It was a fruity, rich wine, odd-tasting, and not much to his liking, and not from his own cellars, he was certain. Had they scoured the wine cellars of Castle MacGinnis, looking for this particular quite potent burgundy?

If she was trying to get him drunk on wine, she had quite a task ahead of her. How intriguing. Men were supposed to seduce sweet young damsels by plying them with an intoxicating beverage. Maybe she was trying to dull her own senses. She herself was drinking the wine as if it were water. Her eyes were on his. They fell. She reached for his glass, and he allowed her to set it beside her own. She brought her hands to his face, cupping it. Then her palms fell to the V of his robe, her fingers teasing his flesh before her hands pressed flat against it.

He'd known for a long time that she was beautiful. And desirable.

He'd never imagined what such an intimate touch could do to him.

Heat raked him. Muscles spasmed within him. By sheer will alone he kept her from realizing the extent of the tremors she had sent racing through him. Yet, if she stood any closer...

"You mustn't prosecute Alistair."

"Why mustn't I prosecute him?"

"Because he is young and foolish," she whispered.

"That's all?" he asked harshly. "I mustn't prosecute him? What have I to gain for my magnanimity?"

"I've asked you here so that we can discuss it," she reminded him.

A nasty possibility having dawned on him, he reached behind her, switching wineglasses as he handed one to her and kept one himself.

"I see. We're making a trade. I give you something, you give me something. A bargain—sealed in wine."

"Must you be so hateful?"

"Must you be so ridiculously hypocritical? You came half-naked to my room. You want to bargain. Bargain," he told her, taking a sip of wine.

"Bastard!" she hissed beneath her breath, then realized he heard her. He watched as she quickly lifted her wineglass to her lips, taking a sip.

She was definitely nervous. Her sip became a long swallow. He took her glass and set it down once again with his. If she'd been attempting to drug him, she'd go out before he did, for certain. It was time to get down to basics.

"Bargain, Lady MacGinnis. Just what is it you've got to offer?"

"I'll marry you," she told him quickly.

He laughed out loud. He could see that he'd offended her. Apparently, her pride overruled her intent, and she raised a hand to strike him. He caught her wrist before the blow could fall, but her words spilled from her furiously.

"David Douglas, how dare you—"

"Shawna MacGinnis, my homes and lands are far richer than yours. I've been offered the daughters of counts, earls, dukes, immensely rich merchants, and even the lovely offspring of an Indian chief or two. I will marry for no bargain."

No matter how tempting you may be, my beauty, he thought, turning from her to start from the stables.

But her anger was not so great that she did not attempt to waylay him, placing a hand upon his shoulder. He stood still, his back still turned to her. "Nay, you cannot leave, David!" she cried softly.

A smile she couldn't see curved his lips, but he spoke harshly. "You've something else to offer?" he demanded, annoyed when he heard his words somewhat slurred. He blinked as it seemed the earth wavered for a moment as well. But then she spoke again, distracting him.

"I—" she began, and he could hear her biting down on her teeth as she fought now to control both her pride and her temper. "I—damn you, I offer whatever it is you might want. It doesn't have to be marriage. I—I can—surely, you must feel something for me?"

Indeed, he did. And in turning back to her, he found that she was so close she was almost standing on top of him. There was a clean, floral, haunting scent to her hair, the scent of lilac to her flesh. Half in anger, half in longing, he set his arms about her, pulling her close. Letting her know how dangerously she played. Letting her feel the extent of his arousal. Letting her feel...

Oh god, what was he doing to himself!

Harsh, bitter words formed on his lips. He meant to tell her to guard her own honor more tightly, her cousin was a fool, but a fool he'd not punish before the law.

Yet something goaded him, and he could not give the truth to her so easily. "This does grow more and more intriguing. However, I wouldn't want to accept anything blindly. Is it your intent, then," he demanded angrily, "to show me something of what I am being offered?"

"Aye, something!"

"What?" he demanded.

"Something—of what you desire to see!" she exploded, aggravated. She tried to pull free, taut with fury. He shook her once, staring at her hard.

"Let's be more specific. What?" he repeated icily.

"Something—of me!" she cried furiously.

"Know what you're doing, girl!"

"I—" she began but broke off. He should have let her go then. Walked away. Left the stables. Dealt with her and her kin come morning.

"Leave me be, Shawna," he warned her sharply. "Don't seek to bargain when you've not—"

"Wait! I do intend to—to give you everything I've offered," she insisted, yet she gasped again as he jerked her closer, hard against his body.

Her eyes were on his, her lips were parted in surprise at the feel of him, and he found her so tempting that he crushed his mouth down upon hers, his tongue parting her lips. God, but she was lush, breasts so full, firm against his chest, legs lithe as they pressed against his. He groaned, just slightly lifting his lips from hers, aware of a dizziness pervading his body, yet making every sensation all the more acute.

He felt...too much.

Yet not enough. Something was wrong. It didn't matter.

His hunger was too great. The sensations were too strong. His sex throbbed against the juncture of her thighs. He looked down at her face to find it pale, her eyes closed. Her lips remained just slightly parted, inviting his in return. He threaded his fingers into the lustrous black mane of her hair. Found her mouth again.

He picked her up while he still had strength to do so. He stumbled to the wooden bunk against the wall, falling onto it with her. His head spun, but his body hungered. The smell of fresh hay seemed to fill the room, then the sweet scent of lilac soap and a woman's flesh.

"Wait...!" she gasped.

Wait? When his heartbeat thundered throughout the length and breadth of his body? When he ached with a longing that seemed to tear into his flesh and his soul? There could be no waiting. It seemed incredible now that he had ever intended merely to hear her out—and leave.

"David?"

He was aware that she whispered his name, that she suddenly sounded confused and uncertain. And in some dim recess of his mind, he remembered that he had switched the glasses, that they had both drunk from a glass filled with wine intended only for him.

Filled with...

So sweet and potent a vintage that it did not matter. Nothing mattered.

No matter what either of them had actually intended.

"Perhaps the bargain is met," he told her.

Nay, hold back! some sense within him warned.

But he could not.

The momentum of the sensations sweeping into him was overwhelming. The scent and feel and taste of her filled him.

The world became a blur.

Of hunger.

Of feelings so acute.

Of desire so fierce that it had become like a flame, destroying his ability to think.

A sound, he heard a sound, a whisper on the air behind him and then...

Pain!

Shocking pain, striking him so suddenly. Sharp, horrible, excruciating, at the back of his head. Sensation that had been unbearably sweet was now unbearably vicious. Staggering.

Paralyzing.

He thought he saw her. Her eyes, sky blue above his. Her face. Angelic in its beauty.

Then the bitter realization hit him. The MacGinnises never would have confronted him face-to-face. They knew his temper, his sense of honor—and his strength.

Just as they had known his weakness. Shawna.

Oh god, never again.

No, never, for seduction had not been their true intent, he saw with startling clarity. Their true intent had been murder.

Suddenly he realized that the burning pain in his skull had been caused by something other than the blow to his head.

He was surrounded by heat.

And fire.

Oh god, yes. Fire! Flames, shooting all around him. And he couldn't move, couldn't twist or turn, he could only feel the bursting agony within his head. He could see nothing except for the shooting red tongues of flame that rose against the blackness.

No, more.

He could see what a fool he had been. And that he had been betrayed. Oh god, yes, with what must be his dying breath, he could see so clearly what a fool he had been and that she...

Aye, she had damned him. To all the fires of hell.

Horses neighed and shrieked. From somewhere in the darkness of a never-ending pit, he heard her, heard her screams, rising, sweeping, tearing from her throat...

Then, despite the flames and the heat, darkness began to encompass him. The void of death would come to claim him before the searing fires of hell and damnation reached out to fire his soul again...

Blackness settled upon him.

And all around him the flames continued to rise, until the crackle of the blaze rose to a roar.

And the fire consumed the night.

CHAPTER 1

Castle Rock, The Highlands—Fall, 1875

Night had fallen. Mist was rising over the moors, and a strange golden moon sat high in the night sky. Shawna could see the moon through one of the ancient arrow slits in the tower office wall as it played a spectacular game of hide-and-seek with the clouds. It was a fey moon, glorious, mysterious, the type that gave the Highlands a reputation for strange powers, a hint of magic, a haunting beauty.

She should have been asleep, but Mark Menzies had sent her a message, begging a moment of her time when his work was done. She sat behind the giant oak desk in the office, listening intently to his words. He was the foreman of the coal miners and a good, fine man.

"The men will not go into the left tunnel, milady. They are convinced that there is evil within."

Shawna nodded. She well understood his words. They were all Christians in this parish in the Highlands, but they were a people quick to believe in the power of myth and spirits, and she wouldn't force any man to work against his fear. The mining business was dangerous enough without adding a man's spiritual torment to the brew. "Perhaps," she suggested, "the men will not be so uncomfortable if we have the Reverend Massey bless the opening of the new shaft..."

"Perhaps," Mark said without conviction. "They claim they hear hangings and the like. They think that something dangerous may reside within the earth, something we don't know so well as men, don't understand, and should not taunt." He was a big man, broad-shouldered, craggy-faced, with gray-dusted long hair and lines grooved into a face made handsome by integrity and pride. Shawna had liked him all her life. She had only come to know him well in the last five years. What the people in this part of the Highlands referred to as the Fire had taken place five years ago. Laird Douglas's elder son David had died in it, and the laird had begun to spend more time in America, placing his castle and his lands in the care of the MacGinnis clan. Traditionally, though the Douglas laird had held the greatest wealth and power in the area, his distant MacGinnis kinsmen had been his right-hand men. When the Douglases were unable or unavailable to lead, the MacGinnises did so in their stead.

The night of the Fire, however, had changed everything. It had, perhaps, changed her more than anyone or anything else. She had remained at Craig Rock—the walled village in which both Castle MacGinnis and Castle Craig stood—in horror and misery for some months after the terrible night, then had fled to Glasgow. But she'd been home now for nearly four years, and during the last two years she had asserted herself as the head of the MacGinnis clan and taken a hand in the affairs of Craig Rock. The recent death of the elderly Laird Douglas had further altered the situation. While Laird Douglas had left an heir—his younger son, Andrew—that young man was half-Sioux and deeply embroiled in the affairs of his own country. Shawna knew that Andrew's heart remained in the American West and the wild terrain of his mother's own "savage" people. When he had asked her to continue to manage the Douglas estate for him, she had agreed to do so. As "the MacGinnis," the Lady of the clan, she had responsibilities to the people who lived and worked on MacGinnis as well as Douglas land. Although she had many male relatives—her great-uncles and cousins and second cousins—the title and the MacGinnis property, which bordered that of the Douglases, had become hers upon her father's death. She'd been young at the time and had been willing then to take her lead from her great-uncle Gawain. Then the night of David's death had nearly destroyed her. The months following his demise had been hell. But she had discovered in Glasgow that there was no running away from oneself, and there was nowhere in the world like home—especially when home was the Highlands.

"We all fall prey to superstition now and then," Shawna said with a smile. "It's part of our character as a people, part of our charm, in my opinion," she told him, ruefully grinning. "We are near the Night of the Moon Maiden, when the November orb rises full and the demons may fall upon the virtuous lasses if they don't take care. Once, it was a time to fear, and now we do our best to celebrate and feast. Mark, you and I know that there are no ghosts, goblins, pookas, or the like living in the mines. We must convince the men that the banging is some natural occurrence, as we know that it must be. But tell me, have you spoken to my great-uncle Gawain about this problem?" she asked.

Mark nodded. "I'm afraid your great-uncle does not understand the hearts of men as you do, my lady. Gawain says that I should tell the lads to work the tunnel or forget their pay. You know as well as I that the men must have their money in order to live."

"Aye, I know."

In Shawna's opinion, there was no place more beautiful on all the earth than the Highlands of Scotland. No place wilder, more unique, finer. But the Highlands were losing her people. Industrialization was causing them to desert the lands they struggled to farm and to seek better livings in the cities. Still, the Highlanders remained fiercely bound to their families, and many stayed because they were responsible to older parents, injured relatives, or young children. Many stayed as well because the Highlands were home as no place else could be.

"The blessing of the coal mines is that so many may live on account of them," Shawna told Mark. "We must make the men feel it is quite safe to work. As safe as we can make mining, that is. Well, I shall see to it that the Reverend Massey comes out first thing in the morning. I'll talk to the men."

"And to Gawain? He is distraught already that you have set limits upon the time the children may work."

Shawna nodded without saying anything. Gawain did not much appreciate her interference with what he considered men's affairs. She didn't want to fight her great-uncle, and she didn't want to hurt him, but she was determined to have her say in how the mining business was conducted. "Leave it to me, Mark Menzies. I will see you, and the men, tomorrow at the site."

"Thank you."

He rose to leave; even as he stood, the office door banged open, and Gawain strode into the room.

In his late fifties, this younger brother of her grandfather remained a tall, broad-shouldered, able, and powerful man. His dark MacGinnis hair was still only peppered with gray, falling long and thickly to his shoulders. He dressed in the Highland manner, kilted each day, and Shawna could well imagine him as one of the war chieftains of old, entering into ruthless combat with any enemy who dared threaten the sanctity of their homeland. He was a fierce man, bound strictly to the land. He knew how to wrest the best crops from their land, how to raise the best cattle. He was equally able as a businessman, and though Shawna was titular head of the family, it was the nineteenth century, and she, Gawain, her other great-uncle, Lowell, and her cousins Alistair, Alaric, and Aidan were all involved in managing the family's interests.

"Ah, Uncle," Shawna murmured. "You're in good time. Mark has come to talk to me about the new shaft. I've suggested that we could have a service—"

Gawain waved a hand impatiently. "Put on whatever pretty show you must, my dear. Menzies, you shouldn't bother Shawna with these difficulties, man, you should be coming to me."

"Beggin' your pardon, sir—" Mark began, but again, Gawain waved a hand in the air.

"The matter is settled for the moment then, eh? Get on with you then, Menzies, back to your own doings if you will, I'm a busy man, and I need a moment with my niece."

"Aye, then, tomorrow, Lady MacGinnis," Menzies said, and quickly quit the office.

"That was quite rude," Shawna commented.

Gawain merely replied, “I’ve other matters of greater importance at the moment.”

“Such as?”

Gawain tossed a letter down upon the table. Shawna looked at her great-uncle, arching a brow. “Take a look, girl. It’s from America.”

Shawna picked up the letter and saw the American postal marks on it. She started to read, but Gawain’s hands landed suddenly on the desk, and her eyes were drawn to his. Blue, like her own. There was a startling resemblance among MacGinnis family members. Ink-black hair with an exceptional cobalt gloss and startling blue eyes marked them almost irrefutably as MacGinnises. Family members had, as well, high, cleanly-defined black brows and a way of lifting them that connected them all as kin.

“Read!” Gawain commanded, his “r” rolling especially deeply with his irritation.

She knew instantly, of course, that it was from Andrew Douglas. As she touched the letter, great waves of guilt seemed to wash over her. She had been in a sorry state herself the last time she had seen him, but she would never forget his pain at his brother’s death.

She quickly scanned the words on the paper, trying to keep her fingers from trembling. He had always reminded her a great deal of David. Although Andrew had definitely inherited certain features from his mother’s family, he still looked like a Douglas and had his father’s build. The brothers had been of the same height and muscle structure, both of them like lions, so powerfully built, so sleek, so agile. Capable of great courtesy—and great violence, she believed, if thwarted.

If known to have been betrayed.

Every word of this letter was polite and courteous. Andrew was coming to Craig Rock. He didn’t know how long he would be staying, nor exactly when he would be arriving. She wasn’t to make any changes in the management of the estates. She had done so well in his absence thus far. She was not to vacate the master’s chambers of Castle Rock, nor depart that residence for Castle MacGinnis. He had recently married again and was happy to be attended by his new wife and friends on his trip to his father’s ancestral home. “If you’ve kept up with newspaper accounts of events in America, you will be aware as well that my mother's people are involved in disputes with the American government. As this makes my own plans rather complicated to say the least, and since I might have to leave Scotland at any time, I especially hope you will not be inconvenienced by my return. I am, at the moment, visiting as any traveler from America and beg you not to be put out by my arrival. I look forward to seeing you."

Recalling that Andrew's first wife, a Sioux woman, had perished from disease a couple of years ago, Shawna looked up at Gawain with a pleased smile. "He has married again. I'm so delighted."

Gawain exploded with impatience. "Delighted? Why, in God's name? Now he can produce little brown savages to come and make claim to the property here!"

"Douglas property has never been ours, though we prosper from it."

"Douglas property should justly fall to you. Andrew Douglas—is he called Laird Hawk, I wonder?—has no dealings here. He's American and half-savage to boot. He should have stayed with his mother's kith and kin, his bows and arrows and buffalo! He should have lived and died on his savage plain, and the property should have rightly fallen to us."

"Uncle, it is his property."

"Aye—his property. But hundreds of years ago, my dear girl, before Robert the Bruce, Highlanders defied what would have been the rule of conquering English kings, and they kept these Highlands free by the sheer brutal force of their fighting power. Douglas and MacGinnis came together then, locked in wedlock, so it was said, and as it has always been, if the Douglas line should die out, then the property goes —by law—to the ancient Douglas kin. The MacGinneses."

"Uncle Gawain, Laird Hawk Douglas seems to be quite alive and well in America."

Gawain didn't seem to hear her. "Trouble in America!" he muttered. "Aye, the Americans intend to decimate their redmen. Their newspapers talk continually of great confrontations. Andrew Douglas should be caught in such a confrontation before he gets a chance to breed!"

Shawna shook her head in amazement. "Uncle, he's a young man who has probably taken a young bride, and I wouldn't doubt that another generation of Douglases of Craig Rock might already be on the way."

"Andrew Douglas is an American, but I have worked and breathed life into this land for all my years."

"When the late Laird Douglas had his heart broken here and returned to America, I promised to care for his property in his absence—as your tradition would have it. But we also agreed to take on the additional work in order to create more wealth for the MacGinnis family," Shawna said quietly. "And God knows, after the night of the Fire, we haven't really the right—"

Andrew slammed a fist on the table, staring at her. "You challenge an act of God, Shawna MacGinnis?"

"Did God suggest I lure David to the stables?" she asked softly.

She thought for a moment that her great-uncle was going to strike her, he looked at her so furiously.

"The Fire, girl," he bit out, "was an act of God. And if you'd drag your whole family down to wallow in self-pity, then God should have taken you in that inferno as well!"

"I don't believe that the Fire was an act of God," she said determinedly.

"Are, you accusing me of setting the Fire? I tell you, girl, I did not!" Gawain declared, his eyes narrowed in fury. "And what is more, the authorities came, specialists all the way from Edinburgh—at the request of your Laird Hawk Douglas, if you'll recall. No arson was proven, lass."

"Then what did happen?"

Gawain planted his hands on the desk and stared into her eyes. "An act of God!" he said with firm fury.

She stared at her great-uncle, shaken by his vehemence. Gawain felt no remorse for David's death, but at least she was convinced of his innocence as far as the Fire went. Perhaps he could put that night behind him. She had tried to do so but could not. It would haunt her until the day she died.

"Would it have been more convenient for you if I had died in the Fire as well?" she queried.

He exploded again with an oath of impatience. "Good God, lass, that you could accuse me so! But the night is past, and your kin live, and these miners live, and two hundred souls make their livings on these lands. If you want to be part and parcel of the future of Craig Rock, then you must get beyond the past. And live for the future."

Shawna watched him and nodded slowly. She looked back at the letter on the desk once again. "I wonder why he is coming now."

"Well, that, girl, I cannot tell you," Gawain said, his arms crossed over his chest as he stared down at her where she sat in the chair. "Or perhaps I can tell you. Every fool one of us sent condolences to him at his father's death. He must have got the idea that he should come home and claim his property, though God knows what he'd rightfully be doing here, or why any MacGinnis would express concern that he come. Unless someone has a different reason for wantin' him here," Gawain mused. "But be forewarned that he is due. Due—with his new wife and 'friends.' A pack of violent, heathen, dangerous savages, I imagine."

"Uncle, Andrew Douglas may be half-Sioux, but he is an intelligent and extremely well-educated man. Whatever his beliefs, he's certainly not a heathen. He mourned his brother's death with what we could certainly consider to be Christian anguish—"

"And demanded an inquest and had us all with our throats bared to the hangman, girl. I had thought that we were well and good done with him." He wagged a finger beneath her nose and warned, "You keep your wits about you, Shawna MacGinnis."

"I'll certainly do my best," she murmured dryly.

"You think before you open your mouth, eh?"

"What could I tell him, Uncle Gawain? What in bloody hell do I know?" she demanded angrily.

"Don't talk to me in that tone, girl."

She knew he didn't like her tone. He didn't like the entire conversation, especially her references to the events of the night of the Fire. Those events had been swept into the dark recesses of their minds.

Coming back now, it seemed, to haunt them all.

"You provided the wine, Uncle," she reminded him with sudden quiet determination.

He stared at her for a long, hard moment.

"Aye, lass, I provided the wine. You were confident you could charm the man to sleep. We needed the documentation of your fool cousin's thievery. I tell you this—I didn't want the man dead."

After all this time, she was startled by the pain that could still seize her. "Then who did?"

"It was a fire, girl, a sad, pathetic thing, nothing more. Have y'not heard a word I've said all night? The Fire was an act of God! And don't you go letting the Douglas make more of it, do you be understandin' me, girl?"

He didn't wait for her reply but exited the office in a blur of MacGinnis plaid.

When he was gone, Shawna looked down at the letter again, and at her fingers, which were still trembling. She let out an oath of impatience at herself. There was brandy in the lower right-hand corner of the desk. She pulled it out and started to search the drawer for a glass. She gave up the search, taking a long swallow straight from the bottle. It seared her throat but warmed her body deliciously. She started to drink more.

She was nervous. When she was nervous, she drank far too quickly.

Just as she had drunk far too quickly the night of the Fire.

She swore again, standing up. She was going to go to bed. She was glad that Andrew "Hawk" Douglas had married again and found solace when he had no one left on the Douglas side of his family. She'd done well with his people and his estates. He owed her his thanks.

Even if she had passed out, drugged, just moments before his brother had died...

She left the office. The castle was quiet as she hurried to the master's chambers.

Once there, she paused. Sometimes, she still wondered what she was doing here, in Castle Rock. Specifically, in the master's chambers.

But the administration of the castle, the properties, and the mines had always been done from Castle Rock. To be lady here, it was necessary for her to live where the people expected their lady to live. And as to the master's chambers, if she was to make her claim to the title of lady within her own family, it was necessary as well that she command the master's space as her own.

Sometimes, still, she shivered to be here.

And sometimes, the pain was oddly poignant. She could remember David clearly. Remember him here. Remember his touch.

She wasn't going to dwell on the past, she determined with an anger that belied the very sentiment.

She shed her clothing and climbed into her nightdress. She was tired, exhausted.

She lay down, praying for sleep.

It was a long time coming.

Yet when she slept at last, she dreamed. Nightmare images flooded her mind.

It seemed that she had barely closed her eyes before she awoke with a start, choking back the scream that had risen in her throat from the force of her dream. In it she had been running in the hills, aware that she was being chased, terrified of what would come at the end of it. When she looked back at her pursuers, all she could see were shadows in the mist.

Like shadows, her pursuers were strange, constantly moving shapes, ever-changing as they came ceaselessly closer and closer.

They might have been selkies, creatures of myth and magic, beasts that could shed their coats and adopt human forms. But they were still dangerous creatures, for they remained beasts inside.

They had kept coming and coming, silent as they ran over the green-carpeted hills. Coming closer, closer, encircling her. They hadn't been selkies at all. Rather, they had been strange human beings, half-naked, bronze and copper in color, wielding axes, hatchets, bows and arrows. They'd been adorned in feathers, and in her dream, she had known that they were savages from America, that they had come for vengeance. The mist continued to swirl all around them, then from that mist there stepped another man, this one clad in Highland colors, kilted and broached, his sword in his scabbard, his dirk set into the sheath at his calf. This one walked straight toward her, this one stared straight into her eyes, and he knew her, knew the truth of all that had happened, and it was then that the scream rose in her throat...

Until she awoke. Hot, yet shivering, her heart beating quickly within her chest.

She rose, trying to calm that racing beat, to slow her breathing.

Dear God, but she was shaken tonight!

She smiled mockingly at herself as she walked to the window, looking out upon the mist-shrouded night. Naturally, she was having nightmares. The new Laird Douglas was coming to Scotland to see to his affairs. Andrew Douglas—Hawk—to those who knew him well. A man who was half American Indian. Her dreams might well be filled with vengeful savages, eager to learn the truth.

What was the truth?

That question had plagued her for five years now, during the time right after the Fire when she had stayed, the time when she had ran to Glasgow, the time when she had returned. And now, knowing that David's brother was coming back, she was starting to live with the nightmare again.

Because she had lured David to his death.

Oh god, not intentionally!

As angry as she might occasionally get with her family, she loved them all. Gawain, Lowell, Alaric, Aidan—and Alistair. Alistair especially, perhaps. He and she were so close in age. They had always been friends. But she'd never meant harm to David, even for Alistair's sake. Her kin had needed time, only time, and she had meant to give them that. But it had been time itself that had betrayed her in the end. Fate had played her cruelly. The only good to come of it was that she would never be so innocent again, never so malleable.

Nor, she thought, would she ever live without the nightmares.

She suddenly felt as if she had to escape the confines of the castle, the heavy stone walls that surrounded her.

The shimmer of moonlight on the loch seemed to beckon her. She slipped her white-fringed shawl from the hook by her door, sweeping it around her. She quietly opened her door and stepped barefoot from her room.

This is madness, she thought. She was like some poor fey creature, rushing out to see the moonglow on the water when it was well past midnight. She told herself firmly that she couldn't run away from the past, the future, or the nightmares.

Still, the urge was with her. She needed to get out. She ran down the steps to the hall.

The great hall of Castle Rock was empty. She stood on the last step for a moment, surveying it. The great hall at Castle Rock had been much the same for centuries. A massive table in the center, carved hardwood chairs around it, and tall-backed chairs facing the hearth that ran at least half the length of the far wall. The stones that comprised the walls were ancient. What ghosts might linger here, she wondered, then shook off the fanciful thought. The hall was simply caught in the stillness that came with the night. The world itself was quiet.

She hurried out the massive wooden doors to the courtyard, through the high gates, and down the slope of rich, verdant grasses toward the loch. Ahead of her loomed the massive Druid Stones.

CHAPTER 2

Though the mist was rising, moonglow fell upon the earth, illuminating the ragged cliffs, the rocks, the sweeping plains and vales of the landscape. Soft light, countered by shadow, fell upon the shimmering loch, where again, great cliffs rose on either side of the shoreline in the central valley.

The night was warm for November in the Highlands, quiet and still. Then the man rose from the water, alone and as naked as the bare rock surrounding him, a man as hard and unyielding as that same rock in shape and form, bred and born to the harsh and beautiful tors and craigs of the land around him. His was both a wild and rugged breed of men, a people who had stood their ground for centuries, battled, won and lost, and even into the present day, preserved both honor and individuality. Like many of his ancestors, he had suffered at the hands of the treacherous. And again, like many of those who had come before him, he had survived the malicious intent of others and come back a more powerful and wary man.

Indeed, he was back.

Laird of all his land.

But none knew it. So far, he mused, he was king of the night. His castle was a cave.

His choice.

For now.

He stood, shaking back a thick length of dark hair. Despite the unseasonable warmth, it was cold enough for him to shiver fiercely, and long for the warmth of his clothing.

Yet he paused, staring upward, suddenly not noticing the chill that assailed him, for from where he had risen from the loch he was given an excellent view of the countryside. Castle Rock to his far right upon the highest cliff, Castle MacGinnis to his far left, both commanding great sweeps of the landscape. Indeed, neither was a manor that would be much coveted by modern standards. Both structures had been built long ago, when Highland lairds had determined to take Norman architecture and use it to their own purposes. When William the Conqueror had seized England and looked to Scotland, wary chieftains had seized upon the talented Norman stonemasons instead, and thus had risen these structures. The years had added hidden alleyways and priests' nooks, since religious wars had been waged and Jacobite princes had had to be hidden, but very little had been done to add the modern concepts of comfort and beauty to the strongholds. Castle Rock was the older of the two edifices, standing upon the highest tor and overlooking the largest amount of property. It was grander in scale, the seat of the Douglases of Castle Rock, a fortress of unique historical significance.

Castle Rock was his.

And he had come to reclaim it.

Yet even as he stared at the castle, he looked at what remained of the old stables, and a fire began to burn within him as fiercely as the inferno which had raged that night five long years ago. He could remember the heat.

And he could remember her.

The whispers, the pleas, the promises, that had brought him to destruction. The ebony of her hair, splayed out upon the bunk. The ivory silk of her flesh, the sky-blue promise in her eyes. He remembered her arms around him, her fevered words. A mint freshness in the warmth of her breath against his lips as she whispered her lies, the fire within her that made him heedless of the warmth igniting around him until he turned, too late...

...and entered into a world of damnation.

Ah, but miraculously, he was back. From the dead. A demon returned from the fires of hell to discover the truth.

She'd not been in it alone. And he'd come back as he had with no word or warning because he intended to know just what had happened, just who had been involved with her. And they would all be made to repent.

Ah...but she would be the first from whom he would demand justice for the past.

She would be the first...

THE NIGHT AIR of autumn was beautiful, crisp, and clear against her cheeks and flesh. It felt good to be out and good to run. She mocked herself, telling herself again that running in the moonlight probably certified her for madness. It would not help her escape the past. Maybe she just wanted to run away from the future, maybe it would be harder to face Andrew Douglas now than it had been when David had died.

She was accustomed to running over this terrain, riding over it, swimming within the cold waters of the loch, but tonight, she didn't seem to have her usual stamina. She was running from herself because she was...

...guilty.

Not guilty! She had never meant such awful harm to come to David. She had been more than halfway in love with him most of her life. Nay! Oh god, how proud and arrogant she had always been around him! But she had been younger. He had been the great laird. He'd known many women. Easy to admit now that she had been jealous, and therefore as disdainful as she could manage to be at all times.

Until that night.

Well, he was dead and buried, and she was at least partly to blame.

Her lungs were growing sore. Her thoughts were robbing her of breath. Even as she ran, she knew that she had to pause. She stopped at the ancient Druid Stones to catch her breath, inhaling, exhaling, raggedly.

Leaning against the stones, she studied them in the moonlight. There were twelve of them, each stone standing at least ten feet high. Time and exposure had eroded whatever ancient writings might have been upon them, but some of the deep etchings of men, women, and animals remained. The stones were quite beautiful, arranged in a circular pattern, with a thirteenth stone set horizontally in the center, like an altar. Just to the side of it was a circular stone weighing a good two tons, a stone that still cast shadows from which people could tell the time of day.

Shawna loved the stones. They had all played here as children, she and her cousins as well as the Douglases, though David had been older and only tolerant of their games rather than a part of them. Shawna had wanted the stones to be on MacGinnis property, but they were not. She had made up stories when she was little that changed the events of history and gave the stones to the Clan MacGinnis. David had told her curtly once that she should not be so fond of them. The altar had most probably been used for human sacrifice in ancient times. She should have realized that—since they still celebrated so many of the holidays around the stones.

Christian holidays.

That just happened to coincide with many of the old pagan celebrations of the ancient inhabitants of the Highlands.

She ran her hand over the cool roughness of the tallest stone. The old ways were enchanting. She was grown now, but she still loved the stories and the legends. Yet as she touched the stone, she suddenly became certain that she heard a noise.

A footstep?

One...

...and then another.

Aye, footsteps. Someone else, out in the night.

She moved suddenly and swiftly from one of the stones to the next.

Again, she thought she heard footsteps.

Someone was following her.

Unease swept through her.

In the middle of the night, when all the world lay still, someone was following her. Someone was coming behind her in the night. Someone...

You are losing your mind, she thought. This is madness! She told herself sternly that she had to be imagining the sounds...no one would come after her so furtively in the night. There was no reason to be afraid.

Again, she moved a few steps forward, moving on to a third stone, and paused.

She just barely caught the sound of shuffling feet before those footsteps paused as well.

This was her home. These were her people. She'd never been afraid of the dark. She'd never been afraid here because she knew everyone who lived in and around Castle Rock.

She kept very still, waiting and listening.

Nothing.

She was afraid, imagining things, because of her nightmares, she told herself. She'd been remembering all the stories they had told and all the games they had played by the stones, which were still considered sacred and mystical by many superstitious villagers. She was letting her imagination run away with her.

No.

She had really heard footsteps. Or something. A rustle in the grass. A soft pounding on the earth.

Fear was settling into her.

"Who's there?" she called out in the night.

In answer, the wind seemed to rise, keening suddenly against moonglow and shadow. She waited, pressed now against one of the stones, but she heard nothing else.

No one would come after her. She had no reason to be afraid!

"Answer me!" she said sharply. "Who's there?"

Still nothing.

She pushed away from the stone and started walking once again. This time, she decided to leave the stones behind her. She moved easily, barefoot over the heather toward the shore. The strangest sensation of unease swept along her spine.

There was nothing at first. No sounds of anyone following her.

Then again she heard a rustling.

She turned back.

She saw a shadow, slipping behind one of the stones.

Or did she?

In the night, light and shadows blended. The Druid Stones cast strange lines against the hills and vales. Had she seen movement? Or had the moon shifted and lengthened the eerie play of light and dark that filled the night?

"Who is it? Who's there?" she cried out sharply.

No reply.

Yet there was someone or something in the night. She was convinced of it.

Looking back at the stones, she was suddenly quite certain she was being watched. Icy water seemed to run in rivulets down her neck and spine.

What kind of fool had she been to leave the castle and run into the night? she asked herself. Not a fool, she countered herself passionately. She had known this land all her life, knew the earth, the stone, the loch, the cliffs and hills and rocks.

Through all her life, she had known nothing but security here. She had never known what it was like to be afraid until...

Until the night the Fire had raged. And the kiss of the flame had been burned into her heart forever.

Oh god. That was so long ago.

And this was now.

Happening. In truth.

She barely breathed, studying the stones that stood like silent sentinels on the hill crest.

Again, she heard movement. And this time she cried out in fear.

The shadow was definitely no figment of her imagination. A caped figure was now running directly toward her.

THE NIGHT HAD BEEN SO STILL. When he first heard the cries, he thought that they were whispers of the rising wind. Then he heard them more clearly.

And he saw the woman running from the shelter of the Druid Stones. Saw her clearly, for the moon chose that moment to break free from the clouds and cast a shimmering glow of light down upon her.

She was dressed in ivory cotton and lace, a gown appearing soft and fragile as it flowed behind her on the wind. Like the sheer gown caught on the wind, waves of ebony hair were caught in a banner flow as she ran. She was fleet and agile, running barefoot across the terrain with the grace of a gazelle. She appeared like an ancient wood nymph, a sprite, seductively magical in the mist beneath the moon, that dark hair of hers, appearing blacker than midnight, floating in her wake, rich, wild, as full of a cloak about her shoulders as the soft knit shawl that covered the soft cotton of her gown.

Dear god. Shawna.

Aye, Shawna.

Come to him already...

It seemed that every muscle within his body went suddenly tense, as if a fire, liquid and wickedly hot, ignited within his limbs at the very sight of her.

How often had he dreamed of seeing her again. Of the fury he would feel. Of the longing to reach out and shake her.

Or just touch her. For it seemed that even now, just the sight of her awoke in him a passion that was fueled by both fury...and hunger.

Shawna...

He would not be swayed by emotion. He would be as hard and steadfast in his purpose as the rock with which the castles had been built.

Yet, she came to him still. Here.

How damned curious.

Then he saw that she was being...chased.

Chased!

Indeed, from the stones burst forth another figure, tall, caped, features hidden beneath a cowl.

What in God's name...

He'd be damned if any other man was going to get his hands on the girl. Not when he'd come back from hell itself for his own vengeance.

He crouched instinctively at the water's edge.

And he watched.

And waited...

THIS IS MADNESS.

She'd lived here almost all her life. She was the lady here. She knew not just every soul who resided in their wild hills and valleys, but knew their life histories as well.

Yet she was being chased.

She had to be dreaming, she told herself. However, this was a very realistic dream. She could feel the dew-dampness of the grass beneath her feet, feel the soft caress of the misty night, the movement of her muscles, the chill touch of the wind...

She could hear the gasping of her breath, the rampant pounding of her heart. She could feel the burning sensation in her lungs.

Oh god, wake up.

She couldn't wake up. It wasn't a dream. She could hear and feel now the pounding on the earth behind her as her pursuer gained on her.

Then she stepped down upon a rock. Screamed in startled pain, staggered, fell.

It felt as if a thousand needles were ripping into her foot.

The footsteps were still coming from behind her. Coming harder.

Coming closer.

Running.

Coming after her with sheer menace.

She staggered back up, found her balance. Ran again. She had given him time, allowed him to get closer and closer. She zigzagged, realizing that she had been heading straight for the water.

A good idea, perhaps? She was an excellent swimmer. Yet, where would she swim? It was more than a mile across. Perhaps her pursuer could swim as well, swim, and drag her down...

She heard a strange rasping sound and turned back. In horror, she saw that the dark figure had drawn a sword. She gasped out again, seeing the sword glitter in the moonlight.

Then suddenly, all light was gone. A cloud had scuttled cleanly beneath the moon, and hills and valley both had been cast into total darkness. She swallowed back a cry and spun, terror filling her heart as she raced along the shoreline.

He was behind her. So close she could hear him, almost feel him, smell him. He was going to reach out, touch her. A scream rose in her throat. Exploded from it.

The cloud slipped slightly. The palest light ventured forth upon the night once again. She veered toward the water, gasping, choking...

Then suddenly, out of the strange glow and shadow of the night, a form appeared.

Tall, massive, in the near darkness.

Huge, growing...

A beast coming from the water. Nay, a man. Nay, a demon.

Rising.

A man's form. Towering against the moonlight, dripping, broad-shouldered, formed as hard and solid as a Greek statue that might have been thrust up from the loch.

Naked—save a sword.

A massive, naked form, risen from the water.

She had lost her mind completely.

But the vision didn't go away.

And she could not stop herself. Her momentum was such that she couldn't stop, nor could she veer away. She saw the sudden, startling, impossible form, and then she crashed straight into the man, beast, or demon who had risen like the mist from the water's edge.

He was real. As solid as rock.

She shrieked in terror.

Hands gripped her shoulders. Powerful, rough hands. Cold as ice from the water. Hard pressed against the figure, she could feel muscle and flesh.

She shrieked again, yet before she could fight the steely hold upon her, she found herself cast aside and falling down to the damp softness of the earth.

She tried instinctively to turn as she fell, to watch what was happening, to discover if she was being rescued—or damned.

She had to catch herself, had to fight for herself, if she was going to survive.

But she could not stop her fall.

Her body struck the ground against a cushion of grass. Her head struck a jagged piece of rock.

Sharp pain exploded in her head.

As her vision blurred, she saw the naked figure of the man who had seemed to appear like a selkie or demon from the water quickly raise the sword he carried. His steel sliced the air just split seconds after he had cast her aside.

The hooded figure was upon him already, his sword slashing as well.

Slashing air...

Where she had stood just a breath of time before.

The two came clashing together now in a roar of steel.

She saw that much.

But saw them in mist, everything spinning.

Then dizziness seized her completely.

And she saw nothing but ebony mist engulfing her, blacker than the night.

CHAPTER 3

Oh god, would this wretched nightmare never end? Her head was spinning.

She lay somewhere between sleep and awareness, yet she could not fully awaken.

She was dreaming again, and the dreams were becoming horribly real. She was dreaming that there would be a reckoning. The surviving Douglas was coming from America, bringing his savage kin. He was not so civilized. She lay upon her bed in the ancient master's chamber of Castle Rock, and he and his kind surrounded her. Redmen in vibrant war paint. Feathers protruding from their heads. Their faces garishly colored in crimson, blue, black, their half-naked bodies painted as well. Each carried a weapon, a bow with arrows, a knife, a pistol. Each aimed his weapon at her. One lurked by the wardrobe, two flanked the window steps. One hunched down by the trunk at the foot of her bed. One...

One somehow different from the rest stood framed by the moon-glow upon the old stone steps that led to the balcony window.

He was the most chilling of them all.

Somehow so familiar...

They had come to kill her.

A scream rose within her again with a terror so great that she awoke fully. Gasping, she sat up in bed. The savage at her side faded away. No war-painted brave perched by her wardrobe.

Her heart seemed to stop. Her head pounded. Her shawl lay on the floor, muddied and damp. Her cotton gown was damp as well, clinging to her flesh.

She hadn't dreamed all of this! She had risen. She had walked to the water. She had run from the cowled man and crashed into the demon from the loch.

And somehow come back here.

A sound, a whisper on the wind, alerted her. She looked up. To the window.

And froze.

The savages were gone, oh, aye. Faded back to the realm of her imagination, from where they had sprung.

But a man remained framed in the window. Different from the savages, for he wore no breechclout but stood there framed in a silhouette of light and shadow that clearly donned his Highland boots, scabbard and sword, and kilted mode of dress.

He, too, would fade, she thought.

She prayed.

Yet he did not. For long moments she stared at him, waiting for him to do so, both her limbs and her tongue frozen.

He'd come like a ghost. No, dear God, he was real. Silently come into her room. Ghost, selkie, beast, demon, man—did it matter which? He watched her from her window, in the silence of the night, and watched her with a menace that seemed palpable in the night air.

Fool! She chastised herself—whoever or whatever, the figure in the window meant her harm. She needed assistance, fast. She leaped from her bed, ready to race to the hallway, scream, and cry for help. Too late, for the Highland demon had sprung from the old stone steps, accosting her before she could reach the door. Her scream became a gasp, the very air wrenched out of her, as he reached for her and caught her. She heard the cotton of her gown ripping yet heeded it not in the least as she determined to race onward to escape. But no matter what the strength of her will, it seemed his was stronger, for his hands were on her again, this time seizing her with such force she was spun around into his arms. When she managed to draw breath to scream in earnest, his hand clamped hard upon her mouth. She struggled fiercely, to no avail. She found herself swept up and down and pinned by his massive strength as he straddled her on the bed. She twisted, arched, fought wildly. The clouds were again covering the moon, and she could see form and shape but no substance. She couldn't free her mouth to scream, and she couldn't wrench or writhe enough to free herself from the grip of his thighs. Lack of breath was making her strength wane. She feared she would black out again. It seemed she had been rescued only to be assaulted anew by a terrible and ruthless strength. A Highlander indeed, and certainly a man, flesh and blood. He was bare beneath the kilt. Her torn wet gown eluded her more and more with each of her own frantic struggles. But she couldn't cease to fight, she could not, could not...

"Ah, my lady, what then is this? Why, this is so strangely similar to the last time we met. Ah, yes, similar, but then different. If I recall the occasion, you were enchanting then, intending to give so very much! Perhaps not quite as much as you did give me that night, but then, timing is everything, is it not? And my own was rather pathetic at that! But then, I was distracted."

She went dead still. Her blood seemed to freeze within her veins. It couldn't be.

Dear God, no, it couldn't be. She had lain beside his charred remains, smelled burning flesh. She had somehow been dragged from the fire alive. He had not been dragged from it until he had been nothing but the charred remnants of a human being.

He could not be alive.

His hand no longer covered her mouth. He sat quite comfortably straddled atop her now, arms crossed over his chest.

He was, in fact, so very comfortable that he leaned against her, taking a match from the bedside table to strike against the stone of the wall and light the candle upon the small table there.

The room was suddenly flooded with the soft, ethereal, golden glow of candlelight. And she was free. He did not hold her. He straddled her still, staring at her, arms crossed over his chest once again.

Yet now she could not move. She did not attempt to do so, nor did she think to try to scream. She was far too stunned at first to do anything other than stare upward at him and wonder if his face, the voice she heard, could possibly be real, if, indeed, he could be the Douglas.

Returned from the grave.

David, oh god, David, it couldn't be, but it was, David, sweet Jesus, David...

A gasp of pure disbelief and absolute amazement echoed from her lips.

"Have I distressed you by my appearance? Your heart does seem to be beating quite quickly, my lady. How's the head? Surely, it wasn't so hard a blow. Nothing to compare with the blow I suffered that fateful night."

Her head reeled. "You are dead!" she whispered. "I saw you dead!"

"Then I am a ghost, risen from the loch in flesh and blood. Vengeful blood."

"My god, how have you come to be here?"

"God does, it seems, work in mysterious ways."

"You rose out of the loch! You came naked out of the water—"

"Rather good timing this evening," he said dryly. "Wouldn't you agree?"

"But here now, tonight. In my room—"

"Oh, pardon me, my lady. If you will recall, it is my room."

Once again, the fickle moon moved in the heavens. Now it seemed that the room was alive with light, and she saw his face quite clearly. Broad cheekbones, set high and ruggedly hewn. Ink-black brows a clean dark arch over eyes the fierce deep green of the forest. Long straight nose, hard squared jaw, generous mouth now compressed to a taut slash against the sun-bronzed darkness of his flesh. The faint line of a scar now ran across his left temple toward his eye. Where the whole of his face had been handsome before, it was hardened now.

He was real, no ghost, no dream. Real, alive.

Something within her leaped with joy. Alive. He was alive. And she was tempted to throw her arms around him, to allow the warmth and happiness that seized her to guide her. She was so grateful to see that he had not died a hideous, terrible death. She wanted to hold him, tell him how glad she was.

Yet she refrained from moving, for he stared down at her with hatred and fury seeming to burn as the very life force within him. And she was afraid, as she had never been before.

She didn't know him anymore. At all.

She didn't know the stranger who stared at her with such hatred.

The man who oh-so-apparently assumed that she had somehow attempted his death in that fire!

She was suddenly chilled.

He was here, no mistake about it.

But he hadn't come to try to help her understand what had happened that night.

He had come, having already condemned her.

"You're back, but you've become a demon then," she told him. "Fierce and cruel. It's in your eyes. Nothing more than a beast—"

"A selkie, would you? Ah, lady, you've yet to see the beast fully furred, taloned, and fanged! Indeed, what irony! I come to wrest my own revenge only to discover that I must first seize you from another man intent upon severing you with his sword. Tell me, Lady MacGinnis, have you not fared so well then since you achieved my supposed murder?"

"I have fared quite well—"

"So, you do admit to attempted murder?"

"Nay, I do not!" she cried furiously.

"Ah, how strange!" he murmured, easing himself from her prone and tattered form. He strode some distance from her, hands folded behind his back. He swung back to look at her and said politely, "Yet you thought me dead?"

"I saw you dead!" she whispered.

"Alas, my dear, you did not. And you claim to have done so well, yet when I am eager to strangle you myself, I find I must first battle an unknown thug."

"The man who chased me!" she gasped. That David was alive was a shock. That she had been chased by another assailant as well was simply too incredible to be fathomed.

"Who was he?" David demanded sharply.

"I've no idea, I never saw his face."

"Why did he chase you?"

How in God's name should I know? she asked herself.

Shawna sat up, determined that she must have more dignity for this conversation. She was at such a terrible disadvantage. So stunned. So sweetly relieved and disbelieving to see him alive, yet...so unnerved by his restrained yet furious manner. She tried to draw the torn shoulder of her nightgown upward lest she lose more of her damp gown.

She didn't succeed well.

Because she hadn't replied to his snapped-out demand quickly enough.

He was back before her, wrenching her to her feet by the very hand that attempted to hold her gown in place. His gaze fell upon her breast. She felt the flush of heat that rushed into her face. His eyes swiftly fell up and down the length of her, and a wry smile curved into his lips. His grip around her wrist tightened. The tone of his voice did not change. "Did you not hear me, lass? Why did that fellow chase you? What new treachery has sprung up here in my absence? Who was the man?" he demanded.

"I don't know," she snapped back. Who was he indeed? What was going on? How could she begin to care or think or reason when David was here. Holding her in so merciless a grip.

She forced herself to stare into his eyes and reply heatedly, "You should have asked him."

"I would have enjoyed doing so, but I'm afraid it was his life or my own. We had no time for conversation before I was forced to make his acquaintance through my sword. Pray tell, my lady, just where are your kin? Your great-uncles and cousins? What are they up to these days? Could one of them have now decided that you should have joined me in the coffin those many years ago?"

"How dare you—" Shawna began furiously, but he gave her a hard shake that silenced her, and his green stare sliced into her with the commanding power of a steel blade.

"I dare because you attempted my murder, my lady. The question here is, how dare you?"

She shivered, the fire within him seemed to burn so hotly. What words could she say? How could she cry out that she did not know the truth, that she had suffered like the damned herself when the night had turned from blaze to ashes? His fingers, clenched around her wrist, just brushed the tender flesh of her breast, and she longed to shriek out in protest of the disturbingly sensual touch. One that he did not even seem to notice.

She had to fight for breath to speak. To moisten her lips in order to form words with them.

"I never attempted to kill you," she said.

Yet his eyes condemned her. She thought that there was nothing she could say that would change him.

Still, she tried.

"I tell you, David, I never attempted to murder you, I never wanted you dead—"

"Really? Someone did. And you were the one who lured me to the stables that night."

There was, she realized quickly, no forgiveness within him. Had he brought her back here to make sure she was well aware of who was dealing a deathblow to her when he fell upon her?

"Talk to me, Shawna!" he demanded, his fingers biting into her flesh.

She could no longer bear his nearness, his casual, intimate touch. She drew her fists up between them, slamming down hard against his chest. Talk to him? She'd been trying to talk to him. The truth meant nothing to him. He refused to accept it. "Go to hell, Laird Douglas! You've judged me already. I've nothing more to say." She slammed her hands against his chest again with all the force she could muster, managing to force him back a step. She instantly saw her small reprieve and knew she had but little chance to quickly make the best of it. She spun around, determined to make a mad dash for the door.

She barely moved a step before he caught her upper arm. She was spun roughly back to face him. To meet the glittering green fury in his eyes.

"You might well have been dead now yourself if I had not come from the water! Do you deny that some conspiracy exists here?"

"I cannot deny evil exists in the world! Or that there are evil men who might wish to steal from us, who might assault a woman in that quest. Now, let me go—"

"It may well be your own family."

"It might well have been some wretched beast who has come along with you as your henchman—"

"I fought the man."

"So you say."

"Ah, and you say your family would never harm you."

"You are harming me!" With her cry, she again tried to escape his hold, shoulders straightening against the force of his hands upon her. She tried to pull back, elude him. His fingers slipped from her arms and fell fully upon her breasts, hard calloused palms against her nipples. She shrieked out, amazed at how very desperate she was to avoid his touch. Caught in the menace of sheer sensation, she wildly pummeled his chest, then desperately raised a hand to strike his face. He caught her wrist before any blow could fall.

"Stop!" he commanded her.

"Nay—"

She had the sensation of flying as he lifted her up and tossed her down. There was nothing but air beneath her before she landed upon her back again on the great ancient Douglas bed.

With him over her once again, pinning her there. She gasped, staring up at him furiously, fighting both her fear of the hard man he had become and an even more frightening fear of the emotion that was riding within her.

Her shoulders were bare. Her breasts nearly so. Another move and she'd be half-naked. She struggled to maintain some semblance of dignity in her current position, flat upon her back. She tried not to think of how terribly vulnerable she was or of how she felt with his bare thighs pressing against her hips.

She didn't want to wonder if his anger was so great he would rape her. Most of all, she didn't want to acknowledge the fire within her own body, created by his very nearness. She didn't want to remember the way that he could make her feel. The touch of his fingers against her flesh when he'd had tender feelings for her...

"Shawna!"

No tenderness. Just steel. Merciless.

Lord God, she had to moisten her lips again. He touched her. Touched her in far too many ways.

She lifted her chin, met his eyes. "No one within Clan MacGinnis would ever wish me harm, Laird Douglas. You had best take that to heart. I've uncles and cousins living within these walls."

"Oh, I am well aware of that. Clan MacGinnis certainly had no difficulty moving right in."

"Your father had no heart for this place, your brother no interest! By tradition, responsibility for your holdings fell to the MacGinnises, and we assumed responsibility at your father's request and with his blessing! From this residence, it is far easier to—"

"Rule?" he mocked.

"You are a liar if you say that you are surprised to find the MacGinnises here. Castle Rock has always been the point of protection and administration in Craig Rock. We do not rule, we administer!"

"So, you and your clan administrators have made my castle your home. Indeed, MacGinnises do rule here." There was a curious twist to his voice. Aye, he had expected to find the MacGinnises within Castle Rock. He was bitter. He was suspicious. And very aware he was outnumbered by her family. He did not seem to care.

"Yet you've come here—challenging me!"

His eyes focused on her again in a way that sent shivers racing through her. "I've business to settle."

"Then—"

"With you. First. Then, of course, there is the matter of your clan. Those who have taken over my life."

"Be that as it may. You have been—dead. Gone. We have cared for the place. My kin live within these walls now. David, nothing was taken from anyone. Your family chose America."

"After my 'death.' But I think that you and your kin have failed to remember one fact. While one Douglas draws breath, this is Douglas land."

She had never forgotten that. Nor had she ever coveted Douglas property in any way. She'd spent the past five years in pain and confusion, wishing that she could go back, wishing that she could do anything to bring David back to life.

Well, he was here.

Unforgiving. Menacing. Threatening.

"You, my lady," he reminded her, in a surprisingly soft, husky tone, "have taken over my very bed."

"I've still only to shout, and my kin will come to slay you here and now for daring to so much as threaten me in the intimacy of—she broke off, stuttering suddenly—"these chambers where I sleep."

He arched a brow. "You're referring to my chambers, right? We must never forget the obvious—that you've chosen to take up residence in my chambers. Will your kin have the gall to slay me in my own castle, within my own room?"

"It matters not where. You're threatening me! My kin could easily slay a man for less."

"I can well imagine they might want me dead in truth at last," he said dryly. "Especially considering the fact that you and your kin are all so very well positioned in my house, you, dear lass, I must again point out clearly, within my very bed."

"If you'll let me up, I'll no longer be in it!"

"Umm...I think not. Not at this moment. Indeed, it seems you have been happy enough to be here in the past."

"The care of the castle was left to the MacGinnis clan by your father, proper laird."

"The proper laird—who had no heart for his own ancestral home once his son had died so violent a death within it!"

"You've come back in violence, assaulting me—"

"I—a dead man. What harm can a ghost do?"

"Since you are dead no longer, pay heed to my warning. If you do harm to me, my kin will kill you!"

"I'm quite difficult to kill. Surely you realize that now."

The way that he looked at her made her afraid.

Afraid of what he would do to her. Afraid as well of what she might want him to do...

"Get up and away, Laird Douglas. One shout will bring them to me."

He did not move. For the first time, it appeared that he was capable of smiling, even if only in a mocking manner.

"Have you gone quite daft? What is the matter with you?" she demanded. "Move, man!"

"Umm...I think not."

"You don't understand—"

"No, you don't understand. I carried you to where you now lie. Although there are other means of entry—as we are both well aware—I walked through the gates, the great doors, up the stairs, and to this room, awakening no one. I think you'd have to shout quite a bit to raise any assistance. And you know full well I'll never allow you to shout for very long."

"One of my kin will challenge you tomorrow!" she threatened.

"Then one of your kin will die tomorrow, Lady MacGinnis, and I will not blink an eye in remorse."

The deadly cold menace in his words frightened her.

"Leave me be," she told him earnestly. "Reclaim your inheritance, and the MacGinnis clan will naturally leave the care of the property to you. Leave me be, and the room reverts to you, Laird Douglas." She hesitated, then told him passionately, "I had nothing to do with what happened to you!"

"On the contrary," he said quite softly, "you had everything to do with what happened to me." He touched her cheek lightly with his knuckles. For a long moment, she could not look away from the power of his eyes. Then she realized just how thoroughly he blamed her, how very suspicious he was, and perhaps, even, that he had a right to blame her for the events that had occurred.

"I lured you, yes!" she whispered passionately, vehemently. "That and no more. Aye! We meant to search through your rooms, the office. We needed time—"

"Which you would get plenty of—once I was dead," he said dryly.

No matter what she said, she realized, he wasn't going to believe her.

"But you're not dead!" she reminded him.

"No."

"So, you sit here and accuse me of attempted murder while you live! You have lived elsewhere. You have left us to believe that you died cruelly. How dare you! It is your place, Laird Douglas, to beg my pardon, and explain where you have been all this time!"

CHAPTER 4

"Where have I been?" he repeated with a raw fury that caused her to tremble so violently inside, she nearly betrayed the fear she was attempting to hide.

"Aye! Where have you been? I said that it was your place to beg my pardon—"

"Beg your pardon!" he all but roared, then lowered his voice, his green eyes afire. "My lady, were you to crawl buck naked through layers of ground glass to kiss my feet, you'd not manage to beg my pardon with enough humility!"

"It shall never happen, I do so swear—"

"Indeed? We shall see. And you know this—where I have been is not your concern. Suffice it to say that though I was not dead, I did most seriously dwell in hell here on earth! And by God—"

"We are living in the nineteenth century," she cried. "If you've some accusation to make," she warned, "you had best do it through the courts! We'll wake everyone in Castle Rock and let it be known that you have returned, and then you may make your case against me or my clan if you will."

He shook his head. "Nay, Lady MacGinnis. I've no intention of letting it be known that I have returned as of yet. My brother will shortly arrive from America. As Laird Douglas."

"As Laird Douglas. Aye! You are so quick to cast blame upon me and mine."

"Where else would I cast blame?"

"Perhaps it was your heathen brother who wanted you dead!"

She spoke the words, then fought hard not to allow herself to cringe into the bedding, for she regretted them the moment they were out of her mouth and with good cause. His hand was raised, as if he would strike and strike a stunning blow. But he gained control, and his knuckles fell tauntingly upon her cheek.

"So now you would blame my brother?"

"Who gained here by your death?"

"Milady, you are sleeping in my bed."

"I am a caretaker for the surviving Douglas—"

"You—and your kin—hold the power here in my brother's absence. Any man—or woman—who was patient and well aware my father's and brother's hearts lay in America, would benefit well from my demise. My father's death was naturally coming soon enough. Age would see to that. Here you are, living with your kin within the castle. I imagine that more and more Douglas cattle find their way into MacGinnis hands. Then there is the matter of the disputed land, which I daresay might be at the very heart of the matter, for unless I miss my guess, there are even more tremendous coal deposits on that property than any of us had imagined, and in our nineteenth century industrialized world, coal is worth a king's ransom and certainly a lesser man's death. Then, I imagine, the laird's share of tenant produce here most probably finds its way into MacGinnis coffers. But then, what argument do I need to bring up with you? You wished to see me the night of my 'death.' Alone. My assignation that evening was with you, was it not?"

Aye, God yes, it had been. Yet he was here now, quite menacingly so. Aye, she had lured him on Gawain's urging, only because she had been desperate to help Alistair.

She'd not known what would happen next. Truly, she had not.

Words suddenly sprang desperately and unbidden to her lips. "Sweet Jesus, David. It was long ago. You must realize, I don't know what happened. There was the fire. There is so much I don't remember—"

"Ah, lass, but I have remembered, and I have remembered you! Through what agonies you cannot begin to imagine!"

She remained still, biting into her lower lip to maintain what dignity she could. Through what agonies...where had he been? What had happened to him in all that time she had thought him dead? Why hadn't he come back before? Why hadn't he let her know that he was alive?

"David, truly, I meant you no ill—"

"Ah, but you are a sorry liar, milady!"

"I tell you—"

"Nay, lady, I tell you!" He leaned close, his green eyes glittering in the moonlight. "I am alive—demon, man, or beast—and I will discover exactly what happened that night, how I came to be buried while suffering all the tortures of hell at one time."

Shawna swallowed hard, willing herself not to tremble. She was afraid. She was fascinated. She couldn't forget the feel of him when he had touched her with passion, searing into her with fierce fire and raw determination.

And desire.

She had to speak, had to escape his touch. The memories.

She moistened her lips. She had to make him move away.

"I meant you no harm."

"Ah, but you did!" No good. Now the soft stroke of his fingers smoothed back a lock of her hair. His voice remained husky and soft, causing the burning within her to heighten. "You lured me to the stables."

"I've admitted as much. I needed to talk to you."

"We didn't do much talking. You lured me to seduce me. To my death."

"I never intended to seduce you—"

"Umm, perhaps not as far as you did. You intended that I drop from the drug in the wine before matters could go quite so far as they did."

'The wine—"

"Was very definitely drugged. Are you denying that?"

Her lashes fell. She had difficulty breathing.

"Shawna?"

His whisper touched her face. The feel of his thighs around her hips distracted her.

"I—I—meant to talk. I've told you that. We were trying to help Alistair. But I tell you, sir, in truth, I don't know—"

"You knew enough, and you brought about my damnation, Lady Shawna MacGinnis. And by God, you will be part and party to all that I require—nay, demand—now!"

"You are mad if you think that you can demand anything of me, Laird Douglas! I will not—"

"You will not what?" he queried softly, leaning even closer, the flash of his teeth caught in the moonlight now, his smile like a satyr's grin.

"Just what is it that you would demand?" she asked.

"Everything, Lady MacGinnis. Everything. Flesh and blood and bone and more."

He was closer. So close that his lips hovered just above hers.

His fingers again brushed her cheek. They ran down the length of her like tendrils of a flame.

"I demand...you, milady," he said flatly. "Indeed, I have come back and would begin again where I left off. I demand you. And how very damned convenient. Just what I want—so easily delivered to me. You are, after all, sleeping in my bed."

"I offer my heartiest apologies. By some miracle, you have returned. The bed is yours. I can most certainly leave it."

"I think not, Shawna. I think not. Most certainly, milady, I think not tonight."

"This is absurd. You don't understand—"

"You don't understand, my lady. I was set up. Attacked. Left for dead, yet somehow alive. Alive to reside in absolute hell. The guilty parties must be made to pay."

"But—"

"Tonight, my lady, paying begins. And it is your turn. You first. Oh, aye, you first. For others may be involved. Others must be discovered and proved. While you, my love—you are guilty as all hell."

"Damn you, I didn't—"

"Damn you, you did."

"I tell you—"

"I lay in this very room, Shawna, while you came to me in the moonlight and beckoned me to hell. How quickly, how easily, you forget!"

"I did not forget!"

"Neither did I."

"David, I'm telling you, I don't know what happened. I don't know how you can be alive. I—"

"Well, we'll have to all discover the complete truth of the past then, won't we? But in the meantime, tonight, lady, you begin to pay."

She knew him. He was so familiar.

Yet he was a different man, and she feared she didn't know him at all.

He could very well mean that he was about to wind his fingers around her neck and slowly, surely, squeeze her life from her.

Her breath caught as she met his eyes in the nighttime play of light and shadow. No deep dark warmth of forest green met her stare, but a glitter as sharp as emerald gems, as cold as stones from within an icy depth of the earth. And still, she despaired to feel a searing of heat within her veins, her limbs. He was a stranger, but even after five years, he was a familiar stranger. Flesh, bone, and muscle, she knew him well, knew the man with her. The power in his eyes she knew, yet it was clear that whatever gentler emotions he might once have felt toward her had indeed died that night. The sharp light in his eyes as they met hers came from the demon death had made of the man. His touch upon her was equally as cold. Yet that did not douse the fever that had possessed her, born of fear, and dread, and fury, and...anticipation.

She was the daughter of a people who had fought forever, she reminded herself. A people who had died for their rights, for their pride, for their beliefs. Whatever he sought, vengeance or murder, she would fight until she could fight no more...

"I'll not pay for what I haven't done!" she whispered heatedly. "You'll demand nothing from me. You'll—"

His finger fell against her lips, and he spoke coldly and harshly, as if he hadn't heard a word of what she had said. "I shall tell you, my lady, what will and will not happen. You cry to me of your innocence while admitting your guilt."

"I was guilty only of—"

"You were the pawn, Shawna. The bait. Perhaps you didn't strike the blow, someone did."

"I swear to you, I don't know—"

"Someone tried to kill me."

"But you didn't die. Where—"

"That's not important right now."

"Perhaps no one did try to kill you. There was an ungodly fire."

"I was struck with what was intended to be a deathblow to the head, Shawna."

"A rafter must have fallen—"

He let out an expletive with such explosive fury that she fell silent.

"I swear to you, I know nothing about any attempt to murder you—"

"Prove it."

"What do you mean?"

"Keep your silence. Help me find the truth."

"How?"

"For the time being, just watch and listen."

"And if I don't help you?"

"If you don't..." he mused, leaning close, low against her. She was aware of the texture of his face, the tension in his features and throughout him. A strange heat riddled him now, like a low-burning fire that could at any time rage out of control. Could she have moved, she might well have been tempted to leap out the window to escape the portent of violence that seemed to burn and simmer within him. But he sat back upon his haunches again, atop her, yet easily keeping the pressure of his weight from her. "I promise you this, my lady, if you don't keep quiet, I'll make you very, very sorry, indeed. And aren't you forgetting something?"

"What?"

"It seems you are in deep and deadly danger yourself, Shawna

MacGinnis. There lies the corpse of a man by the loch who meant to do away with you. So again, I warn you, Shawna. Keep your silence."

A recklessness suddenly ignited within her. She was tired of being threatened. "What will you do, David? Slay me? Beat me to death? Rape me?"

He arched a brow. Cool green eyes swept over her. He suddenly angled down against her, his face just inches away so she again felt the warmth of his breath and the tremendous power of his body. The warmth and pulse of his sex. He touched her face again, fingers sculpting her cheek, brushing her lips, moving over her throat until she scarcely dared to breathe. His fingers curled in a sensuous cradling motion around the mound of her breast, drawing a startled gasp from her lips, which he ignored. "Rape you?" His voice was a mere taunting whisper. "Hmm. Were it my design, lady, my choice, I'd have had you by now. And I don't think it would have been rape. After all, my lady, I do believe, in the past, it was you who seduced me."

She was startled when he suddenly rose. So startled she could not speak. He stood above her, his eyes meeting hers for a last time.

His eyes sweeping over her.

"Hmph."

He reached toward the candle and pinched out the flame.

She could swear she blinked, and then he was gone.

Gone. Gone!

Just like that. He had left her. Just when she had become convinced that he would never do so that night, not until he had taken from her... her.

She leaped out of her bed and stood by it, not at all sure if she was completely relieved...or disappointed. He had just walked away. He'd threatened her and left. He didn't want her anymore.

He had wanted her. Oh, aye, he'd wanted her.

As she hadn't even really realized just how she had wanted him.

Once...

Now he was a ghost; a man risen from a grave he was convinced she'd managed to dig for him.

"Oh god!" she whispered aloud.

She ran to the window, looking out to the night beyond. There was no sign of him. She pressed the stone on the secret door just beyond the window and looked down into the stairway. The stairway was blacker than ebony, and not even the slightest sound echoed back to her from it.

Had he departed the normal way—by the door?

She returned from the balcony and threw open the door to her room, scampered into the hallway and then to the balustrade looking down on the great hall below. Again, there was no sign of him.

She couldn't stand around in the hallway, she determined. Her gown was damp and shredded, and she was half-naked, and if any of her kin were to appear, she might well find herself residing in an asylum for the insane.

She slipped back into her bedroom, closing and bolting the door, and pacing the floor.

David had returned. It was impossible.

She shivered, discarded her torn, wet gown, and dressed quickly in a fresh one while staring at the remnants of the old. She realized she had to get rid of the ripped gown.

Only if she intended to keep secret the fact that David was alive. That he had returned.

David was dangerous.

Maybe he had a right to be. Where had he been for the last five years? What had happened to him? How had he managed to come home and rise from the loch at precisely the moment she needed him?

Had he really been there at all?

She groaned softly, rolling up her shredded gown, determined to hide it until she decided what to do with it. She stuffed it beneath her bed for the time being. She couldn't report to anyone that David was alive.

She had no proof. Already, there was no sign that the man might have been in her room. If she betrayed him, she realized, she'd definitely be sorry. For one thing, no one would believe her. They would all doubt her sanity, as she was beginning to question it herself. No one would believe what had happened to her tonight. She had run out She had been chased and nearly killed by a tall dark shadow near the Druid

Stones. But she hadn't been killed because a dead man had risen from the loch to slay her would-be assailant...

She needed a drink, she decided, if she was ever going to sleep for the rest of the night. And she had to have some rest. The world, at the very least, had gone mad. And she had to cope with it all somehow.

She slipped from her room, returned to the office, found the brandy bottle, and returned with it. The fire in her hearth had burned down to practically nothing, but she sat in front of it, shivering, trying to rouse up the last of the embers.

She was going to drink the brandy properly out of a glass, sit calmly in front of the fire, and think.

She did pour the brandy into a glass. Throwing her head back and swallowing down the contents in one long sip wasn't exactly proper.

She'd do better with the second glass.

Actually she did do better. With her feet and legs curled beneath her, she stared into the small, flickering flames. He'd come back. He was alive.

Or was he? She shivered fiercely. Her nightmares had been torturing her for so long. He was gone again without a trace. How could she be so certain...

In the morning, there would be no doubt. Someone would find the corpse by the loch. And what? Was she supposed to pretend that she knew nothing about it?

David believed that she had been part of a conspiracy. That she had been the lure, the bait, so that someone else could come along and murder him unaware, in cold blood. He was watching her now to see who she would go to...

There was no murderer, she tried to tell herself. A rafter had fallen, another man's body, burned beyond recognition, had been discovered, and it had been assumed that the charred remains had been David. No one would have tried to kill him.

But David was alive. How could he be alive, back after all this time?

She drank another very long swallow of the brandy.

Her limbs, at the least, were no longer cold. What remained of the fire, and what sweet flames the brandy could create, warmed her at last. Any more and she was going to awake with a pounding headache just when she would need to have her wits about her.

She set the glass down on the arm of her chair, leaving the brandy bottle by the side of it. She stood in the middle of the room for a long moment. Nothing was different. Nothing had changed. She might have truly dreamed that he had walked back into her life.

She knew she hadn't just dreamed of David. He had walked back into her life.

For revenge.

CHAPTER 5

Shawna awoke to brilliant sunshine pouring into her room. She sat up with a sudden jerk, looking around her.

Had she dreamed it all?

She leaped out of bed, searching for some evidence that David Douglas had been there the night before.

But there was no sign of David's existence.

Shawna stared at her bed. The pillow on the right side, where she had slept, carried the telltale indentation of her head. Naturally. Yet her covers were torn apart as well, as if she had waged war there.

She fell to her knees, looking beneath the carved frame structure of the bed for the gown that had been torn and soaked during her midnight foray. There it lay.

"Shawna?"

Shawna banged her head, trying to rise and turn as she heard the voice of her lady's maid, Mary Jane Campbell.

"Shawna, are you quite alright?"

No, she wasn't all right. Her head had been spinning in confusion since she'd awakened. Now, it was killing her.

She stood, rubbing her head, facing Mary Jane. Her maid was just a few years her senior, and they had been together, except for when Shawna had left Craig Rock, since they had been children.

"I'm—fine. Thank you. No, actually I'm not fine. I, er, had a rather rough night."

"Oh, aye, strange night, wasn't it?"

"I'm sorry?"

Mary Jane walked on into the room, drawing open Shawna's wardrobe, setting out undergarments and toiletries so that Shawna could wash and dress. "The moon," Mary Jane said, flashing Shawna a quick smile. She was a slim, pretty girl with light green eyes and dark brown hair. "The moon, the way it kept coming and going behind the clouds. It kept me up half the night as well."

"Did you...see or hear anything unusual?" Shawna queried.

Mary Jane shook her head. "Shawna, y'know me well. I lay in my bed, covers to my chin, and I didn't move the night. What would I see or hear in my bed?"

"It seems amazing what one can see or hear from her bed," Shawna muttered.

"I beg your pardon?"

"Never mind. I'm sorry. I suppose I'm quite late. Get a message out for me, will you? The miners should take some free time this morning."

"Free time?"

"Aye, free time."

"They work for hourly pay, Shawna—"

"And they shall be paid for these hours."

"Your great-uncle runs a tight ship."

"Well, that's true, but it is the nineteenth century, and it is my ship to direct. Gawain will understand. Time is lost every day now when the workers argue over going into the shafts. So, this morning they will have free time. They should have tea with their wives and babes."

"Shawna, that is brilliantly generous."

"I'm afraid it isn't. I wish that I had thought to be so generous, but actually I overslept. I meant to be up and about far earlier, but...well, you know, there was that wretched moon. Anyway, I shall get the reverend, and we'll have a service at the mine in, say, two hours."

"Shawna?"

"Aye?"

"I don't mean to overstep my bounds..."

"Since you've been doing so all our lives, why on earth would you want to stop now?" Shawna inquired.

"Fine!" Mary Jane said, laughing. "You must realize, your great-uncle will be furious about the lost time."

"Uncle Gawain will have to go hang."

Mary Jane flashed her another smile. "I shall hope and pray that he does not decide to shoot the messenger."

"He may grumble, but he'll save his anger for me. Go quickly, please. I'm certain many of the men will have left for work already. Oh, wait!"

"Aye?" Mary Jane queried.

"You've been up and about awhile?"

"Aye, that I have."

"And there have been no reports of anything unusual?"

"Like what?"

"Well, you know, the miners have been so nervous about the shaft."

"Yes?"

"Well, has anything at all unusual occurred? Sightings in the graveyard? Reports of ghosts perhaps—or bodies lying about?"

Mary Jane shook her head. "Bodies lying about! Nay, Shawna, there's not been a report regarding a single corpse, and that's a fact!"

"No one has been reported missing?"

"Missing?"

"Aye, a villager who didn't return home from the pub or the like?"

"Shawna, are you quite alright?"

"I'm...just concerned about what's going on with the miners. That's all."

"You think there are ghosts in the mine shafts?"

"Of course not...I'm just looking for logical explanations."

"I see. Well, we've no missing husband who lost his way home and fell into the mine shaft to beat against the walls. None that a wife will admit to, at that."

With a last smile, Mary Jane closed the door to Shawna's room.

Shawna walked up the steps to the balcony and looked out upon the day. The Druid Stones looked bright beneath the rising sun. Hills and valleys sloped and rose in emerald beauty, studded with the colors of wildflowers. The loch shimmered in the light, and the craigs and cliff rising from it to spread across the hilltops were caught up in glittering silver color, stalwart as steel. Cattle dotted the fields. The landscape had never appeared more serene. As if the tempest of the night could not possibly have occurred.

Yet knowing that it had, that David was out there somewhere, Shawna hurried down from the steps, approaching her washstand, ripping her nightgown over her head. She sluiced her face and throat with cold water, shivered, soaked herself again, and paused.

She had imagined nothing. The subtle, but unmistakable unique male scent of him lingered about her body. She trembled and grew warm, then picked up her water pitcher and doused herself with the chilly water from head to toe.

What in God's name was she going to do?

What could she do? David had cleanly disappeared. There was no body by the loch. And if she betrayed him again in any way...

Yet, she could not believe that anyone in her family had set out to kill David.

So, what had happened?

God, she yearned for the truth!

And perhaps the truth could be found in helping him.

There was but one thing to do for the moment, she determined.

Get past the night.

And begin the new day. Forewarned...

And forearmed.

She did begin the day. Definitely late.

But by ten-thirty, Shawna had summoned the Reverend Massey, and she stood by his side at the entrance to the main tunnel dug out of the rugged cliffs near the loch.

The miners and their families were assembled nearby, the men with their caps in their hands, the women with their heads bowed.

"Shawna MacGinnis, do you think that this will work?" the Reverend Massey asked worriedly.

Shawna lowered her eyes, hiding a rueful smile from Massey. Would it work? She was trying to convince miners that a shaft couldn't be haunted while she was halfway convinced she was mad and carrying on with a ghost herself.

"Reverend, whether it 'works' or not, a blessing on the mines would be a good thing, would it not?" she asked.

"Aye, aye," he said after a minute of thoughtful frowning.

"Be strong!" Shawna told him encouragingly as she looked at the crowd of sixty or so people who had come to hear the blessing. Her great-uncle Gawain, flanked on either side by her cousins Alistair and Alaric, were watching them, waiting. Alistair caught her eyes upon him. He grinned and winked.

Shawna had managed to depart Castle Rock without seeing Gawain, Alaric, or Alistair. She was determined to follow her own way, and it seemed more prudent to have her own way now and argue about it later, rather than risk a public argument.

"Please proceed, Reverend," Shawna urged. The people were beginning to grow restless.

"Uh-hmm!" the Reverend Massey said, clearing his throat. He lifted his hands to Heaven. "My good people, let us pray!" he invoked, then dropped rather slowly to his knees.

Everyone followed suit. Before closing her eyes in prayer, Shawna saw that her great-uncle Lowell and cousin Aidan had come as well and were kneeling at the far left side of the crowd. Aidan offered her an encouraging smile as Alistair had done, and Lowell, as gentle a man as Gawain was rough, winked as Alistair had done. It was a pity. She didn't see nearly as much of her great-uncle Lowell as she did of Gawain. Lowell and Aidan had maintained residence at Castle MacGinnis to keep up the MacGinnis ancestral home.

She wished now that she had stayed there herself. But along with all the business-related reasons for her maintaining her residence at Castle Rock, the recently deceased Laird Douglas, David's father, had asked her to do so himself. No matter what, she wouldn't have been able to have refused him. Since Gawain had run many of the affairs of both estates for years, he had decided to move to Castle Rock too. His two sons, Alistair and Alaric, had joined him there.

From across the crowd, she saw Aidan arching a curious brow at her. She realized that she had been frowning.

She tried to smile.

She should have remained in her own home, no matter what the old Douglas laird had asked of her, no matter that he and her father had been the closest of friends. She should have known that "ghosts" could come back to haunt Castle Rock.

"Father in Heaven," the Reverend Massey intoned, "we ask for your blessing on these thy children who work the earth. We ask your blessing on these coal mines which offer so many here sustenance. Oh, Father, hear our prayers, through the infinite goodness of your son, Jesus Christ, grant us your goodness and mercy. Bless this work we partake of in the name of the Father, the Son, and the Holy Ghost. Be with us in all our endeavors, bless each man, woman and child who works within the mines..."

The prayer went on and on—once the Reverend Massey had got started, he found passion in the event. Shawna found herself opening her eyes. Alistair's eyes were open as well. He was still watching her, his expression amused. His blue eyes sparkled. His handsome face was cut by a broad grin. She shook her head in warning, and he lowered his eyes dutifully.

At last, the prayer ended. The Reverend Massey implored them all to go and work dutifully and in peace. When they stood, Massey was approached by a young woman with a baby on her hip, and Shawna discovered that Mark Menzies was at her side, thanking her for the arrangements that morning. "The men are enthusiastic about their work once again." He lowered his voice. "Aye, and still, it would be best if I knew myself what causes the sounds that haunt the mines at times!"

"You've heard these sounds yourself?" she asked.

Mark started to reply but paused, and she realized that Gawain had come up behind her.

"I was thanking m'lady for the prayer, MacGinnis," Mark said politely.

"If a blessing matters to the work, then a blessing there must be," Gawain said.

"Aye, the blessing will work well," Mark said, smiling at Shawna with warm admiration, "as will milady's care that the men be' given a few special hours, paid hours, with their wives and bairns."

"Aye, my niece does have a woman's sympathies and sensitivities!" Gawain acknowledged, smiling. The smile was a fierce one. It meant that she should have discussed her plans with him.

"M'lady Shawna, would you have some of our tea?"

Shawna spun about to see that the speaker was Gena Anderson, young and very pretty if somewhat fey, one of the village lasses whose father had worked in the mines. The girl was offering her a steaming mug. The miners' wives, it seemed, had brought tea and scones, as if the blessing constituted a celebration, a reopening of the mines themselves. She took the warm cup from the woman, thanking her. As she did so, an arm slipped around her waist, and she spun about to see Alistair at her side.

"You're jumpy this morning, eh?"

"Am I? Sorry."

"You needn't be sorry. Ah, cousin! The lady bountiful—you do it so well!" he teased. Though they were actually second cousins, since Gawain was her great-uncle, they had always referred to one another as cousin, as she did with his brother, Alaric. Aidan, likewise, was Lowell's son, and Lowell was her great-uncle as well, but in the Highlands, the word "cousin" could easily stretch several generations.

He lowered his voice. "And you must have run like the wind down the steps to escape the castle and the walls before Father could stop you and offer his opinion on your generosity!"

"I simply walked out," she lied. "None of you happened to be about."

"How convenient! But I do believe you've done quite well."

"We are responsible for these people's lives, you know," she reminded him primly. Looking about, she saw one of the very young children who worked the exceptionally narrow corridors of some of the tunnels. She knew that children were drastically overworked everywhere—in the big cities such as Glasgow, London, and even New York—but it still horrified her to realize that the very little ones went into dangerous places. She had fought her great-uncle tooth and nail on the matter of the children, and here, they were allowed to work no more than a few hours a day.

The little lad she noted now was one of her favorites. Though he was one of the Andersons of Craig Rock, it was obvious that the boy had MacGinnis blood as well. He had the telltale ink-black hair and blue eyes. More. He had the handsomely shaped eyebrows that distinguished her family members. In fact...

She glanced sharply at Alistair, who had been known to seduce more than a few of the village maidens. There had been a rumor at one time that he, one of the gentry of the manor, had seduced the very pretty, young Gena Anderson. Whatever had happened, much of it had taken place while Shawna had been away and talk of it had ended.

"Have you had more to do with the lives of some of these people than I might have previously imagined?" she demanded of Alistair.

Alistair laughed, shaking his head, completely unashamed of whatever his sins might be. "Now, cousin, you go too far! Would you blame me, fair cousin, for the fact that too much inbreeding has occurred throughout the centuries in our secluded Highlands, eh?"

"Inbreeding, my—" she began.

"Ach! Such language from the lady bountiful!"

"M'lady!" Mark Menzies called. "Will ye come? The Reverend Massey will give a special prayer for the left shaft!"

"Of course!" she called.

Alaric, Alistair's older brother, was beside them then as well. "Menzies, I'm not sure Shawna should go into the mines!"

"No, no!" Shawna insisted softly, squeezing Alaric's hand. "I must go. If it's not safe for me, then it's not safe for the men."

"Shawna, there are differences here!" Alaric told her firmly. He was far more like his father than Alistair, very serious in all his endeavors, a big, gruff, Highlander. From the time they had been children, he had been serious. He was a handsome man, much like Alistair in appearance, but he lacked his younger brother's quick grin and easy style of living. Like her great-uncle Gawain, Alaric reminded her of a Highlander of old, a man who could easily be a savage warrior, painting his face, shrieking out a battle cry, and rushing into the fray with little but raw courage behind him. She smiled at the thought. Her cousins were so different. Alistair and Alaric, Gawain's sons. Alistair the charmer, Alaric the hulk. Alaric nearly ten years older than she was, Alistair just four. Then there was Aidan, Lowell's only child, a decade older than Shawna like Alaric, the very quiet and thoughtful one, steady as a rock. They, with her great-uncles, were her family, and she loved them all. She missed her father dearly. He had been somewhat of a cross between Alistair and Alaric, built like a warrior of old, gruff—and charming. Shawna didn't remember her mother, who had died before she was a year old, so these men were her closest kin. And now, Alaric was determined to be as protective as a father, speaking to her firmly. "You're Lady MacGinnis. These men are miners. These men know the mine, and you do not, little cousin."

"I am Lady MacGinnis. I must go," she said firmly. She smiled, knowing he spoke from affection, but slipped by him quickly, escaping his reach before he could physically attempt to stop her.

Entering the mine, she found herself wishing that she were elsewhere. The air was tight and stale. Even with lanterns, it was difficult to see. The walls were dark with coal dust. She knew that she would walk from the mine covered in dirt, almost as black as the little urchins who worked the mines when they crawled out from the narrow tunnels.

Mark Menzies was there along with a few of the other miners. Shawna realized that Alistair had come with her as well. He would dare the mines and the devil himself, she thought.

Alistair. She longed to shake him. She wanted to shout that David Douglas was back, demanding vengeance for the fiasco that Alistair had created. But she couldn't cry out, and despite everything, she did care deeply about Alistair. Of all her kin, she loved him best. He had got her into plenty of trouble, but when she had been hurt, he had been there for her as well for all of her life. And though he remained a man quick to taunt and tease and charm, what had happened had changed him, irrevocably. He'd become extremely responsible, no matter what lightness he might portray.

The Reverend Massey quickly began his benediction.

He didn't pray long at all, and his words were very fast. She realized that he was as anxious as she was to leave this place where so many men spent grueling hours every day.

"Amen!" she heard Massey say, then he was hurrying from the shaft. Menzies hurried after him. Shawna felt Alistair's hand at her back, urging her from the mine in the wake of the others.

"Let's leave here, eh?"

She hesitated, not quite ready. This was probably the best possible place to have a truly private conversation with him. She turned around to wag a finger beneath his nose. "If that adorable little Anderson child is actually yours, I want you taking full responsibility."

"Oh, now you're going to preach to me! You, fair cousin, after what you did—"

"What I did!" she gasped. "I should hit you in the jaw and blacken your eye!" she informed him. "What I did, I did for you!"

"What you did, you did because David Douglas always attracted you like a moth to a flame, and you thought that you were powerful enough to get what you wanted out of him without risking anything."

She gasped, unable to admit his words were true.

"Why, you ungrateful wretch!" she accused him.

"Shawna, Shawna, I'm sorry, truly, I'm sorry, I had no right. It's just that you're so quick to jump on me. The lad isn't mine, so maybe you need to speak to our pious cousin Aidan—or my good serious brother, for that matter. Then again, half of Craig Rock is populated by Highlanders with blue MacGinnis eyes and black hair, while the other half seem to bear green Douglas eyes and auburn hair. Maybe we have a few variations of each, what do you think? Shawna, I am sorry, please do forgive me?"

They were alone. Even their whispers echoed eerily. It seemed that the mine shaft was closing in around Shawna. "You are, indeed, a sorry wretch, but I keep forgiving you, so I might as well do so again now."

She started to turn away. He pulled her back. "Shawna," he said, speaking quickly, "I was always grateful for what you did for me. And I swear, I have spent the time since that tragedy trying to make up for what I did. I keep the books meticulously. When Andrew Douglas arrives from America," he said somewhat bitterly, "he'll discover that his funds have been managed with more care than he would have given them himself. And I swear to you, I come into this mine often enough with the men. God's truth, Shawna."

She studied his eyes, so like her own. She nodded. She realized that it was important that she not betray the fact that David Douglas lived. David needed to see how Alistair had changed.

"I oversee the bookkeeping for both estates, Alistair. I know that you have been scrupulously honest."

"Penance," he said.

"For me?"

"For what happened to David." He hesitated, then took a deep breath. "I wasn't so upset that he might take out charges against me. I wanted to talk to him myself because he was a friend."

Startled, Shawna asked softly, "Why didn't you?"

"You know Father. And MacGinnis honor."

"God, Alistair, if I only knew what truly happened!" she exclaimed passionately.

"It's all in the past," he said firmly.

She found herself shivering. "Please, let's do get out of here now."

They left the mine shaft together. Just outside of it, Gawain stood talking with Lowell, Aidan, and Alaric. The women had returned to their homes. The men were organizing for the day's work.

"Shawna, we'll have a conference in the Castle Rock great hall," Gawain said firmly. "Now."

"Aye, Uncle, we'll have a conference if that's what you wish," she said, but his autocratic way disturbed her.

She was determined not to act like a child or to let her great-uncle bend her to his will, as he had once done. "But you'll notice I'm covered with mine soot. We'll meet in the great hall in the early evening over supper. I'd like to bathe and attend to a few other business matters now."

The mines were no more than a mile around the loch from Castle Rock, but it had seemed a long mile that morning, and Shawna had ridden to the blessing. She hurried past Gawain then for her horse, not willing to give her great-uncle a chance to change her decision.

Mounted, Shawna turned back.

Her male kin were all assembled together. Gawain, Lowell, Aidan,

Alaric, and Alistair. They stood tall in their Highland stances, legs slightly parted, backs very straight, shoulders squared, arms crossed over their chests. Together they were a handsome, powerful lot. Men in whom she could take great pride.

For some strange reason, she shivered.

She lifted a hand and waved.

They waved in return.

She turned her horse and rode hard for the castle.

CHAPTER 6

They were gathered around the long table in the great hall—Gawain at one end, Lowell at the other, Alistair and Alaric on one side of the table, Aidan on the other with a chair at his side that awaited her. They were, as she had thought earlier, an impressive group, all of them tall, large, well-muscled men, no matter what their ages. Dark-haired, light-eyed, powerful men, sure of their purpose. Highlanders, a different breed.

They rode like the wind and could run over hills and valleys nearly as quickly as they could ride. No matter what befell the world around them, they often went their own way, bowing to authority only long enough for authority to go away. The Highlands were wild and rugged, and not for everyone, but equally, the Highlands had always been a place too difficult to tame, and the most stalwart of conquerors had often chosen to ignore them and their people rather than pay the price of trying to subdue them.

MacGinnises were proud. A part of their land.

And these fine, fierce men were her kin. Her protectors, as they saw it.

Her rulers as well, or so Gawain seemed to assume, she thought wryly.

Still, she assured herself, they all meant well. Every last one of them, no matter what the particular quirks of their individual personalities. She loved them and was proud of them.

To a man, they stood courteously when she appeared.

The table was set for supper, and the food had been served. It was obvious that Gawain had given the order to Myer, who served as butler in the castle, and Anne-Marie, his head housekeeper, that they weren't to be disturbed during the meal.

Dirty laundry was about to be aired, Shawna decided.

But she couldn't hover at the foot of the stairway forever, and she wasn't afraid of facing Gawain. They argued frequently.

But tonight...

Tonight was different.

David Douglas was alive.

She walked quickly into the great hall and to the dining table.

She smiled at Aidan as she hurried around to the chair that he had pulled from beneath the table so that she could slip into it.

He smiled in return. Rather sternly.

"You're late," Gawain said firmly.

"Am I, Uncle? I'm so sorry. I'm afraid I don't remember having specified a time."

He wagged a finger at her. "Shawna, you forget, I am your great-uncle. Your father's uncle. He entrusted your care to me. I will have your respect."

"Will I have yours?"

Aidan, with his quiet, calm sense of responsibility, cleared his throat. "Perhaps we could fight this family battle of wills at another time. We are all Clan MacGinnis here and should respect one another."

"Aidan is quite right," Lowell said firmly, offering a stern glance to both his brother and his great-niece. "Now, I was under the impression that we gathered tonight to plan for the arrival of Andrew, Laird Douglas?"

"Shawna made some decisions today without thinking to ask our advice," Gawain said, watching her, still angry.

"I didn't see you this morning before the blessing, and you knew last night that I had assured Mark Menzies I would have the reverend down to the mines."

"You might have let me know you were planning on giving the men time off. What I didn't know might have made a fine fool of me, girl."

"I awoke late. I had no choice."

"You had the choice to inform me."

"I am sorry."

"You will do so in the future."

"I certainly did not seek to make you look foolish in any way."

Lowell let out a crusty "Hmm! Shawna, you must remember that we are family. We work together. Back to the business at hand, for I've had a long day, would have a good supper, and get some sleep. We need to plan for the arrival of Andrew Douglas."

"To plan?" Shawna said. "But, Uncle, what is there to plan? Andrew is Laird Douglas, and he's coming to see to his holdings!"

"Andrew Douglas doesn't belong here," Lowell said firmly.

Startled by the vehemence of his comment, Shawna stared at the younger of her two great-uncles. He smiled at her, shaking his head. Like Gawain, Lowell had kept a headful of hair that was barely peppered with gray, but his face was far more gauntly cast, and tonight he looked tired, both age and weariness visible in his countenance.

"'Tis true, lass," Lowell said, catching the surprise in her eyes, "that the American has no place here. He knows it as well."

"But Douglas lands are his heritage," Shawna said. "Perhaps he wants them for his children."

"Maybe," Alistair said cheerfully, winking at Shawna, "his new wife will be barren."

"Maybe," Alaric mused dryly, "we should consider trying to buy the property from him."

Alaric's statement was greeted with a moment's silence.

"Buy the property..." Gawain repeated.

"Now that," Aidan murmured, "is quite a concept. Truly, Andrew Douglas has no interests here. He's always made it quite clear that he belongs with the Sioux people. Alaric, buying the property is a sound idea."

"Andrew Douglas does not belong here, that much is certain.

Lowell is entirely right," Gawain said, as if they all agreed upon law. "And I agree as well. Buying the property would be an excellent idea." He shook his head, staring hard at Shawna as if all their difficulties were somehow her fault. "Primogeniture!" he exclaimed. "Ah, but the Normans introduced a great idea when they brought feudalism to England. Sons inherited. And when daughters were all that was left, the closest male kin inherited."

"Andrew Douglas was Laird Douglas's closest living male kin when he died," Aidan reminded Gawain, who was still staring at Shawna.

"This modern world will be the downfall of us, women inheriting the same as men," Gawain exclaimed.

"We were never like the English, Uncle," Shawna reminded him. "And though Scotland became a part of Great Britain by the Act of Unity, we've always kept apart. The Conqueror never quite made it to the Highlands, as you'll recall, and even Scottish Lowlanders think us a breed apart. Women have been the heads of many great Highland families in the past."

Gawain sniffed disdainfully. "Thank the good Lord, lass, that you've the lot of us."

"I love you all, Uncle Gawain," Shawna said sweetly, "and therefore, I do thank the Lord for you all."

"Ah, but could you be saying that you have no need for your male kin, Shawna?"

"I've never said that, Uncle Gawain."

"But you fight me every step of the way. You forget you're a MacGinnis time and time again."

A new wave of guilt washed over her. Was she forgetting she was a MacGinnis at this very moment? David Douglas was alive, and she wasn't saying a word about it. These men were her family.

But someone had chased her, someone had tried to kill her.

Not her family!

Still, she couldn't speak about David.

Not yet.

Aidan cleared his throat. "Once again, perhaps this isn't the right time to argue primogeniture and the rights of men and women, or our arguments with one another."

"Ach, women!" Lowell murmured, smiling as he shook his head.

"After all, Queen Victoria is sitting upon the throne, and poor Albert is but a prince!" Alistair provided.

His father shot him a glance that was dagger sharp.

"Then there was good Queen Bess!" Alistair continued. "Good God, she ruled forever!"

"And here," Aidan added dryly, "we had good Queen Mary, who nearly brought about the downfall of her people!"

"Ah, but good Queen Mary of Scots produced the future King James I of England, whose blood even now runs through the veins of royalty!" Shawna pointed out. "Besides, Mary might not have had quite so many problems if not for all the men conspiring behind her back."

Shawna was startled to feel a twinge of unease as she felt all her male kin staring at her.

Did they all resent her? It seemed a pleasantly joking conversation, but was it? Gawain did seem aggravated that she had inherited the title of Lady MacGinnis and was traditional titular head of the family. He'd never hidden that fact, but it had always seemed more an annoyance to him than anything else.

Certainly it would not drive him to...

Murder.

If she died, Gawain, as the oldest of her grandfather's surviving brothers, would inherit the title. After Gawain, Alaric, and then Alistair. And after them—unless someone was to have a child—Lowell would inherit, and after him, Aidan.

Was she a fool, believing in family, in blood? After all, there had been a man following her last night, a man who had drawn a sword...

Who had meant to kill her.

But no body had been found.

David had done away with the body. Obviously.

"Wonderful," she murmured aloud, looking around the table. "You all resent me."

"Nay, lass, 'tis not that," Gawain said with a weary sigh. "Men are more likely to deal with business well, and you should be part of our business—we should be acquiring a proper and fitting husband for you and the like. What is, is, and we do well enough as a family. And we'd do well to acquire Douglas holdings. Aidan, look to our family resources and see what we could offer to buy out Douglas. Maybe he'll want money quickly to arm his heathen family. Maybe we will have a chance. Alistair, take time to compose what we must tell him to convince him that he would be better off to leave this property and its problems to us. Alaric, take inventory of our property to see what we might sell for ready hard money."

"Aye, Father," Alaric agreed.

"Well," Shawna murmured, "at least we're planning to buy him out —rather than kill him off."

Dead silence met her words.

Then Gawain warned angrily, "You, my dear, will mind your manners!"

"And is that my assignment in all this?" Shawna inquired.

"Nay, lass," Gawain commanded, leaning toward her with his blue eyes bright with anger, "you will plan the homecoming for the Douglas and see to it that we offer all possible hospitality."

"Will I?" Shawna murmured.

Aidan suddenly covered her hand with his own, and she found herself looking to this quieter, older cousin. Child of a quieter, gentler, great-uncle. His eyes were a lighter blue. and his hair was closer to auburn than the near black that graced most of the MacGinnises, as if even his coloring was of a gentler nature. "Shawna, don't you think it a good idea that we seek to buy the Douglas property?"

"We run the property. We live and breathe and die by it. And truly, you know as well as I do, that Andrew Douglas wants to live out his days on his father's American property."

"Yes, I suppose that's true."

"Then?" her great-uncle Lowell prodded gently, lifting his wineglass to her.

They were never going to be able to buy the property because David Douglas was still alive.

"Shawna?" Aidan said, frowning.

"Yes," she said quickly. "I—I suppose we should try to buy the property."

"Pass the meat," Gawain said.

Irked by her great-uncle's peremptory manner, Shawna felt disinclined to obey even so simple a command as this one.

Aidan and Alistair, however, did not seem bothered by Gawain, for Aidan passed the platter of meat to Alistair, who then set it before Gawain. Shawna discovered that she wasn't particularly hungry.

But she did imbibe in their dinner wine quite freely.

Alistair commented on how well the blessing went. Aidan asked him if he'd any idea what was causing the "haunting" noises in the mines. Gawain discussed the merits of cattle with Alaric. Shawna sat, feeling like screaming.

Sipping more and more wine on an empty stomach.

"Shawna, are you well?"

Aidan, at her side, softly asked the question. She glanced at him quickly to find his light eyes filled with concern. "You're quite flushed," he told her. "This morning, you were far too pale."

"I'm fine."

She stood suddenly. "Will you excuse me, please? I didn't sleep well last night."

Gawain looked at her, frowning. "You're well?"

"Aye, Uncle. Extremely healthy. Robust," she assured him dryly. "I'm just tired. Good night." She gave Lowell a quick kiss on the cheek. He patted her hand where it lay on his shoulder. She kissed Gawain as well, and he in turn caught her hand, staring at her. "You've been pale all day, lass."

She shrugged. "I'm fine, really."

Alistair was arching a brow at her, a quizzical curve to his lips.

Alistair knew her best. She was going to have to avoid him.

She hurried from the hall. Let them talk out their plans alone.

And talk about her.

And about what a pity it was that a lass held their property.

She intended to get some sleep.

But she wasn't going to get any sleep, she realized quickly.

Her room had been prepared for the night. Her fire blazed warmly. A nightgown had been left out on the quilted cover of the master's bed.

A soft glow of moonlight streamed in from the balcony window.

For hundreds of years, moonlight had come through that window just so. There had never been a way to close or lock it. In winter, a heavy tapestry hung over it to keep out the cold. The weather had not become so harsh yet that a cover was necessary. In ancient days, there was no danger from the window because the stone walls protected the castle. And, unless one knew of the existence of the secret stairway, there was no way to reach the balcony—other than to walk up sheer walls. The hidden stairway had been a secret passed on only to the Douglas heir...

Except that David had told her about it. Years ago, when her father had died, and she had been so hurt and lost. He had come to the services for her father and had sat with her after her father's body had been interred in the vault at Castle MacGinnis, and he'd distracted her with stories about the old days when so many of the Highlanders had been Jacobites and often, in their hearts, Catholics, and they had done their best to protect and hide both fleeing priests and Stuart aspirants to the throne.

She'd always admired David. Naturally. He was the overlord, he was older, he was tall, striking, handsome, everything a laird should be. Her fear that he did not appreciate her, the younger lass, had always kept her from revealing that she admired him.

That night, after her father had died, when he had been so gentle, was probably when she had begun to care much more deeply about him.

And just maybe, Alistair had been right. She had been more than glad to take on the task of seducing him from the castle. She had been glad for any opportunity to play the siren with him.

She had never imagined the consequences...

The nights, ever after, when the dreams plagued her and she wondered.

She walked out to the balcony. The night was quiet.

Yet he was out there. Somewhere.

"Where are you?" she murmured aloud.

There was no answer for her other than the whisper of the night wind.

She walked back down the steps.

Looked behind the screen, under the bed. Nervously, she shed her clothing and hurriedly slipped into a nightgown, waiting for him to pounce from the shadows at any moment.

He did not appear. She lay down to sleep. And stared at the balcony window.

She and David were the only ones who knew about the stairway and passage. Or so she thought. At least, she was fairly convinced it was so. Yet someone had chased her last night. Someone who'd wanted to hurt her...kill her.

She leaped out of bed, convinced there was a way to jam the secret doorway cut into the stone from the balcony.

If David needed her help, he could ask her by daylight. She wanted no more nocturnal visits from him. She dug into her drawer for a handkerchief, then sped up the steps to the balcony, and out into the night. She dropped down to find the stone that triggered the mechanism to open the passageway. She slid the handkerchief into the metal workings and closed the stone with the edge of the handkerchief on her side. She was pleased then to discover that she had managed quite well. The mechanism was jammed by the fabric, which couldn't be seen from the inside, but which she could remove quite easily.

Incredibly pleased with herself, she curled back into her bed.

She closed her eyes.

But she leaped back to her feet and hurried to her hallway door, then slid the ancient bolt.

No one would be coming into her room by either the chamber door or the secret entry. She could sleep in safety at last.

She lay down again and stared into the night for a very long time, thinking, not wanting to think, remembering, and praying not to remember. A soft fire still burned in her grate. The room was filled with shadows, yet the gentle flames cast an orange-and-gold glow over the room as well.

She was so tired.

Yet David lived. And her life was a tempest again.

Where was he?

Not in her room, she was safe!

Safe? Yet unnerved.

Still, eventually...

Her eyelids began to flutter.

She began to drift.

And fall asleep...

She awoke in sudden terror. The stairway entrance had been jammed. The door had been bolted.

There had been no possible entry to her room. Yet she was not alone. A dark shadow hovered over her in the night. Then fell upon her. Silencing the scream that so nearly tore from her lips.

CHAPTER 7

"Hush it's me."

He was atop her, then the hand that had covered her mouth was lifted from it, and David Douglas fell to her side.

She was shaking like a leaf caught in a fierce north wind, terrified and amazed. She came up on an elbow, creating all the distance between them she could manage on the bed.

"How did you get in here?" she demanded.

"I have my ways."

"How—"

"Ghosts can come right through walls, can't they?" he inquired, rolling from her and rising.

He had changed from his Highland garb, she saw. Tonight, he was decked out in a black cotton shirt, form-hugging black breeches, boots, and hooded black cape.

Shivers shot along her spine.

He looked a great deal like the shadowy form that had chased her from the Druid Stones.

"What did you do with him—the dead man?" she demanded.

"Weighted him down."

"And?"

"Well, I'm sure he's joined the remains of many another man who perished by righteous or illegal means throughout the centuries. He lies at the bottom of the loch."

"Why?"

"Did you want it known you're aware someone is after you? Do you think I want it known who rescued you?"

"My family can hardly take the proper steps for my safety if they are unaware that I am in danger."

"What if someone in your family is creating the danger? What if they all want you dead?"

She slipped out of bed, standing very tall and determined as she faced him. "They don't want me dead, and I refuse to listen to you."

"You will listen to me."

"I won't. You've no right to accost me in the middle of the night after all these years with no explanation—David, no!"

Despite her protest and her desperate determination to back away, he was upon her in a flash. Her words were lost as he caught her wrists, drawing her hard against him. "Listen!" he commanded.

She wished fervently that he had not chosen such a way to force her to do so. A hot weakness pervaded her. She was far too aware of his warmth, his touch, the feel of his body against her own.

Far too aware of what had been in the past, and of the feelings that tormented her now.

"David—"

He was angry, not ready to release her. "Don't speak, listen! I've every right to come here and more, my dear."

"But where have you been all this time?" she cried.

"I've no intention of relaying my past. I seek to forget it, and I do truly suggest you cease trying to make me remember! Pay me heed, my lady. You have to listen to me, Shawna, you've got no choice. For all that has been in the past, I am determined I will be with you, and I will keep you safe as we discover the exact truth of what happened here!"

She was silent for a moment, trying not to shiver while she studied his eyes. Dear God, what had he gone through? She wanted to touch him. She desperately wanted to reach out and touch his cheek, smooth his brow. His anger with her would never allow it. He wanted no tenderness from her, and if he wanted her at all, it was with that same anger.

He sought vengeance.

And still, he didn't understand. Terrible things had happened, aye, but no MacGinnis could be capable of murder.

"You're asking me to believe that my own flesh and blood are trying to kill me. I can't believe you. Let me go, David. My god, David, think about it! It is absurd that my kin would want to harm me, why should I believe you—"

"Because I, at least, intend to keep you alive."

"Why? To use me, nothing more. While you tell me that the family I've lived among my whole life are all out to do away with me."

"I didn't suggest that every MacGinnis is trying to kill you."

"Then—"

"One of them is."

"Who?"

"I don't know."

She wrenched away from him, hugging her arms around her chest as she walked to the window, keeping her back to him. "Why are you so certain that someone in my family is guilty?"

"Shawna, who else has power here?"

She spun around. "You. You walk through walls. Your brother. He plans a trip here, and suddenly strange men are appearing out of stone and trying to cut me down."

"My brother isn't here yet."

"You are in this room—when there is no possible way that you can be here!"

"Obviously, it's possible."

"Why—why are you here again?"

"To protect you—understand that. I will protect you. God knows, there might well be some link between the danger threatening you now and what happened five years ago. Accept the fact, my lady, that I will be with you, protecting you, despite the fact that you seem not to appreciate my efforts."

"It seems you're the only one I need protection from when I'm in this room."

"I threaten you?" he queried softly, and she realized that he had silently come to stand behind her. His hands fell upon her bare shoulders, and his soft, husky voice burned her earlobes. "You, my lady, are the dangerous one. One way or the other, you were the first to solicit my affections. Remember? And you have certainly weathered them without ill effect."

She braced against his hold. "Oh, you have no idea of the consequences—"

He spun her around, his hold upon her firm as he told her, "But I do know the consequences of seeking heaven with you."

Shawna gritted her teeth, trying valiantly to struggle from the tight hold he had upon her. "Oh! Yet last night you seemed ready to dare it again. What incredible courage."

"Ah, my lady, I weigh all risks."

"If you think—"

"I think that someone made a very great effort to kill me. I don't know why someone attempted my murder, nor do I know exactly why I'm alive. I'm equally certain that someone is determined to kill you. I know every secret passage, tunnel, stairway, nook, and cranny in this castle—it is, as you will recall, my birthright. So, I think that I will come and go from this room as I please, and I think that, under the circumstances, you should do your damned best to accommodate me in any way possible."

"Accommodate you!" Shawna gasped.

"Ah, my lady!" he teased in mock horror, eyes raking over her. "It may not be such a wretched thing. Indeed, it did seem that you enjoyed my presence when last we met. You may discover what revenge I would take against you to be sweet indeed."

"Let go. You are brutal—"

"Ruthless," he corrected. And again his eyes swept her in a way that seemed to create an inferno within him. "And very, very determined."

"Determined on vengeance?"

"On truth," he said softly. A curious light touched his eyes, and his tone was even huskier. "And, aye, vengeance. Naturally, I will take all that vengeance at my leisure."

He still held her tightly. Perhaps he heard the thunder of her heart, felt the way she trembled. She struggled fiercely against his hold, advising him furiously, "Go to the authorities. Go to the queen! Take back your birthright—"

He shook her hard, once, to still her. Her eyes met his. She was aware that he did not tease now, that his green eyes were sharp, and his handsome features were rigid. "If I go to the authorities, Shawna MacGinnis, I will seek out the very best solicitor in the country, and I will accuse the entire MacGinnis clan of attempted murder, and since the very fact that I am alive stands well for evidence in my favor, it is likely a good portion of your family will hang. Not to mention the fact that you were quite definitely part and parcel of the conspiracy."

Determined to respond with dignity rather than the bursts of fear and fury that so easily ruled her when he was near, she tried to pull free from his hold. He let her go. She faced him from just a few feet away. "So come and go as you please, Laird David Douglas. Slip in and out of the room—and I shall do my best not to perish from the shock of your sudden appearances before we've come to the end of this quest. Just keep your distance, Laird Douglas, and I'll argue this no more. We'll find out what truly happened in the past and what is happening now."

"Aye, lass, I'll keep my distance. You keep yours."

"I don't keep slipping through your window and crawling atop you in bed."

"Ah, but you did teach me that it was the way to reach someone privately in the night."

It would always come back to that. And Shawna was dismayed to realize that the very strength of her fury against him made her want to touch him. She wanted to pound against him, and then...

Feel him. She was on fire. So very angry, yet so very much alive and wanting.

She carefully backed away from him again. "Would you like a pillow and blanket for a place before the hearth?"

"No. Would you?"

She caught her breath. "Surely, you don't mean to sleep—in the bed?"

"We've agreed it is mine," he reminded her politely.

Damn him.

"I will sleep before the hearth," she heard herself say.

"Go ahead then, my lady. Whatever pleases you."

She plucked her pillow from the bed and dragged off the quilted coverlet. She did her best to make herself comfortable in the chair before the fire.

David cast off his cape and boots and lay down upon the bed.

"Good night," he said pleasantly.

"Go to hell."

He ignored her, stretching out comfortably.

She could scarcely believe it.

Seconds of night ticked away. His eyes were closed. He seemed comfortable and at ease.

She was wretched in the chair.

But he did sleep, so it seemed. She was unbelievably uncomfortable. Surely, it would have been better to attempt to sleep with him near her on the bed. Nay...that would have been even more wretched!

She threw her pillow and coverlet upon the floor before the hearth and tried to curl up there. The stone was cold. She watched the fire and prayed for sleep.

HE DIDN'T SLEEP, not so easily.

He remained very still as the night passed, determined that she would think him quite naturally at rest. When she finished fidgeting in the chair and curled down upon the floor, he continued to remain still for a long time.

Then he halfway sat up, eyeing her prone form. This was a strange anguish when the temptation was to swear impatiently, wrench her up, and pull her into the warmth and softness of the bed with him.

And then...

It would be a far better thing for him were she not to realize that he found her quite so tantalizing.

Wanting her had indeed, once upon a time, sent him into all the blazes and tortures of pure hell.

David lay back down upon his pillow, closing his eyes tightly. He pressed his thumb and forefinger against his temple, as if he could squeeze away the pressure building in his head.

God, he had lived that night over and over again in the years that had followed it!

He could see her every time just as she had come to him that night. Through the secret stairway. And she had stood, framed by the moonlight, whispering his name.

"David..."

And he had agreed to meet her at the stables.

He closed his eyes, wishing that he could not always remember with such startling clarity so much that had taken place that night.

But he would always remember.

Every word.

Every whisper and movement.

Going to the stables. Drinking the wine, changing glasses with her.

Their argument. Over Alastair.

"Must you be so hypocritical?" he had demanded.

"Must you be so hateful?" she had returned.

And he had tried to walk away. In all honesty, he had tried to walk away. But she had called him back. "I do—I do intend to show you... something...give you all that is offered..."

The sensations became overwhelming. She was in his arms. He had her lips, and then he had her down upon the poor bed in the stables, and she'd been all that mattered. He'd known he was drugged, but the very essence of the drug had kept him from caring.

How curious now that he could still remember every little nuance of that night. Remember, see her, feel her...

She twisted beneath him as he kissed her, discovering that he couldn't know her lips enough. Her gown inched up. He dragged it farther, his hands caressing her naked hip and thigh with growing passion and demand. His robe parted. He kissed her throat. She whispered words he didn't understand. He slipped her gown from her shoulder, her breast. He fastened his mouth upon her nipple, laving the hardening peak again and again with his tongue. She gasped and shuddered, fingers ripping into his arms. He thrust her gown far above her hips and abdomen, buried his face against the soft, vulnerable flesh there, delved his fingers into the raven black triangle of hair until he touched her with unbearable intimacy. Shudders ripped the length of her, words escaped her, words, having no sense and no reason.

"...just show you..." she gasped.

The flesh of her belly was unbelievably soft, silken fascination. He moved his lips upon it, traveled, delved. The brush of his fingers became bold, demanding, intimate, that of his lips even more so. She filled him, she was every breath, every caress, every beat of his heart, sweet, fragrant, musky. She twisted, writhed. Words ceased to come from her. He heard her frantic intake of breath, felt her fingers digging into his shoulders and hair. She cried out, her body as rigid as steel, and the honey of her seemed to fill him again with intoxicating sensation. He rose over her, knees parting her thighs. She didn't open her eyes. Her face was pale and beautiful. He groaned with a shudder that seemed to rise from him with volcanic volatility, enwrapped in her, thrust himself fully, deeply within her.

The sound that escaped her was a breath, no more. He looked into her face again. Her eyes were opened, glazed.

"Shawna..."

Her name from his lips was pained. What was done he had not intended.

What was done he could not have avoided. And even now he didn't seem to be in his right senses because what had been done did not matter. He wanted her. Could not withdraw from her, had to have her. Again, sensation was painfully acute, desire was desperate. In a distant corner of his mind, he was angry with himself. He was a man, not an animal with no reason or logic. Anger didn't matter, what pain he might have caused her didn't matter. She twisted. He held taut. She cried out suddenly, her arms coming around him, her face pressed against his shoulder. Pain had stunned her. He could have withdrawn, yet she was suddenly the aggressor, clinging to him. Crimson light and fury seemed to fill him. He moved with desperate energy against her, sheathed, filled, urgent, reveling in every movement, wanting more and more. Climax built wildly within him, spiraled. He was vaguely aware of the rough wool blanket beneath them. The world still smelled sweetly of new-mown hay, more sweetly still of flowers and the woman and the musk of their bedding.

Her face remained buried against him. He caught her hair, forced her to meet his eyes. Hers remained blue and glistening with unshed tears. He found the sweetness of her mouth once again, forcing her lips to part to his. And they did, and she met the hunger of his kiss with a thirst of her own, hesitantly at first, then more fully, until he thought that he would drown in the seduction of her. Then the force of the climax that had been building within him burst wildly upon him. Muscles constricted and taut, he held above her and within her as wave after wave of release seized him, shook him, spilled from him, and into her. As he stared down at her then, he was dimly aware that Shawna had never intended for her game to go so far.

He started to brush her face with his knuckles, to tell her that if her bargain was marriage, then so be it. She was far too anguished, he thought, and he was far too proud to tell her that she had just aroused and seduced him like no other woman. Such admissions with a lass like Shawna could be far too costly for a man in his position at this time. She was still a MacGinnis, lady of the Craig Rock MacGinnises, and dangerous in that holding.

Her eyes closed. Her body glistened in lamplit crimson beauty.

Sated, soaked, both satisfied and aware he'd be wanting far more, he opened his mouth to speak.

No words came from him.

Just the pain. An ungodly pain within his head.

He saw red...

He touched his hand to his temple, and it came away covered with blood.

The color before him turned to black...

The world began spinning into deeper and deeper shades of crimson and black before him.

Yellow, gold, orange, blue...

Fire.

There was fire. He didn't know if he felt the searing pain in his head and then the fire immediately, or if there had been time between the two. He felt the heat of the fire, and he struggled to clear his mind...

Black again. Ebony. A void...

Death...

Aye, death, it was what someone had intended, and in a way, he was indeed to die that night.

Aye, it was death, and the coming of it slow and miserable. He tossed. He felt pain. He felt nothing. Terrible cold, burning heat. Darkness...

No, color again. Color...blue, the sky, the sky at morning. The sun was in his eyes, causing his head to burst with pain once again.

He could hear the lap of water. He was on a boat, he realized. Out in the loch?

"Get this one up and moving, there, man! There's work to be done on the sails."

He jumped as he was viciously kicked in the ribs. Despite the pain that continued to rack his head, he managed to leap up to a squatting position.

Sunlight filled his eyes, nearly blinding him. He realized that he was naked and filthy. And indeed, he was upon the water, on a large ship. Seamen surrounded him, doing the bidding of a peg-legged man who stared down at him now with contempt.

"Get this murdering, ragged-ass bastard up and about!" the peg leg shouted. He had an accent. A strange accent.

David tried to stand, tottered, nearly fell. He saw that he had been lying on a pallet. He staggered to his feet once again, in agony, but was ready to leap for the throat of the peg leg. "Do you know whom you address?" David demanded in a rage.

"Aye, you jackanapes! You're going to live, you sorry bastard, but 'tis my belief you should have met with the hangman in Glasgow."

"The hangman?"

"For murderin' that poor wee lass."

"Murder..."

He did leap at the peg leg. The man shouted, choking. In seconds, half a dozen brawny seamen were atop David. He fought them off, had no strength. He fell back to his knees, a wave of nausea and dizziness sweeping over him again. The peg leg had remarkable balance and struck David with his wooden limb, knocking him to the deck. David barely felt the pain. What were they talking about? What had happened after he had been knocked out in the stables? He could remember nothing but the smell of fire. Had someone come and done harm to Shawna? "Murder!" he cried, pushing back to his knees. "If she's dead—"

"Aye, the wee lass is dead, you cut her throat on a drunken binge on a cold Glasgow night, my man, and in my care, I bloody well swear that you'll pay for it!"

"Glasgow!"

"So drank he canna remember his own crime!" Peg Leg muttered with disgust. "Mr. Phipps!" he cried to one of his men. "Take the bastard back to the hold for the next few days. He's been in a fever too long to be much good to us yet. But mark me, Mr. MacDonald, I'll wring flesh and blood from you yet, I will."

"MacDonald!" David roared. "I am not a MacDonald. I am David Douglas of Craig Rock, heir to the laird!"

Snickering from the seamen who had gathered round him greeted his words.

"Get the bastard below!" the peg-legged captain shouted with disgust.

"Have me touched again, you pathetic piece of pig shit, and I'll murder you, I swear it!" David promised.

Peg Leg seemed to take the threat to heart. "Shackle him, wrists and ankles!" Peg Leg commanded.

The first man came toward David. David managed to deal him a telling blow to the left jaw. He spun in time to catch the man to his right with an elbow jab to the ribs. He kicked the one before him, slammed the one in the rear with both fists.

But there were four more to fall atop him. He was shackled, and a solid blow with a fisherman's sinker sent him spinning back into oblivion once again.

He came to stretched out upon dirty, molding straw. A stench surrounded him. He had been wrapped in the remnants of a blanket. A small, ragged little man with sharp features and huge eyes was attempting to spoon some kind of tasteless gruel between his lips. David coughed, sputtered, and managed to lift a hand to stop the man.

"Water," he croaked.

The little man provided it, watching him anxiously. He drank, forcing himself to be careful. His voice remained a sorry croak as he asked, "What manner of ship is this? Into what pit of hell have I fallen."

"A sorry pit, indeed," the little fellow said. "You're on the convict ship, Revenge, bound for labor in Australia, mate."

"Sweet Jesus, heads will roll for this! I am the heir to Laird Douglas of Craig Rock!"

The little man was still. In a fury, David knocked the bowl of gruel from the very hands that had tried to help him. "Why will no one believe me, man?"

"The Douglas heir was killed in a fire a good two weeks ago now."

"What? The fire was two weeks ago—"

"The laird's son is dead and buried, MacDonald, and most men aboard think it's blasphemy that you, the murderer of a young woman, dare to use his name."

"What young woman was murdered? Shawna of Craig Rock?"

The man shook his head in confusion. "Nay, MacDonald! The serving wench you met in Oarmsby Tavern!"

"I met no serving wench, and I haven't been to Glasgow in years! If we can but turn this ship around, I can prove—"

"Shh! Shh!" the little monkey of a man warned him. "Some think as how that fever you suffered has you daft now, man, believing you're a laird and able to put on airs and all. But the captain, he's a fierce man, and he says that from now on, every time as how you start claimin' to be a Douglas, you're to receive twenty lashes with a cat-o'-nine-tails."

"I am David Douglas!" he roared.

There was a bursting sound as the swinging door to the hold was thrown open. Peg Leg maneuvered down the ladder, wrinkling his nose at the stench of the hold. He was followed by a number of his seamen, one of them the nasty-looking fellow David had previously struck in the jaw.

The seaman's face was still swollen. David had probably cost the fellow a number of teeth.

"MacDonald, I'll have no more of your mad cries on board my ship!" Peg Leg roared. "See to him, men."

Again, David fought. In the end, he was too weak to face so many men. He found himself dragged up, still naked, bound to the center post in the hold.

And the threat of the twenty lashes with the cat-o'-nine-tails was carried out. The man with the swollen face was to carry out the punishment, but even he paused, voicing a protest to Peg Leg. "'E's half-dead, now, Cap'n. Twenty lashes will kill him."

"He stands tall as an oak, and he's muscled like a fighter. He used that strength against the innocent. God will judge him. If he dies, so be it, but I'll watch each strike—he's a fine one for work in Sydney, and worth more to me alive than dead. Carry on."

Each lash bit cruelly into David's flesh. In his weakened state, the pain was unbearable. He blacked out before it was over.

He came to with the little man by his side, staring at him sorrowfully. "Your name is Collum MacDonald," the little man warned. "Ach, sir! Be you the laird's issue in truth, you'd best forget it for now. Captain Barnes will kill you like as not if you give him more reason! Work the sails, scrub the decks as he commands you. Live to tell your story where someone might care to hear it!"

"I am David Douglas, eldest son and heir to the laird of Castle Rock, Craig Rock, the Highlands," David insisted.

"Fine, man, and I'll believe you. But if you've a mind for livin', answer to the name 'MacDonald,' sir. And try to eat this broth. Something's got to keep you going. They'll be draggin' you up to work soon enough."

David stared at the little man and frowned.

"Who the bloody hell are you, and why do you care, man?"

The jackanapes smiled. "Once upon a time, I was Dr. James McGregor of High Street, Glasgow. But that was before a great man's mistress chose to abort his child, then come for my help. She died as I tried to staunch the flow of blood pouring from her womb. The great man let the courts convict me, but the mercy of a judge sent me aboard this ship rather than straight to the hangman. Now, sir, they'd not believe my story, and they'll not believe yours."

"Doctor," he mused.

"They call me murderer now."

David stared at the little man, and at last saw the wisdom in his words.

"I am MacDonald, eh?"

"Aye, that I beg of you."

David shrugged. "Not a bad clan as clans go. Even good families must throw out a bad egg now and then, eh?"

"MacDonald. A good enough name to live by if you'd seek to retrieve your own."

Indeed.

There was but one way for him to find justice and vengeance, and that was to survive. His rage against what had happened, against her and those who had conspired with her, would not help him now.

Had he been supposed to die?

But he had not perished.

Yet it did not seem that he had lived.

He had found hell on earth.

But he was going to survive it. He was going to survive it because he was going to go back. Find out who had sought to kill him, and who was buried in his stead. Discover what evil cunning and conspiracy had brought him to this pit of eternal fire.

And he was going to enter her life again.

And God help him...

She would have all the fury of hell to pay, and he would see to it that they were damned together.

David awoke with a start. He was no longer aboard a ship, nor was he any man's prisoner. He had found his freedom, and he was back in his room at Castle Rock.

In his own bed.

He looked quickly to the floor. She slept.

All those years...

All those years he had waited to come back, and she had been both the focus of his revenge and the spirit that plagued his sleep, for though he longed for his revenge, he had found himself simply longing for her as well. Her scent had haunted him in the night. Memories of the satin-smooth feel of her flesh had come to him in the darkness, along with those of the soft brush of her hair against his limbs. And now...

He still longed both to hold her tenderly and to shake her. When she had been younger, he had cared for her as an unruly, headstrong, beautiful child.

When she had grown and matured, he had desired her.

Aye, he had wanted her, therein had lain his weakness, and therein now lay his thirst for revenge.

Yet again, it was Shawna twisting his heart and senses and reason.

He rose from the bed and walked to where she slept now upon the cold stone of the castle floor. He gently picked her up and laid her upon the bed.

And because he could not help himself, he gently placed his lips against her mouth and there tasted her sweetness with the breath of his kiss.

Fool! he charged himself.

And he departed the room in the same manner by which he had come.

CHAPTER 8

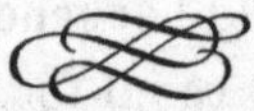

Shawna sat in the office, scrupulously going over each individual set of books kept for both estates. As far as she could tell, not a single shilling had been miscounted since the day David Douglas—or the charred corpse that had supposedly been David Douglas—had been buried.

She sighed, setting down the books, rising, stretching, looking out of the large window that was so similar to the one in her bedroom. Steps led to it, and beyond it was a stone balcony. The balconies naturally offered a fine method of defense for the castle, but to the best of her knowledge, they'd never been used so, for in the days when feudal wars had plagued the Highlands, the outer walls had stood strong against any attempted invasion.

She frowned, staring at the window, hoping it would give her some insight as to how David was coming and going from her room.

Since she had awakened the second morning after his arrival—back in the bed—three days had passed.

Tense days for her.

She continually waited for him to appear.

He did not.

Yet she knew he came at night. Very late, she thought. She would find some subtle reminder that he was near.

THE FIRST MORNING, she found a bunch of wildflowers lying by her pillow. The second morning, the pillow by her head was indented, and she realized that he had lain beside her the night before, leaving behind a small, beautifully wrought Celtic cross on a delicate chain, a Douglas family heirloom, she was certain. The third morning, she found a delicate silk handkerchief—along with an empty brandy glass which sat upon the old trunk at the foot of the bed.

She wondered about the gifts, half-tempted to throw them one and all in the fire.

But he had left them for her. To taunt her, perhaps. No matter, she wore the cross, kept the flowers by her pillow and the handkerchief in her pocket.

It infuriated her that she found herself so pathetically unnerved and unable to sleep—then unable to awaken when he made his irritating appearances.

He was about, somewhere during the day, she knew. She was quite certain that he was slipping in and out of the office here as well as at the stables and the mines. He could probably even come and go from Castle MacGinnis as he chose, though she had never heard of secret passages within her own family's home.

But what was he doing? What was he discovering?

She realized that although she was angered by his easy movements and although she dreaded their encounters in which he insisted on blaming her family for the evil afoot, she was anxious to see him again.

She didn't want to long to see him.

But she did. In the most curious manner, she ached. He was in her thoughts day and night.

She heard footsteps coming hard and fast up the stairway to the second floor, and she spun away from the balcony, looking toward the office door as it was flung open. Alistair stood there, his handsome face completely free of any hint of a mischievous smile.

"There's been an accident. At the mine," he told her.

She walked quickly to him, ready to pass him to reach the stairway. "My god, what happened? How many men are down?"

"The men..."

"What? Tell me, Alistair, please?"

"There are three men in the shaft, but the others are already digging for them. They've done a good job, and we're going to reach the men."

"There's more, Alistair, tell me!"

"Daniel was searching a passageway."

"Daniel!" she gasped.

"The little Anderson fellow."

"Oh god!" she cried. Turning swiftly, she went flying down the stairway.

Just outside the main doors, Alistair caught up with her. He took her firmly by the shoulders. "The horses are here. We're ready to ride. But you must get hold of yourself. It will do the lad no good if you kill yourself on your way to reach him!"

She nodded numbly, then mounted up swiftly. She was somewhat in control again, and Alistair knew that she was an exceptional rider. The two of them streaked over the hills, valleys, and fields like bolts of lightning. Twenty feet from the mine entrance, Shawna leaped from her horse and went racing to it. Mark Menzies caught her at the entry.

"Lowell, Gawain, Alaric, and Aidan are within, m'lady. Ye cannot dig, as the men can."

"Where's the lad, Mark?"

"Still within, they're trying to reach him."

Alistair passed by her, hurrying to the entry.

"Keep her out, Mark. Let her comfort the wives if the men do not make it," he said firmly.

Shawna let her cousin go, then she looked to Mark.

"Mark, let me pass."

"M'lady—"

"You must let me pass," she said firmly.

Reluctantly, he let her go. Shawna raced on into the shaft, where lanterns provided an eerie light. Aidan, covered in coal dust and supporting a completely blackened man, was coming from the shaft.

"Shawna, take yourself out of here!" he commanded. "We've opened the shaft. We're getting the men."

"The boy?" she inquired.

The blackened miner who had been caught in the cave-in shook his head. "Not yet,'ees in a natural shaft we've not taken to yet."

"Oh god!" Shawna breathed. She ignored Aidan and the miner, moving deeper into the eerie light and darkness of the shaft. Men were working with support beams. Each of them called to her. She ignored them until she came to the place where the men had been working. Now, they dug, her kilted uncles tearing at the coal with a strength to match that of any man there.

There was a cry as they dug through to free another man. "Me leg!" the miner cried.

"I've got him," she heard her cousin Alaric say, hunkering down to pick up the man in his arms as the fellow groaned, but cleared the coal around him.

Wiping his blackened brow, Gawain turned and saw Shawna. "For God's sake, lass, are you seeking death? Alistair, I said to take her outside—"

"And I left her outside, Father. She's a stubborn wench, and you know it."

"Get your cousin out—" Lowell began.

"Nay, I'm here now," Shawna pleaded. "Where's the boy?"

"Back in there," a voice croaked.

"Angus—where are you?" Alistair demanded.

"Here!"

Alistair and Lowell crawled to where the last of the trapped miners still lay beneath a mound of rock and coal. "We've got you, man!" Alistair assured him.

All of the men were safe.

But a child remained.

Shawna crawled over the dirt and rock and coal to a tiny, incredibly narrow shaft above the spot where the last of the buried miners had been caught.

The men could not explore such places. Only children could do so.

And women.

She was slim enough to manage the space, she thought. Instinctively, she started to crawl into it. She was dimly aware of her great-uncle Gawain swearing from behind her.

"Daniel?" she called softly. She shouldn't shout. She knew that the shaft would be vulnerable now to whatever had caused the cave-in that had plagued the larger tunnel.

"Shawna, get out of there!" Gawain demanded.

"Daniel...Danny? Are you there?"

She heard a soft whimpering sound. Oh god, the boy sounded so very far away!

"Danny, it's Lady Shawna. Can you hear me? I know that you must be very frightened. We're going to get to you. If you could talk to me, it would help. Are you there?"

She heard a whimpering again and then a soft, "Aye!"

"I'm going to reach you..."

"Y'cannot," the little boy said.

"Why?"

"A—rock fell. A big rock."

"We're going to move the rock."

She heard the whimpering again. The soft cry of a child, a little boy. But then she heard words with soft resolve. "Don't come. You'll get caught, too."

"Daniel, I'm not leaving you in there."

She wasn't going to leave him. But there was suddenly a firm tug on her ankles, and she heard her great-uncle's angry voice. "Shawna, get out of there. I care not if you're the lady. I'll wrench you out over my knee if you do not choose to obey me before the whole of this place falls! The walls must be shored up, you know nothing of mining—"

"I know this child will smother if we don't get him out!"

Her own words died away. She gritted her teeth and pulled hard against the rocks in the shaft floor, dragging her ankles out of his reach.

She heard Gawain swear vociferously.

Then, as the sound of his voice faded, she went still, because the little boy was talking. To someone else.

"Aye!"

To her amazement, she heard childish laughter and again another, "Aye!"

"Danny?" she whispered.

"I'll ride the beastie!" she heard.

"No, no, Danny, listen to me."

"Can y'not hear the water?"

"Danny!" she cried with alarm. She heard his laughter again, fading away. Then it did seem that she heard a lap of water against rock.

"Danny!" she cried. "Danny!"

No answer. The boy was gone. He had been deluded in the darkness. He had gone mad from lack of oxygen. He had crawled farther into the shaft, he had fallen into some kind of an underground waterway, and he was...

"No, no, oh god, no!" she cried. Then she gasped. Someone had come behind her.

"Leave me!" she cried, fighting the hold upon her. "Danny!" she cried again. "Danny?"

Still no answer. Nothing. Nothing at all.

She was firmly tugged upon. Still, she fought to free herself. To no avail. Someone had a solid hold of her ankles, and she was being dragged from the shaft.

"Danny! Answer me!"

But there was no answer, and time was against her. Seconds passed, minutes.

"Danny, Danny, Danny, please."

She was ever more firmly gripped. Black coal, ragged, rocky dirt dragged and tore at her. She was barely aware of it. She was in tears when she found herself falling back onto a pile of pure coal, freed from the shaft. She was pulled up.

She looked into the pitch-black of Alistair's face, dimly recognizing her cousin only because of the startling blue of his eyes.

"The boy..." she whispered.

"Shhh..." he said, holding her against him.

Suddenly, they became aware of shouts from outside the tunnels, muffled as they entered into their underground world.

"What now?" Shawna heard the gruff demand come from Gawain.

"Alistair—" Lowell began.

"Don't worry. I've got my cousin," Alistair said.

"We can't just leave!" she protested.

"Shawna," Alistair said, "we can do no more." He started forcing her along the pathway. They had barely left the caved-in area of the shaft before one of the miners hurried up to them. "Come out, come out, quickly now. The boy is outside. Sweet Jesus, little Danny Anderson is just outside the shaft."

"What?" Gawain thundered. "'Tis true, he's outside. The wee lad is alive."

"How?" Shawna breathed.

"God alone knows," the miner said. "For 'tis sure, there's not a one of us can tell!"

Shawna tore out of the cave. Mark Menzies, as coal blackened as the rest of them, was kneeling down in the grass, a distance from the shaft, with the boy, while he was surrounded in an outer circle by miners and their families. A blanket had been placed around Danny, and his little face was smudged beyond recognition. His dark hair was soaked and plastered to his head. Shawna went running to the pair in the deep grasses, falling to her knees before the child, lifting his hair from his forehead to study his enormous blue eyes. "Danny, Danny... you are alive!" Impulsively, she hugged him tightly, then managed to sit back again, studying him. "Danny, how did you get out?"

"The beastie," Danny said solemnly.

A cup was pressed against Shawna's hands. Someone had brought warm, milk-laden tea. She forced it to the little boy's lips, which were almost as blue as his eyes. He sipped the warm tea and his shivering somewhat subsided while his eyes remained on Shawna.

She was suddenly determined the boy wasn't going back into the mines. She didn't give a damn what happened in the rest of Scotland, Great Britain, or the world at large. They would be sending no more children into the mines at Craig Rock.

He finished the tea, returning the cup to her. Shawna looked up as a hand reached down to take the cup from her. Gena Anderson was standing there by her side, looking down at her and the boy solemnly. Shawna felt a twinge of guilt. The boy was supposedly one of Gena's own brood of sisters and brothers, a child of Fergus and Charity Anderson, but Shawna was convinced that Gena was actually the child's mother. She should step away and let Gena take the little boy into her arms to comfort him, but Gena didn't seem to mind the attention she paid him.

"Danny, lad. What beastie was this that could pluck you from the tunnel?" Mark Menzies asked.

"The beastie that lives in the cave," Danny said, as if explaining that the sun rose each morning. "He talks. He heard m'cryin' he said, and he told me to come with him. I did, and he lifted me through the earth. He's a huge beastie, but he's not a mean one."

"The tunnel is haunted by some spirit or creature!" came a woman's fierce cry. It was Charity Anderson.

A shawl thrown over her graying hair, she broke through the crowd, kneeling by Shawna to give her a reproachful glare and take the boy tightly into her arms.

Danny seemed to struggle a bit against that hold, and Shawna quickly sat back. Charity Anderson was not an attractive woman, she never had been, though she and her husband had produced a handsome enough brood. Charity possessed a long, horse-like face. Her eyes were gray blue against her ashen coloring. Her hair had once been her only claim to beauty, but she cared nothing for it now, and it was merely wild and unkempt and gray. There was a strange look about the woman now. She half smiled, and yet she was grim. Her look seemed to say that Shawna might be the great lady, but she was the lad's mother, and she was taking him, and that was that.

Shawna stood, aware that people around her had started whispering, and some were speaking more boldly.

"'Tis true, the damned mines are cursed in some way!" cried a miner.

"Haunted," agreed another.

"Haunted, be damned!" Aidan suddenly cried out in aggravation.

"My cousin is right!" Alistair decreed. "My god, are you all daft? If any spirits reside in that mine, they are surely the most benign in all the world. A shaft caved in, yet all three men caught were dug out of it, and even a little mite of a lad caught in a narrow exploratory tunnel was miraculously saved—by some beastie. Sweet Jesus, if we've ghosts or the like, we've got the nicest group of the damned creatures in all of Scotland!"

It occurred to Shawna then that there was no mystical creature within the mine shafts.

David Douglas had found the boy, and David had saved him. David —who had risen out of the water like an ancient selkie just in time to save her. David, who managed, with incredible stealth, to be everywhere.

For Danny's sake, she was grateful. Incredibly grateful.

The silence that had fallen was suddenly broken by Mark Menzies.

"Aye, men, if we've a spirit, it's a kind one, and that's a fact!"

"Aye! And we've a lady of the house willing to blacken herself like any man on behalf of us all!" cried out one of the injured miners, who still hobbled near her cousin Aidan.

"Aye, to our lady!" went up a shout.

The men were suddenly closing in around Shawna. She caught Alistair's grin of approval before she found herself being lifted and set atop her horse. "Will you drink with us at the tavern, Lady Shawna?" Mark Menzies asked.

A drink at the tavern was a customary event when any possible tragedy at the mines was averted.

Just as a drink at the tavern was customary if tragedy was not averted. The lords of the manor always drank with the miners after a funeral service.

"Indeed, I shall be glad to drink with you," Shawna said. "But I am dusty as pitch—"

"'Tis part of the celebration," Mark said, winking.

"Then we shall drink," Shawna assured him.

The tavern was not large enough to accommodate all those who came to it, but many of the men and their wives took their ales and stouts out to the grass and the tables beyond the walls of the establishment to make way for everyone. Shawna managed to wipe some of the coal from her face, but not all, and she found herself smiling as she saw the faces of her family around her. Alistair was certainly comical in his coal coloring, but Aidan made her laugh out loud, he was so encrusted with the coal dust.

She was proud of her family. Each and every man of her kin had been in the mine, working, digging, determined none should die. When she was given an ale, she met Gawain's eyes across the crowded tavern. She lifted her glass to her fierce, crusty great-uncle and was pleased to see his smile of approval in return. She swallowed down some ale, then realized that she was standing by a stranger, a man in dull, brown friar's garb. He was very tall, but also very old, with thick silver-white hair and one of the thickest, richest beards she had ever seen.

"'Tis honored I am to stand by the lady of the land," he said, his voice throaty and accented with the lilt of an Irishman. "And on a day of such high excitement. Tell me, how is the lad who was trapped?"

Shawna smiled her relief. "The lad is fine."

"A miracle."

"Quite possibly."

"Yet, I've heard y'have strange spirits about the place?"

Shawna swallowed down a long draught of ale, then looked at the stranger. "Nay, we've no spirits here...friend. I'm sorry. I don't know you. What is your name?"

"Brother Damian," the man supplied.

"And what are you doing here, traveling our Highlands?"

"Pilgrimage," Brother Damian said. "Please, tell me more about your spirits."

"We don't have spirits."

"Ah, but my lady, you are a superstitious lot! You have a Night of the Moon Maiden—so I've heard tell."

"We enjoy feasts and merriment and happily celebrate some of the ancient holidays," Shawna informed him, somewhat annoyed. It was one thing to admit to Mark Menzies that they certainly were superstitious, far closer at times to very old ways than they were to contemporary society. But their thoughts and beliefs were a part of them, and she would not be mocked by strangers traveling through their Highland craig. "We enjoy our entertainments, Brother Damian, but we have no spirits here, no pookas, ghosts, or the like. I imagine that the boy found his way through some opening within the tunnel. He is very young. Little more than a babe and certainly imaginative. Far too young to work the mines." She hesitated and set down her ale. There was a point she meant to make here and now. "In fact," she said softly, more to herself than to the visiting friar, "there will be no more children of his age working here!"

"Ah, and you are the lady here, so it is your decision, is it?" the man inquired. He drank down a long swallow of his own ale, then set down his glass. He shrugged at her. "One hears things as he travels. The mines are owned in large part by a Douglas, are they not?"

It wasn't her place, in truth, to run around making decrees regarding what was largely Douglas property. "The current Laird Douglas is in America, Brother Damian, not often able to see to his affairs. He trusts my judgment."

"And that of your fine, courageous kin."

"Indeed. Why do you ask?"

"As I said, one hears things...well, quite frankly, there is still talk of the great fire that raged here so many years ago. The Douglas heir killed, consumed in flame! Perhaps he comes back to haunt his land, seeking justice."

"Justice? The stables burned. No one knows exactly what happened, but there was an inquest. The authorities believe that a lantern must have fallen, creating an inferno. God's will—and none can seek justice for that," she said angrily. She could still see her uncles and cousins, deep in the most dangerous part of the shaft, digging away to save lives when even the most experienced of miners had left the caved-in section. "There was a fire, a tragic accident, and that's that. Welcome to Craig Rock, Brother Damian. I pray you enjoy our village. Now, if you'll excuse me," she said. Even if she hadn't been taught to respect all religions, Shawna would have instinctively felt that she must be courteous and welcoming to any man of God, especially any pilgrim making his way through the Highlands. But this old fellow was irritating, more so due to her present circumstances.

She left him, excusing her way through the miners—who were reliving their own parts in the day's excitement—to reach the table in the far corner of the tavern where Fergus Anderson was sitting.

Fergus had long been into his ale. He didn't work the mines. He didn't work at all, allowing his boys—the eldest being eighteen now and the youngest being little Daniel—to work in his stead. Fergus claimed to have hurt his leg several years ago when crawling from a tunnel. However, he hadn't turned to farming, nor did he tend sheep or cattle. His wife and daughters grew vegetables on a plot of land they tenanted on the far outskirts of MacGinnis holdings, and between the work of his sons and the women in his household, the family ate, and Fergus kept himself in money enough for the beer and ale that, according to him, kept him from feeling the pain that plagued his leg.

He should have had plenty of money to ease all his sorrows. He had hurt himself many years before, and David Douglas had given him an abundant allowance for living when he had claimed himself injured in the mine.

Today, he was unshaven, and though he was not covered in coal dust like the miners, he was nearly as dirty. He had dark beady eyes, silvering hair, and a florid face.

He looked up, startled, as Shawna suddenly slid next to the man on the bench across from him.

"I'll be having no more bairns in the mines, from this day forth, Fergus Anderson."

He seemed to note the challenge in her voice, but he answered her courteously, well aware that the tavern was filled with not only her kin, but well-toned workingmen who had admired her courage for entering the mine alongside of them.

"Ah, now, m'lady, 'tis a privileged man I am, hearing the fine likes of ye say that me lad is special and will not be lost in that black cave of dankness! But, blessed Lady Shawna! There's many a man of us could not feed his family without the help of even his most precious, wee-est bairn!"

"You can survive quite well, Fergus."

"Alas! Sweet lady! Y'are young and a beauty, and ye've never known the heartache of pain, of being a man and half a man, at that."

"I'll have no more little ones in the mines, Fergus."

"Well, Lady," he said, his fingers winding more tightly around his ale, "we'll have to see as how that goes, eh? 'Tis my understanding that the Douglas is on his way from America. The decisions here will come from him now, eh?"

Shawna clenched her teeth together furiously. "I'll give the lad work at the castle."

Fergus arched his brow. "Ye'd have him be fetchin' and carryin' for ye, m'lady?"

"Aye."

Fergus smiled broadly. "And ye'll pay the lad well?"

"Aye."

"Then I bow to your great wisdom, Lady MacGinnis!"

Miners were still talking around them, laughing, bragging, celebrating. Shawna no longer felt like celebrating. She stood up and hurried from the tavern.

She reached her horse when she heard her name called. She turned to see Alistair behind her.

"I'll ride back with you," he said.

"I'm all right."

"Perhaps," Alistair said. "And perhaps you should have an escort."

"Why?"

"Intuition. Let's get home."

As usual, she searched her room.

Today, she was exceptionally irritated. She had never been dirtier in her life, and though she remained incredibly grateful that the miners, and especially Daniel, had survived, she remained irritated by her encounter with Fergus Anderson and maybe a little bit unnerved as well. There was something about Fergus Anderson she didn't like. It wasn't just that he was a lazy man who abused his family. She didn't like the lasciviousness in his eyes or the little edge of something sinister that seemed to taint his voice.

Her encounter with Brother Damian had not pleased her either. She was annoyed that there was rumor in the countryside that the fire had been set on purpose.

Just as David believed. David, who'd managed to be in just the right place to save Danny.

But her family was innocent. Perhaps not absolutely, completely innocent, but innocent of murder, at the very least.

Mary Jane arrived in her room, clucking over her state, yet complimenting her on her rush into the tunnel in hopes of helping to save the men.

"They'll all think of you as an angel now, you know. You do know how to manage men."

"Do I?" Shawna inquired of her wryly.

"Aye, that you do!"

Mary Jane put a few drops of rose oil into the bathwater, then supplied Shawna with a warmed linen towel and washcloth and sweetly scented soap before leaving her. Shawna sank deeply into the heated water, dousing her hair and scrubbing it, then working strenuously at her blackened flesh. She didn't linger in the tub. It quickly filled with the blackness that had covered her. She stood over it, rinsing her hair and body with fresh water from the pitcher, then drying herself briskly. Wrapped in her towel, she moved toward the window, filled with an eerie sensation that someone was watching her.

But there was no one there. The room was empty.

She walked to her freshly made fire, sitting before it to untangle the black skeins of her hair before its warmth. She wondered if she should have changed tactics with Fergus Anderson so quickly. David might want vengeance against her, but he would surely back her decisions regarding the mines. As would his brother. Unless men felt differently about children.

They could not. She could accuse the Douglases of ready tempers or a certain arrogance, of having implacable wills and being incredibly stubborn and even pigheaded at times.

But they were not avaricious men, and surely, both David and Andrew would have stood beside her against Fergus, just as her family would have done.

She had simply been determined that she was going to have things her way, she realized.

Without having to ask for help.

She wound her fingers around the arm of her chair tightly. She hadn't done anything wrong. It was going to be good to have the little boy growing up around the castle. She'd see to it that he received better schooling. She'd have more opportunities to help him.

That was true.

But she hadn't wanted Fergus going to a Douglas for anything.

She didn't want to owe a Douglas, and she didn't want to ask a Douglas for anything. At all.

She sighed, suddenly very, very tired. It had been a long week.

The longest week of her life since...

Since the Fire.

Suddenly there was a loud knocking at her door, and she heard Mary Jane calling to her anxiously. "Shawna!"

"Aye, come in."

The door burst open. Mary Jane entered, cheeks flushed, eyes bright.

"He's here."

"He—who?"

"Andrew, Laird Douglas. Fresh arrived from America with his new bride and her sister. The Sioux is back in the castle, Shawna, do come, do hurry!"

She didn't hurry. She couldn't move for a moment.

Oh god, Hawk was here already. Between Hawk and David, she would surely lose her mind completely. Did he know, was he aware that David was alive?

Had he seen David?

Should she tell him?

"Shawna!" Mary Jane cried.

"I shall be down directly," she said, trembling but praying that she'd kept dignity in her voice. "You can go, Mary Jane. No, wait!"

"Aye, can I help you dress—"

"No, I can manage on my own, but..."

She looked around the room.

"There are a few changes I must make here quickly, if you will give me just a second and lend me a hand..."

CHAPTER 9

"Shawna!"

Andrew Douglas had been seated before the fire in the great hall along with Alistair, Gawain, and two women she didn't know. He'd risen upon seeing her, setting a brandy snifter down upon a table to greet her. He strode to the base of the stairway and caught both of her hands, holding her at arm's length while his eyes swept over her. Then he pulled her into a gentle, encompassing hug. She pulled away, praying that she didn't start to shake with the weakness she was feeling. He was a striking man. In height and build, in his expressions and movements, he bore an ungodly resemblance to his brother. The sharp planes of his face and the copper tone of his skin gave evidence of his Sioux heritage, while his forest green eyes were all Douglas.

His gaze upon her was very tender, like that of a brother greeting a sister after many years.

She was quite certain Andrew Douglas had not seen his brother as yet. Andrew knew that she'd been caught in the fire that had killed his brother. She'd told him as much herself at the funeral. Had she wanted to do so, she couldn't have lied about having been at the stables the night his brother had died—too many of the villagers had seen her prone form next to the charred remains of the man they had assumed to be David Douglas. Andrew, she knew, had been well aware that she had cared for David, even if she'd most usually and carefully pretended to disdain the heir to the great laird.

Apparently, he'd believed that his brother had felt something for her in return. Even if it had been nothing more than a growing intrigue and desire.

Surely, Andrew Douglas had no idea now, though, that his brother believed that she had been partly to blame for his "death." He would not be greeting her so warmly if he did.

"Hawk," she managed to murmur, and then it was easy to smile, because if it hadn't been for the current strange circumstances, she would have been glad to see him. He had grown up in America, but he'd come here often enough. He was older than she by several years, yet still closer to her in age than David. He'd been her friend, and she'd been honest with him, caring for him deeply, all her life.

Until the night of the Fire.

After which, she had never really been able to face him again.

"Hawk, I'm so glad to see you," she said. She looked around him. "And meet your wife."

The two women who had been seated by the fire beside him with Gawain and Alistair were standing now as well. They bore a resemblance to one another in their slender physiques and facial features, but one was a golden honey-blonde with striking silver eyes while the other possessed rich, dark auburn hair and eyes that seemed to range from turquoise to cobalt with each flicker of the firelight. They were both young, elegant, and very beautiful. Only one could be Hawk's wife—unless he had truly embraced Sioux ways—and she was started to find herself wondering how David would respond to the unwed American beauty who had just entered his household.

Annoyed at herself, she swallowed down the surprising pang of jealousy. "Hello, welcome to the Highlands," she said to the two women, walking toward them and offering her hand.

Hawk followed her, his hands set gently upon her shoulders as he directed her first toward the blonde. "Shawna, my wife, Skylar, and my sister-in-law, Sabrina."

"How do you do?" Shawna murmured. "Welcome to your Scottish holdings."

Sabrina smiled and murmured a thank you. She seemed pleasant enough, yet somehow distracted. Skylar Douglas, however, was enthusiastic. "I've just been telling your uncle and my husband how incredibly impressed I am with the way your family manages to handle so very much and do it all so well. Thank you for all that you do for us here."

"It's...so little," Shawna said. She saw that Gawain was staring at her sternly over the top of Skylar Douglas's head. She tried to focus on what she was saying. "The estates have been entwined for so long, managing them as one is quite an easy feat actually."

"Perhaps," Hawk said, "but these castles are ancient. And it is surely a feat in itself to keep both in such a sound state of repair."

"Indeed, the buildings are very old," Gawain said, coming around to address Skylar. "The Vikings came to the Hebrides and the Isles and taught us to erect sound defenses against them. Then the Norman conqueror seized Hastings and began to build defensive castles out of stone throughout England so that he could be sure to rule a people who continued to rebel against him. He battled the Lowlander Scots often enough, as did his heirs. In the Highlands, we've always been a breed apart, living in so northern and rugged a land, our own great cliffs and rocks and hills help to shield us from our enemies. But we learned from those enemies who ever sought ways to attack us that we needed strongholds as well. Your home was officially built as Grayfriar Castle, Lady Douglas, yet has been known since the twelfth century, when it was completed, as Castle Rock, for few structures have ever been built more solidly."

"It's quite fantastic," Sabrina commented.

Alistair joined them as Gawain had done. "But small," he said somewhat apologetically, "when compared with such structures as those found in London, Edinburgh, and the like. I'm afraid neither Castle Rock nor our own Castle MacGinnis compares to the truly grand castles and palaces that were built later."

"Ah but there's more to the place than the size of the castle," Hawk said, smiling at his wife. "Highlanders are unique, as is the countryside."

"There is no country like this anywhere in the world," Shawna said. "You'll see tomorrow. The hills sweep out in endless shades of green with mauves cast in where you come upon the fields of wildflowers. The sky ranges from bright blue to silver to gray and is streaked with pastels at dawn and dusk. The rock by the loch gives a cast of gray to various areas, and the water itself shimmers and dances beneath the sun." Shawna flushed, aware that her passion for her homeland had grown with her speech. "Well, you shall see," she murmured lightly.

Myer, as tall and straight and dignified as any butler might be for one of the grander castles to which Gawain had referred, appeared, clearing his throat. By habit, he glanced toward Shawna and Gawain, then remembered that the true laird of Castle Rock was home.

"M'laird. Supper is prepared. May we serve?"

"Indeed, please, it has been a long ride," Hawk said.

They assembled themselves at the table, Hawk at one end of it, Shawna facing him, her cousin and uncle to her left, Skylar and Sabrina to her right. Conversation flowed freely enough, with Shawna asking questions about America and the sea voyage and Skylar and Sabrina describing their trip, while Hawk gave Gawain and Alistair more serious queries regarding the estate and the mines. Shawna was very grateful then for the presence of both Gawain and Alistair, for although they might have designs on the Douglas lands, they were both being honest and sincere tonight, and keeping the homecoming for Laird Douglas all that it should be.

"Hawk," Shawna asked at last, "how is your situation at home?"

His smile faded, and he glanced briefly at his wife before turning back to Shawna.

"The situation at home is extremely difficult, and I fear it grows worse daily."

"I'm truly sorry to hear that. I wish that there was something I could do to help."

He smiled at her from his distance down the table, a grim but accepting smile. "You do well for me here, Shawna, you and Gawain and your MacGinnis kin. You leave me free to attend to matters in my mother's country. I'm grateful. As I said in my letter, I'll not be here for long. I have to return home very soon."

"How soon?" Gawain asked quickly. He cleared his throat and added politely, "You've just come."

Hawk nodded. "We'll stay just past the Night of the Moon Maiden, then we'll have to head back."

"The Night of the Moon Maiden..." Skylar repeated, offering Shawna a beautiful smile. "It sounds wonderfully romantic and mysterious."

Shawna laughed. "Ah, yes! Just three days away now! It's wonderful that you have come in time for it, but remember, it's just an ancient custom. Like dancing around a maypole. It's harvesttime here, you see. And I suppose in the olden days, that meant surviving the winter to the Highlanders, so they celebrated, and they thanked their gods. It all began way before Christianity came to the Highlands, of course, yet some things do linger. It's a charming night," Shawna supplied.

"And to the lairds of old, it was a prosperous night," Alistair interjected, "for many bairns to work the land in times to come were conceived upon that night."

"A madness with a reason behind it," Skylar commented.

Her sister choked slightly on her water.

"I'm sure you'll enjoy it."

"At one time, of course, a Moon Maiden was sacrificed," Alistair said.

"That practice ended many, many years ago," Shawna said firmly.

"Well, that's quite a relief," Skylar said.

"You would have been quite safe as the laird's lady," Alistair told her with a mischievous grin. "Now, the lovely Sabrina, an innocent foreigner...she might have done well. But..."—he turned to Shawna—" the perfect sacrifice would have actually been my fair cousin."

"Alistair!"

Alistair laughed. "In fact, when we were younger, and Shawna proved to be too great a pest to us older boys, we did upon a time or two determine to tie her to the altar known as the Druid Stone—those standing rocks are known as the Druid Stones, plural—and pretend that we actually might get permission to offer her up to the gods."

"Alistair!" Shawna protested.

But Hawk was laughing, and even Skylar's sister seemed amused at last.

"Actually, I do remember an occasion when they did have you on the Druid Stone. You were spouting away furiously, ready to draw blood, and I think David came along and suggested that you must be let up before your father came out and saw to it that we were all switched for good measure," Hawk told her.

"Aye, and thank God you taught them about playing cowboys and Indians instead," Shawna said, turning to Skylar. "In your husband's games, my lady, the cowboys always lost."

"Knowing my husband, I'm quite sure anyone who went against him lost," Skylar said with a wry smile. She caught herself then just before yawning. "I am so sorry...I guess...if you'd be so good as to show us what sleeping arrangements have been made for us, I'd appreciate it very much."

Shawna glanced down the table to Hawk. "I've vacated the master's chambers for you and your wife, and Sabrina shall have the room to the left of them."

Hawk frowned, glancing from Shawna to Gawain. "I wrote that you were not to disturb your own living quarters, that I could not stay that long."

"I did not have my niece make changes, Hawk. Indeed, it seems I have little enough influence over the lass these days."

"I'm old, Uncle," Shawna said sweetly.

Hawk winked at Gawain. "'Tis true, she's nearly decrepit."

"I'm twenty-four," Shawna said.

"You shall decay within the week!" Hawk assured her, smiling, but then adding seriously, "We cannot stay, that's why I asked you not to bother unduly with changes."

"I merely moved a few of my things to leave room for yours," Shawna said as she rose. "If you like, I can escort you—"

"I do know the way," Hawk murmured somewhat dryly.

"Of course." Shawna smiled. "Then if you'll excuse me, we had a bit of a trying day here as well."

"I heard," Hawk told her, staring at her in a way that unnerved her. His green eyes were so like his brother's. "We stopped for an ale at the tavern; I understand that you are quite the heroine among the people, rushing down into the shafts and trying to crawl into the narrowest of the tunnels to rescue a boy."

Shawna flushed. "We were all within the tunnels, Gawain, Lowell, Alistair, Alaric, Aidan, and I. It is our responsibility, we run the operation, nothing more."

"It is much more," Hawk assured her. He rose as well, as did the others. He set his hands upon his wife's waist in a gesture that was both possessive and tender.

"Well, thank you, I shall accept the compliment," Shawna said. "And I will bid you all good night, since you do know the way." She kissed Gawain and Alistair on their cheeks, bidding them good night. She walked to the foot of the stairway, looking back. Hawk remained at his wife's side. They were a gloriously beautiful couple, she so blonde and delicate in appearance, he so dark and powerful. Shawna was suddenly quite glad for his happiness, and wretched in her own knowledge that Hawk would soon know that she would have a great number of good deeds to do ahead of her to make up for the treachery she had once practiced.

"Good night, Sabrina," she said as well.

Sabrina smiled. "Good night. Thank you for your care and hospitality."

"It's your sister's home," Shawna reminded her wryly.

"Still, it's in your care."

"I hope you'll allow me to show you some of what is MacGinnis property as well," Shawna told her.

"I'd be delighted."

"Do you ride?"

Hawk laughed. "Sabrina is a demon on horseback."

"I look forward to seeing this land through your eyes," Sabrina assured Shawna.

"Tomorrow, then," Shawna said. She looked at Hawk. "When we've finished with the books, of course."

She started up the stairs at last, slowly at first, then fleeing when she reached the second-floor landing. She hurried down the hall to the narrower stairway that led to the attic rooms and found the one she had chosen in the north turret. She entered her room, bolted it, and started pacing.

There was sufficient room to pace. Once upon a time, prisoners taken in warfare had been kept here, sometimes for months at a time, since Highland feuds could entail the necessity of a fair ransom before a hostage might be released. The room was circular in shape, with two windows. Both were smaller than the window in the master's chambers, but the one boasted steps and a small balcony as well, allowing the castle's "guest" to look out on the world where he or she was no longer free to roam.

It was fitting that she had come here. She felt like a prisoner.

She should have returned to Castle MacGinnis, she thought. But then, she'd departed the master's chambers here with such speed that she couldn't possibly have planned a great deal.

But now, this deed was done.

She sat upon the bed, shaking. Hawk was home with his wife. And David would find the real help he needed in his brother now. She had lost complete control of her world, and there was nothing she could do about it.

She rose, distractedly shedding her clothing, donning her nightgown. If David made any of his mysterious appearances tonight, he would crawl into his brother's bed.

It was what she had wanted, what he deserved.

What she had planned.

Yet she felt anxious now, worried that she had lost all chance of communication with David, that, in fact, she had lost David.

But she'd never had David. And what had once been something of a relationship had been lost five years ago.

Shawna doused the lights. Mary Jane had seen to it that she had a warm fire here. She curled up in the bed and stared at the flames. She closed her eyes against the light, anticipating a night of uninterrupted sleep.

WITH THE DOOR closed upon the master's chambers, Hawk walked up the steps to the window and balcony while Skylar looked around the room, at the ancient rock walls, the furniture that was hundreds of years old, and the Victorian touches that had added an element of elegance to the room.

"It's spectacular," Skylar said. She saw where Hawk had gone, and she quickly climbed the steps to join him, slipping her arms around his waist from behind him. "You are truly a diverse man, my love. I've now bedded in the most elegant manor home, a tipi, and a castle." She laid her head against his back. "I pray that David is alive, Hawk. I know what it will mean to you."

He turned at her words, taking her into his arms. "I pray that he lives as well."

He still had no more evidence that his brother was alive than the mysterious message left with his attorney by a supposed "little jackanapes of a man" that he should come to the Druid Stones on the Night of the Moon Maiden.

That and his brother's Douglas insignia ring.

He kissed his wife's lips lightly, then found that his mouth lingered upon them. "Let's get some sleep, shall we?" he said. "The journey has been agonizingly long, and I want to show you my father's ancestral home tomorrow." He was exhausted, but he wasn't sure he wanted to sleep yet. What he'd intended as a gentle brush of affection had created a slow burning within him. He was tired, but not too tired to desire his beautiful wife. "Well, let's at least get to bed," he suggested.

Skylar moved down the steps, her fingers unfastening tiny buttons on her bodice. "There's a great deal here that's stunningly beautiful," she agreed. She turned back to him. "Like Lady MacGinnis."

Hawk couldn't help but smile. He'd thought the tempestuous days that had begun their marriage were in the past.

She still questioned him with just a touch of jealousy.

He came down the steps to her, sitting at the foot of the bed and drawing her against him as he worked at the tiny buttons himself.

"Shawna is beautiful. She grows more lovely with age. Yet, even when she was just a babe, she was beautiful. Her eyes are so incredibly blue, her hair like ebony."

"So, you have noticed this about her, of course," Skylar said. He realized she had ceased undoing her buttons and was now redoing them just as quickly as he was attempting to unbutton them.

"Naturally."

"Oh god," Skylar groaned. "Was she a part of your past?"

He laughed, realizing that although Skylar had learned a great deal about his life in America and probably knew his soul better than anyone else alive, she knew little about this part of his past despite all that he had told her on the way to Scotland.

He met her silver eyes, drawing her closer against him. "I never slept with her, Skylar."

She frowned. "How curious that there was not...something."

He shook his head. "Not curious at all. She was infatuated with David when she was a child. He was amused by her at first, then..."

"Then?"

"Well, she grew up. And she was stunning and full of life and very proud, and she was charming and flirtatious and reckless. She drove him halfway insane, but I think that she really cared for him. And she taunted him so fiercely because she was jealous."

"Jealous?"

"David was his own man. He would not be tricked, coerced, or taunted. He had a place in the government waiting for him, he'd been in the military, he was welcomed in political circles in all of Great Britain and America. I think Shawna was always afraid that she'd give everything to him, then find herself rejected if he discovered himself falling in love with a young woman of greater sophistication elsewhere. But still..."

"Still?"

He grinned. "If anything, she's like a little sister to me, and I felt terrible for her after my brother's funeral. She was lost then, completely broken. She could barely talk, even to me. Maybe especially to me."

"She was very charming tonight."

"She was."

"Yet, it seems most apparent that there's some mystery involved in what happened the night your brother was presumably killed. Could the beautiful Lady Shawna have attempted to do away with your brother?"

Hawk shook his head slowly. "I think not."

"Why not?"

"Because I believe with my whole heart that she was in love with him."

"Then we need to look suspiciously at the MacGinnis men?"

"Whatever we need to do, we can do in the morning. Douse those lights. And come to bed."

"Demanding, aren't you?"

He shrugged. "For tonight, my love, I am the laird of the castle."

Skylar sniffed, then gasped slightly as he suddenly leaped past her, dousing all the lights within the room, then crashing upon her to land on the bed. For the longest moment they lay together, entangled in silence as his lips found hers in a deep, slow, sensual kiss.

Then there was the strangest sound. A rasping so faint Skylar thought she might have imagined it.

But then, in the shadows of the room, so close to her she could almost feel his heat, she heard a muttered, "Damnation."

Skylar nearly shrieked aloud. Someone was in bed with them.

Then she heard her husband speak, his voice trembling. "David?"

"Hawk?"

Skylar had been about to scream. She leaped up instead, grasping a match and lighting it in the fire to set the candles aflame once again.

As the glow illuminated the room now, she realized that she wasn't Lady Douglas.

David did live.

As tall as her husband, as dark, as broad in the shoulder, as trim in the hips. Dark hair touched by auburn where Hawk's was black, his green eyes incredibly the same, his features equally handsome in their European planes and angles as Hawk's were with their Indian heritage. The two men stared at one another, then embraced warmly, and the seconds ticked by.

At last, they parted. With no introduction, David Douglas turned to Skylar at last. "Dear God, I am sorry. I was most anxious to meet you, but I didn't intend to crawl into bed on you."

"Why on earth did you crawl into bed?" Hawk demanded.

David arched a brow. "Well, I—"

"You were expecting someone else?" Skylar suggested.

"Naturally," Hawk moaned, staring at his brother. "Shawna. So, she knows you're alive."

"She does."

"My god, then...does she know what happened to you, where—David, where the hell have you been all this time?"

"Shawna knows only that I'm alive. She refuses to see that someone in her family intended to kill me and is trying to kill her now. And as to where I've been..." He glanced at Skylar. "It can be a long tale."

"By God! Then the MacGinnises are guilty!" Hawk exploded. "And Father and I handed everything over to them—"

"Hawk, wait. I don't believe that the entire family is guilty of evil. Oh, they will protect one another—they are Highlanders. But though I'm sure the entire family was trying to protect Alistair from the possibility that I might bring charges against him for tampering with the books, I'm equally certain that they are not all so callous as to ignore an attempted murder."

"Alistair! I should slit his throat!" Hawk said passionately.

"Wait, now, I'm not at all certain that Alistair was guilty of anything more than being young and careless. From what I've discovered since I've returned, Alistair appears to have become a fastidious, hardworking businessman. And one willing to risk his own life for others."

"Then who is guilty?" Skylar asked softly.

"I don't know, but I will find out the truth. It's a long story, but I'll make it as short as possible. I met Shawna at the stables that night because she wanted to talk. Someone knocked me out before the fire started, yet someone dragged me from it alive, allowing everyone to believe that I was dead. I was given the identity of a Glasgow murderer and sent off on a ship bound for Australia. When I first woke up aboard the ship carrying me to Australia, I fought to convince the ship's master that I was David Douglas, but I was nearly killed for my efforts. I'm not sure it mattered who I was once I came aboard that ship. The man whose identity I had been given was supposed to have been hanged. The captain of the ship thought himself God's vengeance, I believe, while he sold men into virtual slavery in a manner that was not quite legal, making escape all the more difficult. I worked as a convict in Australia for more than four years before finally escaping with a friend, Dr. James McGregor, the little fellow I sent to America with my ring. We escaped with nothing and began working our way across the seas as sailors. In all that time, I'd never been able to convince anyone—other than Jamie McGregor—that I was David Douglas and not the murderer, Collum MacDonald." David hesitated a minute. "It didn't help matters that we had finally managed our escape because I killed the guard on duty, a vicious fellow determined on whipping another man to death on the rocks. I had to get out of Australia quickly, and I knew that I was going to have to come back to Scotland in person to prove who I was, yet it was a long journey, and my friend Jamie was not well. When I heard from some Scottish sailors we encountered that Father had died, I sent Jamie to you while I came here as quickly as possible, took up residence in the caves, and began to keep watch at Craig Rock."

"You've indeed been through hell, but you should know that Father died of natural causes," Hawk assured him. "Skylar was with him," he added.

"It was his heart," Skylar said quietly.

David's fists clenched at his sides. "So, he died, and I never saw him again, and he endured the pain of believing until the last day he drew breath that his eldest son had burned to death."

"Father was a fighter, remember that," Hawk told him. "He was busy manipulating my life with his last breath, so he was assured that his line would continue, at the very least."

"He didn't stay here," David said grimly. "He chose to live more completely in America—and since then the MacGinnises have ruled here."

Hawk set a hand upon his brother's shoulder. "David, we will find out the truth." He hesitated. "Is Shawna guilty in this?"

"Shawna was guilty of bad judgment."

"No more?"

"She's yet to prove her complete innocence."

"But she's part of this now, she knows you're alive, and she has kept the secret?"

"So I believe. I've managed to keep an eye on the MacGinnises when they don't know I'm about."

"We'll find the truth," Hawk repeated determinedly.

"Aye." David clasped his brother's arm. "Aye, that we will, and yet I am nearly sorry that I sent for you. I didn't know at the time that you had a wife or that you would bring her here. I pray I haven't put you in danger."

"He is forever determined to put himself in front of someone's gun or bow," Skylar commented about her husband. "He can surely be in no greater danger here than at home."

David smiled at her. "But what of you, Skylar?"

"I shall be careful, I swear," she promised.

"And that you will be," Hawk warned.

She sensed or saw something in his eyes. For a long moment, she stared at him, then seemed to draw her gaze from his and clear her throat. "So, this is where you sleep as well. We shall have to make some arrangement—"

"No arrangement, Skylar. I apologize again for so rudely interrupting you. I've business elsewhere tonight."

"But—I believe others may still be about. You can't just walk out if you wish to keep yourself hidden—"

"The castle is riddled with secret passages, Skylar," Hawk told her.

"Oh!" Skylar said.

Hawk studied David. "You've business with Shawna?"

"I keep an eye on her. The night I returned, she was hunted by a man and nearly killed."

"What man?"

"I didn't know him, and I was forced to kill him."

"What did the constable say?"

"I didn't leave the corpse to be found."

"But Shawna refuses to see that she's in danger."

"She refused to admit a MacGinnis could be involved. Now that you are here, however, I will have even greater freedom to search both castles and try to discover what was done." David studied his brother, drawing in a long, deep breath. "I've kept up with the newspapers. I know what is happening in America. And I thank you for coming here. When this is solved, if I can be of any help, I will gladly go to your Sioux lands with you."

"I might let you do that," Hawk said. His voice lowered, and trembling slightly, he added, "And I thank God, brother, that you're alive."

The two brothers embraced again. Then David turned, smiled at Skylar, and kissed her on the cheek. "Do forgive me, lass."

Skylar gasped softly as he turned again to the wall by the side of the bed, touched a stone there, and caused a small doorway to open into a black void.

He disappeared into that void, and with the same faint rasping sound she had heard earlier, the stone closed back into a wall, and the passageway might never have been.

"My god!" Skylar breathed. "Your brother is alive. And something horrible is going on here."

"It is. Thank God we've come, though David would have prevailed on his own, I am certain."

"He seems very assured and powerful."

"He is. More so now. He must have suffered greatly. He has hardened."

"He bears a slight scar. But he is still..."

"Still?"

"Extraordinarily striking. He is a handsome man, despite his hardness."

"Really?"

"Indeed."

"So, he's quite good-looking—and not even a savage."

"Something tells me he is quite capable of being very savage."

"Should I be jealous?"

"It would definitely serve you right."

"I'm afraid I can't be jealous."

"Why is that?"

"I trust my brother."

"But not me?" She hit him with a pillow.

He laughed, catching her, kissing her. The desire that had been so abruptly cooled burned through him once again. Yet she pulled away from him.

"You mean that the castle has these passages...everywhere."

"Many of them. We were Jacobites in days of yore."

"Jacobites?"

He smiled. "The Scottish Stuart line ruled Scotland and England. The line came down to James II, and for his second wife, James took a Catholic princess. The English people, and many of the Scots, refused to accept their son as an heir to the throne. James II himself was forced to abdicate when his daughter, Mary, and son-in-law, William of Orange, came to England to claim the Crown. James fled to France. His son became the 'Pretender,' then eventually, when he had his own son, he became 'the old Pretender.' None of James's descendants ever did reclaim the throne, but many Highland families supported the Stuart's efforts for years. Stuart supporters, priests, and others often had to be hidden. In places like Castle Rock, they could easily hide. The passages were a godsend."

"Ah, but how very...disconcerting they might be now!" Skylar said.

Hawk grinned, pulling her back to him once again. "Don't worry. David will not be back." He left her by the bed, turning to extinguish the lights once again.

Skylar heard him returning. Then he paused and laughed softly in the darkness.

"What is it?"

"Disconcerting..." he repeated. "Come to think of it, Shawna did look a bit on edge tonight. Quite disconcerted."

"And what does that mean?"

"It means that my brother does not completely trust Lady Shawna MacGinnis. And it also means that..."

"That?"

"Whether he trusts her or not, he is seeking something from her."

"Revenge?"

"Perhaps."

"Poor girl."

"It's a problem they'll have to work out themselves."

"I'm simply familiar with Douglas tempers."

"Don't you dare take her side, my love."

"I'll dare what I choose."

"We'll see, won't we?" He didn't give her a chance to argue any further.

SHAWNA SHOULD HAVE SLEPT QUITE EASILY.

Maddeningly, she did not.

She lay in bed for what seemed like forever, staring into the fire. And in the flames there, she saw the past. In her mind's eye, she relived the fire that had occurred so long ago. She remembered wakening beside the burned corpse. She could still hear her own scream.

She closed her eyes against the colors of the fire, then opened them, frowning. She hadn't slept, she'd heard no sound, but she was suddenly afraid that someone might have come into the room.

Coward! she silently charged herself.

But she slipped quickly out of bed and looked around the room. No one. She still had the uncanny feeling that she was not alone.

She spun around in a circle, looked under the bed. She walked to the window and looked out on the night. The moon was high in the sky. So nearly full.

She shivered and was certain that she heard movement in the room.

Chilled, she ran back to the bed. She crawled back beneath the covers, staring across the room to the fire once again. A startled gasp tore from her lips.

It was impossible.

She had been right. She was not alone.

He was here.

Clad in a black shirt and black breeches tonight, he sat in a chair before the fire, one long, booted leg cast haphazardly over the arm of the old Queen Anne chair as he stared into the flames.

Oh god, he was there...

And she didn't know whether to scream with rage and frustration...

Or simply to pray.

CHAPTER 10

He turned his head.

"Ah, my lady!" he said, his voice quiet and deep. Almost a whisper in the darkness.

"My god!" she breathed, still stunned. "You can't be here!"

"I'm well aware you intended me to surprise my brother and his bride in their bed."

Shawna hesitated uneasily.

"And did you?"

"We've had a discussion."

She lowered her eyes quickly, biting her lip. Perhaps it had been a foolish move on her part. She had managed to surprise him.

And anger him.

"I assumed you wanted to see your brother as quickly as possible."

"Y'er heart was in the right place, eh, lass?"

The edge to his voice kept her from imagining he might have meant the words. "Perhaps you should cease accosting people in the middle of the night."

"I don't accost people in the night."

"Only me," she whispered.

His green gaze seared her. "Only you," he promised.

"But..."

"But what?"

"How did you manage to get into this room? It's simply impossible—"

"Ah, I beg to differ. Ghosts and selkies and beasts will go wherever they choose."

Beasts...

Shawna leaped out of the bed, coming around to stand in front of the fire, staring at him.

"Beasts...beasties!" she repeated. "Aye, at least as a creature of lore, Laird Douglas, you are doing some good. You got Danny out of the mine somehow. For that, I am eternally grateful."

He stared at her, then shrugged, his eyes piercing hers once again. "Aye, indeed, I got the lad out. And he'll have a long and far healthier life, I imagine, since you took it upon your shoulders to decree that he will no longer work in the mine."

Shawna had the truly uneasy feeling that he was managing to hear every word she uttered. "I was right in what I said and did. Fergus would work his children to the bone and sit upon his..."

She broke off, weary. Andrew Douglas was here now, and David was alive. Her serving as the lady of the manor with the right to make decisions was all a charade.

"You were right in what you did," he told her surprisingly. And to her amazement, his voice gentled. "The lad is a charmer. Handsome little thing and bright as can be. He only lived because he listened to me and did as I told him. He might have drowned, but he held his breath and swam exactly as I told him."

"I couldn't reach him," Skylar said.

David was suddenly on his feet, angry as he approached her. "What in God's name were you doing in the mine?"

She set her hands on her hips but found herself backing away as he neared her. "I—I had to go in. I knew that there was a child stuck—"

"You seem too easily misdirected and misguided by the needs of wee ones, Shawna. You should wed, bear a few of your own, and have done with the madness of trying to care for all those in the world."

"Thank God you've apparently not found the time to marry and procreate! You'd make a wretchedly cold-hearted parent!"

"I am aware that I cannot save the world."

"One child was at risk, not the world."

"The child survived. You're not to go in the mine."

"But I must. If I am lady here—"

"You are not."

"What I am," she informed him angrily, "does not depend on Douglas dictates. I most certainly am Lady MacGinnis, and my father made that so, and I am tired of battling wretched men over that fact!"

"I don't care if you're the bloody queen. While I live, you'll not go back into that mine."

"But you don't live—you've chosen to remain dead."

"You know full well that I am very much alive," he reminded her.

She found herself backed up against the cold stone wall of the turret room. There was no place else for her to go, and he was all but leaning against her as he stated his warning. She swallowed hard as she felt his fingers thread into her hair, lifting her face to his. She started shaking and told herself it was the cold of the stone while she tried to meet his gem-sharp stare with dispassionate dignity.

"You've not been alive for five years. And since you've chosen to remain dead, you have little power here."

"Really?"

"Dead men cannot make decisions, nor issue ultimatums."

"Well, my lady, rest assured that I am one corpse who will do so—most especially where you are concerned."

She gritted her teeth but refused to fight the hold he had upon her. "If you're so bloody concerned, what in God's name has taken you so long in coming back from the dead?" she demanded furiously.

Then she wished that she had not spoken, for his features hardened. His jaw locked, and she saw the powerful cords in his neck straining with tension.

"Circumstances over which I had little control," he said flatly, his fingers curling more tightly into her hair. "You don't want me to remember where I was for the majority of the last five years."

The coldness of his tone sent a chill sweeping down her spine, reminding her that he had returned for what was his—and vengeance as well.

Shawna studied him, recalling the word he had used for where she had cast him.

"Hell," she whispered.

"Hell," he agreed harshly.

"But I don't know how you came to be...in whatever hell you found yourself!" she swore fervently. "David, you say I must listen, but surely you must realize that someone else might have come into the stables that night, not my family. You should have seen them today, David, all of them—"

"I saw them."

"You cannot see everything—"

"Far more than you would ever imagine," he assured her.

"There have been no further attempts on my life," she reminded him.

"Aye. I have sat guard each night, waiting for the time that will come when someone tries to enter your chamber despite that bolt."

"No one will hurt me. No one except—"

"Oh, aye?" he challenged angrily. "No one except?"

"You!" she assured him.

He smiled grimly, no thought of releasing her as yet seeming to cross his mind. "There is no hurt I would inflict upon you, my lady, that could begin to compare to the pain you brought down upon me."

"If I could go back, I would undo what I did that night, by God, I swear it. Sweet Jesus!" To her horror, she felt tears stinging her eyes. She fought them with a tremendous effort.

She couldn't falter. She'd never tell him what she had gone through after that night. Never.

"I would endure your hell for you, if I could, Laird Douglas!" she hissed angrily.

"Would you really?" he demanded, arching a brow. "I'm quite glad of it, for, though I haven't it in mind to condemn you to hell, I think I'd like the bed tonight. A chair before the fire isn't exactly torture, but it isn't comfortable, either."

To her incredulous relief, he released her, turning away, striding to the bed.

He plumped up one pillow and tossed the other to her. She caught it, her anger growing.

"Would you be so good as to toss the blanket, too?" she inquired.

He threw the blanket casually to her, turning away. It landed atop her head. Furiously, she pulled it off, and before she could control the urge, she found herself rising, ready to fly at him.

She caught herself just in time, for he spun around to face her again. She stood dead still, hands clasped behind her back, chin high, voice scathing as she spoke. "You overbearing, wretched bastard! This castle abounds with rooms and beds, and you have easy access to any and all of them—so it seems!"

He arched a brow. Smiling and with a curious taunt to his voice he repeated, "Overbearing, wretched bastard?"

"Indeed! There are at least a dozen beds you can choose from, but instead you savor the act of throwing me upon the floor!"

He lowered his lashes for a moment, then gazed at her once again, a teasing light in his eyes. He played with her, she thought then. Cat and mouse. He played a game. "Throwing you upon the floor," he murmured, taking steps toward her.

They seemed predatory steps.

Menacing steps. Slow. Easy. Calculated. They brought him directly to her.

Then circling around her. "I've yet," he said quite softly, and she felt his eyes raking over her, head to toe, "to throw you upon the floor, though the idea does have its merits!" he assured her. He remained at her back. She spun swiftly around to face him, unnerved to have him behind her, feeling his every breath against her neck.

"You've stolen my bed. Mine—not yours. This is not your room. So, in a manner of speaking, you have thrown me from my bed," she accused him indignantly. "It is one and the same."

"Is that how you see it?"

"Aye."

"But the castle, we've agreed, is mine?"

"Aye," she murmured uneasily.

"Then every bed within it is mine," he stated.

"Not when it is occupied by someone else!"

"Then pray, if I have thrown you from your bed, let me throw you back into it!"

She gasped, nearly shrieking aloud as his hands fell upon her. There was no violence in his touch, no brutality to his hold, yet he lifted her, casting her indeed, and sending her flying.

She landed upon the bed, stunned, breathless, afraid to move, and afraid to lie still. She gasped again when he was suddenly next to her, a muscled leg thrown over her hip, his arm barring her from rising then as he observed her from a position upon his elbow. "My dearest Lady MacGinnis, since the act of 'throwing' you upon the floor seemed such a cruel behavior on my part, I welcome you back to the bed. I wouldn't dream of putting you through the torture of a night on the floor."

His eyes were green fire. She didn't know if he spoke with anger, or if he taunted her still. She only knew his nearness alarmed and excited her. She was very afraid of moving, even breathing, for she could feel him within every fiber of her being. He spoke in a pleasant, evenly modulated voice, yet there was an edge beneath it, as if he seethed beneath the surface, as if the fire within his eyes burned throughout him, and his cat-and-mouse game was about to come to an end.

She gasped in a long, desperate breath in order to manage a reply.

"Actually, I think I rather enjoy the cool feel of stone at my back."

"You are kind and courteous. You say that only now because you have so suddenly determined to be generous with the bed."

"I don't mind the floor."

"I simply cannot throw you there. I'm afraid you've betrayed your true feelings on the matter."

The green in his eyes remained wickedly glinting.

Dangerous.

Still afraid to move, she vowed to keep control of her temper. She was not going to allow the whirlwind of sensations ripping through her to overrule her pride, dignity, or courage. "Would you be going there, then?" she asked hopefully.

"I would not."

"Then?" she inquired, the word scarcely a whisper.

"We will both sleep in comfort."

"Here, together?"

"Ah, my lady, you are indeed blessed with keen powers of observation and comprehension."

So much for carefully maintaining her temper and control. She had to escape him. With sudden, wild impetus, she attempted to leap free of his hold. Yet she could not, for he was as swift as a tiger, and apparently, he had been awaiting her attempted departure. In one smooth motion he seized her, drawing her against him hard, her back and derriere flush to his chest and loins, her right arm caught beneath her own weight, her left wrist captured firmly in his grasp.

"This seems comfortable enough," he commented.

For him. He had the benefit of clothing. Her gown had risen surely with every twist and movement. She could feel the fabric of his linen shirt brushing her flesh through the thin material of her nightgown... and the coarser fabric of his form-hugging breeches lower against her where the gown had risen. She swallowed hard, remaining still as a statue. She could feel the moist heat of his breath against her nape, touching her earlobe. He held her wrist just below her breasts, and it seemed she could feel his fingers brushing against her flesh, though surely, she could not. To her incredible dismay, she became aware that her nipples had hardened and strained against her gown, that a sweeping rush of fevered heat raced through her veins.

She was so very afraid that he would touch her further.

And so terribly agonized that he might not.

"I—I really would enjoy the floor," she stammered.

"I wouldn't hear of it," he insisted.

She held still. Then burst out with, "I've got to sleep on the floor!" And again, she desperately tried to pull free from his hold.

"I think not!"

And she found herself slammed back down into the softness of the bed, this time, with him atop her. She was imprisoned by the force of his body.

For brief seconds she met his eyes, and she tried not to breathe.

Then despite herself she inhaled and twisted. Her movement caused his fingers to brush against her breasts, knuckles riding softly against their swollen crests. She gasped at that contact and twisted further against it, only to realize that she had turned right into his touch, turned against him, into his body. His clothing did not feel like such a barrier then. His arousal was quite hard against her abdomen despite it, the muscled expanse of his chest and arms beneath linen seemed to be on fire. His eyes remained hard, green gems burning in the night as well. She opened her mouth to speak but never found words. He covered her lips with a hungry, bruising kiss.

And she quickly realized just how high her gown had risen for his hand was upon the dark triangle of her mound, fingers deftly delving within it, parting, stroking, thrusting. She wanted to push him away. Somewhere within her, she knew full well that sex could have very little to do with emotion. He had told her to find a husband and bear children, his suggestion surely being that the husband should be some man other than himself. Yet within her own heart and soul, loving David, Laird Douglas, and wanting him had been one and the same for most of her lifetime. Losing him had shattered her dreams and her desires.

And though she halfway hated him for his accusations against her and her family...

She wanted him still.

She was dimly aware that his mouth had left hers and had moved to kiss her throat, pausing at the thundering pulse there. She tried to speak, yet he continued to touch her, his fingers stroking within her.

"No" formed on her lips but found no substance.

And yet...

She wanted, oh god, she wanted, the scent of him was filling her, the feel of him...

She should have attempted a true protest. She should have stopped him. Fought him, wildly, determinedly. She should have stopped this. She should have bitterly decried so intimate a touch as that with which he so easily stroked her. He had come seeking vengeance, nothing more. Revenge. Was part of this revenge to seduce her into the flames...

As she had done with him?

Her gown was open. All slim barriers she might have possessed were gone now. His hands were cupping her breasts. His tongue bathed one and then the other. His body moved against hers. The wetness of his caress moved erotically over her abdomen, rising, falling, rising... wetting, licking, touching her while he stroked within her...

"Is this revenge?" she managed to whisper.

He groaned softly in turn, rising against her. His green eyes captured hers with passion, and he told her, "From hell I dreamed of you, Shawna, longing for revenge. Longing to see you again, and you are here, and I am newly seduced by the perfection of your face and form, even knowing that your beauty can be as deadly as the captivating brilliance of a fire!"

"I tell you—"

"Tell me nothing!" he charged her. "For revenge, my love, can indeed be sweet."

The heat of his body seemed to be a fire, and that fire burned from the green of his eyes and into her. His lips fell upon hers again with fierce demand, bruising first in their passion and ardor, suddenly gentle, then demanding once again, seeking, delving, into the heart of her. Revenge, perhaps. But he was right, for it seemed that the violence of his kiss was unbearably sweet.

His hands, oh god, they were rough upon her, yet so strong, holding her. They moved with trembling strength into her hair, then against the soft flesh of her cheeks, stroking her shoulders, drawing her tighter against him, running the length of her body.

Seducing...

Pressing her against his body, against the fever that burned in him now like an inferno, consuming, taking her with him into a conflagration. She felt the strength of his muscled power, the erotic hardness of his arousal. She could scarcely breathe. The pressure of his mouth demanded and ravaged, his tongue brought liquid sweeps of searing heat that seemed to awaken and arouse the length of her.

She could not do this.

She pressed her hands against his chest. He didn't seem to feel them. She tried then to find words to protest, yet the force of his mouth against hers gave her no chance to speak, no breath with which to do so.

In time she realized that his mouth had left her lips again to travel an erotic trail down her throat. Her gown was shoved to her waist, and the rough, calloused touch of his hands was against the bareness of her flesh, caressing her breasts, thumbs teasing and rubbing her nipples, sending exotic shafts of fire and light to sear throughout her like the rays of the sun. His lips, his hands, were everywhere. Ever more intimate. Whispered words escaped her at last, yet she could not comprehend them herself, and he did not hear or heed them. His thumb created a line down her abdomen from her navel, intimately invaded once again, thrust deeply within her. Again, some cry tore from her lips, and whether a cry of pure sensation or the dying gasp of a struggle she could no longer seek to wage, she did not know. She felt the gentle pressure of his teeth teasing against her upper thigh, the stroke of his tongue, a liquid fire that circled the center of her desire until she thought she would die, then stroking directly upon it until the sweeping sensations rose in a wicked explosion within her and a cry erupted from her lips.

He was atop her then, fumbling briefly with the buttons of his black pants. His mouth seized hold of hers once again, capturing her lips, her tongue, and her breath with whatever whispers might have escaped her. A deep, trembling shudder swept into her at his next invasion, for he thrust within her with the burning shaft of his sex, blunt, hard, bold. She might have shrieked aloud again at the deep, knifing sensation that filled her, but she could not, for his kiss continued to absorb all sound.

To seduce and arouse anew.

God help her, she was swept into his demand. And then, she discovered, she demanded in return, she was seeking herself. She wanted him so urgently. Forgetting him, forgetting herself, time, place, past, present, and all reason. She hungered, she ached, arching and writhing to meet his every thrust, to feel his every touch.

He covered and filled her, still dressed, with only his dark breeches loosened. Her flesh seemed almost unbearably vulnerable to the touch of fabric against it, and yet everything within her seemed drawn as well to that place where bare flesh met bare flesh, where his body stroked into hers with a thundering urgency, hard, wild, seducing no more, suddenly demanding everything. She clung to him, feeling as if she rode out a storm. His very fever touched her again and again, along with the driving relentlessness of his demand. The very force and power that filled her seemed to awaken in her the clamoring to have more and more, to reach surcease. His body constricted in a massive wave of tension and heat, then it seemed that sunlight rushed within her, triggering the sweet explosion of her own climax. `The feelings burst upon her, so incredibly wonderful, like a blending of all the hot, brilliant colors of the fiercest blaze within her body. She drifted in the sweet, warm fires, shaken again and again by a series of little rapid-fire convulsions, until she seemed to fall into the deep softness of the bed again.

David moved quickly, as if he had realized his weight just as she began to feel the pressure of it. He lay at her side, his face completely in shadows. Still clothed. She felt him button his breeches, then stretch out, his fingers laced behind his head as he stared at the ceiling.

"Oh god!" she breathed suddenly, realizing what they had done. Despite his flowers and gifts, he still accused her and her family.

And he had come for revenge. This, then, was nothing but revenge.

"Damn you!" she cried out, springing up to leap out of the bed.

She didn't manage to do so.

He caught her upper arms, flinging her back down upon the mattress. "What do you think you're doing now?" he demanded irritably.

"Getting up!"

"Why?"

"Because—because—" she sputtered. "Oh, damn you!" she cried again, a balled hand landing against his chest. She stared into his eyes and whispered vehemently, "I did not seduce you, Laird David Douglas!"

"You seduce me by being, Lady MacGinnis!" She felt his eyes sweep over her. "And I'm not sleeping in any damned chairs anymore, and you're not going to catch pneumonia on the floor and expire on me, either."

She was shaking, trying to fight when there was no fight left within her.

"You can't—"

"Did I hurt you in any way?"

He couldn't begin to know how he was hurting her.

"Say yes, m'love, and I'll call you a liar. Our greatest danger here tonight was that one of us might have shrieked out loudly enough in pleasure to have given us both away."

She gasped, ready to hit him. He gave her no chance to do so, drawing her to him.

"You had every chance to deny me," he told her.

"You're wrong. You seldom give me a chance at anything."

He stared at her in the darkness, then his knuckles brushed her cheek, and his thumb moved over her lower lip. "Maybe I don't dare give you any more chances!" he whispered softly.

"We can't—let this go on," she said fervently.

He shook his head, frowning. "You think that you can take back what happened between us."

"You don't understand—"

"Nor do I care to."

"There can be—consequences!" she told him.

"Not this time. I will not be taken this time!"

Shawna lowered her lashes, but she couldn't hold her tongue. "I don't mean you!" she lashed out.

"What, then?"

The truth she couldn't bear to share with him retreated within her. "Nothing."

"Damn it, what are you talking about?"

She shook her head vehemently. "Nothing!"

"Nothing," he murmured. "Nothing will change the fact that one of your kin is guilty, and I will discover who. Sleeping on the floor will not help you. My spending the night awake on a window seat will not change anything for anyone either."

In the flickering light of the fire, she saw him looking at her, his eyes filled with anger and passion and determination. She trembled, wishing that he could not feel her every little movement.

"If you intend to continue to accuse my family and expect my help, you'd better intend as well to keep me advised about what is happening, what you're doing!"

He smiled. "You know I've been with you every night."

"Aye, the flowers, the necklace, left upon my pillow." She tried to study his face in the firelit shadows. "Why?" she asked very softly. "Part of your revenge?"

His teeth flashed in a white smile. "Most definitely," he told her.

She studied him gravely. "Five years ago—I did not mean to seduce you. I—perhaps that isn't exactly true, but I didn't intend—"

"You intended to seduce me, you simply didn't intend to consummate anything you started," he said bluntly.

She shook her head, then twisted away from him, lying with her back to him when she spoke again. "I didn't intend to seduce you into the hell you discovered. And I do fear your revenge—"

"Perhaps my revenge, my lady, is partly to make you want me as I wanted you when that fire began."

His husky tone sent warmth cascading down her spine. She swallowed hard, fighting a strange surge of tears once again. He couldn't know how she had wanted him. How she had missed him. How she had longed for him. How she had needed him with her.

"Perhaps, Laird Douglas," she whispered in turn, "I am determined not to let you take revenge so easily. Perhaps I shall refuse to want you —I didn't seek to seduce you now, and so help me, I will not do so—"

"No?" he queried.

His tone was oddly tender and yearning.

Yet his touch was firm as he rolled her back to him, suddenly straddling her in the darkness.

"Then it seems that I will have to seduce you," he promised her heatedly. "And I will want you. Again and again..."

He did want her.

And he did seduce her.

Expertly. Shedding his clothing that time.

And sleeping naked beside her when he was done, holding her close to his warmth through the hours of the night.

CHAPTER 11

Naturally, David was gone come the morning. Shawna hadn't actually expected to see him when she awoke, and she was glad for once that he'd disappeared. As the sun filtered into her room, she tried to make sense of the tempest his most recent visit had created within her heart. She had thought him dead once and the pain had been so intense she had hardly wanted to go on living herself. And now it seemed that he was intent on arousing every conceivable emotion within her again. Revenge. He didn't know it, but he'd had his revenge against her years ago. She couldn't begin to imagine what he'd been through—especially since he wouldn't speak about those lost years—but neither did David know what he had left behind for her to deal with alone. Did he use her now? Was making her want him the vengeance he sought? Or was his passion caused by a deeper, far different feeling? She didn't want to admit how deeply she felt for him now, and she didn't want to admit that nothing had really changed. She had always loved him. When she had believed him dead, she had been half-dead as well.

A light tapping at her door brought her flying out of bed and hurrying to it. She leaned against it, listening. "Aye?"

"Shawna? It's Mary Jane. I've brought you fresh water. Is something amiss?"

Feeling foolish, Shawna started to slide the bolt. She realized that her nightgown had wound up on the floor during the night, and she raced for it, quickly slipped it back on, and returned to the door, sliding the bolt and opening it. Mary Jane offered her a curious smile, her pretty face speculative. "What on earth is going on with you, Shawna? I don't remember you bolting doors before this last week!"

Shawna shrugged. "I—I hadn't even realized that I'd bolted it," she lied.

Mary Jane stepped into the room, bringing a fresh ewer of drinking water. She set the water down, then walked to the window, looking out. She shivered but offered Shawna another smile. "Maybe we're all a little excited." Her eyes widened, and she said dramatically, "The Night of the Moon Maiden draws near!"

"As it has every year since just about forever," Shawna said dryly.

"You seem unnerved by Laird Douglas's appearance."

"Umrnm...possibly," Shawna agreed, thinking that it was the understatement of all time. But since Mary Jane didn't know that a different Laird Douglas had actually arrived straight from the grave, she couldn't understand just how seriously unnerved Shawna could be.

"Well," Mary Jane told her, "You are usually the most ardent supporter of tradition and ceremony, so I hope you'll not forget what an important occasion the night is. Actually, I'll not let you forget!" she promised. She walked back to Shawna and kissed her cheek. "Shawna, smile!"

So, Shawna offered her a smile and assured her, "I'm quite enthusiastic about the coming occasion, I promise. We've guests this year as well. Not guests—since Skylar Douglas is actually lady here."

"You will always be lady here," Mary Jane said loyally.

"Skylar is Laird Douglas's wife," Shawna said. "But the point is, we must involve her and her sister in the festivities."

"We will embrace them fully!" Mary Jane promised happily. "Well, let me leave you to dress then. Don't let the men—your kin or the new arrival—wear you down!"

"I'll not," Shawna promised her, and Mary Jane departed.

As soon as her maid had gone, Shawna bathed and dressed quickly. When she went downstairs, she saw that Andrew Douglas and the men of her family had already breakfasted. She spent the morning in the office with Hawk, as Andrew preferred to be called, Gawain, Lowell, Aidan, Alaric, and Alistair. It was a good meeting, she thought. The MacGinnises had kept sound control of Douglas interests, showing a profit in the various enterprises, while also managing the domestic affairs of the properties equally well. Hawk listened during most of the meeting, asking a question here or there, then remaining thoughtful as he considered the replies he received. When the meeting broke up, it was decided that they would have dinner in the great hall together, then Hawk would spend the afternoon showing his wife the haunts of his Scottish youth. As Shawna's kin departed the office first, she and Hawk were left alone for a matter of minutes.

Shawna was startled when he leaned across the desk to her and bluntly told her, "If you know anything about what happened, you had best speak now."

Shawna was alarmed and dismayed by his tone of voice. She had expected his anger and his scorn for her once he knew she had played a part in the events that led his brother's "death," but nonetheless, a wave of despair settled over her. Rather than dissolve into tears, she straightened her shoulders and stared at him fiercely in return. "If I don't? Shall I be scalped on the spot?"

Hawk leaned back. "I expected far more from you."

She lowered her eyes to the desk and whispered desperately. "I don't know what happened."

He reached over, lifting her chin. "If you betray him again, it will not be me you have to fear," he warned quietly.

She met his eyes, then sat back in the chair, crossing her arms over her chest. "I don't know what happened that night, and that is a truth that I cannot change. I—I haven't betrayed his presence, though it is my own family, my clan, my kin, I deceive. A dead man crawls in and out of my window without my leave to do so, and still I have kept my silence."

A smile suddenly flashed across his dark features. "So, of course, you are glad that he's alive."

Shawna flushed and hissed softly, "Of course I'm glad that he's alive."

He suddenly seemed satisfied and stood, indicating with a sweep of his arm that she should precede him from the office. She did so. When they entered the great hall, she found Alistair in the act of charming Sabrina Conner, while Lowell and Gawain were giving Skylar Douglas a description of the Highlands in contrast to the Lowlands and of the frequent historical differences between the two regions regarding policy and politics. "Oft enough," Gawain was saying, "the Lowlanders were first to accept the English ways, and English rule—they were low on the border there, you see. Many lairds in those parts came from England, and their financial holdings are entwined with English interests. 'Twas the Highlanders—mainly—kept fighting for the cause of the Jacobites, protecting the rights of the Catholic strain of the line. Now, of course, we've laws to protect the religious interests of all our people, but it was often the Highlanders who hid the priests when they were in peril during those olden days when religion and politics were often one and the same."

"Aye, and the Highlanders were the ones who practiced witchcraft as well," Lowell commented with a twinkle in his eyes. "We've still a number of witches about the place."

"Witches?" Skylar inquired.

"Uncle Lowell," Shawna protested, entering into the conversation, "you'll give Skylar the wrong idea."

"They are witches," Lowell muttered.

Shawna smiled. "He is referring to those ladies who practice Wicca, not to broom-riding crones who would cast deadly spells upon the earth." She gave her Uncle Lowell an exasperated frown.

Smiling at Skylar, Alistair explained further. "Before the advent of Christianity, so many peoples settled here. Gaels, Picts...the Scoti from Ireland who gave our country its name. Druids ruled here, the Norse invaders brought their old gods, and in the days before Christianity, many people practiced Wicca."

"The earth is honored in the religion," Shawna said, "along with Mother Nature, and herbs are used for healing, stones give strength, and beauty and peace are found in the ground, sky, and water themselves."

"We burned our last witch just about a century ago," Lowell

commented. Her great-uncle was teasing her, Shawna saw. Taunting her because she liked to defend the right of people to live as they chose. Lowell was a staunch member of the Scottish church, and that was that.

She imagined he might like the idea of burning witches once again.

Hawk Douglas slipped his arms around his wife. "Many of the Wiccan practices are similar to our Sioux beliefs," he mused.

"If Wicca is such a benign religion, what caused the furor over witchcraft?" Sabrina inquired, accepting a glass of wine from Gawain as they began to draw together.

"Satanists!" Lowell advised, adding a dark roll to his voice.

"Father," Aidan said patiently, smiling at their visitors as well, "the point here is that Satanists and witches are not one and the same."

"The Pope," Gawain offered dryly.

"Gawain, y'canna go blaming the Catholic Church—" Lowell began with irritation, but Alaric nobly interrupted in his father's defense.

"Uncle, I don't think my father intends to attack the Holy Roman Church," he assured Lowell. Alaric, sound and steady as always, intended to allow no real arguments here before guests.

Whereas Alistair loved a good rousing discussion, Alaric was quite Victorian in his outlook—dignity and protocol above all else.

Gawain, however, seemed in a peaceable enough mood himself—though he did intend to get his point across.

"I greatly respect the Roman Catholic Church, brother, but I can't change history! At one time there were two popes—men can be corrupt creatures, even in God's own church, and in all the frenzies of righteousness that have gone on in past centuries, men who were not corrupt were sometimes misled. Then, whether 'holy' in calling or not, there existed men within the Church who were simply cruel, thriving upon the pain and agony of others. In the 1400s, there was a document called the Malleus Maleficarum, decrying the practice of witchcraft, and the hunt was on. Witchcraft became associated with devil worship—two different things, the gentle practitioners of true Wicca will assure you. In Spain, the Inquisition brought down thousands upon thousands of innocents. Our own James—that would be VI of

Scotland and I of England—was terrified of witches, and they were persecuted fearfully."

"Uncle Gawain!" Shawna applauded. "How very well explained."

"Aye, for yer great-uncle Gawain is fond of Edwina McCloud, who, it is whispered, heads a coven of witches here in our midst."

Gawain eyed Lowell sternly. "Right is right," he said sternly, sounding very much like the staunch Scotsman, and still his words brought laughter from them all.

"Why, Father! I did not know!" Alistair said. He glanced at his brother Alaric. "Did you?"

"Aye, I had a few ideas."

Alistair sighed. "Father likes you better!" he said teasingly.

"Father trusts him more than you not to taunt an old man to death, and that is that!" Gawain said, drawing laughter from them all. Shawna found herself smiling, actually relaxed and happy. Although eccentric and strong individualists, her family could be charming when they chose to be so.

"Would Wicca have anything to do with the Night of the Moon Maiden?" Sabrina inquired.

Shawna frowned. "Well, aye and nay. The Night of the Moon Maiden is older than any other Highlands celebration. The truly ancient peoples here celebrated it—that's when there was actually a sacrifice on the main Druid Stone. But, of course, through time, the Night of the Moon Maiden has evolved, and now it's simply a special night that celebrates the harvest."

"And fertility," Hawk reminded them all wryly.

"Well, aye, of course, that. We must be fertile," Lowell agreed.

"I do suppose," Sabrina murmured.

Myer entered the great hall, informing them all that supper was served. They continued to discuss local customs, Highlanders versus Lowlanders, and Americans versus the British while they ate. When the meal was finished, Sabrina reminded Shawna that she had promised to show her some of the property.

"You can ride with Skylar and me," Hawk told his sister-in-law.

"You two should ride your empire alone together."

Hawk frowned. "That's not at all necessary—"

"I think it would be more romantic for the two of you to go alone—and more fun for me to go with Shawna. If you don't mind, Shawna?"

"It would be my pleasure," she assured Sabrina.

"Well, then, why don't we all be about our business?" Gawain suggested. "Perhaps we could meet up again at the tavern, give your lady and her sister a taste of fine Scottish ale and mutton stew, Laird Hawk?"

"Indeed, that sounds like a fine idea," Hawk agreed.

"I'm to the mines," Aidan said.

"Aye, me as well," Alaric agreed.

"Perhaps the ladies desire an escort—" Alistair began.

"Brother, we men are to the mines," Alaric advised.

Alistair grimaced. "Aye, then, brother." He bowed charmingly. "We men are to the mines." He followed his brother and cousin from the hall.

Shawna and Sabrina agreed to meet at the stables in an hour. Shawna changed into an olive-green riding habit with a velvet banded hat, dressing uneasily, as she feared that at any minute, David would make one of his startling appearances. He did not, and she met Sabrina without incident.

The American girl was pleasant, courteous, and polite, and seemed truly happy when they raced haphazardly across open fields and over the hills and along the shore of the loch. Shawna showed her Castle MacGinnis, explaining that it might even be a bit older than Grayfriar Castle—or Castle Rock, as the Douglas stronghold had come to be called—but that it was smaller, and with fewer windows lacked a great deal of the daylight that made its way into Castle Rock. "An office is far easier to keep within Castle Rock, so we MacGinnises have tended to reside there since..."

"Since David 'died,'" Sabrina suggested dryly.

Shawna nodded, gazing at Sabrina. "So you know."

Sabrina shrugged. "Naturally. My sister and brother-in-law would not bring me here and not have me be aware of any potential danger."

Shawna looked at the castle walls. "I can't believe that you could be in any danger here." She smiled somewhat wryly. "You'd make an exquisite virginal sacrifice on the Druid Stone, perhaps, but as we said before, we did cease that practice long ago."

"Well, I'm not so sure I'd make such a fine sacrifice anyway," Sabrina murmured. "Let's move on, shall we? Perhaps to that tavern of yours? I've acquired quite a thirst."

They rode again, turning toward the village. The sun was quite bright for an autumn afternoon in the Highlands, casting brilliant light upon the sloping hills, which were richly green with long grasses in some areas, and blanketed in purple wildflowers in others.

"It's quite beautiful," Sabrina said. "I could imagine living here forever."

Despite herself, Shawna shivered. Her mind played havoc with her heart. Sabrina Connor was young, charming, beautiful.

Innocent of complicity in attempted murder.

She and David didn't even know one another.

But they would soon enough.

They arrived at the tavern before Hawk and Skylar. Shawna warmly greeted the woman who came to serve them. It was Edwina McCloud—the gentle, pleasant woman with whom she had just learned her great-uncle was romantically involved.

"Edwina! How lovely to see you. This is Miss Sabrina Connor, who is the sister of Hawk Douglas's new lady wife. Sabrina, Miss Edwina McCloud."

"'Tis a pleasure," Edwina said. "And what might I be getting you? Ale, perhaps..." Her voice trailed slightly as she studied Sabrina. "Cider maybe. We've fine cider."

"Ale," Sabrina said. Yet, to Shawna's astonishment, as Edwina continued to stare at her, Sabrina seemed to change her mind. "Perhaps I shall try the cider."

"Cider. Will ye eat nothin', then?" Edwina inquired.

"Aye, but later." Shawna watched the older woman's face. She had once been a stunning woman, and though time had ingrained numerous lines upon her countenance, she was still beautiful, with silver-gray eyes to match the streaks in her abundant auburn hair. She farmed on lands that she tenanted from the MacGinnises, but she worked a few nights a week as well for her cousin, Evan McCloud, who ran the tavern—on land tenanted from the Douglases. "My uncles, cousins, and Laird Douglas from America will be here shortly with his new bride. We'll have something then."

"Aye, then," Edwina said, not seeming to react to the news that Gawain would arrive shortly. As she moved behind the tavern bar to get their drinks, Shawna studied her curiously. Was Edwina aware of Gawain's regard? And did it mean anything? Gawain might have defended the practice of Wicca nobly, but he was a still a proud MacGinnis, from a long line of ancient Highland chieftains, and Edwina was a tavern maid.

Albeit they were both aging a tad.

"The tavern is quite pleasant," Sabrina said, smiling.

"A bit rustic compared to what you've become accustomed to in America?" Shawna asked.

Sabrina shook her head with a wry smile. "I've most recently been with my sister in Dakota Territory—this is high civilization by comparison. Well, I don't mean that exactly, my brother-in-law is quite sophisticated, of course, but it is Indian country, and I can assure you that many of the Indians are not civilized. Well, they're different, I mean. I don't mean to be insulting, they're simply..."

"Savage?" Shawna suggested.

"Definitely. At least some of them are."

"You're—you're quite welcome to stay here, of course," Shawna said, then she broke off.

Brother Damian was back in the tavern. He sat in the corner across from them. He lifted his tankard of ale to her, his cowl shrouding his thickly furred face.

"Who is that? Another local character?" Sabrina asked.

Shawna shook her head. "An irritating visitor," she murmured.

Sabrina turned around. "That harmless friar?" she asked. She smiled at him.

Brother Damian nodded gravely in return.

"M'ladies?" Edwina said.

Shawna smiled at Edwina and was startled to see that Edwina was regarding Sabrina intently. It gave her a little chill. Some people believed that Edwina's being a witch meant far more than the simple practice of her Wiccan religion. Edwina did have special talent. She could heal sores and blisters and all manner of sicknesses. She was said to have "the sight," and very often, she had made predictions which had come true, most of them regarding the birth of a calf, the arrival of a storm, or the like. The Reverend Massey himself said that she was "touched by God's hand," and though he frowned upon her lack of interest in the Scottish church, he enjoyed debating with her, and stated frankly that he admired her abilities to heal—though, like others, he seemed uneasy with her ability to predict the future. Luckily, Edwina was blessed with the good sense to keep much of what she knew to herself.

"The cider is delicious," Sabrina said, "though I might just as well have tried the ale."

Edwina kept her eyes steadily upon Sabrina. "Cider's good fer the bairn. I've seen far too many goodwives imbibe too freely when with child, and seen children born the more poorly for it."

"Edwina, this is Miss Sabrina Connor," Shawna said, frowning, then realized that Sabrina had gone as white as a sheet and was simply staring at Edwina.

"I don't—I don't know what—" Sabrina began.

But Edwina merely shook her head, glanced around and lowered her voice. "As you wish, Miss Connor. But your child is in danger, as are you—and you, milady."

"Edwina—"

Edwina didn't need prompting. She was anxious to speak quickly and be done with it.

"I had a dream about the young Laird David. I wandered into the Douglas crypt, and he was there, banging at the lid of his coffin, demanding it be opened. He lay there atop the corpse of another man. You were there, Lady Shawna, and he was beckoning to you, demanding that you help him. He said, 'I live, I am laird of the castle, and I'll not lie here murdered and moldering!' But there were people in the shadows of the crypt, and they wanted Laird David to remain dead—and Lady Shawna, they wanted you dead as well and—" She broke off for a moment, shaking her head. Again, she stared at Sabrina. "I don't quite understand my own dreams all the time, but you, Miss Connor, are in grave danger as well. Somehow, it is all connected. And I am telling you this simply because you must take the greatest care."

Shawna stared at her, stunned. She looked around to see whether Edwina might have been overheard.

Brother Damian remained in his back booth, eyes upon them. Shawna turned and was dismayed to see that Fergus Anderson had taken a seat up at the bar, and was smirking now, indeed having heard every word the woman had said.

"Did ye hear that, Evan, eh? Y'er cousin Edwina here is telling our fine Lady MacGinnis that David Douglas lives!" He fell into a gale of laughter. "Alas, Edwina, be off with you! Leave the poor lady alone. They say the pair were destined to marry, yet what horror she'd have with a burned and shriveled corpse of a man!"

"Fergus!" came a roar from the tavern's door. Fergus cast his hand to his eyes to shield them from the sudden last streaks of golden daylight that flooded in upon them from the opening of the door.

"Why, 'tis the savage!" Fergus muttered to the man at his side.

Sabrina Connor was suddenly up, slapping Fergus across the face. "Don't you call my brother-in-law a savage, you sodden dreg!" she snapped.

Shawna was just as quickly up beside her, coming between Sabrina and Fergus as the man leaped to his feet to do drunken battle. But it didn't matter. Hawk Douglas had been at the door, and he now advanced among them, catching Fergus by his lapels and drawing him close. "I don't take kindly to drunkards discussing my brother—alive or dead. You've had enough. Go home, Fergus."

Fergus stood dead still, staring at Hawk. "Lairds, ladies—and savages!" he muttered. "They rule over all and think that they can take your life, your time—aye, even a man's bairns!"

"Nothing's been taken from you, Fergus," Shawna said angrily. "Everything's been done for you!"

"How's me wee boy doing, Lady Shawna?" Fergus demanded.

"Your lad is in fine hands," she assured him.

"Go on, Fergus, get out," Hawk said, releasing the man.

Fergus adjusted his collar rebelliously, then left the tavern. Shawna was startled at the way Hawk's eyes touched hers, for he seemed neither distrustful nor angry. "His lad?"

"The child nearly died in the mines the other day. He was rescued by—" She hesitated. "He miraculously made it out. I've given him work at Castle Rock. I hope you approve."

"Immensely."

By then, Skylar Douglas was at her husband's side, Gawain and Aidan had arrived, and a fair amount of confusion began in greetings and explanations.

Shawna noted that Brother Damian seemed to have slipped out

And that Sabrina Connor remained an ashen shade throughout the evening, her color changing only when she happened to glance Shawna's way.

Then her cheeks turned crimson.

FEELING EXCEPTIONALLY tired and eager to be alone, Shawna managed to leave the tavern ahead of the others.

Night was just falling when she rode back toward Castle Rock. Beautiful yet eerie streaks of light in shades of gold and crimson seemed to splash down upon the landscape, reflecting off the distant Druid Stones. Enchanted by the sight, Shawna drew her horse to a halt by a shadowed copse of trees and there dismounted, leaning against a tree and staring toward the hill where the Druid Stones rose.

She was there several long moments before she turned to gaze at the crest of a small hill just at the end of the copse. A man stood there. A kilted Highlander, caught in a silhouette in the strange shadows of the dying day. He seemed very tall, facing the wind, as strong as the rock upon which he stood. Then quite suddenly, he moved, and Shawna realized that he was coming toward her. She recalled in that instant that an attempt had been made on her life, and she turned swiftly in panic, determined to reach her horse and ride hard for Castle Rock and safety.

"Shawna!" she heard, and she paused, spinning around. The Highlander had come down from his hill. David walked toward her in the golden glow of the setting sun, handsome in the radiance of color in which he had been caught. She had seen him only in darkness until now, she realized. Only in shadow.

By daylight, she thought, he was as dazzling as the rays of the sun. She wanted to run to him. She wanted to throw her arms around him. She wanted to be plucked up in the strength of his arms, held tenderly against him. But suspicions and accusations remained, and only in the shadow of night could she allow herself to touch him.

He paused before her, the breeze catching his dark hair, blowing it against the strong contours of his face.

"David. In the flesh. By daylight. My laird, I am honored," she said and curtsied, a small smile playing upon her lips.

"Honored, indeed!" he retorted, and she was suddenly where she wanted to be, lifted into his arms, held against his chest...

And hurried into the shadows of the copse.

Still, the sweet scent of the foliage surrounded them. Streaks of crimson and gold fought their way through the high-arching branches of the trees to continue to cast the colors of daylight upon them. He strode with her to a group of huge rocks that sat by a bubbling stream as if they had been cast there by the careless hand of a Titan. He seated her upon one, then set his own booted foot upon it before crossing his arms over his chest in what seemed to be the stern mode of the Highland men who filled her life.

"What in God's name are you doing alone?" he demanded.

She smiled, smoothing back a stray strand of hair. "I'm not alone. I'm in the company of an extremely powerful and annoying ghost."

He cupped her chin, raising her face to his. "Shawna, not even powerful ghosts can be everywhere. You've—"

"You seem to have a knack for being everywhere."

"Well, my lady, I do try—but I fear that not being among the truly dead, I am not infallible. Shawna, you are not to ride alone."

"But David—"

"You are not to ride alone!" His touch upon her tightened. She gritted her teeth, ready to argue. But he released her chin, stroking her cheek with his knuckle, and he repeated himself softly. "You are not to ride alone!"

"I had to get away from the tavern, from the others," she said.

He shook his head. "Never alone, Shawna, and never with just one member of your family."

"David—"

"Please."

She sighed.

"There is an answer, and I will find it. Bit by bit, the secrets that have been kept by people here will begin to unravel."

"What have you discovered?"

He hesitated. "Let's say for the moment that I've discovered new ideas regarding where to search," he told her.

"Where?" Shawna demanded.

"When I've a better idea of exactly what I'm up to, I'll tell you."

"Really?"

"I promise to keep you advised. If you promise not to be alone."

"As you wish, Laird Douglas," she told him, not trusting herself to say more. She lowered her lashes, lightly biting into her lower lip. She looked at him again. "But, David?"

"Aye?"

"I have ridden here now, and there are remnants of daylight about us. And it is really beautiful here, David, isn't it? The rocks strewn about the valley, the crystal stream, the color of the coming night. It's something of why we've always fought to be Highlanders, fought for Craig Rock itself and her people, isn't it?" she asked wistfully.

He smiled. Leaning toward her, he again touched her face, this time, his palm cradling her cheek. His face was very close to her own. Within the copse of trees, it felt as if they were alone at the ends of the earth, the shift of the breeze and the bubbling of the brook a melodic song about them. His mouth touched hers...so gently at first and then his tongue caressed her so deeply, awakening a delicious ache within her.

He suddenly drew away from her. "Horses," he said.

"What?"

"The others are coming from the tavern. I can hear the horses. There, that way, get your horse, and join them."

She hadn't heard a thing, but as she turned in the direction he had pointed, she heard the sounds of laughter and voices in casual conversation. She turned back to David.

But he was gone.

The brook continued to bubble. The breeze rose and whispered.

Her ghost had vanished along with the last golden streaks of daylight.

CHAPTER 12

Shawna quickly leaped from the rock and found her horse, mounting just as the others came around the outskirts of the trees.

"Shawna!" Gawain said with a frown. "What are y'doing here alone, lass?" he demanded. She was somewhat startled to realize that Gawain didn't seem happy that she wasn't safely within the walls of the castle.

"Dusk is such a beautiful time in the Highlands. I stopped to watch the sun fall. But I shall rejoin you all now if you don't mind."

"You must do so," Hawk told her.

Shawna urged her horse along with their party. Sabrina, she noted, was riding ahead just a bit. Concerned, Shawna trotted her mount until she had caught up with her. "Sabrina?"

The young woman turned to her, startled. Still ashen.

"I..." Shawna began awkwardly. "I just want you to know that it's all right, really." She realized she was blushing herself. "I mean, Edwina does tend to be right about such things, and if you are expecting a child, I don't intend to say anything to anyone. I understand—"

Sabrina slowed her horse and swung on Shawna. "No, you don't understand, you can't possibly understand. How could you even begin to say that you understand this, Lady MacGinnis?"

Consequences...Shawna thought. She couldn't begin to explain.

But she tried to keep her peace and her temper. "Fine. I don't understand. But I won't say anything to anyone since it's apparent this is one matter you've not chosen to share as yet with your sister."

"I haven't yet shared it honestly with myself," Sabrina murmured, her beautiful cobalt eyes closing for a moment as she pressed her temples between her thumb and forefinger. "Everything happened so quickly. My stepfather's death, the trip out West, the journey here..." She opened her eyes, glancing sharply at Shawna. "I'm sorry. But truly, you don't understand."

"Does the father know?"

"Good heavens, no!" Sabrina said in horror.

"Then perhaps—"

"This is nearly impossible!" Sabrina said, more to herself than to Shawna. "How in God's name could that woman know?" She stared at Shawna then. "And she—she knew about David."

"Yes. And Fergus heard her. The entire village will be running around, whispering about David's rising from the dead."

"Well...he did rather do that, didn't he?"

"Yes, but he's really alive."

"Perhaps he should just be alive then," Sabrina said.

"I've suggested that," Shawna murmured. "But he's determined—"

"That someone in your family tried to kill him, and he doesn't intend to be killed again?" Sabrina asked.

Shawna flashed her an angry glare, only to realize that Sabrina was sitting on her horse easily and watching her sympathetically. "He's wrong," Shawna said, alarmed to realize that her voice held a note of uncertainty.

"Then you have to prove him wrong," Sabrina said. "Shawna, if you'd already been left for dead once, you'd be very careful in the same circumstances a second time."

Shawna shook her head. "You can't have the same circumstances a second time. And you've managed to talk about me instead of yourself."

"Have I? Well, there's not much to say about me at the moment."

"The father really has a right to know—"

"Indeed, he does not!" Sabrina hissed with an anguished vehemence that silenced Shawna for a moment.

"If I can help in any way—"

"You can't. I shall manage. I'm telling you, you can't begin to understand—"

"I'm telling you, I can."

Sabrina shook her head. "You don't know—him. Or the circumstances. It was entirely accidental. I can't—I just can't believe this!" she whispered.

"But—is the father a terrible person? A madman? A monster of some sort—"

"No, no, nothing like that."

"Well, is he a handsome man? A young one, an old one?"

Sabrina looked at her irritably. "Oh, he is quite striking," she murmured, then her words suddenly came forward in a rush. "When he walks into a room, every woman there is instantly aware of his presence. He is tall, lean as a whipcord. He can be quite incredibly charming, but he can be completely merciless. He is unique in all that he is, and we met under the most ridiculous circumstances. Oh, it's all so ironic!"

"But you don't despise him?"

"Yes. No. I don't know. He is so self-assured, so set in his ways, and so caught up in his own conflict! I don't—I don't think that we can solve my dilemma at all right now. Thank God I'm here, and I've got time to think. And—please, I don't want to talk about it anymore!"

Shawna decided that she had best let the matter drop. She was being far too personal.

Yet, so was Sabrina Connor, for—glancing back to assure herself that the others still rode far behind them—she again turned the conversation to Shawna's past sins.

"You've raked me over the coals. Now it's my turn. What exactly happened the night when David was supposedly killed? If you could recall everything in minute detail, perhaps—"

"I have recalled everything in minute detail thousands of times. And I still have no answers."

"Tell me what happened. Maybe I can help. Looking in from the outside, you know."

Shawna felt her cheeks coloring. "Alistair had been guilty of shifting some money. I was quite sure of myself, certain that I could keep David talking long enough for my uncles and cousins to remove any incriminating evidence that might be found in either his office or the castle's master's chambers."

"So, what went so wrong?"

"I don't know."

"See, you're not giving me details. You kept David in the stables?"

"Oh, aye. But then...I don't know. I had closed my eyes. Everything seemed surrounded by darkness. I had—" She paused, shrugging unhappily. "The wine we were drinking was drugged. Mine wasn't supposed to have been drugged, but David suspected I was up to something and switched the glasses. I was with David, then suddenly, I was not. I remember darkness and shadows—then the fire. And waking up. Next to..."

"A charred corpse," Sabrina finished.

"God, it was awful," Shawna remembered.

"But it's quite incredible. Someone substituted a dead man for David in the stables. Well planned, don't you think?"

"Evidently. But Alistair did no such thing, of that I'm certain. I think that David's death hurt him incredibly. He felt terribly guilty for what he had done to begin with, then he was ashamed of the way we planned to undo it—and then when David was discovered dead...or we thought he was discover dead..." She broke off, glancing at Sabrina again. "That's what Laird David doesn't understand," she said angrily. "He has simply condemned MacGinnises and has no idea what we went through, assuming he was dead!"

"Shawna, you have to see that someone here did want to kill him."

"Then why is he alive?"

"That is the baffling part," Sabrina admitted.

"Do you have an answer?" Shawna demanded.

Sabrina thought a minute. "I've a hunch."

"Oh?"

"I think that several people must be involved—"

"My entire family?" Shawna queried, a rush of anger rising within her.

Sabrina shook her head. "I'm not saying that. I'm saying that a lot of things happened for just one person to be involved. The others are coming closer," she warned, lowering her voice, then keeping it quiet but fierce. "You mustn't say a word to my sister or brother-in-law, do you understand? I beg of you, you must keep quiet about—me."

"Sabrina—"

"You must promise me."

"It's not my place to say anything," Shawna told her.

Sabrina exhaled, then turned back to address Hawk and Gawain, nearing them as they rode.

"What a beautiful night."

"Not so lovely as the Night of the Moon Maiden will be!" Gawain assured her.

"It's a guarantee, a promise," Alistair averred, riding abreast of them then. "We've never had rain, or fierce cold, or a touch of snow or frost, on the Night of the Moon Maiden."

"Coming within the week," Hawk added.

Shawna felt his eyes on her, and a sense of unease swept through her.

"Three nights from this very evening," she agreed softly.

That night, her tower chamber was empty when she arrived there.

Mary Jane had left her a warm bath, which could easily be made hotter by heating a few kettles of water at her own hearth. She stoked the fire burning there, heated her water, bathed, all the while, waiting.

Expecting him...

But he didn't come.

When she slept, it seemed inevitable that she would dream.

Tonight, she ran across the valley from Castle MacGinnis to Castle Rock, cresting that hill, well aware that someone was after her. She passed by Castle Rock, hearing a rustling, feeling the earth move with the heaviness of the footfalls upon it. Far, far before her, she could see the moonlight shimmering down upon the loch. She needed to reach the water's edge. A selkie would rise from the depths, its fur shed, its form that of a man. The selkie, though half-beast, perhaps demon, would save her...

But the Druid Stones lay between her and the water. The main stone, the altar stone. She didn't know that she ran to it, but she was suddenly there, and she stumbled down because her would-be assailant was so close.

So close she could feel breath upon her neck...

So close she could feel warmth...

Fingers reaching out to draw her back, curve around her throat, steal the life from her.

She fell upon the altar, but rolled, determined to rise upon the other side. Yet, as she turned, a vision of pure horror greeted her. She lay beside a corpse. Burned, charred, the face contorted, blackened mouth opened in a final, horrid scream of agony and death.

She jerked herself awake, shaking, gasping, praying that she hadn't screamed aloud. Then a second cry nearly tore from her lips as she felt strong arms come around her.

"What is it?" came David's deep whisper from the shadows, and she felt his weight as he sat by her side.

He had been with her, she realized. Sitting sentinel before the fire, as often was his way.

Taking her by surprise.

Coming in silence while she slept, like a wraith.

A selkie, risen from the water, slipping in upon her when he chose, disappearing again when he so chose as well. Determined and taking complete advantage.

"Shawna?" he prompted.

She shook her head blindly. "It's nothing. Dreams, nightmares."

"Of dead men?" he queried.

She pulled away to try to study his face in the dim light of the fire. His eyes looked sharp, his mouth grim, yet he didn't seem to taunt or condemn her.

"Dead and buried," she told him.

"And burned?"

She shivered fiercely. How uncanny. It was almost as if he had been where she had been, heard what she had heard. "Edwina McCloud spoke to me tonight."

"She did?"

"She spoke of a different body lying in your grave."

"A perceptive woman."

"How can she be so perceptive?"

"How has she ever been so perceptive?" David queried. "Yet perhaps..."

"Perhaps what? Perhaps it is time to announce that you live, that you were never buried."

"That's not quite what I had in mind."

"Then?"

"Well, I think I would like to try to ascertain if the man who lies in my grave is the convict whose life I led in his place."

"Convict?"

"A long story. And it does not matter tonight."

"It matters to me."

"Well, I'm not in a mood to share it at this time."

"I want to know—"

"Shawna, you tell me," he asked gravely, "what happened to you on the night of the fire?"

"I was dragged from the stables. I don't know by whom. I only know that I awakened outside—next to your body."

"It would seem, then, that there were two powers at work that night," he mused. "I was supposed to die in the flames, and it was made apparent that I did. But somehow, my body was exchanged for that of another man."

"Perhaps some member of my kin attempted to save you," she suggested.

"I'll allow that. But you needn't say it with such superiority!"

"Really, my dear Laird Douglas. Well, what can you expect? It's incredibly distressing that you are just suddenly here—that you never so much as knock upon the door—or even the bedpost!"

"Ghosts cannot be expected to knock."

"Then perhaps ghosts should not expect to experience other earthly sensations."

"How rude, my lady. Especially considering the fact that I sat in a chair, awake, and keeping watch throughout the long hours of many a night, ever attentive to your safety."

"Aye, for indeed," she taunted wryly, "if I'm to be throttled, you would choose to be the throttler."

"That I would."

"Then if you would keep watch," she told him evenly, "keep watch." She did her very best to keep her eyes completely level with his. Yet she felt herself shivering again, and her lashes fell to cover her eyes. Why was she so uneasy tonight?

"You are afraid," he told her, "But you needn't be. Because I do keep watch. And because you're quite right. If you're to be throttled, I shall be the throttler."

"Laird Douglas, your eloquence with women is unmatched. Please, do feel free to take your seat before the fire, where you so nobly and happily kept watch before I rudely interrupted you with my cry."

"I was not happy where I sat."

"A pity."

"I didn't wish to disturb your sleep."

"How kind. Then—"

"You are no longer sleeping," he reminded her.

Warmth pervaded her. She longed to tell him that she wished for nothing other than to find the deep solace of sleep again.

But she didn't think that she could sleep now. Not with the visions that haunted her mind. She wanted to feel the flesh and blood of the living man, lie down with powerful arms around her, in order to shake off the fear of the cold and clammy grave that had settled upon her.

She slid into his arms with a soft, glad cry. For a moment, she felt the sheer comfort and security of his embrace. Then more...

So much more...

His fire burned within her and without her, and when the sweet violence of climax seized them like the shimmering of sparks given off by a bursting log split apart by the intensity of a blaze, she drifted ever downward.

Yet retained his warmth...

He would leave, she knew. Leave by the first hours of dawn, and she would not know where he went.

Only that he continued to see and hear...everything.

She roused, ever so slightly, when he rose from her bed at last. The room remained heavy with shadows, but faint streaks of light were beginning to touch upon the stone of the castle.

She felt the heat of his lips upon her brow, then the warmth was gone. He seemed to disappear, as cleanly as a dream. His touch nothing more than a memory.

She closed her eyes and felt an awful emptiness. She wondered if he could ever really be more than a dream to her.

SABRINA COULD NOT SLEEP.

How long had she tried to ignore the queasiness that had plagued her on the ocean voyage? How long had she tried to pretend that the obvious could not be?

She lay down to sleep, then rose. She slipped a robe over her nightgown and began pacing the room before the fire. Oh, dear God.

Sloan!

She could remember every detail of their first meeting in his hotel room. She was so desperately trying to hide from her stepfather while Sloan was under the assumption that she was the "new" girl, sent from the nearby whorehouse! She could scarcely explain her position, which had become steadily worse and worse until she...

Well, she had managed to remain hidden from her stepfather. And she was alive, wasn't she?

Alive and now responsible for another life within her!

"Oh god!" she whispered aloud, shuddering.

The night had been bad enough. Come the morning, he'd known nothing different than what she had told him—nothing. And his assumption had remained that she had come from the whorehouse and...

It wasn't that he had been horrible or cruel. He had roused her from sleep, and she had been sensually seduced before she had fully wakened. Yet that had been it! One night, one morning! And then, of course, the horror of discovering that he wasn't only a half-breed cavalryman with a heart and will of steel, he was her brother-in-law's best friend. Destined to be near her frequently. A single man, confirmed in his bachelor status, accustomed to the company of any woman he chose, white or red. Sloan could be exquisitely charming when he chose and ruthlessly pigheaded when he chose as well. She was obliged to him for his help as well when her stepfather had done his best to hunt down and kill her and Skylar.

Sabrina hugged her arms around her chest. And he was a half-breed. Part of the Sioux Nation, torn by the conflict approaching them. She wasn't afraid of him, she told herself. She wasn't afraid of anything.

But she was. She was afraid of the savagery of the Indians, and despite his exquisite manners, she was certain that a fire burned deeply beneath the civilized surface of Sloan Trelawny, as fiercely savage as that within any feathered and painted redman on the plain.

Sabrina searched her room, going through the handsome cherry wardrobe and desk, hoping to find a bottle of brandy or sherry. Whiskey would do just as well. Then she paused, remembering how Edwina had told her what drinking could do to a child. Just one little brandy...she was going to have a bastard anyway.

The thought brought a choking sensation to her, and she hurried to her window, anxious to inhale the night air. She was no naïve child, and she hadn't been when she'd desperately traveled west from Maryland to reach her sister. She could be hard and determined herself, since she'd grown up with the manipulating man who'd managed to murder her natural father and get away with it smelling like a rose, a man who had become a renowned politician. A man with so many connections he'd followed her trail west. Rather than let him discover her, she'd wound up in a room with Sloan Trelawny—drinking whiskey to stall for time. And when the following morning had come, she had been furious. Furious with herself, for not trying to explain the truth, for allowing Sloan Trelawny to believe she was a novice prostitute. Furious with him. Because she could have lived with herself if she could believe she had made a sacrifice for Skylar's and her own life. He had made the encounter more. He had made her see what making love could be, yet he had done so assuming he was educating a whore. When she had managed to depart at last, he had surely dismissed her as easily as his morning coffee. And when they had met again, she'd been stunned. And hateful herself. And now...

She could never tell him.

Fine! Then what was she going to do? Convince her sister that she was about to have history's second virgin birth?

She could lie, of course, and tell Skylar that there had been a man back in Maryland.

Then she'd have to leave her sister. Skylar, now, of course, had Hawk.

And a world about to explode on them, the Sioux situation in the West was so tense.

Still...

Her head was killing her. She didn't want to think anymore. One little sherry or brandy wouldn't hurt her babe, she determined. It would definitely help her sleep, and she was desperate to sleep.

She pulled her blue velvet robe around her shoulders, quietly departed her room, and hurried down the stairs.

In the great hall, she saw a brandy decanter with glasses on a tray in the center of the huge dining table. She hurried to the table and poured herself a brandy.

A small one.

Edwina's warning still disturbed her. She touched the glass to her lips, just tasting the brandy. She started then, swirling around, certain she had heard a noise coming from the hallway that led to the castle's chapel. "Hello? Who's there?" she demanded.

She thought she heard a sniffling sound in return. The cry, perhaps, of a lost child. "Hello, I won't hurt you!" she called softly. "Who's there, can I help you?"

She continued to hear the sniffling sound. She set down her glass and started down the dark corridor.

In her cottage, Edwina awoke with a start, staring up at the shadows of light and dark that played upon the ceiling.

She wondered what had wakened her.

She rose and moved restlessly to her window, looking out at the night. The moon was so nearly full.

An unease settled around her. Evil was afoot. She wished that she could do something about it, but she had no proof, no knowledge, just a feeling.

She had warned Shawna. And Sabrina Connor as well. And she had been overheard and taunted by the village drunk and ne'er-do-well for her pains!

That didn't really matter, she told herself. She had been mocked before. Frequently. She should have told Lady Shawna more. She should have told her about the boy.

The wind suddenly rose. The door to the cottage suddenly banged inward.

A man towered in her doorway.

"You have come," Edwina said.

He entered her cottage and closed the door behind him.

The wind continued to moan.

Clouds passed over the moon, then shifted away from it. It glowed yellow in the heavens. So very nearly full.

Sabrina found the door to the chapel open, and she slipped through it, certain that she could still hear a child crying. A lantern blazed on each side of the altar, but another beam of light cast a glow into the ancient chapel, and she saw that the door leading to the cemetery beyond had been left open. She knew that Shawna had recently brought a little boy to live at the castle, and though she mocked herself that it was too early for her to be feeling maternal instincts, she was still definitely worried. She couldn't bear the sad, frightened sound of the sniffling.

Sabrina hurried through the chapel, past the thick castle walls, and into the cemetery.

It looked as ancient as the chapel. The remnants of ancient wooden crosses remained alongside stone Celtic crosses. Marble angels sat guard among simpler stones. Tall mausoleums rose to greet the dead of one family or another. Tombstones rose with dire messages for the living chiseled most sternly upon them.

Sabrina shivered. By day, she had thought the cemetery magnificent. By night...

If a child had awakened in the night and lost his way here, he would quite naturally be terrified.

The sound came again. It seemed to be originating from just beyond a large, full-winged angel about a hundred feet from the castle wall.

"Hello! Let me help you!" Sabrina called out. She started to pick her way through the cemetery toward the angel, her robe and hair flowing behind her in the rising wind.

As she hurried across the dew-damp ground, she thought she heard footsteps following in her wake. The wind picked up, and the moon was suddenly covered by a dark cloud.

Sabrina spun around.

Too late.

She never screamed, for a foul-smelling cloth was clamped over her face far too quickly.

CHAPTER 13

"It's the shaft to the northwest of here which is supposed to be haunted, is that right?" Hawk was posing the question, and though Shawna was aware that he was speaking, she didn't immediately respond. A huge yawn prevented her from doing so...

"Shawna?" he repeated, frowning. "Shawna, this is the shaft which is supposed to be haunted, right?"

She couldn't believe it, but she had actually been nearly asleep. Nearly asleep and standing. Deep in one of the tunnels of the coal mine.

But then, she hadn't had much sleep in what was beginning to seem like a very long time, this morning less than usual. It was just barely dawn. She couldn't have closed her eyes for more than a few moments after David had left before she had heard a pounding at her door—his brother, determined on touring the mines before the workers started for the day.

"Aye," she said quickly, "this is where the trouble has been, where we've had the accidents, though I believe it is your brother who has done the 'haunting.'"

"Perhaps. But this is where the cave-in took place?"

Shawna lifted the kerosene lamp she carried to shed more light around them. "You can see where they have worked to shore up the walls here." She pointed out where carpentry had been done with solid columns of sturdy wood to prevent any more rocks from falling from above. "We're not far from the loch now, of course, and many of the tunnels beneath are waterways. So far, we've had no problems with the tunnels getting flooded. You've already heard that we nearly lost a child in the cave-in, but luckily, your brother was nearby 'haunting,' and he rescued the boy."

"The lad who works at the castle now?" Hawk queried.

Shawna shrugged.

"He's the look of a MacGinnis about him," Hawk commented.

Shawna felt a rush of warmth sweep through her. "So do many hereabouts. Just as we've a plentiful group of green-eyed, auburn-haired children among us."

Hawk didn't reply. He frowned suddenly, pressing a finger to his lips. "Perhaps we should cease to discuss matters pertinent to either the Douglases or the MacGinnises," he murmured. Then they both heard a tapping. It seemed to be coming from the north, where the shaft made a natural, curving turn.

"Do you hear it?" He barely mouthed the words.

She nodded.

He started forward, and she quickly followed him. They had come here alone. Skylar was waiting at the entrance to the mines, ready to warn them when the workers began to arrive for the day, but within the mine itself, they should have been completely alone.

He paused after a few steps, listening again.

There came a tap, then another.

Hawk moved his booted feet over the ground, moving in a circle. He stopped. The sound came again.

He watched her, a curious smile curving into his features.

"We're being lured!" Shawna murmured.

Hawk nodded.

She shook her head. "We shouldn't move forward," she said. "We should go back. Get help—"

"And add to the belief that the mine is haunted?" he asked her lightly.

She exhaled. "If we go forward..."

"I won't let anyone hurt you," he assured her.

"I wasn't—"

"What?" he asked.

"I wasn't worried for myself."

He arched a brow to her. "I have handled myself well against the US Cavalry, Rebs, Crows, and others. Would you have me run from a tapping in a mine shaft?"

Shawna nodded strenuously. He laughed softly, pulling her close for just a moment to set a brotherly kiss upon her forehead.

"We have to find out what's going on."

"It's probably David, preparing his morning tea," Shawna murmured dryly.

"Shush!" he warned her.

"Oh, aye. We don't know who might be listening!"

He proceeded forward again, amazingly silent though he wore boots. She crept quietly behind him with a deep sense of dread. She was afraid. Not just for herself. For them both.

Ahead of her, Hawk paused. Listened.

The tapping came again. More persistent. As if whoever was tapping had become annoyed because the noise wasn't causing them to react swiftly enough.

Hawk turned, lifting a hand to stop her.

Even as he did so, a curious gust of air suddenly burst into the tunnel.

And Shawna's lantern was extinguished.

Total darkness instantly fell upon the tunnel shaft.

For a moment, there was silence.

The tapping began again.

"Shawna!" Hawk said softly.

"I'm here."

"Don't move. Don't move, do you hear me?"

"I won't move. I can't move. I can't see anything at all. Hawk? Don't you move—"

"I have matches," Hawk said. "I've got to reach you to relight the lantern." A small burst of flame appeared against his cupped hands, and he called out irritably, "I told you to stay still!"

"I am still!" Shawna said indignantly.

"I can see your shadow. Shawna, dammit, get back here!"

The match went out. Shawna heard footsteps, his, moving hard and boldly in the darkness toward the natural curve of the shaft.

But she hadn't moved a muscle. She was still grasping her extinguished lantern, her back now against the wall as she stared blindly around her.

"Hawk!" she cried, ascertaining with panic that they were not alone, that he was being lured forward by more than just the tapping noise. Someone was with them. Someone who had misled Hawk into thinking that she was the shadow moving forward.

"Hawk! Stop—" she began.

Too late. She suddenly heard the sound of breaking, splintering wood beams, and she heard him cursing as he fell. Screaming, and moving blindly then herself, she started inching forward in the darkness.

"Hawk—"

"Shawna, stay still!" he thundered back to her. "Stay still, or you'll wind up down here."

"Where are you?"

"A few levels below. I can't see a thing down here. And naturally," he said, then paused in embarrassment, "I've dropped my matches."

"I'll get help."

"I can hear the water."

"Is there a way out?"

"Not that I can see. Well, if there was, I'm not so sure that even I could see it." He suddenly swore with a vengeance. "The water is rising in here. There didn't seem to be water when I first fell. Now it's over my ankles."

"Oh god!" Shawna breathed. "It's the tide."

"The tide?" Hawk repeated. "From the loch? Oh god yes, from the loch!"

Shawna knew that he'd forgotten the peculiar phenomena of Craig

Loch. It was connected with the Irish Sea through several underground rivers, and they were close enough to the open water for the tides to cause great changes in water levels in the caves that rose at the edge of the loch.

"Oh my god! I'll get help."

"You can't get help. You'll kill yourself trying to maneuver in the mine in the darkness."

"No, I won't! I can see better now..." she began, but her voice trailed away as she frowned and turned desperately to try to see around herself.

Then she screamed in wild panic as she suddenly felt hands roughly upon her, settling upon her shoulders, spinning her around.

She dropped the lantern, wildly trying to free herself, gasping and screaming again in protest, fighting to no avail. She suddenly felt herself being shaken hard, and the voice grating out to her finally penetrated through her panic.

"M'lady, cease and desist, now!"

It was David. David—whose voice was less than reassuring at that moment.

"Get the lantern!" he ordered.

She was shaking and found it nearly impossible to locate the lantern she had dropped. She heard him striking a match against the stone of the tunnel wall, saw it blaze. She had managed to get the lantern. He managed to light it. She was vaguely aware of green fire in his eyes as they briefly met hers, then he was moving past her.

"Hawk!"

"Here!"

Following him, Shawna saw where the cave flooring had given way to a break, and where that break had been covered over by a thin plank of wood—one that had cracked easily beneath Hawk's weight.

David didn't follow his brother into the breech. He flattened himself to the ground before it, waving the lantern over the gaping hole until he saw his brother.

The water was now up to Hawk's knees.

"What the hell are you doing down there?" David demanded.

"Wading?" Hawk suggested pleasantly.

"Indians are supposed to be able to see in the dark," David reminded hawk.

"I did see in the dark. I followed Shawn—" He broke off, apparently aware before Shawna realized herself just how angry David was. Why?

Because he had assumed that she had led Hawk here, that she had known about the break in the flooring within the cave.

She wanted to shout at David, to tear into him. But the water was rising, and Hawk remained trapped below.

David set the lantern by the hole, pushing himself quickly to his feet. He spun around suddenly, grasping Shawna's wrists. "Get rope. There's sure to be some in the front tunnels. Get back here as fast as you can, or I shall take you apart piece by piece myself, I swear it."

She wrenched free from him with an energy born of pure fury, somehow maintaining complete dignity as she did so. "I'll get rope because I'd do anything in my power to save Hawk."

She squared her shoulders, plucking up the lantern and hurrying down the tunnel as fast as she could go. As she hurried along, she heard David say, "I'll have her yet, I swear it! She'd best get back—"

"I can swim," Hawk reminded his brother. "If the currents don't sweep me from the opening."

He probably could rescue himself, Shawna thought, hurrying down the mine shaft. He was strong, and resourceful, and now David was with him. Whether she did or didn't find rope, Hawk would escape. But she remembered passing a heavy coil of rope when they had entered the outer tunnel, and as she ran through the shafts, she could picture it exactly in her mind's eye.

She paused at a fork in the tunnel. The main entrance to the mine was just to her left, yet she had to pause to catch her breath. She leaned a hand against the stone wall of the tunnel, inhaling deeply. Skylar was at the entrance to the main shaft, and Shawna wondered if she should tell her quickly what was happening. But as she paused, she heard a tap.

Tap.

Then, in a deep, low, unearthly tone...

Her name.

"Shawna..."

A whisper she might have imagined. She started to spin around.

But she smelled something before she could turn. Before she could look.

Something cold and wet and clammy landed over her face before she could see anything.

A sickly, sweet smell seemed to overpower everything else, and she felt herself falling, and falling, and falling...

And once again, the darkness was absolute.

A knife flashed in lanternlight in the tunnel. But before it could touch Shawna's flesh, the hand that wielded it was drawn back.

"Fool! What are you doing?"

"She is to die—"

"Not here, not now! Take her."

Arms reached out for Shawna, but the tunnel shaft was suddenly flooded with light from the entrance to the main shaft. "Hawk, Shawna! Hawk, Shawna!"

"Someone is coming! Hurry!"

"Leave her!"

"We must have—"

"We'll find another opportunity. Come on, we cannot be caught! We've got the other lass, but he wanted M'lady MacGinnis very especially. We'll take her when the opportunity is better! We must not be found here!"

The two figures hurried down the shaft of the tunnel.

Just outside the main entrance, Skylar anxiously played her lantern around in circles.

She prayed that her husband and Shawna would quickly emerge.

"WHAT IN GOD'S name can be taking her so long?" David demanded irritably. He had come to know the mine shafts very well. He was very familiar with the tunnels that led from the caves by the loch, bordering the cliffs where the miners dug. He'd been in them often enough, and still, with the lantern gone, the darkness was almost overpowering.

And he could hear the water as the tide filled the tunnels. Hear it rising.

As if reading his mind in the darkness, Hawk spoke from the void at his side.

"She didn't lead me here. I was the one determined to get into the shafts before day broke."

David leaned against the wall of the cave. "You said you saw her moving."

"I thought I saw her moving."

"If we both die, this property all reverts to the MacGinnises."

"But you're alive, and Shawna knows it."

"Aye, but since no one else is aware that I do live, my death a second time around would not be much of a bother."

"She's innocent. I swear it."

"Knowing full well that she duped me the night that I did 'die?'"

"Ah, well, now, there's the crux of the matter, eh? Lady MacGinnis duped you—so perhaps forgiveness is difficult? David, do you really believe that Shawna intended to lure me to injury or death now?" Hawk queried his brother.

"Sweet Jesus! I don't want to believe such a thing. My god, every time I see her..." He paused, inhaling harshly. "She was involved, Hawk. She was involved in what happened. And until I know exactly who else was involved and how, I have to keep up a certain guard against her."

"She is a part of you, David. You can't deny it."

"Aye, she is a part of me," he said softly, but then added with angry passion, "Yet I will deny it if I discover that she is lying to me now in any way or keeping any secret from me whatsoever regarding her kin." David frowned and leaned over the hole, ready to argue with his brother. But in the darkness, he could see shadows, and the shadow of the water rising was not pleasant.

"I'm going to reach down for you," David told Hawk.

"Wait 'til it rises a bit more," Hawk said quietly. "I'll have a better chance of reaching you."

"In a few minutes, the current may be too strong."

"All right. One minute then."

"One minute..."

David twisted around, bracing his legs around the rocky edge of the gap, then falling forward with his length, reaching out his arms like an acrobat. He could barely make out his brother's form, but he trusted that Hawk could see shadow the same as he did himself. He could hear the water now, for the strength of the tide was causing it to rush by in bubbles and whispers. He heard movement as Hawk jumped within the water, using it to make himself as light and buoyant as possible, then jumping with all his strength and energy.

At his first attempt, their fingers met and slipped. He heard Hawk swearing as the force of the water carried him northward, and out of reach.

"Hawk!"

"Coming back, coming back..."

"Hawk!"

"Ready."

Again, David heard the sloshing movement, saw the shadow of his brother beneath him. Again, Hawk leaped.

Their hands met, grasped. Their palms were slick from the water. He swore. Grasped harder.

Their grip became firmer. With all his strength, he lifted. Gritting his teeth, he inched back against the stone, levering his brother's body upward. As soon as humanly possible, Hawk released his grasp on David, caught hold of the stone ledge, and propelled himself upward and out of the void. He landed beside David. For a moment, they lay together, panting, breathing.

"Son of a bitch!" Hawk muttered, then said in the darkness, "Brother, you are one competent white man."

David smiled to himself with vast relief. "Thank you. You're quite an acceptable American heathen yourself."

"Which part is worse, the American or the heathen?"

"I shouldn't have had you come here," David said.

"Because of this?" Hawk queried.

"Someone is determined to rid the world—or Craig Rock, at the very least—of Douglases."

"Umm," Hawk mused. "I should have stayed home in the middle of the Sioux conflict."

"You'll go back to it anyway, and you know it."

"Maybe it will all work itself out while I'm here abroad."

"Aye, and maybe the Scots will awaken one day and love all things English." He sat up suddenly, realizing that Shawna had not come back.

"Lady MacGinnis left us."

Hawk leaped to his feet, reaching for his brother's hand. "Something has happened to her," he said worriedly.

"Aye, the greed of her kin," David said, but he was up as well. He was glad of the darkness then, hiding the worry that surely played upon his features. She had come here with Hawk, and he had nearly been killed. She had gone for the rope to save him. she had never returned.

"No, David, I don't believe that—" Hawk began, then broke off with a shrug.

David was condemning her for what had happened here today. But it didn't matter. He was already hurrying along through the tunnel, moving swiftly and easily despite the darkness.

"Get up."

Shawna blinked, aware of the voice nearby and overwhelmingly aware of feeling ill. She swallowed, praying that she wasn't going to vomit.

"Shawna, get up."

"I can't."

Her head was spinning. The more it spun, the more afraid she was that she was going to be sick.

"Shawna—"

Light flooded into her eyes. She blinked and cringed against it. Who had come, who was talking to her? Someone who intended to kill her?

Death seemed a mercy at this moment.

"Shawna!"

Her name was spoken harshly. David. He was kneeling before her, holding the lantern above her face. She couldn't see his features. The light was all but blinding her.

"What happened?"

It was another voice. A kinder, gentler voice.

The kinder, gentler voice of a savage. Hawk.

He was hunkered down on her other side, and she could see without being blinded by the glare of the lantern.

"I—I don't know. I paused to catch my breath...oh god! You're—you're all right."

"Aye, my brother lives."

It was all that he said, yet she was aware that he believed his brother was fine despite her efforts to harm him. Angered, she leaped to her feet. She instantly wavered, feeling again the dizziness and the nausea. She nearly fell— and would have, had Hawk not caught her.

"Shawna, what is the matter with you?" David demanded skeptically.

"Shawna?" Hawk inquired.

"Shawna, talk to us!" David warned. "We'll not play games here as we did five years ago!"

"You must...you must leave me be," Shawna whispered to Hawk. "I'm...sick."

She pushed away from him, staggering along the tunnel. When she burst out of the main shaft, Skylar, who had been waiting and watching from the very edge of the entrance, came hurrying after her. "Oh my god! What's happened, are you all right—"

She broke off as her husband emerged, followed by David. She spun around nervously, trying to assure herself that they remained alone by the mine's entrance. "David, you can be seen here. Hawk, what's going on? Shawna, tell me! What has happened?" she demanded, her voice rising anxiously at the sight of them, Shawna gray, Hawk soaked and muddied, David disheveled and caked with coal dust.

Without waiting to hear the men's answer, Shawna hurried to the nearest bushes. Her stomach constricted in vicious torment, and she was violently sick, so much so that she fell into the long, cool grass once her retching had stopped.

"Poor thing!" she heard. She tried to sit up. The effort was too much. She fell back as Skylar knelt down beside her. She'd had the presence of mind to bring a bucket of water from the mine entrance and dipped her handkerchief in it to bathe Shawna's face. "There..." she murmured. "You're not...well, you're not..."

"Not what?"

"Expecting?"

"Expecting what?" Shawna inquired, then realized just what Skylar Douglas thought she was expecting.

"No, oh, no! I was attacked, drugged!"

"Drugged?" Skylar demanded, alarmed, and Shawna realized that neither Hawk nor David had really told Skylar anything.

"We were tricked in the tunnel. Led toward a gap in the flooring that led to the caverns below that fill with high tide from the loch. When I ran for help...someone drugged me."

"With wine?" came a sardonic voice.

David stood behind her. She knew it. She made it to her feet, though she had to pray that she would maintain the strength to stand. And to move.

"Pray, Skylar, tell your brother-in-law how terribly sorry I am that he does not reside in hell!" she said furiously and started for her horse.

She was going to make it. She was still trying to move too fast. She heard a cry, though it seemed distant. Skylar, she thought.

She started to fall again.

She was swept up. She tried to open her eyes.

David. David was carrying her.

And for a brief moment, his green eyes seemed forest deep with concern.

"Bastard," she mouthed to him.

Then her eyes closed again.

When she awoke next, she was in the tower room at Castle Rock.

Sunlight was shining through the window, and Skylar was seated by her side, reading as she kept watch.

Thinking they were alone, Shawna groaned. She tried to smile at Skylar, who instantly looked at her with concerned eyes.

"Are you alright?"

"Better. Very thirsty."

"I'll get you some water—"

"Here."

Skylar didn't need to go for water. David was in the room as well. Bathed and changed, he wore a handsomely loose-fitting white shirt and form-hugging breeches along with black boots. A stray lock of his dark auburn hair had formed a wild, rakish wave down the center of his forehead, and he impatiently thrust it from his eyes as he pressed a glass of water into her fingers.

Skylar rose. "Well, Shawna, you're looking much better. I guess I had best leave the two of you...er, alone," she finished flatly, looking from one of them to the other.

She didn't flee uncomfortably. Skylar wasn't the type to do so. She turned and seemed to gracefully float from the room.

Shawna sat up, instantly wary.

But she groaned then, burying her face in her hands. "Don't you ever go away anymore?" she whispered painfully.

He sat by her side on the bed, and she felt his eyes on her. She felt his stare. It seemed to be piercing her, stripping her in a manner quite unlike anything she'd ever felt before, even from him.

"Tell me exactly what happened."

"I should not tell you the time of day."

"I don't give a damn about the time of day. What happened?"

"Your brother came to me to see the mines—"

"So he says. But he is a gallant heathen and would protect you."

"He is gallant—and honest."

"Indeed. Go on."

"We heard a tapping. And followed it. And a gust of air doused the light. I heard him calling to me—" she began, then broke off flatly, crossing her arms over her chest.

"Go on."

She shook her head vehemently. "I'll not."

"You will."

"Go plague someone you believe in, Laird Douglas."

"I shall plague you mercilessly until I get my answers. My brother was nearly killed today. That would have made a fine and fitting end to the Douglas clan."

"I never sought to harm your brother. He knows it well. And you know it."

"Maybe I'm afraid I'm finding it far too easy to believe in your innocence, and knowing you, I don't dare allow myself that luxury. What happened to you when you went for the rope to save his life?"

"Someone...drugged me."

He stood, walking to the window. Then he turned back to stare at her.

"How odd."

"What is odd?"

"I found a handkerchief very early this morning in the chapel."

"What has this to do—"

"It still smelled of chloroform."

Shawna gasped. "Chloroform? But whose—"

She broke off, wide-eyed, because he was walking back toward her, and he leaned over her, his arms like a pair of bars on either side of her.

"Yours," he said, before she could voice the question.

"What?" she gasped. "You're trying to tell me that you found one of my handkerchiefs in the chapel—and it still carried a scent of chloroform."

"Indeed. I did, however, search the chapel from top to bottom. And I found nothing more."

"So, you're implying that I drugged myself to keep from saving your brother—then managed to run back here, drop my handkerchief in the chapel, and go running back to the mine to fall flat on my face?"

"I'm implying no such thing."

"Then—"

"I'm saying that it's quite curious that you are drugged by a mystery creature in the mine—and a handkerchief with your initials upon it is found in the cemetery bearing the scent of chloroform."

She pushed his arm aside, trying to rise. She wasn't nearly as dizzy as she had been, but she wavered for a minute before gaining strength by leaning on him. "I have had it! I won't keep secret the fact that you live anymore—I will not betray my own family. How could my kin possibly be guilty when I am master of so much mischief? And you,

Laird Douglas, you may have many rights, but you've got no right to me—"

She was suddenly no longer leaning on him, he was holding her, his hands cupping her elbows as he kept her firmly close, his head somewhat lowered to hers.

"You are sure it is a drug that made you ill?"

"Aye, of course!"

"You're quite certain that you're not with child?"

"Oh, sweet Jesus!" she murmured. "It was a drug. I am not with child!"

"How do you know?"

"I know, believe me, I know."

"You can't—"

"Oh god, stop!" she hissed. She was feeling weak again. She couldn't tell him that she knew full well that this was not a pregnancy sickness! "I was ill from the sickly-sweet scent of the drug, and that is all! Damn you, go! If you cannot believe in me, I insist that you leave me be. Your brother is here—darken his door by night! If you must guard someone by night, find your way to Sabrina's door—"

"That would not be likely."

"She's an exceptionally beautiful young woman."

"Exceptionally so."

She tried to wrench free from him. "Go—"

"My Lady MacGinnis, I think not."

"If—"

"I rather imagine that Sabrina Connor is involved with the father of her child."

Shawna gasped, horrified, trying to remember if she had given Sabrina away with any word or action. Surely, she had not done so!

"So, you know—"

"Aye, that I do."

"But I didn't—"

"You did not."

"But she has told no one, she doesn't want her sister or your brother to know—"

"They do not. Not to my knowledge."

A warm wave of uneasiness swept over Shawna. He heard too much, knew too much! She backed against the wall, watching him, wondering what else he might know.

She never gave away the past, she assured herself. Never.

Not even in her dreams.

There were things she could not bear to remember.

"Ah, so, Laird Douglas, were it not for Sabrina Connor's delicate secret, you might be slipping through her door?"

He frowned, staring at her peculiarly. "You don't think that my nights are well spent?"

"We've both just agreed that Miss Connor is exceptional."

"So we have." He arched a brow. "Ah, my dear Lady MacGinnis? Could you be...jealous?"

"Certainly not. I seek some other poor damsel for you to plague."

He came to her. She found herself backed all the way against the wall. He lifted her chin, meeting her eyes.

"Not jealous, eh?"

"Never. Although..."

"Aye?"

"It easily might have been," she murmured softly. "Your brother's sister-in-law is a very lovely young woman."

"Very lovely indeed."

"So then...who knows what might have been."

"Had she not had a lover—and I not had you?"

"Are you so certain that you have me?"

"I am certain only of the past, my lady. Who knows what might have been had our lives been different. The lovely young Miss Connor has her past, and I have my own."

"The past, Laird Douglas. What of the future?"

"What can one know of the future when we must first survive the present?"

He stared at her, the expression in his eyes demanding and provocative.

Yet then, even David was taken by surprise, for the door suddenly burst open when he was completely unprepared.

Totally exposed.

It was Skylar who had come upon them, anxious and upset—yet still with the presence of mind to close the door swiftly once she had entered.

"Edwina, the woman from the tavern, is here, with your great-uncle. She's very upset. She's come about some very unpleasant dreams, and...oh god!" Skylar buried her face in her hands.

David walked to her quickly, putting an arm around her shoulder. "Skylar, Edwina often has dreams, but you shouldn't be upset, she comes to warn people so that they can be careful when she feels they are in danger."

"No, no," Skylar moaned, blinking back tears. "She came because she was worried about Sabrina and—"

"And?" Shawna said worriedly.

"I can't find Sabrina! I went to get her to talk to Edwina, and I couldn't find her anywhere!"

"Skylar! We'll find her. She's an independent young woman with—with a lot on her mind," Shawna said, trying to be reassuring. But she was concerned herself. "Sabrina is not a part of whatever nonsense is going on here. We'll find her. I'm sure she's fine."

"I'm afraid not," Skylar whispered. "Edwina is certain that—"

"Certain that what?" David asked hoarsely.

"That Sabrina has met with some evil!" Skylar said.

"Why should she be so certain?" Shawna queried, a sinking feeling wrapping about her heart.

"Because," Skylar said, hesitating just briefly, "because Sabrina was somehow woven into her dream. She appeared as an angel in Edwina's dream, whispering to her."

"And saying?" David demanded.

Skylar moistened her lips to speak. "Saying that the charred corpse of David Douglas has come to life and walks the earth. Seeking vengeance. And that, in a reign of death, he shall have it."

CHAPTER 14

Shawna wound up searching through Castle MacGinnis with her great-uncle Lowell and Aidan. Since Castle MacGinnis was far smaller than Castle Rock, it had been involved in far less political maneuvering throughout the years than the Douglas stronghold at Craig Rock. While Lowell methodically went room by room through the ground floor and the crypts beneath, Shawna searched the upstairs rooms and turrets with Aidan.

Working the main turret in a circular fashion, Shawna met up with Aidan in Castle MacGinnis's master's chambers, composed of an office area with desk and file drawers beneath one of the great windows, bedchamber, library area, and dressing room. Aidan looked beneath the desk while Shawna searched the wardrobes.

"This is madness," Aidan said with exasperation at last. "Why would she come here?"

"I don't know, but she must be somewhere," Shawna replied, equally frustrated. "Either that, or Edwina is right, and she has met with some terrible fate, but even if that is so..." she began, her voice trailing away with a catch.

"Even then, we should find her body, is that what you mean?"

"No, of course not!" Shawna cried. She sank to the floor, staring at Aidan. "Oh god, Aidan, I pray so desperately that nothing has happened to her!"

"We're searching the wrong place."

"Maybe not."

"Why would she come to Castle MacGinnis?" Aidan demanded.

Shawna hesitated. "I don't know. I did show the place to her when we went riding. Maybe she needed to get away from her family. I mean, we all need to get away at times, right?"

"She could get away at Castle Rock."

"Who knows what she might have been thinking—or feeling. Maybe she wanted to get away from the Douglas household. This remains the MacGinnis stronghold."

"That it does," Aidan muttered, and she thought there was a note of bitterness in his tone.

"Is something wrong, Aidan?" she asked quietly. "I had thought that Gawain was the only one really bitter about the return of the Douglas."

"Should we be bitter?" Aidan asked, his handsome features curled into a wry grin as he sat by her, his back against the bed. "Let's see, the Douglases hold the choice land, and we work it to reap the benefits for others. We tend their cattle, collect their rents, and give them the larger portion of the proceeds from the mines at every turn."

"Most of their income from the mines is turned back into the property."

"We are little but tenants here, no better than the Andersons."

"How can you say that? We do hold our own property."

"Well, you are Lady MacGinnis."

"If you're angry with me for that, Aidan—"

He exhaled a long, weary sigh. "I'm not angry with you for anything, and in truth, all I begrudge Laird Douglas is America."

"What?" Shawna said, stunned.

"I want to leave," he told her. "I want to see the wild American West, I want to see massive herds of buffalo on the plain, I want to be a part of a new world."

"Dear God, Aidan, I'd had no idea—"

"No one does."

"But why don't you go to America?"

"Because my father is old, and I am all that he has."

"But Gawain is here, and Alaric and Alistair. And I would look after him, Aidan—"

"It isn't the same."

"But—"

"It isn't the same, and that's that. My father is bound to the land, to tradition. Maybe, if I've any youth left once he has passed on..."

"You could go with Hawk Douglas when he returns home," Shawna said firmly.

"Are we so sure that Laird Douglas will return home?"

"Of course. His interests lie with the Sioux people, and there is terrible trouble brewing in America. He—he will go home. And pray God, he will go home with his sister-in-law!"

Aidan squeezed her hand. "She is not in Castle MacGinnis, but we will find her. And Hawk will go home with his wife and his sister-in-law, but will he sell us his property?" Aidan queried.

"I—I don't know," Shawna faltered, looking downward. "But if he does," she said quickly, "you could go to America with him. Just for a visit. Surely, you could trust me with your father so long!"

Aidan smiled, and Shawna was startled to realize the wealth of dreams which had taken root and flourished within him when she had thought him so determined and responsible a man, dedicated to his own homeland and property.

"Surely, I could trust Father with you! Though why we are so passionate to create our dynasties, I don't know. Look how fertile they were in days past, yet now Alaric and I have passed thirty, Alistair will not remain long in his twenties, and even you, dear Shawna, are certainly well into marriageable age—yet not one of us has procreated to keep this great property we fight for in the family!"

"I think all of Craig Rock would have to die out to rid the place of Douglas and MacGinnis blood," Shawna said.

"Aye, that's true enough." He gazed at her curiously. "Tell me, has Cousin Alistair been playing fast and loose with the Anderson clan?

The lad you've taken in at Castle Rock bears a strong resemblance to the family."

"Alistair claims innocence. You've taken me quite by surprise with your dreaming, Aidan. Perhaps you're simply more discreet with your affairs?"

"How politely put, cousin! Nay, the lad's not mine, and though the Anderson lasses be fair enough, their father is a warthog, and I'd have nothing to do with the likes of any related to him."

Shawna came to her feet, reaching down a hand to Aidan. "We're forgetting, Sabrina is missing."

"She's not here, not at Castle MacGinnis." He accepted her hand and stood but then stared down at her with serious concern. "Shawna, you're always defending the ways of others. Highlanders should go kilted when we choose, and in Prince Albert's more somber and gentlemanly apparel if we so choose as well. Presbyterians should leave Catholics alone, and those who damned well wish it should worship at the Anglican Church. And those who adhere to the Wicca should practice their witchcraft. But perhaps their practices are not so benign as you want to believe. Perhaps witches became associated with devil worship for good reason. Perhaps Edwina's own clan of witches has done the lass in, required her for some sacrifice."

"Aidan! Don't even suggest such a thing!"

He shrugged unhappily. "We're about to celebrate the Night of the Moon Maiden. Maybe there's more to their ancient celebration of the event than we've suspected in recent years."

"Aidan! You cannot believe that!"

"I don't know what I believe," Aidan told her. He shook his head tiredly. "She's simply disappeared. With no clue at all."

Shawna turned away from him suddenly. Perhaps there was a clue, yet she didn't dare speak of it now, to Aidan. Her handkerchief had been found in the chapel, laden with chloroform. Someone had taken her handkerchief, soaked it in the drug.

Someone had seized hold of her in the tunnels, and that same person—or persons—had seized hold of Sabrina as well.

"Events have grown quite strange around here in the last few days," Aidan continued. "The cave-in, the boy disappearing in the shaft...

reappearing and speaking about a beast saving him. The arrival of the great Laird Douglas from America."

Events were far stranger than Aidan knew.

At the bottom of the loch lay a dead man, weighted down to disappear, as enemies of the Highlands had been weighted down to feed the water creatures for centuries.

And strangest of all, Laird David Douglas lived, hiding out within the walls of his castle, in the caves beneath the ground. Five years ago, someone had attempted to kill him, but another man had been burned, and David had somehow miraculously escaped...

She kept far too many secrets. From her own blood.

She looked down at her hands. She had no choice.

"Something bad has happened to Sabrina, and that's surely a fact," Shawna said. "We must find her."

"Then again, perhaps she has run off. Perhaps she found love and ran away."

"Not Sabrina."

"Don't fool yourself, cousin. Every woman can fall prey to the sins of the flesh."

The way that he stared at her brought a flush to her cheeks, and she was suddenly anxious to move again. And she knew—as no one else did, except for David!—that Sabrina had a great deal on her mind.

But Sabrina hadn't just irresponsibly disappeared. Shawna was certain of it.

"Let's get your father and head back to Castle Rock."

"As you wish, Lady MacGinnis," Aidan said, bowing slightly, and for just the slightest second, she was afraid. Of her own cousin. Of her own blood.

"THERE ARE FAR MORE underground tunnels than those of which I am aware," David said. He'd met his brother in the mine shaft where the cave-in had taken place, where lines were up for the miners not to cross back into dangerous territory. Hawk was deeply concerned about his sister-in-law, yet he was trying very hard to search for her with his mind focused, not allowing his emotions to cloud his thoughts. David spoke to him about the recent events that had taken place as they searched the mines for Sabrina.

"I brought the lad through the water the other day here—" David said, hunkering down and pointed to where the very narrow shaft gave way to a tunnel below. "It was flooded then, but the distance was short enough, and he's a terribly bright little lad."

"I would imagine," Hawk commented, coming down on the balls of his feet at his brother's side. Staring through the hole he murmured, "He looks like a MacGinnis."

"Aye, that he does," David agreed. He sat back for a moment. "I have the feeling Shawna must believe one of her cousins fathered the wee lad, the way she was so determined to take him in. Then again, he possesses quite a bit of charm, and perhaps she needed no reason to seek to take him in. I was quite taken by the lad myself, and whatever happens here, I'm glad the boy will be safe out of the mines and working at the castle."

"So, Castle Rock itself should be safe enough?" Hawk queried.

David shrugged. "I've access to nearly every room within it. There are peepholes in the tunnels beyond the walls. I can see and hear what goes on within the castle, and whatever evil is at play there, I don't think much goes on within the walls. Whoever seeks to do away with our family tries hard to do so by natural means—to all appearances. Sabrina was outside of the castle when she was taken."

"You're certain?"

David hesitated. He hadn't told Hawk about Shawna's handkerchief because he hadn't wanted Skylar to know about it. He and Hawk had tried to convince Skylar that Sabrina had gone riding and lost track of time and her sense of responsibility. Now he told his brother, "I found a handkerchief soaked in chloroform—one of Shawna's— in the chapel. But I don't think that she was taken from the chapel. The handkerchief was all balled up as if it had fallen from a pocket."

"Surely, you don't think that Shawna actually drugged and kidnapped Sabrina?"

"Of course not."

"Good, since that probably exonerates Shawna from any evil designs upon me in the tunnels, doesn't it?"

David scowled, then shrugged. "Fine, if Shawna is such an innocent, then what is going on, and who in God's name is she trying to protect?"

"Perhaps she isn't protecting anyone."

"She isn't telling me everything."

"Have you told her everything?"

"I don't talk about the years I lost," David said bitterly. "They are best forgotten. They—"

He broke off suddenly, his eyes narrowing as he looked at his brother.

They had both heard the sound. A strange, quick sound, a creaking sound. David drew a finger to his lips and made a motion to Hawk.

It looked as if there was nothing more than a break in the rock wall of the tunnel to their left. As if the cave-in had created a crack. Yet, as David moved around, he could see that the thin break in the rock was complete—and that a man could slip through it. And seeing how the Highland cliffs here were filled with caverns and tunnels, it seemed likely that they might find another extension of the tunnels through the crack.

They approached the break from opposite sides, David reaching it just before Hawk. As he came to the break, he heard movement and swiftly, if somewhat recklessly, crawled through the opening, expecting to fall under attack at any moment.

But whoever watched them, and listened to them, did not intend to attack.

The watcher sought only to run.

"Hurry!" David cried to his brother, entering into a cavern where he found himself in total darkness, but hearing now the steady thud of footfalls upon the earth as the watcher tried to escape.

Trying to adapt to the blackness, David followed fleetly, trusting the earth beneath his feet since he had heard the footfalls upon it just seconds before.

He heard his brother behind him as he closed in on the runner. He catapulted himself forward, his arms thrust out in the blackness.

Encircling a body.

They plowed to the earth together. David drew his knife from the sheath at his calf just as Hawk struck a match against the wall, illuminating the cave.

"Sweet Jesus, you!" David thundered down at the face below him.

"You are alive!" the watcher said in astonishment, heedless of the blade beneath his nose.

"Aye, and anxious to know what goes on—and where the lass may be!" David said angrily.

"Let me up. I pose no danger to you."

David glanced at his brother. Hawk's barely perceptible nod assured him that it would be unlikely that the man could take them both by surprise and escape them.

"All right, MacGinnis," David said. "Get up. And explain why in God's name you are spying upon me."

"Aye, Douglas, I shall do so. If you will promise to explain to me why you wish to make us all think you haunt us when you are a flesh-and-blood man!"

"Let's make these explanations swift," Hawk said softly. "Remember, we still seek Sabrina—unless, MacGinnis, you know where she might be."

"I seek her myself."

"And I seek the truth," David said flatly.

"I'll give you what I have of it."

By late afternoon, all of Craig Rock had been turned upside down, and no trace of Sabrina had been found. Constable Clark had come up from the city, but he had been less concerned than the people of Craig Rock, for he was quite convinced that young women frequently disappeared from small villages at whim, since he'd had a daughter himself who had run off to see the world. He spoke with Shawna, Gawain, Hawk, and Skylar in the great hall at Castle Rock, taking information from Skylar and trying to assure her that Sabrina was most probably quite fine and off on some lark while his own two men continued to search the property and the area beyond with Lowell, Aidan, Alaric, and Alistair.

As the day had passed, Shawna felt a greater and greater sense of dismay.

David had assured her that he would cover Castle Rock with his own search—slipping through all those secret corridors and stairways that were unknown to the others. He had apparently found nothing. While she and Aidan had searched Castle MacGinnis, the others had scoured the village, the mines, the fields, the stables, and more.

"You mustn't fret so, for lasses do these things, Lady Douglas. Perhaps there was a man involved," the heavy-set, florid constable suggested with a wink as he accepted a whiskey against the brisk cool turn of the day in the great hall at Castle Rock.

"There was no man involved," Shawna assured him, glancing at Skylar, who was exhausted and frightened. "And we've had search parties out all day—the miners combed the tunnels, my cousins have gone door to door in the village, we have searched the castles—and we remain quite concerned."

"Ach, now, m'lady, 'tis fitting that all are concerned. But I'll warrant the lovely young American lass appears soon enough."

"We cannot let up on the search for my sister for a single moment," Skylar said. "Edwina McCloud, in the village, has a special sight, I am told. And she has warned me of extreme danger."

"The sight now, is it?" The constable obviously did not believe in the sight.

"Constable Clark, this is a serious matter, and if you don't care to handle it in such a fashion, I'll have to request special assistance from your superiors," Hawk Douglas said.

The constable hemmed and hawed uncomfortably, his cheeks growing very pink. "My report is filled out right and proper, Laird Douglas, and we will do everything in our power to get information out regarding your sister-in-law as far as we can. Now, again, Laird Douglas, you being an American and all, it's quite understandable that ye're not aware of rumor and suchlike of the goings-on up here, but 'tis known across the country that Craig Rock harbors all manners of strange thought and custom. I believe it's true that this Miss Edwina McCloud you speak about considers herself a witch?"

Startled, Shawna stared at him. "Apparently, sir, you don't understand the original meaning of the term 'witch!'"

"Ah, 'tis true, the lady dabbles in the black arts!"

"She dabbles in no black art!"

"I'm afraid I need no further answer, m'lady. I shall have Edwina McCloud questioned. Perhaps the witches of Craig Rock are seeking out a sacrifice or the like?"

"How dare you, Constable Clark, how dare you!" Shawna said, infuriated.

Gawain was before the constable like a bulldog. "You're quite correct, constable, in that Laird Douglas is an American, but he's come here oft enough in his life and the blood of Craig Rock runs through his veins. He knows, as we do, that the ancient Wicca practiced here is gentle and good, a difference of religious opinion, protected now by law, just as Catholicism, Buddhism, Judaism, and more!"

Constable Clark drew his cumbersome body very straight. "I merely say that if some evil is afoot, you will recognize it here far more quickly than any outsider might manage. Craig Rock has always managed well on its own, the only difficulty I remember is the tragedy at the stables, and that now some five years or so past. You must look to your own. I'll leave two men at the tavern to keep up the search with you for the next two days, but well pray, Laird Douglas, that Sabrina Connor is about on a lark exploring our magnificent countryside and will come home in her own good time. If not, perhaps she will be found in a nearby village. I've been constable for twenty years, and I can tell you that young lasses oft surprise their kin, and that is a fact, 'tis the way God made women."

"My sister is a responsible woman," Skylar stated firmly. "No flighty young girl."

The constable arched a brow. "Well, now, I've not implied that she is a fey thing or the like, have I, just that the very best of us can be seduced by various evils."

"She won't be found in a nearby village," Skylar said. "She is here. Somewhere."

"Perhaps she is in hiding then," the constable suggested with aggravation. "And will appear when she is ready to do so. My dear Lady

Douglas, you are an American, but I am an outsider here as well, and as an outsider, I've done what I can for the time. 'Tis you who know your sister, and 'tis you and the villagers and Laird Douglas and the MacGinneses who know the area and where a young woman might be wont to wander. Has anything strange been going on in the last few days? Did Edwina McCloud offer you an explanation of why she is so certain you need be concerned for Sabrina?"

They all looked at one another. Shawna wondered if David had told Hawk about her handkerchief and, if so, why Hawk wasn't presenting the evidence to the constable. But if Hawk knew about it, he wasn't saying anything, and she thought that he might not do so in defense of her. She was deeply glad of his faith in her.

Shawna looked at the constable. "Edwina had been dreaming about David Douglas coming back to life."

"What rubbish!" Gawain said irritably. He shook his head, shuddering, his aging features taut. "We saw him. All of us in this room saw him dead. Thankfully, my great-niece here apparently stumbled from the flames before she met a like fate. Sweet Jesus, must we keep talking about this? With the poor man's brother here, it is cruelty itself to suggest that the man might have lived."

"I thank you, Gawain, but we must discuss whatever will help find Sabrina."

"How curious," the constable murmured. "Perhaps we will have to exhume David Douglas if something is not discovered in time. Is there anything else at all that I should know?"

There was, Shawna thought. He should know that David was alive, that a man had died and was sunk to the bottom of the loch, that their mines were supposedly haunted, that she had been drugged senseless that morning, and that a handkerchief bearing her initials had been found in the chapel that morning.

But the constable was right. He didn't know or understand much about Craig Rock or the Highlanders living there.

"Well, then, I shall return to the village, and see what can be done there," Constable Clark said. "Then I shall strive for a good night's sleep so that I may be of some help in the morning. Good day to you all."

The constable left, Gawain seeing him out. Shawna approached Skylar, whose fear and pain for her sister were heartbreakingly obvious as she sat before the fire. Myer, tall and straight and completely dignified but with stark sympathy in his eyes, brought brandy, and while Hawk watched pensively, leaning upon the ancient stone mantel, Shawna tried to get some brandy into Skylar.

Hawk came to hunch down before Skylar, gently reaching for her hands. "You have to get some rest, my love. Sabrina will be found, and it may well be that when she is, we will all need our strength and energy to help her."

"Yes," Skylar said listlessly. But then she smiled and touched his bronze features. "I love you. I know that you will find Sabrina."

He smiled, caught her hand, and kissed it. Shawna felt a surge of longing. Dear God, that was what she longed to have from David. And Hawk was so much like his older brother that Shawna found that she had to turn away.

Hawk stood. "Skylar, you must get some rest."

Skylar nodded but didn't move. "Whatever that foolish man says, Sabrina did not run away with a man, she is not in hiding. I know her. I'm so very afraid. And my god, Hawk! I brought her here."

"She wanted to come, remember? She didn't want to stay in the Dakota Territory without us. Perhaps she is being held for some reason, and we've time yet to find her, but we must all have our wits about us to do so," Hawk said, looking at his wife.

"And we must have some faith in Sabrina," Gawain said, returning to the great hall from the entry. "She is an intelligent young woman, a fighter."

"Yes, yes, she is!" Skylar agreed. Shawna was glad that her great-uncle's words had seemed to offer Skylar so much comfort.

Mary Jane came into the great hall then, her eyes full of sympathy for Skylar. She came in very quietly, pausing beside Shawna to whisper softly. "I've a hot bath prepared for Lady Douglas in the master's chambers. And there's a large bottle of brandy by her bedside."

Shawna squeezed her maid's hand. "Thank you, Mary Jane," she said softly.

Mary Jane nodded, departing the hall as quietly as she had come.

"Mary Jane says that she has a steaming tub all ready for you, Skylar. Please go up. A long bath and rest can't help but make you better able to keep searching yourself once we have daylight to work with again," Shawna said.

"I'll take you up, Skylar," Hawk said.

Shawna stopped him to whisper that Myer kept laudanum, if it seemed that Skylar would need more than brandy. Hawk nodded and walked Skylar slowly up the stairs. Gawain looked at Shawna, shaking his head sadly. "Sabrina must be found. Quickly!" he announced. He came to Shawna and squeezed her shoulders. "I'm going to Edwina's. God knows, the constable is useless. Maybe Edwina will 'see' something useful in another dream."

Shawna nodded. She poured herself a brandy and stood staring into the fire as she sipped it. A while later, Hawk came back down the stairs.

He poured himself a brandy and swallowed it all in a single gulp.

"Skylar?" Shawna asked.

"Sleeping at last. The laudanum," he said.

"You found nothing today in your search?"

"I wouldn't say that we found nothing," Hawk said, "but I'm afraid we found no trace of Sabrina."

"But what of David's search—"

"Shh!" he warned, bringing his finger to his lips. "The walls do have ears."

"Aye!" Shawna said very softly, staring straight into his green Douglas eyes. "Your brother's!"

"Whatever, we did not find Sabrina. Shawna, you must go up yourself and get some sleep. There's nothing else we can do until morning."

Shawna was dismayed by the rise of hysteria that seemed to sweep through her. She was so worried about Sabrina. "Sleep! I've not had real sleep in a very long time—Laird Douglas."

"Go up. You'll not be troubled tonight."

"Why not?" she demanded suspiciously.

Hawk was instantly aware that she was anxious to determine just where David would be. "I'm sorry," he teased, running his fingers through his hair. Despite the gravity of the situation, he offered her a smile. "Did you wish to be disturbed tonight?"

Shawna groaned. "Sweet Jesus! You, too. David torments me well enough on his own, I assure you!"

Hawk quickly put a finger to his lips again. The main door opened ,and she heard the commotion there as her great-uncle Lowell and her cousins returned to the castle, exhausted from their search for Sabrina.

"The lass has quite cleanly disappeared," Alistair said, wearily rubbing his chin. "Hawk, I'm so sorry, we've learned nothing as yet. Oh, thank God and Myer! Sustenance!" he said as Myer came to the room, bearing whiskey, brandy, hot tea, and a plate of scones.

Aidan stretched his hands before the fire, staring at Shawna as if she had somehow brought it all about. "Shawna, you two seemed to be growing quite close. Was she upset, is there any reason she might have just gone off?"

"No," Shawna said firmly. "She has met with some kind of foul play."

"I pray not, and I do believe there's hope—" He paused, glancing unhappily at Hawk. "We've not found Sabrina's—body," he finished quietly.

"I'd not have you speak so openly before my wife," Hawk said, "but I fear terribly that Sabrina has been harmed."

"Perhaps—her body has been hidden," Alaric said, his countenance as weary as his brother's.

"We've been through the mines, through the village, through the castles, through the fields. We've looked among the cattle, horses, goats—both the animals and the old-timers in the village—and we've not found her," Lowell said.

"There's—" Alistair began but broke off.

"Aye?" Hawk demanded firmly.

"The bottom of the loch," Alistair finished reluctantly.

"Oh god!" Shawna cried. "You mustn't suggest such a thing!"

"Alas," Lowell said, shaking his head sadly, "the loch has welcomed many a murdered man—and surely a woman or two—throughout the centuries. 'Tis said the Douglases—and the MacGinnises, mind y'—have rid themselves of an erring wife that way now and then."

"Father, I think it might be far kinder simply to say good night and depart for the evening, rather than remind us of all of the bodies that are now little but bones in the water. Well, at any rate, I am for home," Aidan said. "I am quite exhausted."

"Aye, that we all are," Lowell said. He finished the scone he was eating and swallowed down the whiskey-laced tea he had taken. "'Tis nearly the Night of the Moon Maiden. Like as not, we will have found Sabrina by then," he said reassuringly to Hawk.

"Good night," Aidan said. "Father?"

Lowell sniffed his dissatisfaction and irritation once again, then left the great hall with Aidan's hand set supportingly upon his shoulder.

"What worries me," Alaric said, "is the mines. Those tunnels are endless. You know how we missed the wee Anderson lad, Shawna? He was swept into the water beneath. Perhaps Sabrina was afraid of something or someone. With all the talk going around that David Douglas has risen from his ashen grave, she might have become afraid of something or someone. If she ran into the mines, hoping to hide, she could venture into a shaft where no one would ever find her. Even if she went by way of the tunnels by the cliffs off the loch—"

"Unless the tide is just right, y'have to swim into those tunnels, brother," Alistair said, interrupting him. "I cannot imagine Sabrina running out of the castle to go swimming her way into a tunnel."

"I suppose not. Still, the mine worries me. I think we should continue to search there tomorrow."

"Aye, that sounds like a fair idea," Hawk said.

Alistair, seated at the table, laid his head down upon his arms there. "We have searched so very hard."

"Yet one could search forever here," Alaric said.

"One could search forever, indeed, and never find what one is seeking," Shawna said, looking at Hawk.

"I don't believe that," Hawk said firmly, returning her stare. "We have to look very carefully at all the facts and leave no stone unturned in all the mysteries that surround the place. Then, the truth will be known—and what one searches for can indeed be found."

Shawna suddenly found herself assailed with icy chills, sweeping in a fury along her spine. Hawk wasn't referring just to the disappearance of his sister-in-law. He referred to her—and the house of MacGinnis.

"What scares me," Alistair admitted, his mind still firmly upon Sabrina, "is that we can search forever now—and then, a decade hence, perhaps—oh god, I keep doing this, Hawk! But we could search forever now and find her bones a decade from now in some small place we missed in our search."

"That won't happen," Alaric said.

"Pray God you're right, but why not?" Shawna asked.

Alaric stared at her. "I do believe that she will appear—dead or alive—by the Night of the Moon Maiden."

CHAPTER 15

By two in the morning, Shawna remained wide awake, pacing her tower room. David had not made an appearance, but then, he hadn't planned on making an appearance. Hawk had told her so—he had simply failed to tell her what David would be doing.

She felt helpless herself, worrying about Sabrina. She assumed that David, most probably with his brother's help, would continue the search for Sabrina throughout the night.

She had to trust in them, and in God, she told herself.

She tried sleeping, tried believing that there would be a method and a plan to whatever David was doing. She tried to tell herself that he wasn't staying away from her because of what had happened in the tunnels, because he had decided she was guilty of deceptions so great that he could not bear to be with her, even to protect her life in his pursuit of the truth regarding Craig Rock.

Sleeping was out of the question.

Pacing the room did nothing to still the restlessness within her.

"David, where are you?" she said aloud to the empty room, but he was hidden somewhere in the walls, he did not respond, and an intuitive sense of emptiness led her to believe that he was definitely not within hearing distance.

In the end, she slipped a white linen robe over her high-necked, smocked nightgown, slippers upon her feet, and exited her bedchamber. She came slowly down the first flight of steps and held very still on the landing. She stood not far from the master's chambers, near the room where Sabrina Connor had slept. And down the hall were the rooms Gawain, Alaric, and Alistair had chosen within the keep. Not a sound, aside from the wind whistling through the turrets, could be heard. Myer, Mary Jane, and some of the other servants kept quarters on the floor above, near her more recent tower abode, yet not a soul seemed to be about at this hour. Naturally. It was the middle of the night. All doors were closed. What went on behind them, no one knew.

Except, of course, perhaps David. Who roamed the walls at will.

Shawna hurried silently down to the great hall. Brandy remained upon a tray on the large, planked table, and she helped herself to a snifter. Gas lamps remained lit there, and something of a fire remained in the great hearth. She sipped brandy, staring at the flames. She looked around at the walls.

"If you're here, come out and talk to me!" she demanded aloud.

She heard footsteps behind her and spun around, her eyes wide.

But David hadn't appeared.

It was Alistair, a snifter of his own in his hands.

"What are you doing here?" Shawna asked.

"Drinking. And you, cousin?"

"I've just come for the fire—and the brandy," she said.

Alistair took one of the high-backed chairs before the fire, watching the flames jump and dance. "It's a curious place we live in, isn't it?"

Shawna, watching him, shrugged. "Not so curious. It's home. We are what we are."

"Highlanders!" Alistair lifted his snifter to her. "A breed apart. We think ourselves great chieftains still, when Scotland and England are joined, when technology rules the rest of the world, and we all seek to rule it!"

She arched a brow to Alistair, convinced that he'd had his share of brandy already.

"I like what we are, Alistair," she told him. "We are more a part of the world at large than you imagine, yet distinct with our tartans, our pipe tunes, and more."

"We work like dogs in the mines," he said flatly.

"We are entrusted with the livelihoods of many."

He smiled, once again lifting his snifter very high. "The great lady magnanimous. Thank God that you are Lady MacGinnis."

"Is that a sore point with you, Alistair?" she demanded.

He shook his head, smiling his most charming grin. "Nay, for I've not your talent for leadership, cousin. And I love you—as a cousin should—with all my heart. I wouldn't begrudge you a thing. If you were not Lady MacGinnis, my father would be Laird MacGinnis, and after him Alaric. And God knows, if it were still the ancient days, Uncle Lowell might well want to battle me for the title, whether Aidan had an interest in it or not. But actually, I do like the sound of the pipes. I like our slightly strange holidays, and I like the wind in the rocks at night and the whistling in the caves and caverns by the loch. I like our tartans, and our dress, and our stories of beasts and sea creatures and more. I just wish..."

"What?"

"Nothing."

"Alistair?"

"I wish that the Night of the Moon Maiden would come and go. I wish that Sabrina would be found. I wish that..."

"What, Alistair?"

"Well, there is evil, of course. And it must be rooted out."

"Evil," Shawna said, growing nervous.

But Alistair yawned suddenly and stood. "Well, I'm for bed," he said quite casually.

"Alistair, wait a minute—"

"You should go to bed, cousin. Did you know that the castle has eyes? They watch you all the time. Ears, too, for it seems that the castle listens..." He cocked his head as if he, too, listened.

"Wait a minute, Alistair, you just said that you want to root the evil out. What are you talking about?"

"Strength," he said after a moment.

"Alistair, please, talk to me—"

"I'm wandering, Shawna, nothing more. Come on, I'll walk you back to your room."

"I'm fine. I can walk back on my own."

"I shall sleep better if I know you are safely in bed."

Shawna sighed. "Fine."

As they walked up the steps together, Shawna studied his face. "You came down just for brandy?" she inquired.

"Aye," he said, then shrugged, flushing. "Nay, I thought I heard something downstairs, something more than the usual creaks and groans."

"What did you hear?"

"Ghosts, I don't know."

"But—"

"Maybe I was dreaming. I heard sounds coming from the chapel, or so I thought."

"Did you go there?"

"I did."

"And?"

"Nothing. Nothing at all. Christ stared down at me from the old crucifix above the altar and silently bade me go in peace. The chapel was quite empty, and the door to the crypts was securely closed. There. Now you know that I have carefully looked downstairs, and you must go to bed and stay there."

They had come to the door of her tower room. He gave her a cousinly kiss upon the forehead. "Go to bed, cousin."

"Aye. Good night, Alistair."

"And stay in there!" he admonished her.

"Aye, cousin. Good night."

The door closed. She waited until she heard his footsteps receding down the hallway, going down the stairs to the floor below.

Then she hesitated.

Wanting to go out again.

And suddenly, very afraid to do so.

THE CHAPEL in Castle Rock was exceptionally beautiful. Situated off the great hall and down a flight of circular stone stairs, it was half above ground level and half below. Massive stained-glass windows that just caught the light of day rose on the upper half of the walls. They had been added during the fifteenth century. Otherwise, the chapel remained just as it had been originally, with old Norman stone design and great archways. The altar top was marble brought from Italy, the beautiful wooden crucifix hanging above it had been carved in Germany in 1256.

Church services hadn't been held there, other than an occasional christening or family event, since Scotland had embraced the new religion years ago—except, of course, in the days when the Stuart "pretenders" to the throne of Great Britain had still held out hopes of returning to rule in glory and the Stuart Catholicism had still held many Highlanders—and Lowlanders, at that—in secret communication. Prince Charles—the son of Charles I, one day to be welcomed back as Charles II—had found haven at Castle Rock along with a number of his supporters. He had sat in the chapel the night he had been hidden here by the Highlanders.

The chapel had always been a matter of great pride to the Douglases.

And staring at the historic crucifix, the windows, darkened now by night, the ancient walls, David was grateful to see that the MacGinnises had maintained it as carefully and lovingly as any family member might have done.

But he hadn't come to savor the beauty of the chapel that night.

Toward the far left of the altar was the iron gateway to the crypts.

The gate slid cleanly open to his touch—the hinges well oiled. The last burial here would have been his own, since his father, by choice, had been buried on his property in America.

Once inside the gate, David set down the steel bar he carried and struck a match, lighting the lantern he'd taken from the chapel. He lifted it high. A second curving stairway with thirty-six steps led down to the crypts below. He descended into the pitch-blackness.

Upon reaching the landing far below, he lifted the lantern once again, looking at the stone corridors that ran in a number of directions from a main hallway. The straight corridor led to steps—twenty-eight of them—at the top of which was a door that opened into the cemetery. But down here, the Douglases themselves were buried, along with priests and servants who had been close to the family. Tombs lined the walls, one for an ancestor who had fought with Montrose against the English, another for an ancestor who had fallen to preserve the life of Mary, Queen of Scots. He paused at the first gateway, where, deep within, the oldest tombs lay, ancestors rotted to bone in their gauzy shrouds. Chilly temperature had preserved what might have been lost, and the insects were kept from their tasks of breaking down the dead by that same cold as well. Services here in the crypt often reminded the living of what was to come.

David paused only a moment, then moved farther down the hallway, seeking his own name upon a vault.

He paused at length. He'd been given quite an extraordinary memorial. Winged angels and serpents guarded the doorway to the crypt where he'd been buried, Latin phrases abounded. Again, an iron gate barred his way to the tomb itself, but like the gate above, it was well oiled.

And unlocked.

He slipped inside.

His tomb sat alone at the rear of the small room, purple drapery over a fine, hardwood coffin. He realized that to the left and right of the room, numerous other coffins and shrouds had been placed as well. Very old burials, some in coffins, some in shrouds, plaques in the artistry of many different centuries proclaiming which Douglas lay upon each shelf. Mary Douglas with five of her children lay to his right, none of them having obtained an age greater than six. They had died by the beginning of the fourteenth century. Laird Fergus Douglas, Mary's husband, lay to his left, alone with Eugenia, his second wife, and four of their children. A second Laird Fergus, son of Fergus and Mary, lay with his lady, Helena of York, below his father's shelf. The script chiseled into the stone stated that Fergus the First had fought with William Wallace, while his son, Fergus, had gone on to fight with Robert the Bruce. Despite the age of the corpses, they were frighteningly well preserved, their features still painfully apparent beneath the gauze of their shrouds.

He had assumed he might have been buried near his mother's tomb, but she was farther down the hallway, nearer the stairs, and there had been two memorials built to her memory, one above ground, and one below.

Despite the fact he lay with ancestors who had been noble warriors, this tomb was now dedicated to him.

And he did not lie within it.

"So, my dear kin, who does lie with you here?" he asked aloud.

He walked forward then, removing the purple sheet from the coffin. He studied the closure of the coffin, then took his bar and began to wedge it beneath the lid. The coffin had been well sealed, and it was difficult to find a wedge, but he kept at his work, beads of perspiration breaking out upon his forehead. Eventually, the lid creaked and groaned, giving way to his efforts.

The noise was loud in the night, in the silence of the crypts.

He was quite certain that it would have sounded like a human moan, reverberating throughout the castle.

He needed to hurry. He set the bar down and lifted the lid of the coffin, wrenching free what remained of the nails. He set the lid aside.

And he stared down in horror at what lay within the coffin.

At his own corpse.

Then he heard the noise.

Footsteps.

He paused. Listened.

Aye, someone was coming. Slowly. Very slowly. Moving down the steps that led to the main corridor of the crypts.

He swiftly doused his lantern.

SHAWNA BROUGHT a single candle from her room, sheltering the flame from the drafts within the castle by cupping her hands around it.

She sped down the stairs silently on her slippered feet, pausing on the second floor to be certain that she heard nothing.

She hurried on down to the great hall then, searching it out with her candle held above her head, trying to be quite certain that she wouldn't run into another of her kin.

The great hall was quiet.

She couldn't bear just remaining in her room any longer. And Alistair had heard something from the chapel. And now, she was certain, she heard noises coming from the crypts as well. Moaning sounds, as if the ancient Douglases cried out in protest of the events occurring now.

The chapel led to the crypts.

She shivered.

Well, she wasn't going to be afraid of the dead. Not when they might hold some secret to aid the living.

She hurried down the steps to the chapel, pausing within. The light from her candle was dim, but it slightly illuminated the windows, casting off soft, ethereal colors within the chapel. She circled around, looking for anyone who might sit quietly in the chapel.

Or for anyone who might stand behind the columns in the nave, watching. Waiting.

No one was in the chapel. Of that she was certain.

She found herself walking to the iron gate to the crypts below. It was closed.

But it opened easily.

She hesitated. There was a heavy brass candle snuffer, at least six feet long, for use on the towering altar candles, lying against the far wall. She grabbed it with her left hand and opened the iron gate with the same hand while balancing the candle in her right.

Slowly, she started down the stairs. She was certain that her footfalls were silent as she went down, step by step by step.

She had been in the Douglas crypts dozens of times. She had come often to bring flowers to set upon David's coffin.

But she had come by day.

She had never seen such Stygian darkness as she walked deeper and deeper into the bowels of...

Death.

She should turn she told herself. Turn and flee back up the steps.

The dead would not hurt her, she reminded herself.

Step by step...

She reached the landing. Iron gates walled in the ancient dead, sleeping with hands folded in prayer throughout the centuries. She tried not to look. She couldn't help but let her imagination fly, for the candlelight was so very tricky. She could swear that she saw movement, a soft fluttering of shrouds.

She could imagine a corpse sitting up, staring at her, accusing her of complicity in murder...

Shawna...

Then, she suddenly heard the sound. An awful groaning. As if a dead man had been struck anew, as if he screamed with pain from the agony of hell.

She nearly screamed herself.

She forced herself to breathe. To look straight ahead. Determined not to see the corpses in their shrouds through the iron gates of the various crypts.

She held her brass snuffer tightly in her hand, moving very slowly, using her free hand to keep herself flat against the wall. Her candle didn't shed much light. The corridor seemed filled with shapes and shadows.

She knew where David's supposed tomb lay within the crypts.

Ten more steps perhaps.

One at a time. She reached the tomb.

Just outside of it, she stood very, very still.

Waiting. Listening.

Then she stepped within the tomb.

She held very still. In the dim flicker of light her candle provided, she saw that the lid of David's coffin had been removed!

She swallowed back a scream, then turned to flee, dropping the brass candle snuffer. But a hand clamped firmly over her mouth and a powerful arm pulled her back to the dead.

Shawna's heart pounded with relief when she heard a familiar voice ask in astonishment, "What in God's name are you doing down here? I've warned you of the danger you face time and time again. Sabrina has been kidnapped, and still, here you are!"

David, she thought dizzily. Thank God, it was David! He released her, and still holding her candle, she turned to face him.

"I was downstairs earlier. And Alistair had heard something—"

"Alistair heard something—and sent you down here?"

"No—"

"That damned Alistair—again!"

"It wasn't Alistair's fault!"

"It never is."

Shawna sighed. "He has no idea that I'm here. I couldn't sleep."

"You missed me."

"Don't be absurd. You plague me to madness, appearing and disappearing into the walls, showing up, not showing up, being there, vanishing into the morning mist."

"Ghosts are supposed to do such things," he said, looking into the coffin again and adding angrily, "You shouldn't be here!"

"Alistair and I both heard noises—"

"So, you felt you had to find out what the noises were?" he queried softly.

"You do seem to hold me responsible for anything that happens here," she said coolly.

He shook his head. "I can't leave you alone for a bloody second, so it seems. You heard noises, so you just walked down into the crypt, completely unarmed."

"I am not unarmed. I brought the candle snuffer—there. I dropped it when you nearly scared me to death."

"Fine weapon!" he mocked.

"It is solid brass and very heavy, and I promise, if I were to whack you on the head with it, you would feel it!"

"It didn't occur to you to stay safely locked in your room where you belonged—especially considering everything that is going on here? You're an idiot."

"How kind, Laird Douglas, how genteel! I pray you, m'laird, do bear in mind! There was nothing going on here—until you returned from the dead!"

"Well, I am returned from the dead, and unfortunately, there are things that I have to do here."

David walked around the coffin. He used her candle to light the lantern he had apparently brought down with him, blew out the candle, and used the lanternlight to study what remained of the man in his coffin.

Her stomach turned in knots.

"Oh god, David, what are you doing?" she whispered.

He glanced her way. "Trying to discover just who this bloke might be. I'm assuming he's the convict whose place I took doing hard labor."

The knots in her stomach twisted more tightly. "You were a convict all that time? Doing hard labor."

David glanced at her, realizing that he'd never even given her that much information before.

"Yes," he said simply. "I'd like to try to figure out a way to make sure that this is the body of Collum MacDonald. Then, maybe I can figure out how and why he and I were exchanged for one another."

"David, this man is burned beyond recognition."

"I'd hoped for a ring, a pendant of some kind."

Shawna shivered. Most of the corpses, so long dead, smelled musty and nothing more. But it seemed that the charred inhabitant of this coffin still carried the horrible smell of being burned to death.

"David, please, there's nothing to be learned from this man," Shawna whispered.

"Charming," he muttered bitterly. "He's been kilted in my best tartan."

"We thought he was you!" she said, her voice trembling with emotion.

"Aye, well, there's nothing left to tell who he might have been! Burned to bone, and not much more. I'm amazed anyone managed to dress this mess of humanity."

"Again, I tell you, we thought that it was you."

He sniffed.

"I awoke next to that abomination after the fire!" Shawna told him with soft, furious vehemence.

She was startled when he suddenly came back around to her, his fingers curling around her wrists. He swore softly. "It makes no sense! What happened between the time we both blacked out—and the fire raged? It seems someone wanted me dead, while someone else just wanted it believed that I was dead. You were rescued, and I was sold into bondage." He shook his head, confused and irritated that he couldn't seem to figure out where the missing piece to the puzzle lay.

She wrenched free from him, unnerved by his manner, backing against the gate to the vault.

"David, I swear, there is nothing more I can say that will help. After the fire, Gawain found me. He—"

"Gawain. And Gawain instantly knew it was my corpse at your side?"

"Well, I did start shrieking and screaming and crying your name. That probably added to his belief that the corpse was you."

He almost smiled. "What then?"

"What then? For God's sake, what do you think, what then? I was in shock. I was sedated, but I knew that you were dead, that I—"

"That you—what?"

Her lashes fell, sweeping her cheeks. "That I had caused your death."

"What else, what then?"

She shook her head, not understanding. "We wrote to your father and brother. They started work on the memorial. We called the undertaker and the constable."

"Aye, and there was an investigation."

"Of course, there was an investigation. Your father was grief-stricken. Your brother demanded no less. He spoke with everyone. He spoke with me. You were buried. Here. In that coffin. And I wasn't afraid to come here tonight because after the fire I came almost every day until—"

She broke off, wincing.

"Until what?"

"I ran away."

"You ran away?" he inquired. "From Castle Rock?"

She nodded. "I—I felt I had to leave."

"Why didn't you stay away?"

She hesitated, knowing she couldn't bear to tell him the whole truth.

"Alistair found me."

"Alistair again."

"All I did was go to Glasgow. I didn't think that anyone would mind much that I had gone away. But Alistair..."

"Alistair what?"

"He eventually convinced me that I had to live on despite the past, that I needed to come home because Craig Rock needed someone to really see to the everyday lives of the people here. He said that aye, he and my uncles and other cousins could easily manage the properties, but that none of them had the heart to keep the character of a Highland village in proper shape and warmth. And I was...I was ill at the time. So, I came home again."

"You were ill? With what?"

She shrugged, staring at the ground again. "Shock, despair, melancholy—I suppose."

"Despair?" he queried, a harsh note to his voice.

"I don't intend to continue insisting that I never meant you any ill. If you don't believe me by now, you have become an embittered madman."

"My lady, it's quite a miracle that I'm not a madman—seeing as how I've lived life for another while I lie here charred beyond recognition."

"I don't know how you came to be where you were!"

He stared at her a moment, then turned away. He lifted the lid back on top of the coffin, fitting it into place, managing to set each nail more or less back into its slot.

"You are always questioning me," Shawna said very softly. "And always refusing to answer me when I ask you questions. David, please, I realize now that someone managed to switch your body with that of a convict, but you owe me more. Please, what happened to you?"

He set down the steel bar he had been working with. Hands upon his hips, he stared at her.

"I don't know."

"You don't know?"

"You woke up that night, next to a corpse. I woke up days later, on board a convict ship with men sentenced to hard labor for murder and other such crimes. I insisted over and over again to the good captain that I was not the murdering bastard he thought me, but by then, news of the 'death' of David Douglas had traveled far and wide, and the fool didn't believe a word I said. I worked his ship in chains for two years, and then I broke rocks in a quarry in Australia for nearly another two before I managed to escape and, with the help of a friend, began to make my way back here. No matter what I said to anyone in all that time, no one believed I was David Douglas, especially not that good captain. But I don't blame him. I supposedly slit the throat of a poor young girl in Glasgow, and apparently, I was spared the hangman's noose because I appeared to be good for heavy labor. I imagine the captain of that ship would have killed me if it hadn't been for a friend with whom I escaped."

"A friend?"

"Aye," he said dryly, "a fellow who managed to keep me alive by convincing me I might find my revenge against you if I did manage to live long enough to escape."

"You've had your revenge these last five years and beyond. I will pay for that night until the day I die," she assured him.

"Will you? Then I can't possibly let you die as quickly as it seems you are trying to do, running about on your own when you know that there is foul play afoot!"

"I cannot just sit still—"

"You will sit still in the future. I promise you."

"Are you quite finished with your corpse?" she demanded as she spun around and hurried to the gate.

Suddenly David was beside her, and his whisper sounded against her ear. "Nay, lady, shush, listen!"

Shawna held very still. She heard footsteps in the corridor beyond the vaults. Footsteps.

At least two sets of them.

And the metallic sounds of swords clanging slightly in their scabbards.

Then whispers.

Whispers...

So hushed she couldn't tell if they were voiced by a male or female. She couldn't hear if they were deeply burred or more anglicized. She couldn't tell anything about the people who were approaching...

Except that their intentions were not good.

David quickly blew out the flame in the lantern he carried, setting it down in silence. He barely mouthed words against Shawna's ear. "Don't move."

The whisperers began to argue with one another. The sound increased, amplifying and echoing as they entered into the vaults Shawna and David had so recently vacated.

"Corpses, all."

"You said—"

"I said that I heard movement."

"You fool! You heard nothing."

"Make sure that they are all corpses!"

Shawna winced as she heard a chilling ripping sound. She could visualize swords slashing into the shelves of shrouded bodies...

"I should have slit her throat before!"

"Y'can't! Y'don't ken what must happen!"

Shawna felt David begin to move forward and heard the sound of his knife being drawn from a sheath at his calf. She grabbed the back of his shirt and started to follow him. He stopped her, his fingers biting into the flesh of her arms.

"Don't move!" he mouthed against her ear once again.

"Don't go!" she mouthed back.

"I must!"

"They've swords, perhaps guns."

"I have my knife and the element of surprise, my lady."

"David, no!"

"Shawna, I beg of you, hush!"

He left her.

The intruders had ceased to talk.

There was no sound at all while the seconds ticked by.

Ticked into minutes.

Endless minutes...

Then there was the sound of gunfire.

A single shot followed by the sounds of a scuffle in the corridor.

Despite David's words to her, Shawna could not remain still. She moved through the darkened vault carefully, but as quickly as she could. There was more light in the corridor—the light from the lantern the whisperers had brought. Shawna made her way to the vault's gate just in time to see David racing after a cloaked figure hurrying toward the stairway that led to the cemetery and the night beyond.

Shawna screamed as a hand suddenly descended upon her shoulder. She turned in time to see a knife rising high in the glow of the lamp. She shrieked again, struggling to wrench free from her attacker.

She twisted and writhed. She was able to fight her attacker, she realized, because he was bleeding. Blood dripped from the hand that threatened her with the knife. Her attacker had already battled with David, she thought.

Thank God, for though the knife fell, it passed just inches from her shoulder, striking the stone wall.

She shrieked in terror as the knife rose once again, and she continued to fight the iron-hard fingers winding around her arm.

She couldn't see the face of her attacker. He wore a cowled cloak, and she didn't dare attempt to dislodge that cowl, lest she allow the knife to fall to her neck.

Once again, the knife plunged toward her.

Bearing down...straight for her heart.

It didn't fall. The hand holding the knife was wrenched cleanly away from her. Just when she thought that death had found her at last in the crypts, David came catapulting against her would-be killer, pulling his knife arm aside, taking him off-balance and bringing him down to the floor. Yet as Shawna gasped for breath, the figure he had been chasing from the tomb returned, tearing back down the corridor. She shrieked out a warning.

But the figure had chosen on flight rather than fight—racing past them along the corridor, it swept up the lantern, swiftly dousing the flame.

The corridor was plunged into sudden blackness.

Then shots began to ricochet in the darkness once again, and

Shawna sank low to the ground, desperately seeking the entrance to one of the vaults.

She heard footsteps moving wildly down the corridor, yet she kept her silence, trying not to let out her cries of fear and terror as she crawled along the floor, seeking David.

A match flared. She gasped despite herself.

"It's all right. I've got you."

David!

"Oh god, I thought you'd been shot!" she cried hysterically, slipping her arms around him.

"And I was afraid you were about to be sliced to ribbons."

"You saved my life again."

"Aye, that means you owe me doubly. But we can't discuss that now. Find the lantern."

"But—"

"Our lantern." He struck another match for her, and she found her way back to the vault, swept up the lantern, and lit the lantern just as her fingers began to burn. She discovered then that David had one of the cowled figures on the floor. As she returned with the light, he pulled the cowl up off the man's face.

David looked from the man to Shawna.

"Who is he?"

"I don't know." Shawna had never seen him before in her life.

The man, obviously badly injured and in pain, somehow managed a mirthless smile anyway. "Nay, a great lady the likes of you wouldn't know me, Shawna MacGinnis. But you'll come to know those of my kind very well!" he taunted. But then he began to cough. Blood spilled from his lips.

Shawna shivered violently. "Where is Sabrina Connor?"

"Ye're anxious to join her, eh, m'lady? Perhaps it will happen soon enough."

David gripped the man by the collar of his cloak. "Is she alive?" he demanded, shaking the man. "Is she alive?"

"Mercy!" the man cried. "She lives!" He inhaled on a rattling breath. "Mercy..."

David eased his hold on the man. "You're dying," David said flatly.

"Tell us where Sabrina is, and perhaps God will look more kindly upon your hell-bent soul."

"God!" the man exclaimed and started to laugh again. He stared at Shawna in a way that chilled her to the bone. "I don't seek God. Hell-bent, indeed! Life and death are close, eh? The living do lie among the dead, do they not, Lady Shawna?" he breathed. Once again, he choked.

"Where is Sabrina?" she cried.

But he didn't reply. He stared at her with sightless eyes.

"Where—" Shawna tried again.

"He's dead," David said flatly.

Then he stood, reaching down for the dead man, hiking him over his shoulder, and heading back into a vault.

"David, what are you doing now?" Shawna demanded.

David returned to the hallway. "A rather instant burial. I don't want him found dead as yet."

"But David, we should call the constable—"

"The constable isn't going to help us. We've got to solve this ourselves." He reached out a hand to her. "We've got to get out of here. I don't know how many are involved in this conspiracy, nor have I fathomed who is at its core. You're truly a fool if you haven't realized the danger you're in by now. You shouldn't have been down here tonight. If you would just learn to behave—"

She had wanted his hand so badly. Just to be touched by him. She had been absolutely terrified that he might have been killed.

Now, he was yelling at her again, as if everything that happened here was her fault.

Shawna shook free of his touch and hurried along the corridor, climbing the stairs to the cemetery outside the castle at a swift pace. Yet when she reached the gateway to the night beyond, he drew her back. She thought he meant to apologize, to speak some words that might be gentle or tender.

He had no such intention.

"Hold, damn it, my lady. Let's assure ourselves no one waits beyond to fire a shot made clear by the moonlight!"

He left her where she stood, opening the gateway himself, slipping out for several seconds before returning for her. "It appears safe."

She ignored him, shaking off his touch. She went out into the moonlight, amazed to see that it remained the middle of the night. Very little time had actually elapsed since she had first entered the crypts.

It had seemed like a lifetime.

Perhaps because she'd been surrounded by the dead and her own life had so nearly ended in the time that had elapsed therein.

She glanced down at her arms, at her clothing. Cobwebs shrouded her in a coating of white nearly as opaque as the shrouds on the dead. Dust...

Bone dust, perhaps?

Death.

Caked over her.

"Oh god! Oh god!" she breathed.

She started to run.

"Shawna?"

He followed behind her, but she did not stop. Her flight was born of a wild panic that went far beyond any rational fear. She was covered in death, suffocating in it, and she could bear it no more.

She ran from the cemetery at an amazing, reckless, haphazard speed, David shouting her name at her heels. She reached the Druid Stones, and she did not pause. He caught hold of her arm, stopping at last, drawing her back to him.

"Shawna!"

"No, no, let me go!"

"Shawna, listen—"

"No! I've got to get—clean!"

"Aye, aye, lass, we will—"

"Now!"

His hold upon her eased. She wrenched free with a wild strength. She ran farther, farther...heedless of the chill of the night, barely aware of the rugged terrain beneath her feet.

"Shawna! Have you gone mad!"

He was directly behind her, but her strength and speed were indeed born of sheer madness. She ran until she reached the loch, and she didn't stop there. She walked until the water came to her knees, then she plunged down into it.

CHAPTER 16

She was dragged back to the surface, gasping for air, staring furiously at David. He was soaked now, too, staring at her in amazement as they stood shoulder deep in the water.

"Are you trying to drown yourself?"

"Of course not! I'm trying to, I'm trying to..." She couldn't speak suddenly. Her teeth were chattering.

"Let me go!" she demanded, struggling to free herself.

He wouldn't let her go. He drew her hard against him, heedless of her wild struggling, until she became so exhausted that she just lay flat against him.

"I just want to cleanse myself of the dust, the cobwebs, the dead people!" she gasped.

"All right, all right!"

He eased his hold on her. She rubbed her arm with her fingers, then grew frantic again, stripping off her torn and dirtied robe and gown. She heard his words, soothing her, felt his fingers, moving in her hair.

Finally, Shawna felt as if she'd scrubbed herself enough. By then, she could barely stand, she was so exhausted. She lay still against him and began to shiver.

"We'll freeze here," he said softly, urging her forward.

"Aye!" she cried, pulling free from him to hurry from the water.

"Shawna!"

She ignored his voice, shivering and anxious to leave the loch. She staggered from the depths of the loch to the embankment, falling against the damp grasses there.

They would freeze. As she lay there exhausted, breathing hard, she realized just how cold the night was, and how wet she was.

Wet—and bare.

Only then did it occur to her that she couldn't go walking back into the castle as naked as a newborn.

She was shaking violently when David drew up beside her, naked as she, but holding his rinsed clothing in his arms.

"My lady, if you run from me again, I swear I'll find a leash—or put you in the dungeon in truth."

"You said—"

"Come on, quickly," he told her.

"Where?"

"Well, back into the water for a moment."

"Nay, I am not going back into that water!"

"You were the one most eager to reach it."

"And I did reach it."

"And went running out, refusing to listen."

"One can only leave the water by walking out of it."

"Not true, my lady. Come with me, now. Quickly, because I am indeed freezing myself!"

He drew her to her feet. "Into the water!" he commanded, lifting her chin.

"No."

"We must."

"Why?"

"'Tis the only way to reach a selkie's lair."

She protested when he drew her back from the embankment to the lapping shore. "I can't. It's freezing."

"Ah, my lady, you should have thought of that in your madness. This is the only entry when the tide is high."

"The only entrance...I cannot go!"

"You've a better suggestion?"

"Aye, surely—"

"Lady, we cannot stand here longer! We might be seen."

She gasped as he swept her up off her feet, carrying her into the loch despite her protests. She gasped when he let her fall into the depths, but she then found herself swimming after him, and swimming strenuously to stave off the cold that gripped her so viciously, heading into what appeared to be solid rock on a cliff wall.

"Catch your breath!" David commanded her then. "At this time, there's about a twenty-foot stretch beneath the rock. You're all right with it?"

A fine time to ask her, she thought.

"Aye!" she snapped out, treading water.

She dove beneath the surface with him. They swam below the rock and stone, and the distance did not seem unbearably great. They emerged into a cavern within the cliff. As she stumbled to the rocky shoreline there, Shawna realized that this was where David had come when he had first returned. Where he kept his clothing, where he came for refuge when he was not with her or haunting the secret passageways within the castle.

He rose from the water first, casting his soaked clothing down upon the earth and sweeping up a blanket from the ground to throw around her shoulders as she emerged from the water. From the top of a traveling trunk, he picked up a length of folded tartan, expertly kilting it around himself.

Cloaked in her blanket, Shawna just stood shivering and staring at the water's edge.

David ignored her and went about the task of building a fire within a pit he had obviously used for a similar purpose many times before. Smooth, level rock surrounded it. David warmed his hands at his freshly made fire, then looked to Shawna with impatience. "Come. Sit. Get warm."

She managed to move, coming to take a seat before the fire with the blanket wrapped around her. She set her hands before it, letting the warmth radiate throughout her body.

"That was horrible," she told him.

"What shall be horror is just beginning," he told her curtly. "They came for you, Shawna, and they will not give up. You must learn to be more careful."

"I don't understand any of this. Why try to kill me in the crypts? Someone could just as easily come to my room—"

"You bolted the door to your room. In the castle, where others sleep nearby. Many others—including my brother."

"Why wasn't I killed in the tunnels?"

David shook his head thoughtfully.

"Perhaps my brother is supposed to believe you're trying to kill him. Then, when you are out of the way, the new 'Laird' Douglas can hardly regret the passing of a shrew who was trying to do him out of his inheritance."

"But I'm assuming that Hawk is supposed to die as well."

"I assume the same."

"But my family discussed buying the property from him!"

"Perhaps it's all deeper than any of us imagined. The man spoke about others of his kind. What kind? As to the tunnels, maybe they weren't trying to kill you. Maybe they were just trying to capture you, as I assume they've captured Sabrina. You never saw that man before tonight, yet he very definitely felt that you are destined to die soon."

"He did say that Sabrina was alive," Shawna said.

"We have to find her quickly. I'm concerned that there is a cult in action here."

"Edwina's group of witches are good women! I cannot believe that—"

"I accused Edwina of nothing. I said that I'm afraid a cult exists here. I am not accusing her of having a part in it. And I still believe that someone tried to make you appear guilty to my brother. Remember, I wasn't with you in the tunnels, when Hawk was nearly killed, until the trouble started."

Shawna fell silent. David opened his trunk and drew out a bottle of good Scotch whiskey. He took a seat upon the trunk then and offered the bottle to her.

"Straight whiskey," she murmured.

"My lady, I do apologize. My offerings here are few," he murmured. "I do have a castle of my own, but alas! It rests in the hands of others."

"You, M'laird Douglas, are a sorry, wretched bastard. Not in the least nice. Straight whiskey shall be just fine." She swallowed hard, gagged, coughed, but felt better. Then she shivered fiercely again.

"Oh my god, what is going on?" she demanded in a stark whisper.

"Think carefully, Shawna. You've really got no idea? No idea at all?" he asked her intently.

"I swear to you," she said wearily, "I do not!"

David took the bottle and swallowed down a large draught of whiskey himself. He set the bottle down and saw that she was still shivering. He let out something like a growl of impatience and reached for her. She stiffened against his attempt, then let out an aggravated cry of frustration as his strength outweighed hers, and she found herself seated between his legs, dragged down in front of him with her back to the trunk. He rubbed his hands briskly with the blanket over her arms and shoulders, vigorously flooding warmth back into her body.

"Better?" he asked, his word against her ear, bringing a different kind of warmth along with it.

She nodded, not trusting herself to speak. His body sheltered her. She was definitely warmer.

"They'll know you're here now. Alive. Whoever was in that crypt tonight will know."

"I don't think so," he reflected.

"But the attacker who survived knows—"

"He—or she—might well think that it was my brother. We're enough alike. And it doesn't matter. I've decided I'm going to keep my presence a secret only a wee bit longer."

"Oh?" She twisted around, trying to read his features.

David nodded grimly. "The laird of the castle is supposed to reign as royalty on the Night of the Moon Maiden. He is master of all that happens. I do think that I shall appear for the festivities."

Shawna wondered why that announcement made her feel so uneasy. People—gentry and villagers alike—usually dressed in costume for the occasion. The night was wild with feasting, drinking, and ribald merrymaking. People went wild.

Perhaps dangerously so.

"David, I'm not sure—"

"You've wanted me to make it clear that I am back at Craig Rock. What more dramatic entry back into the world of the living could I make?"

"But—"

"I thought that I would find something—or someone— by keeping my silence. I've gone through the papers at Castle MacGinnis, and I've torn through the office at Castle Rock. I've watched throughout the day, trailed the passageways by night. I've eavesdropped on men in the mines, I've lived like a mole, seeking answers. I've discovered nothing—except that evil designs most assuredly do still exist here. There is very definitely a conspiracy afoot. But it seems I can discover nothing further by keeping watch. All that is left is for me to make my appearance and stake my claim to all that is mine. Then seek to know exactly who tries to steal it from me and mine by any means, including murder."

"Perhaps we should tell the constable everything."

"Right. Because he was so competent when my corpse was found after the fire? Shawna, I've already told you, we must solve this ourselves."

Shawna sighed. The constable was a good man, good at arresting drunks, good at bringing stray children home, good at correcting youths who might mistakenly think the life of a robber superior to that of an honest laborer. He was not, however, capable of dealing with the machinations of a truly evil mind, so it seemed.

"Surely," she murmured, twisting around to meet his eyes once again, "we will find some clue in the crypts tomorrow. David, shots were fired. Shell casings will be found."

"And it will prove that someone was down there shooting a gun in the crypts, nothing more. Hawk and I will find the shell casings tomorrow."

"But they do prove that something is going on."

"The fact that Sabrina is missing proves something is going on. The fact that I am here proves that something is going on." He hesitated a moment, moving his fingers in her hair. "The problem," he said softly, "is that it seems as if many people are involved in these evil deeds."

She stiffened. "MacGinnises?"

He shrugged. "Most obviously, not all. You did not know the man tonight. But there is organization here. Remember the man who tried to kill you by the loch?"

"The one who is now deep at the bottom of it?"

"Aye."

"Well?"

"He was clad exactly the same as the men—or women—who came down to the crypt tonight."

"In a black cowled cape."

"Aye. They were all exactly alike."

"If you're going to run around trying to be invisible in the darkness, a black cowled cape is probably a good choice of apparel."

"Yes, but..."

"But what?"

"They were exactly alike."

"So, these people all use the same tailor," Shawna said with exasperation.

"The two I killed were men. But I think the cloaked figure accompanying the man I killed tonight was a woman."

"Why?" Shawna demanded.

"The figure was quick and light on its feet. And much more determined to run than to fight."

Shawna shook her head. "I don't know. I didn't see anything. I was —was trying to stay alive."

"Umm," he murmured, his fingers tightening upon her shoulders where they rested. "Tomorrow—or today as it may be—you're not to leave my brother, do you understand?"

"But if you intend to appear as yourself—"

"I do, but in my own good time."

"What difference is there in a day?"

"I want to find out a few more things, if I'm able."

Shawna sighed with exasperation. "But—"

"Do not leave my brother's side. Do you understand?"

She pulled away angrily from his touch. "I understand that I have gone through my own hell for many years now! I understand that you have frightened me, bullied, condemned me, and mocked me, and still—"

"Ah! And saved your life upon occasion!" he reminded her, a sizzling spark in his deep green eyes.

"Only to torment me longer!" she accused him.

A smile curved into his lips. "'Tis pride," he said softly.

"What?" she murmured suspiciously, drawing her blanket more tightly across her breasts.

"Pride, my lady." He left his seat upon the trunk, hunkering down before her on the ledge, not touching her, yet meeting her eyes with a wickedly strange green fire in his own. "I was the heir you see, the fine young Douglas, groomed to take his place in the political and social echelon of the Highlands! I was supposedly such a strong man, destined to be a leader. And one night a lass comes to me in a sheer gown...and I am made the fool. Very nearly killed—but sent to a strange—yet living—hell instead. It was not easy to forgive you."

Shawna shook her head, searching out his eyes. "But I swear to you—"

"I believe you."

"What?"

"I believe you," he said very softly. "I believe that you were as arrogant as I—"

"Indeed!"

"Indeed!" he said and smiled deeply. "Arrogant, in that you thought you could flirt, kiss, and tease—and keep the laird's young heir busy while your family saved your cousin's arse."

"Oh, really!"

"Aye!" And he laughed then, drawing her suddenly against him. "You did not intend what you got, any more than I might have imagined the result of the night's work."

"David—" she gasped in protest, yet the shiver that shot through her as he drew the blanket from her shoulders, letting it fall to the earth, was not from the cold. He pressed her firmly back to the ground, the length of his body following hers, blanketing it. His eyes remained locked with her own, amused, amazingly tender.

"M'laird..." she whispered, suddenly wondering why this should seem so different, why she should feel so vulnerable. She had risen naked from the loch with him and been so accustomed to him that she had hardly noted her state. Yet his tone now seemed so tender that it brought a strange fear racing into her. She wanted that tenderness from him. Yet circumstances between them remained so very tense, and she was afraid to reach for what might be far too quickly snatched away again.

"Aye, m'lady, 'tis hard to forgive a woman for making a fool of a man. Especially when he craved her far too deeply when he fell!"

"David—"

His mouth covered hers, slow, gentle, at first, then forcing her into a deep, wet, open-mouthed kiss that seemed to go on forever, his tongue plunging deeply, ravaging subtly, then moving with sensual, gentle abandon again. Her hands had laid against his chest. Now they moved, stroking the deep, rich, crisp dark hair that grew upon it, easing away the swatch of Douglas tartan crossed over his flesh. He shifted against her, touching in turn, the stroke of his palm and fingers cradling her cheek, his thumb running from her throat to the valley between her breasts. His thumb and forefinger found her nipple, rolled and rubbed it, sending fiery bursts of flame and heat through her breast to her whole body. She moaned against his kiss, instinctively arching toward him, her own fingers falling lower upon his chest to tangle into the rest of the Douglas tartan that covered him.

Impatiently, he tossed away the woolen fabric himself, drawing her hand down to encompass the fullness of his arousal.

She was cold no longer. The fire he had built in the cavern seemed to warm the length and breadth of it. Golden light bathed them in a sweetly burning heat. His very breath was a touch of fire, singeing her flesh.

Her lips brushed over his chest. His fingers dug into her hair, for she teased with her kiss and her tongue while her fingers stroked and manipulated. Life and fire seemed to burn within against her touch.

The strength of his ardor created a new trembling within her, a growing hunger that coiled and burned into the center of her being.

"Aye, lady...I can bear no more!" he groaned, his whisper deep and guttural as he captured her wrists, drawing her hands above her head as he straddled her body. "'Tis safe, I think, to say that you do, indeed, seduce..."

"Laird Douglas!" she whispered in protest. "In truth, you know that you are the one to prey upon the weakness in a lady who..."

"Aye?" His fingers curled into hers, holding them fiercely. His eyes impaled her there, as did the tension in his features.

She shook her head. His lips found hers again, slow, deep, passionate.

"I have wanted you forever, you know," he whispered softly against her mouth.

She shook her head.

"Nay...I had not known..."

His hand ran up and down her body, cupping, teasing, caressing her breasts. Stroking her hip, covering the black triangle of her pelvic hair. Then stroked her thighs and slid between them.

"Forever..."

"Aye?" she gasped, struggling then against his hold, anxious to bury herself against him, desperate to end the torment that burned into her now, desperate as well for it to go on and on...

His lips were close to hers again. His touch...was wickedly intimate. Her breath came in gasps, she burned, she writhed.

"Aye, lady, you were young, you were impetuous, you were so very arrogant! But I was waiting, you know, because I supposed that I had loved you forever."

"In...deed?" she gasped.

"Loved you, wanted you. And one way or the other, Shawna, would have had you..."

His whisper carried on the flames within the cavern, soft, echoing, sweeping around her. Then play ceased, and he was over her and within her. She didn't feel the hardness of the earth beneath her, for the blanket that sheltered her back was as warm as the flesh that encompassed her, and she had again been seduced to such a point that she was desperate for fruition. The earth seemed to rock with the grinding rhythm of his hips, the fever inside of her spiraled until she was aware of nothing but her need for him, and the golden fire that seemed to spill throughout the cavern and into her. He stroked and withdrew, stroked and withdrew, found her lips, her throat, her breasts...She arched and thrashed and climbed until the wild rhythm exploded into a pinnacle of fiery light, bursting sweetly upon her so that she clung to him as she drifted back down to the reality of hard stone beneath her back and the chill of the cavern with only a single fire burning against the cold of the night.

But she fought not to shiver, for he lay at her side, holding her, trying to keep her from the cold, silent then as his eyes kept focus upon the rock above them. She stroked the contours of his face.

"'Tis a pity I am the one left without a coat of fur," she said softly. "For 'tis said that I would control you, if you're a demon, beast, or selkie, that is, if I could but steal that Douglas tartan perhaps, hide it away, and have you in my power."

A slow smile curved into his lips, and he turned his gaze to her. "You don't think that you've enough in your power, my lady?"

She shook her head. "I hold only what you give, Laird Douglas, and you are capable of being quite stingy!"

He laughed and held her more closely. Then his expression sobered as he said softly, "I lost everything once, including my own identity. I fear to lose everything again, life itself this time, if I do not take the gravest care. You are among what I can most easily lose."

"Does that mean then, m'laird, that I am something you wish to have—and keep?"

He rolled toward her, twirling a strand of her hair in his fingers. "I have come back for all that is mine," he informed her. "And you will note, I believe, that I am quite willing to fight for what is mine. I will not be betrayed again, and though I do believe in your innocence, I promise as well that I will readily kill any man guilty of treachery against me again, and if a woman were guilty, my love, I do swear that she would pay the price."

"But—"

"Shawna," he said, his touch then upon her chin so that their eyes met, "I have told you, I believe you. You say that you have told me the truth, that there is nothing more you know, there is nothing more at all that you can tell me about the past. Then I believe you."

She found it very difficult to breathe. She wanted to be as they were then forever. His warmth, his strength—his tenderness—all given to her. The curve of his smile serious yet gentle. His touch...a lover's touch. The warmth that remained when passion was spent.

"I swear to you..."

His lips touched hers.

"I believe you."

"I love you, David."

"Sweet Jesus! How long it took to draw those words from you!" he exclaimed.

She flushed, pushing suddenly against his chest. "It might have aided you in that quest, Laird Douglas, had you thought to speak such words yourself!"

"I told you quite clearly that I had wanted you forever."

"Wanting is not the same."

"Ah, well, I wanted you because I loved you."

She smiled slowly, her lashes lowering. She had never thought she'd feel such happiness.

Yet a feeling of unease fluttered within her stomach. She had kept nothing from him that mattered. And perhaps, one day she would share with him the years they had lost as openly as she prayed he might share the pain of his past with her.

But not now.

"You were speaking of the years before when you spoke of wanting me," she said very softly.

"Aye."

"Well...that was then," she said matter-of-factly, meeting his gaze again. "This is now."

"Dear God, are you never satisfied?" he demanded gruffly.

"Indeed, but—"

She gasped as he rolled atop her once again, his eyes boring into hers, bright with passion once again. "You were a gorgeous child, headstrong, impetuous, annoyingly so—I thought you needed a good switching many times."

"If this is a declaration of love—" she protested.

"Hear me out. Where was I? Ah! Then, you were no longer a child. You grew into a woman—gorgeous, headstrong, impetuous—and arrogant."

"Now, really—"

"And I wanted you. You were young Lady MacGinnis, and I cared for you. Then you were the very beautiful young woman I had known and cared about all of my life, but you had changed, I had aged, and I wanted you. I admired you. I loved your determination and your courage and aye, even your reckless loyalty to your family. In my heart, I knew that the day would come when a goodly distance could be kept no more, when you'd finally tease too far, and I would have what I wanted—all quite properly, of course. I had intended eventually, I'm quite certain, to ask Gawain and Lowell—and you, of course—for your hand in marriage. You seduced me into wanting you, but just by being yourself, with your pride and your sense of duty and loyalty and energy and all those other things about you—you seduced me into love. Five years has changed nothing. I've had you, and I want you more. I was in love with you before, and I am deeply, grievously in love once again. Now, my lady, will that do?"

Her eyes wide upon his, she smiled.

"Quite well!" she whispered.

"Good. Because such an impassioned, rousing speech has impassioned and aroused other things as well. My lady, you may feel free to simply whisper again—with tremendous ardor, of course—that you love me, then you may proceed to show me with that desperately fevered ardor."

She still stared into his eyes.

"Well?"

"Oh, aye! I love you, David, dear God, you cannot believe how deeply, how desperately—"

"I'm quite willing to be shown," he whispered. And he kissed her.

And made love to her.

The fire blazed red and orange across the stone walls.

Until finally, the fire burned out, and the soft light filling the cavern was pink and gold.

The tide had receded.

And dawn was breaking.

Shawna was loath to leave the cavern, but David was anxious to return her to the castle.

"I still don't understand why you don't just announce your presence today."

"There are still things I must discover," he said.

"But how am I to get back into the castle? I can't just walk through the front door naked—"

"I would flay you alive," he assured her. "I've shirts in my trunk and plenty of tartan. You can walk through the forest to the passageway entry kilted in Douglas plaid. I'll escort you back to your tower room."

He dressed himself in a black shirt and breeches, then helped her don a cotton shirt and his tartan. The water was shallow then in the cavern, and David, wearing his boots, carried her through the foot or so of water that still pooled within the cavern until they came out to the embankment of the loch beyond. He caught her hand, quickly leading her around the loch and into the depths of the forest, where they entered the passageway together, taking it back to the castle, and therein, through the secret stairways and corridors of Castle Rock until they came to her tower room.

Once there, he paused long enough to hold her and kiss her very deeply once again.

"You go nowhere without my brother, Shawna, do you hear?"

"Does your brother know of this?"

"Aye, he will. But on this, you must obey me, Shawna, do you understand?"

"Aye. But I don't understand what—"

"Shawna, for the love of God, have faith, I beg of you!"

"I do have faith," she said softly.

She did have faith. She loved David. She had loved him all her life, she thought. And he had whispered those same words to her. Tall, dark, towering, fierce, so striking with his bronzed muscle, flashing green eyes, dark auburn hair. That he did not just want her, that he had told her he loved her, was a dream that she'd not dared wish might come true.

But she was afraid. Uneasy. She didn't know why.

"David—"

"I must go."

He smiled, brushed her lips with his own once again, and disappeared through the shifting break in the stone that led back to the secret passageway.

Shawna watched him go.

Then she felt a strange sensation of dread sweeping through her.

He would not be betrayed again.

She had not betrayed him!

And still...

She was afraid.

Something was going to happen.

And there would be nothing she could do to stop it.

CHAPTER 17

Brother Damian stood at the bar in the tavern, slowly sipping ale, listening to the farmers and sheep and cattle herders gossip and speculate in whispers as they sat at the various planked tables about the tavern. Some ate the mutton stew offered by the tavern's kitchens for lunch, others drank ale, seeking not nourishment, but companionship.

"If y'be askin' me, 'tis simply more of the same," one old-timer said quietly, his head bowed low so that his voice might be heard just by the comrades at his table. The old man was leathered, his hair and thick beard more white than gray. He had bright blue eyes, and despite his seventy-odd years, he remained straight and sturdy as an oak. He was a Menzies, Ioin Menzies, father of Mark Menzies, the foreman of the miners. "There's strange things brewing in the castle on the hill, and that's a fact."

"Since before the old Laird Douglas died," protested a handsome younger man in his twenties, Hamell, one of the Anderson lads. He looked carefully around the room.

Brother Damian, standing with his ale, thought that the lad might be looking about to see if his father was in the tavern.

Hamell Anderson leaned forward, barely mouthing the words to old Ioin. "It began the night of the Fire."

"D'ye think it's the witches?" Ioin demanded.

"Are y' serious, man?" Hamell demanded.

"The American lass is gone, isn't she?"

"Aye."

"The Night of the Moon Maiden comes tomorrow. Perhaps the lass is intended to die on the altar."

"Ach, old man! Ye've lost your mind, surely!"

"Strange things been brewin'."

"Aye, like the lad."

"The lad?" Old Ioin looked puzzled. "Ah, y'mean your brother, Danny, the wee thing caught in the mines?"

"Aye. I mean Danny," Hamell said quietly. He looked down at the table, not meeting old Ioin's eyes. "Danny...came out of the mines with the help of a beastie."

"Things do indeed haunt the mines. My boy has told me so," Ioin said grimly.

"Well, no one will be slaying a lass on the Druid Stone. We'll all be about to see that it not happen," Hamell said harshly. "And don't you go ruinin' the holiday for us all! I've my costume and mask set. The servants at the castle have been setting out the kegs of wine and ale all morning in preparations for tomorrow night. I've worked on me caber throw for the contests, and I've a lass to meet for the dancing! Don't go making something eerie of the fun we've planned on havin'!"

"It's the lass you're planning on havin', eh, boy?"

"I intend to ask her to wed," Hamell said indignantly.

"After the...er, festivities?" Ioin suggested.

"Now, Ioin—"

"I'd not spoil a celebration, and that's a fact. I'm not the trouble. 'Tis the witches," Ioin said.

"The witches?"

"Aye, Edwina and her lot, talking Mother Nature, making their herbal cures and potions and all! You look to it, boy—'twill end that the witches have some shenanigans and say in all this!"

"Don't you be talking such rubbish!" came a sharp, feminine cry from the door.

Brother Damian, who had been deeply involved in the men's

conversation, turned in surprise to see that Edwina had come into the tavern. She wore a cloak against the chill of the November day, yet as he watched her, Brother Damian's eyes narrowed.

"Ah, now, Edwina—" Ioin protested, his cheeks flushing.

"I've done nothing but good for you, Ioin Menzies!" Edwina said, coming straight to the table. "My herbs have cured those carbuncles upon your back many a time, and my remedies have soothed your old feet many a night as well."

"Now, Edwina—"

"Don't you 'now, Edwina' me, Mister Menzies!" Edwina said angrily, and sweeping off her cloak, she went back behind the bar, drawing a pitcher of ale for a farmer who hailed her across the tavern.

Brother Damian took his chances and slid into the seat alongside Ioin Menzies. Menzies looked up at him, surprised and wary. Brother Damian smiled reassuringly. He'd been a bit of a fixture at the tavern for several days, coming and going, and building up something of a trust among the people here.

"She's worried, you know. About Laird Douglas's sister-in-law. And we must still find the lass."

"Aye!" Ioin said, looking at the table.

"In truth," he said quietly, "you know, Menzies, that I've come on pilgrimage to do a bit of studying on the lore hereabouts, and quite honestly, the ancient sacrifices were associated with Druid practices, and not with the Wiccans."

"She'll be mad at me, now," Ioin said, sniffing toward where Edwina worked at the bar. "She'll let my old body rot before she gives me aid again."

Brother Damian drank deeply from his ale, then looked across the table at Hamell Anderson. "There's been no clue here in the village as to the missing girl, eh?"

Hamell shook his head and sipped foam from his ale. "But Ioin may have a point. If witches were out for a sacrifice, they'd want the likes of an important young maid, don't y' think, Brother Damian?" Anderson's eyes lit seriously upon him. "But then again, wouldn't they be seeking the likes of someone even more important perhaps? Like Lady MacGinnis herself? Unless of course..."

"Aye, and of course, what?" Brother Damian demanded.

Hamell Anderson shrugged uncomfortably. "Well, if someone deeply believed in his or her religion—not minding what that belief be—he or she would follow it faithfully."

"Aye, a passionate man follows his religion with great faith," Brother Damian agreed.

"I don't ken what you're off about, boy!" Ioin said, exasperated.

"Perhaps the Lady MacGinnis is not all that she seems."

Ioin took exception to that as well. His glass hit hard upon the wooden table. "Don't y'be sayin' a word against the likes of Shawna MacGinnis. She's proved herself as fine in spirit as any man in taking to the likes of watching over us all. Why, she is using her own income to see to the welfare of your grandfather, young Hamell. She's sending him to that special hospital, soon as the arrangements are made. And didn't she just take your wee brother into the castle?"

"Aye, me brother," Hamell muttered bitterly.

Old Ioin stared at him. "Then your nephew—if young Danny is your sister's illegitimate issue."

"The lad is not me sister's—"

"Be that as it may, Lady MacGinnis has cared for you and yours," Ioin insisted.

"Oh, aye, the great lady, that she be!" Hamell agreed, and he hesitated, still looking unhappy.

"Son, just what are you trying to say?" Brother Damian persisted.

Hamell shook his head. "Just that, well, we're not always what we appear to be, and that's that, I'll say no more—"

"Ye've said nothing!" Ioin snapped in total exasperation.

"Fine, I'll say this, then! One would assume Miss Sabrina Connor to be an innocent maid. And if strange things have been happening, well, aye, they've been happening since the Fire, since David Douglas died. Lady MacGinnis was with David Douglas that night, and it's my belief that Lady MacGinnis was with the laird's heir that night in the carnal sense—begging your pardon, Brother Damian. So, if some practitioner of the black arts seeks a sacrifice—an innocent sacrifice—then Sabrina Connor would certainly be a fair choice."

Brother Damian arched a brow, wondering if the truth regarding Sabrina Connor's condition might save her life.

"What if Miss Connor is not so innocent a lass?" he suggested. "She had scarcely arrived here before she disappeared. What could any man know of her past?"

"Indeed!" old Ioin exclaimed. And he stared at Brother Damian, then at Hamell. He sniffed once, very quietly. Then he sniffed loudly and rose, walking away from the table to the bar.

Most probably, Brother Damian determined, to make his peace with Edwina. It might be one thing to rue the practice of witchcraft, but it was quite another to suffer through the pain of carbuncles.

"Ah!" Hamell Anderson murmured unhappily. "I should have kept my mouth shut. I've offended the old goat. He does truly love Lady MacGinnis!" He glanced at Brother Damian. "I don't mean offense to Lady MacGinnis. I don't. God's blood—sorry, Brother—but all I say is that she and David Douglas were like sparks flying together. Not a civil word, yet they couldn't keep apart. I suppose to you, good friar, 'tis sin, but then, like as not y'don't quite ken what it is between a man and woman that draws them together."

"I do my best," Brother Damian said dryly. "As I assume you do yourself."

"Wait, now there, are you tryin' to imply that young Danny might be me own lad?"

"I wasn't implying anything of the like," Brother Damian assured him. "I just suggested that—"

"I took no innocent maid and gave her issue!" he said, then lowered his voice, looking around. He was terrified of his father, Brother Damian thought. "Look at the lad, and look at the MacGinnises, will you!" he said and quickly stood. He started to leave, then hesitated and added quickly, "If you seek answers here, Brother Damian, look to the lady herself!"

ALISTAIR STOOD IN THE CHAPEL, inhaling, exhaling, staring at the crucifix.

There was no help for it. He was going to have to go down to the crypt.

Because things were beginning to happen. The past was tormenting the living and beginning to eclipse what there might have been of a future.

He didn't want to go to the crypts. He had to.

Yet even in the daylight, he despised going there.

He shuddered fiercely.

Then the sound of the chapel door opening off the great hall sounded, and he spun around.

Hawk Douglas had come.

"Alistair!" Hawk greeted him, his hands on his hips as he stared up at the crucifix as well. Then he glanced Alistair's way, his green eyes sparkling. "I hadn't thought you so religious as to spend time in the chapel."

"I—" Alistair began and paused, then arched a brow. "I hadn't thought you so religious. In fact, don't you people—" He hesitated again, smiling ruefully. "Sorry. Don't the Sioux have a rather different religion?"

"Aye, gods and goddesses, the power of wind, the rain, the earth," Hawk said, taking no offense. Alistair thought it uncanny that in his height and build, and even in some of his movements and mannerisms, Hawk could so resemble his brother, while still having the look of his mother's people about him as well. He was dressed very much like the American today, in a light blue denim work shirt, darker breeches, and American-made boots. Hawk grinned at Alistair. "I'm still quite convinced that there is one great power—and it's all the same, no matter what we call our religious choices."

"So, you have come to the chapel to commune with this 'great power?' If so, I shall leave you in peace—"

"I've not come to commune with anything—I'm passing through."

"To—?"

"The crypts."

"The crypts?"

"I understand that you heard something coming from the chapel last night but found nothing."

"Aye," Alistair said. He shrugged. "You know how these ancient places creak and groan."

"I know—and so do you. Far better than I, since you've been living here. If you heard something, I'm sure there was something to hear."

"I found nothing—"

"But you didn't look down in the crypts."

Alistair shrugged.

"Well, I want to investigate there. Come with me. I'll appreciate the company."

Hawk Douglas started for the gateway, lighting a match to set flame to a lantern hanging from a hook on the wall. "Are you coming?" he queried politely. He turned, pushed open the iron gate, and started down the steps to the crypts.

Alistair felt a trickle of sweat slipping down his neck.

He followed Hawk Douglas.

DESPITE HER EXHAUSTION, Shawna hadn't imagined that she'd be able to sleep that day, especially since dawn had nearly broken when they had reached the castle, and David had departed.

But it felt as if she had barely been in her room long enough to shed David's tartan, wash enthusiastically with soap despite the small amount of water in her ewer and washbowl, and lie down to close her eyes before there came a tapping on her door. She awoke in something of a panic, froze, then quickly called out, "Who is it?"

"Mary Jane."

"One minute!"

She leaped out of bed, saw to it that David's tartan was kicked firmly behind the dressing screen, and hurried to the door.

Mary Jane smiled, but she looked quite tired. "Good day, Shawna. Laird Hawk has sent me to see if you'd be so good as to join the family for a late breakfast, before everyone sets off to search for Miss Sabrina again."

"Aye, certainly. I'll be down."

"Good. You look so tired."

"You look exhausted."

"Well now, we've all been up, worrying about poor Miss Connor, so it seems. Though, of course, perhaps the constable was right—we none of us quite know what will happen if the right man comes along, now, do we?"

Shawna glanced at Mary Jane, arching a brow. "Not Sabrina Connor," she said.

"Ah, but why would Sabrina Connor be different from any other lass?"

It was on the tip of her tongue to say that she knew Sabrina had been kidnapped, but as close as she and Mary Jane had been throughout the years, she remembered that David had chosen to hide the body of the man he had killed in the crypt. He didn't want others knowing what they had discovered.

"Look at you, m'lady, begging your pardon!" Mary Jane said softly. "You were willing to risk much for the late young Master David Douglas. Aye, and for the MacGinnises as well. But look at all you endured—for want of a man."

"Mary Jane!" Shawna said uncomfortably. "That was all quite long ago."

"Well, shall I lay out your clothing for you?"

"No, no...I'll be fine on my own," Shawna said. She was determined to hide David's tartan before anyone in the household could come upon it and ponder its presence in her room. "Please tell Laird Douglas I'll be right down. What—what of Lady Douglas? How is she faring?"

"She is tired but well and quite determined. Thankfully, she is convinced that her sister is alive, and she is determined to find her."

"Good," Shawna said. David, she was certain, had seen his brother and sister-in-law and told them of the events last night in the crypts. "I shall be right along."

When Mary Jane had gone, Shawna dressed quickly. She folded David's tartan and hastily slid it into the one drawer in the tower room's eighteenth-century wardrobe.

When she exited her room, Gawain was waiting there. "Uncle!" she said in surprise.

"I'll escort y'down, lass," he said.

He slipped his arm into hers, seeming both very worried and far older today than usual. "No clues, no hints of anything regarding Sabrina, nothing?" she asked him.

"None. And we've the celebration coming up so quickly now. It means so much to so many. Everyone is worried about Sabrina, but Lady Douglas has just come here for the first time, and she and her sister are foreigners, and the people are restless because, although they care, they don't want to be cheated out of their feast and a day's rest. We must use most of our manpower to continue to search for Sabrina, but the castle staff must make preparations for the Night of the Moon Maiden."

They were the last to enter the great hall. Hawk and Skylar Douglas were already seated, he at one end of the table with her beside him to the right. Skylar looked drawn, but as Mary Jane had said, she looked very determined as well as composed. Alistair and Aidan were seated to the side of Skylar, Lowell and Alaric were across from them. The place at the other head of the table awaited Shawna, and Gawain seated her there while taking the empty chair next to Lowell at her side.

"Good morning, Shawna," Hawk said, watching her with his sharp green eyes. She was convinced then that he had spoken with his brother. David would have gone to Hawk before leaving the castle to carry out his plans for the day. "Poor thing, she looks exhausted, don't you think, Skylar?"

"Simply exhausted." Skylar managed something of a smile. "Aye, quite exhausted."

"We are an exhausted group!" Gawain said.

"It'll be a harder day today, mark me," Lowell said. "Eat up now, all of you."

"Aye, it will be a busy day, searching for Sabrina while the preparations go forth," Alaric said, glancing down at Laird Douglas. "It will be the first time you rule as laird at the Night of the Moon Maiden, Hawk. Will you and your lady come in costume?"

Shawna cleared her throat. "I don't think that Skylar wants to be bothered with the Night of the Moon Maiden right now—" she murmured, but Skylar interrupted.

"Thank you, Shawna, but I like to have my mind occupied, and I don't mind hearing more. Hawk will not let me go searching again until I've eaten, so please, I'd like to hear about the local customs."

"Well, then," Shawna said, "aye, people come costumed. We've trunks filled with old clothing in one of the tower rooms. Mary Jane can help you find something later if you wish. Hawk, what would you come as to rule over the night with your lady wife?"

"Do I rule?" Skylar queried. "I thought the Moon Maiden had to be a young village girl. A lass, a—"

"A virgin?" Alistair suggested. "Remember, they quit sacrificing a Moon Maiden centuries ago!" he said impatiently.

There was an uncomfortable silence at the table. Shawna felt Hawk staring at her, and she knew he was worried that someone might well intend for Sabrina to be a sacrifice. She spoke quickly.

"The laird and lady—when there exist both a laird and a lady—have special chairs placed on a dais from which they open and guide the festivities. The laird chooses his lady, of course, to rule with him, but then the people choose a lass for Moon Maiden, and the laird and lady give her a crown of flowers—and a horse from the Douglas stables."

"A horse?" Skylar said.

"Aye, a fine horse, so that she can ride throughout the year and observe her domain," Aidan said.

"I crowned Gena Anderson Moon Maiden last year," Shawna said.

Gawain sniffed. "Ah, and thank God, for it seems she was no sacrifice. She walks around alive and well. She does, doesn't she, Alistair," he said, staring at his son.

Alistair arched a brow. "Indeed, Father. To the best of my knowledge." He lifted his hands in a defensive gesture. "Father, Danny is not my child."

Gawain grunted.

There was another moment of uncomfortable silence. Forks could be heard scraping against plates as everyone suddenly pretended to be greatly interested in the food.

But then Hawk set his napkin upon the table. "Gentlemen, if you'll excuse me, we've all got a busy day ahead of us. Shawna, may I have a word before we get started?"

He rose and awaited her. Shawna rose as well, following him as he headed toward the stairs. "What is it?"

"Come along with me," he told her.

She was startled when he started up the second flight of stairs to her third-floor tower room.

"Hawk—"

He stopped in front of her door, opening it. "Go in now," he said.

"You've summoned me—to go to my room?" she queried.

He smiled. "I heard you had an exceptionally eventful evening."

Shawna felt a soft tide of red seeping over her features, and she wondered just what information brothers shared. Was he speaking of events before or after they'd swum to the cavern?

"Aye, that! In the crypts—"

"I've been there briefly, but I have to return to search the place more thoroughly."

"I'll help you—"

"No, Shawna, I've brought you here because I want you to lock yourself in for the time being. I can't be with you right now."

"But, Hawk, there's so much—"

"Shawna, I'll not leave you locked up in a tower all day, I swear it. But I have promised my brother to keep you out of trouble, and he seems to think that you have a ready penchant for falling into it. Please, bear with me for the moment. We need to know you're safe, and you surely need some sleep."

"But I'm not—"

"You are tired. You look like hell!"

"Well, thank you, Laird Douglas."

"I'm not Laird Douglas, and you know it well. Despite that, Lady MacGinnis, I am giving you an absolute directive—if you've any care for my brother or yourself, pay heed to me, I beg you. I'll send someone in the late afternoon, after you've slept. All right?"

He wasn't really giving her a choice.

"All right."

She stepped into her room. He closed the door. "Slide the bolt, my lady."

She did so. She heard him walking away.

She was never going to sleep. Never.

She was wrong. She lay upon her bed, but her clothing felt too constraining. She changed back into her nightgown and lay down once again. She stared at the ceiling, telling herself once again that this was torture, she was never going to sleep. Her mind was filled. With David. With the things he had said. With the way that he had touched her.

With Sabrina, poor Sabrina. Where was she?

What was happening here?

She would never sleep...

But she had lain there for just a few minutes when she realized that she was drifting.

Then she was sleeping.

And dreaming...

This time, she was running, but there were sounds coming from all around her.

Bagpipes...playing a mournful tune upon the air.

Shouts, laughter...

She ran to the high hill, where the Druid Stones lay.

And there was Sabrina, stripped naked, stretched out upon the stone while a cowled creature stood over her, bearing a knife, ready to tear into the girl's throat.

She started to scream. "Nay, not Sabrina!"

Then the creature saw her. She couldn't see its face, so she didn't know how she knew that it was staring at her, but she did. And she was aware that it was smiling with evil intent and beckoning to her.

"It should have been you, you, you, m'lady, it should have been you...but you defiled yourself so long ago! Still, your blood would so well feed the earth!"

Then the creature was suddenly coming after her. She could still hear the bagpipes, the shouts, cries, laughter. All across the hills, men and women were dancing, drinking, laughing...

None of them heard her scream. Then she was running. And running. She turned back. The cowled creature was nearly upon her.

She turned to run faster...

Another creature was coming...

And another, and another.

Cowled creatures, tall figures in their capped black cloaks, were emerging from everywhere.

Chanting her name.

They surrounded her. She cried out, trying to find a different way to run, but in each direction, there was a figure.

And each figure bore a knife. Indeed, as she spun around, she saw them all raised. Huge knives, with razor-honed blades glistening beneath the glow of the full moon.

"Shawna, Shawna, Shawna..."

She cried out, swirling around.

She stood directly beneath one of the cloaked figures. She could see the face.

The face of a burned corpse. The horrible, decaying face of the burned corpse she had awakened beside all those years ago.

"No!" she shrieked.

The cowled creature began to laugh.

In a circle around her, they all began to laugh.

And again, they began to move, closing in on her.

Chanting her name, raising their knives...

Seeking her blood...

"Shawna, Shawna..."

CHAPTER 18

Shawna awoke with a start, bolting to a sitting position and swallowing back a scream of terror as she shook herself free from the horror of the dream.

She stood and walked to the window, looking out on the landscape and shivering. Was David right? Was someone seeking a sacrifice? She couldn't deny that the man killed in the crypt last night had been very scary indeed, as his words had been. But she had been friends with the witches of Craig Rock all her life. They were not killers.

Someone was.

She hugged her arms to her chest. If a cult needed a virgin sacrifice, Sabrina was not it. But she hoped desperately that Sabrina didn't tell her kidnappers about her condition. They might simply kill her quickly to get her out of the way.

Shawna shivered. The man had said that they wanted her as well. That she would see Sabrina soon enough. Yet, she would hardly be the proper sacrifice at all herself. She wasn't an innocent maiden. She had borne and lost a child.

Consequences.

Most of the time, she didn't even allow herself to remember the consequences of their night in the stables. It was far too painful.

She bit into her lower lip. She should have told David last night about the child she had lost after his death. She had run away from Craig Rock when she had discovered that she was going to have his child. She had desperately wanted the babe—she had believed herself that she had been responsible for David's death, and having his child would in some way give life back to him. She wasn't going to have anyone pressuring her to give up her child. They would have expected her to do so. She was Lady MacGinnis. Milkmaids had illegitimate children. Ladies did not.

But running away hadn't mattered. Because her infant had died at birth. She had felt as if even God were mocking her. And she had come home then because Alistair had come for her, offering her a brotherly love and care she needed very badly at the time.

How did she tell David now that he'd had a child, but that his child had died? When he had just come back from the dead himself.

The dead among the living.

The living among the dead!

She gasped out loud, suddenly realizing that the dying man had given her a clue as to Sabrina's whereabouts after all.

She tore about her room, digging into her wardrobe for her clothing. She paused, realizing even in her hurry that she didn't see David's tartan. She dug beneath her own belongings, certain that it shouldn't have been buried so deeply. Just when she was truly afraid that someone had come in and found the tartan, she discovered it herself.

She exhaled a sigh of relief. She brought the wool against her cheek, and for a moment, she trembled, just feeling its warmth.

Then she set the tartan aside, dressed quickly in a deep purple riding habit, and slipped quietly from her room, hurrying down the stairs.

Yet when she came to the foot of the stairs, she was startled to find Skylar there. She'd assumed that Skylar would have been out looking for Sabrina with the men.

"Skylar!"

"Aren't you supposed to be locked in your room?" Skylar queried her.

"What about you? It was your sister who was kidnapped."

"They wouldn't let me out of the castle," she said mournfully.

"Has anything new been discovered?"

"Nothing I know about," Skylar said. "Gawain and Alaric have ridden south to search through the forests and stop by and speak with some of the forest folk. Lowell and Aidan are still searching the tunnels with the miners. There are so many shafts."

"Aye—and caverns. The mines are very near the caverns and cliffs at the loch's edge. They actually all tie in together. The cliffs here give access to so very much going on beneath the earth. It seems that there are more ways than one to get into or out of anyplace on the property," Shawna said. "Except for..."

"Except for what?"

Shawna shook her head. She came very close to Skylar and whispered, "Where is David? Do you know?"

Skylar shook her head. "I've no idea. I was told to stay here—watch you when you came down. But surely, Hawk knows where David is."

"Aye, I must find Hawk then."

"A bit later. He's in the crypt now. And I was told to keep you here. I will not take you to the crypt. It's very nearly dark, and the night seems to be an especially dangerous time in these parts."

"How do you feel about the chapel? We could wait there if you're afraid of the crypts."

"Actually, I pride myself on being hard as rocks and afraid of nothing. If we must, we'll go to the crypts."

"Thank you. I've just had an idea. About Sabrina. But I don't want to ask anyone but Hawk or David to help us."

"Pray, God, she's not in the crypts!" Skylar said anxiously.

"Nay, not in the crypts, but somewhere very close, and it may be important that we reach her quickly!"

"You think she is still alive?" Skylar demanded bluntly.

"I think she's alive now, but I'm afraid someone may think she'd make a good sacrifice. We must hurry."

Yet just as they were about to slip away, Myer, who had stood as butler at Castle Craig for nearly fifty years, made an appearance in the great hall. "Lady Douglas, Lady MacGinnis! Anne-Marie requests your presence in the kitchen for just a moment. She has one quick question regarding tomorrow."

They glanced at one another and silently agreed to go to the kitchen as requested, since neither woman was supposed to be anywhere other than at the center of activity in the castle.

Anne-Marie was bustling about. She was as plump as Myer was thin. She was as chatty as he was taciturn. Anne-Marie was preparing all the traditional treats for the Night of the Moon Maiden, and she had half a dozen village girls in the kitchen and young Danny Anderson and three more little tykes washing away at the dishes and flatware to be used for the feasting and turning a spit with a haunch of venison upon it.

"Ah, Lady Douglas!" she said with delight, seeing Skylar first. "I canna fer the likes of me figure Shawna sleeping so late on such a day as this, but she'll be along! But then, well she did tell me when she first heard you were coming that you were the lady of the castle, and that you were to be the one givin' the instructions." Anne-Marie rolled out a round stretch of dough, powdered her hands, and clapped them so that her flour dusted the air and all around her.

"I'm here, Anne-Marie," Shawna said.

"Ah! Well then, ye can both give me assistance!" Anne-Marie said with a rosy smile. "Now, tomorrow, for the prime beef cattle to be roasted on the spits near the Stones, will we be needing three or four animals?"

Skylar looked at Shawna and arched a brow.

"Four," Shawna said. "If any meat is left over, the villagers may take it home."

"Fine then. I'll make sure the herders know. Today, Lady Douglas," Anne-Marie informed Skylar, "we're working on our scones and meat pies and sweetmeats for the morning. We'll have our traditional haggis, a delicacy made from a sheep's heart, liver, oatmeal, onions, and seasonings—and all prepared in a sheep's stomach. But if it doesn't appeal to an American appetite, there'll be so much more to choose from. The roasted meat is exquisite when done so long over an open fire, and my shortbread and scones are the finest in all the Highlands, I do promise!"

"Skylar will enjoy everything," Shawna said, anxious to lead Skylar from the kitchen and to the chapel. She put a hand on Skylar's shoulders to move her along, then paused, seeing that an old man in a friar's garb stood at the doorway to the kitchen, which was open because of the intense heat from the hearth and ovens. *Brother Damian!* she thought with irritation and dismay. This would delay them still further.

"Why, 'tis Brother Damian," Anne-Marie said with delight, looking around. She lowered her voice. "'E's up to our parts on pilgrimage. I have him in for tea when he drops by." She crossed herself. "'Tis good luck!" she assured Skylar and Shawna.

"Well, then," Skylar said, "we'll have to have him in."

"You have him in," Shawna said quickly. She couldn't stand to be drawn into a conversation with Brother Damian right now! "Skylar, I'm going—to pray," she said, disappearing through the kitchen door before Brother Damian could see her, or Skylar could stop her.

Skylar had no choice then but to walk to the door, extending a hand. "Brother Damian. I am...Lady Douglas, wife to Hawk Douglas, in from America."

"My lady." Brother Damian took her hand in his own and bowed. "Forgive the intrusion. I understand your sister is missing. I intend to join the search as soon as I leave here. Anne-Marie is oft kind enough to give a wayfarer a cup of tea."

"Of course," Skylar said politely. "Please do come in."

Brother Damian entered the kitchen, and Anne-Marie quickly padded over to greet him, smiling broadly. "Come now, my good Brother Damian, and sit. You will be good for Lady Douglas, who must keep her mind off her fear! The scones are fresh, just this minute out of the oven. What a fine day for you to visit here at the castle, since ye've such a keen interest in local fests and the like! You'll see all the preparations for the food."

She winked, managing to sit both Skylar and Brother Damian at the long table where the servants usually took their meals.

Skylar longed to jump up and go running after Shawna.

Yet Shawna evidently thought that she could find Sabrina. And she didn't want anyone other than Hawk or David to know where she intended to look. Maybe she was afraid of someone's realizing that they were about to find Sabrina.

And maybe she was afraid of what might happen to Sabrina if someone else reached her before they did.

Two minutes, Skylar decided. She'd give Brother Damian exactly two minutes, then she'd find some excuse to go after Shawna.

Taking the kettle from the fire, Anne-Marie deftly brewed and strained tea, saying, "We've all manner of contests as well, a çaber throw, traditional dance, archery—ah! And imagine! Laird Douglas is part Sioux, can ye imagine such a thing here, Brother Damian? But think on it—archery, with an Indian in the family!" She laughed delightedly. "Our Laird Douglas will surely take the prize this year!"

"I imagine he will," Brother Damian said, smiling at Skylar as he lifted his cup of tea.

She smiled uneasily, lifting her cup of tea in return. Something about Brother Damian was vaguely unnerving, but she couldn't tell quite what. He was clean and neat enough, but his whiskers were so rich and his hair so long and bushy that they all but consumed his face. Still...

"So, there's great feasting—and a great deal of sinning as well, I've heard!" Brother Damian said.

He didn't say the words much like a friar. He seemed amused by the rumors of what went on.

"Now, such a complaint did not come from these parts!" Anne-Marie said in protest. She set a hand on Skylar's. "Lady Douglas, you must not fear for your sister. We'll find her, I know it in my heart. The Night of the Moon Maiden is a night of joy, and we celebrate the harvest, and all that is rich and wonderful and plentiful—"

"And fertile?" Brother Damian suggested lightly.

"Well, then," Anne-Marie admitted, "we need a fertile harvest to keep us all in food!"

"And a night of abandon here and there to maintain a population in the Highlands as well," he said with a smile.

"Well, the night, it brings about a share of marriages, Brother Damian, but for the most part, the births that result from the Night of the Moon Maiden are legitimate by the time they occur!"

"What do you think of these festivities, Lady Douglas?" Brother Damian asked.

"I've yet to experience the night. I'm sure it will be interesting," Skylar said. Brother Damian, she noted, though ostensibly paying attention to her and Anne-Marie, was now watching the lads turn meat at the hearth.

"They're young," he commented.

"Aye," Skylar agreed. "But Anne-Marie takes great care with her kitchen help. The lads have been taken from the mines, where their own parents sent them. Lady MacGinnis, who tends all of our interests as my husband is most often in America, no longer allows the young children to work in our mines. Our dear Anne-Marie runs the kitchen as if it were a school," Skylar said and smiled at the plump woman who was, as always, bustling about, working upon her dough once again. "The lads work with her an hour or so—and then rot their poor little teeth on the pastries she makes for them."

"It's good that they're out of the mines," he agreed. "That's the lad who was lost in the mines just a bit ago, isn't it?"

"Danny? Aye, that's him."

"May I talk with him for a moment? I can give the boys a hand with their work, if I may..." he inquired.

He stood, striding to the fire where little Danny and another boy, perhaps three or four years older, turned a spit. "If you twist so," Damian explained, hunkering down by the lads to show them how to roll the spit rather than lifting it, "it will be much easier work."

"Thank you, Brother," said the older lad.

"Aye," Brother Damian said, nodding to him.

He tousled Danny's hair, looking at the boy, his expression oddly intent. "You've been fine since the day you were stuck in the mine shaft, eh, lad?"

Danny nodded. "Aye." His eyes were wide, solemn. "The beastie saved me."

Brother Damian smiled. "Well, you were saved. That's what matters."

Danny looked at Brother Damian and said something very softly. He smiled, obviously happy and comfortable in Damian's presence.

She thought that she heard the boy say something more about a beastie.

Damian replied, but Skylar couldn't hear as he lowered his voice, talking to the boy. Damian studied the lad's face, laughed, and curiously, turned the lad about, studying him. Then lifted the boy's hair from his neck once again, studying the hairline at his nape with great intensity.

Unnerved, Skylar stood, afraid that, despite his easy way and gentleness, the friar had some evil designs upon the poor lad.

"Brother Damian, what is it? If something is wrong—" she began.

The old man said something gently to the boy, then stood, turning back to Skylar.

His expression, beneath his thick whiskers, was livid. She noted that his hands were tensed, rolled into tight fists at his sides. Once again, looking at him, she found something quite unnerving about the man, but she couldn't quite put her finger on what it was.

Maybe it was his hands. They were very strong, very powerful hands. Long-fingered, his nails clipped and cleaned.

She should know something about this man, she was certain she saw something in him, in his face. There was something about him that was familiar.

"Brother Damian?"

Where in God's name was Hawk when she needed him?

Damian didn't seem to see Skylar. He didn't seem to see anyone or anything at all, other than whatever vision it was that played in his mind.

"I shall kill her!" he said furiously. "I shall very nearly do the damned deed myself!"

Then, before Skylar could reply, he grabbed both of her hands, his eyes focused on her now. "Skylar," he snapped, dispensing with all formality, "keep the lad here, keep an eye on him, don't let him go off anywhere with anyone, none of the Andersons or the MacGinnises or anyone, do you understand?"

"Brother Damian, I would hardly let a child this age go off alone—"

"Nay, you're not listening! Don't let the boy go anywhere until arrangements have been made for him, do you understand? Don't let his—his father come for him, or any of his sisters, any of the Andersons. Or—or the MacGinnises. It will all make sense, just watch him closely! Swear it!"

The man was a madman, and still—

"Swear it to me, for the love of God!"

"I—I swear!" Skylar said, frightened by the friar's passion yet somehow compelled to give him her promise.

"I will watch the lad, I swear it to you," she said.

He squeezed her hands, then released them.

With a speed and agility most amazing for a man of his age, he turned and left the castle.

She was going to have to find Hawk, that was all there was to it. She would take the boy with her and find her husband down in the crypts.

CHAPTER 19

Alistair MacGinnis seemed exceptionally uneasy in the crypts. "I can't quite imagine what you're looking for down here," he told Hawk.

"I don't know myself," Hawk said. He hesitated. "But there was some commotion down here last night—and I'm certain there's a connection between what happened last night and Sabrina's kidnapping. Besides, on the day that Sabrina disappeared, there was talk of my brother's corpse rising out of its coffin, I've been told. I'm considering having the body exhumed."

"Exhume the body?" Alistair repeated.

"You don't think that doing so might put to rest some of the strange happenings here?" Hawk queried.

Without answering, Alistair pushed open the iron gate to the crypt. He set the lantern upon a hook, then walked to the coffin that bore David Douglas's name. Nervously, he set his hands to the lid. The nails screeched but gave.

Hawk watched him curiously for a moment, then hurried over and helped him. Together, they lifted the lid from the coffin.

"It's..." Alistair began.

"Gone," Hawk concluded flatly. He closed the lid. "Someone has stolen the corpse."

"Hawk!" came a cry as the two men stared at one another. "Hawk!"

Hawk glanced at Alistair. Shawna was coming. They quickly re-covered the coffin.

Shawna burst into the vault.

"Hawk!" she acknowledged, then looked at her cousin, attempting to conceal her surprise to find the two of them together in the crypts. "Alistair!" she said. "What—what are you doing down here—both of you, together?"

"Shawna, you were supposed to be in your room or with Skylar in the kitchen," Hawk said.

"I had to see you," Shawna explained. "I've an idea. About Sabrina."

"What is that?" Hawk queried.

"We've—" She hesitated, glancing at her cousin again. "We've got to look through the cemetery. The Douglas crypts are down here, but the cemetery has many vaults belonging to the individual families. Burial has been very important here in the last hundred years or so. Even the poor families vie to have the most beautiful vaults built. There's a McCloud vault above us, which is exactly where we must start, since it seems that Edwina McCloud and her Wicca practitioners are being blamed for events."

"Shawna—" Hawk began, frowning.

"Hawk, what better place to hide someone than a vault?"

"Dead or alive," Alistair murmured.

"All right. Let's go," Hawk said. He started back for the corridor, then turned to Shawna. "Keys?"

"There's a set in the chapel," she said.

"Let's get them," Hawk said.

As they reached the chapel, Skylar was just coming into it, leading Danny Anderson. The boy was clean, well fed, his ink-dark hair groomed. His wide blue eyes were grave, however, and made him look far older than his few tender years.

"Hawk, I must speak with you," Skylar said.

"Daniel," Shawna said, stooping down to the child's level. "You look very well indeed. Tell me, how is the castle? Are you glad to be here? Is everyone being very good to you?"

He nodded gravely. "I like it very much here. Anne-Marie makes good things to eat."

Shawna laughed. "She does, doesn't she?" She picked up the boy, smiling as she rose. But the others weren't smiling at all.

Skylar was concerned as she talked to her husband.

"There was a very strange old man here who calls himself Brother Damian. He suddenly became overwrought with worry about Daniel. He told me I wasn't to leave the boy for a minute, and then he dashed out of the castle. Hawk, I must admit that my encounter with that unnerving man really frightened me."

"Brother Damian said to watch the boy?" Hawk asked, frowning.

"Brother Damian was there, in the tavern, just before Sabrina disappeared," Shawna said worriedly. "I don't think that the man is what he pretends to be at all. He's always about when there's some trouble. We've forgotten Sabrina! Please, let's hurry and look into the McCloud vault."

"But what about Danny?" Skylar asked.

"Daniel, you don't mind coming on a bit of a hunt with us, do you?" Shawna asked.

"Shawna," Alistair said, "we're going to a mausoleum, and not just that, but how do we know what we're going to find?"

"You're right. The boy shouldn't come," Shawna said.

"I have to look for my sister!" Skylar whispered, pained.

Hawk took Daniel from Shawna's arms. "I'll tell Anne-Marie that she must forget her scones for the evening and take the boy up to her room and lock herself in. Don't start without me," he told the others, "But be ready when I get back."

Hawk took Danny from the chapel, and though he returned quickly, each minute he was gone seemed like an hour.

Alistair slipped a ring of slightly rusting keys from a peg near the altar when he saw Hawk returning. "These should do it," he said.

"Let's go then."

"Wait!" Shawna said.

Hawk, Skylar, and Alistair waited, staring at her expectantly.

"We should go back through the crypt. We'll run into fewer people that way."

"Shawna, it's dusk, nearly completely dark. How many people are you expecting to find in the cemetery?" Skylar asked.

She shook her head. "I don't know, I just think that it's safer if fewer people know what we're up to."

Alistair stared at her hard. She returned the stare. Had Hawk Douglas decided to trust Alistair—or had Alistair just happened upon them?

Shawna didn't know which, but Alistair was, it seemed, a member of their search party now.

"We'll go back through the crypt," Hawk said. He took a lantern and his wife's hand and led the way back down the stairs and through the corridor of the crypt to the stairway leading to the cemetery. Shawna glanced nervously at Alistair as they walked. She was glad that her cousin was with her...

And still slightly afraid.

She should trust Alistair, she taunted herself. She had claimed him innocent often enough to David.

Yet...

She prayed he was innocent. Because she loved him.

Darkness was falling, but the moon, which was very nearly full, rode high in the heavens, casting eerie shadows upon the faces of cherubs and seraphs that had been carved into the gravestones. Sculpted angels cast strange forms upon the earth. Larger, bulkier, even more mysterious shadows were created by the vaults of the dead. The vaults themselves, though eerie in the moonlight, were handsome exhibits of architecture, many of them built in Greek or Roman fashion, with fine white columns and meticulous scrollwork.

The cemetery faced the northwest, toward the dense forest there. As it happened, or perhaps by some ancient design, it was tucked away in the corner of the property, and here now in the moonlight, it was difficult to believe that not more than several hundred yards around the stone base of Castle Rock was the grand entrance to the great hall of the castle.

The air was crisp and cool. A ground fog was rising, adding to the ghostly feel of the shadows that fell upon the ground from angels and archangels. Their footsteps, even against the grass, seemed loud in the night. No sounds from elsewhere seemed to penetrate into the moonlit haze of the cemetery.

"McCloud, there it is, just ahead," Shawna advised, seeing the family name in large, sculpted letters atop one of the mausoleums that stood before them. Her voice seemed loud in the night.

Hawk strode ahead to the vault, walking up the three steps that led to the heavy door at the entry. The others followed just slightly behind him, watching as he went through the keys. "Is there any way to identify the proper key?" he queried, looking back at Shawna.

"Rainor—the undertaker from the village—knows them all. I'm afraid I don't."

"We are at a Douglas holding," Alistair reminded him. He shrugged. "I've no idea which key."

"It's trial and error," Shawna apologized.

Hawk nodded and tried a key in the lock. He went on to a second key, and a third. The hardwood door to the vault groaned open.

Yet, even as it did so, Hawk suddenly spun around, hearing something Shawna had not heard. He cried out a sharp warning to them all.

"Down!" he thundered.

He fell atop his own wife, pressing them both to the earth. Shawna heard Alistair swear. Then, to his credit, her cousin cast his own body atop hers, bearing them both to the earth. A clump of mud flew up against her just as a hail of bullets went crashing through the cemetery, ricocheting off stone tombs, angels, and death's-heads.

"Sweet Jesus!" Hawk muttered, his head just above a tombstone.

"Someone is shooting at us—in the cemetery!" Alistair said incredulously.

"Do you see anyone?" Hawk called.

It seemed that the fog had rolled in more thickly the very second Hawk spoke. A field of clouds seemed to lie on the ground where they had fallen for protection.

It surely did offer them protection from the bullets. But it blinded them as well.

"Shawna, Alistair...creep this way. Down on the ground, snakelike. Get into the vault!" Hawk commanded.

"Go!" Alistair urged Shawna.

"But you—"

"I'm right behind you. Go!"

Shawna instantly obeyed. Old, broken headstones clawed at her clothing, blades of grass tickled her nose. She all but tasted the mud of the earth. She heard Alistair inching along right behind her.

She stopped, cringing, as the sound of a bullet bouncing off stone just beside her rang loudly in the night. A shadow loomed huge above her as Hawk stood—just long enough to return a barrage of fire from a gun he had apparently been carrying discreetly.

"Get in the vault, all of you!" Hawk commanded, falling back to the earth again, behind a large headstone.

Shawna saw Skylar rise to a crouching position and run up the three steps and slip into the vault just ahead of another round of bullets that came crashing into the masonry and shrubs that surrounded them. Shawna lifted her head just in time to see a creature in a cowled cloak slip behind the vault far to their left.

"My god!" she breathed, incredulous. "To our left!" she cried to Hawk.

"Will both of you get in there!" he cried back. She realized that he was reloading his gun. "Now!" he said, and she saw him rise, now firing with rapid precision in the direction she had pointed him.

"Shawna, go, get in the vault," Alistair hissed.

"Alistair, did you see—"

"I saw."

"Who—"

"Up, cousin, now, quick!" Alistair urged her. He drew her to her feet. A bullet crashed into stone right by her head as she dashed into the McCloud burial vault, Alistair right at her back, pressing her forward all the way.

"Down here!" Skylar whispered, slipping her arms around Shawna and bringing her down to hunch low just behind the heavy wooden door.

Hawk fired rapidly then, rising as he did so, backing his way toward the vault. He slipped through the doorway which they'd kept ajar for his entry. He leaned against the cold stone of the vault then, inhaling deeply. "There are at least three of them."

"Them—who?" Shawna gasped.

"Your cloaked figures." Hawk looked down at them in the shadowy darkness. "There's no other way in here—and no way out—other than this door?"

Shawna shook her head. "There's another room to our left, but no other way in, no other way out."

On the ground, she crept closer to where he stood just inside the doorway, carefully trying to look out. She covered her ears and leaned flat against the stone as the firing started up from outside once again, bullet after bullet grazing off or plowing into the mausoleum.

"They're trying to make me return fire, run out of ammunition," Hawk said.

"Will you—run out soon?" Shawna asked.

"I have a couple more rounds on me, but...well, we could use some help down here..." he murmured. Bullets crashed into the stone again. Hawk angled out the door, taking careful aim. He fired, then leaned back against the stone as more bullets came flying their way.

"I've got my dirk, if they come close," Alistair said.

"Eventually, they'll have to come—here," Hawk said.

"I don't think they know that we're all in here yet," Shawna said. "The fog is so thick...they were surely as blinded as we were."

"As we are!" Alistair said.

Once again, Hawk inched nearer the door. To their left were another three family vaults. A number of hemlocks grew in the area, and stone sarcophagi littered the earth along with angels, archangels, and more.

Then, for a moment, framed in the moonlight, was one of the cowled figures. The hood was low over its face.

A cloaked figure, its features hidden by the fall of its cowl. A figure, just like those figures she had seen in her dream.

Calling her name.

Coming for her...

"There!" she cried to Hawk.

He took aim. A cloud inched over the moon. Hawk fired and fired again.

His bullets, like the others, ricocheted in the night.

Yet, against that sound, Shawna was certain that she heard another. Pounding. A pounding against the earth.

She stood carefully, gripping Hawk's arm. "Someone is coming."

Someone was coming...

Friend or foe?

Three horses thundered into the graveyard.

Guns blazed.

One horse reared directly in front of the vault as its rider—easily recognizable to Shawna—fired off a gun from its back toward the mysterious cowled figures who had been firing at the group in the tomb.

Shawna gasped, falling back where Skylar was crouched down by her husband's feet.

"It's Brother Damian!"

"My god, is he going to help us or kill us?" Skylar demanded.

"Help us—I think," Shawna said.

"He's not alone," Alistair warned quickly.

"Aye, there are two more riders with him. I don't know either," Shawna said.

Gunfire sounded, then ceased entirely. The riders went galloping over stones and angels alike in pursuit of the cloaked figures.

Skylar called out to Hawk, "What's happening?"

"Rescue," he said flatly.

"I'd say quite in the nick of time," Alistair murmured.

"But what is going on, Hawk?" Shawna asked.

"Our rescuers have gone in search of our attackers. I think we're safe to stand now."

The riders returned. Evidently, the cloaked figures had managed to disappear into the darkness afforded as the moon once again made a fickle disappearance behind a cloud.

"None of them!" a voice muttered with furious disgust. "Every last one of them managed to disappear right into thin air!"

The horses with their three riders came to a halt in front of the McCloud vault.

Brother Damian was off his horse, hurrying up the steps toward them, moving furiously and swiftly for such an old man. He was quickly followed by a slim little man with a face so ugly it was endearing. Behind him came a very tall, straight, lithe but well-muscled man, wearing a railway frock coat over blue denim breeches and white cotton shirt, a plumed slouch hat sitting at a rakish angle atop his head.

Shawna tensed, wondering what designs this trio might have upon them. She gritted down on her teeth and studied the curious Brother Damian, yet she was startled from her observations when Hawk murmured a pleased, "Sloan! I will be damned. Sloan!"

Hawk strode from the vault, laughing as he embraced the tall, lithe newcomer with ebony dark hair, sharp handsome features, and mahogany eyes.

Shawna stared in stunned amazement at the two. Her nightmares had entered into the realm of life tonight. She'd dreamed of savages arriving en masse to do her in for her part in the "death" of David Douglas.

All this fellow needed was a bow and arrow.

"My god. Another...Indian!" Shawna murmured.

"Another half-breed," Skylar said quickly. "He's a friend, a dear, good friend!" she explained happily, and followed her husband out to embrace the stranger, kissing his cheeks as he enveloped her in a hug.

Apparently, Shawna reflected dryly, staring at her cousin who returned her wry assessment, the newcomers did not seek to kill them.

"Shall we find out what's happening?" Alistair suggested.

"Definitely," Shawna agreed.

She ventured out, Alistair directly behind her. The small, slim man —with features so wrinkled that he had a troll's look about him— smiled. It was a nice smile. Shawna smiled back.

"When did you arrive?" Hawk was asking the half-breed Indian newcomer.

"Not thirty minutes ago." He appeared quite tense and worried. "We arrived to discover that there was, indeed, trouble here. This good fellow here is Mr. James McGregor, bearer of the ring sent to you previously and very anxious, when he made my acquaintance back in Gold Town, to find out about you. I had assured him you had left for

Craig Rock, and his story was so intriguing, I determined that I must accompany him here."

"Sloan, what a very good friend you are!" Skylar said. "It's so good to see you."

"And your timing was impeccable," Hawk assured him. He then turned to Brother Damian.

"How did you know to come here?"

"I didn't know. We heard the commotion," Brother Damian said. Except that there was no longer a pleasant Irish lilt to his voice.

It was a different voice.

David's voice—deep and husky and all Scottish.

Shawna gasped, realizing that he had deceived her all along. He had gone about by day, spying on them all. Not just in the passageways of the castle, but wherever he chose to be, walking among them all. His deception had been complete. She'd not recognized him in any way, shape, or form. He had been at the tavern, drawing her out. She was furious that he had deceived her so easily.

Apparently, he had deceived others, too.

"My god! David!" Skylar gasped. "Why didn't you just tell me who—"

"The disguise was important, Skylar. I didn't know who in the household I dared trust. It's been the only way I can move around by light of day. Skylar, where is the boy?"

"Danny?" Skylar gasped. "He is with Anne-Marie. I pray God that—"

"I pray God as well, but I do believe that Anne-Marie is innocent of any wrongdoing."

"I gave him over to her," Hawk said. "We couldn't bring him here."

Skylar continued to stare at David. "I thought I was insane, wondering what it was about you that was so familiar. Now I know. Douglas eyes! I feel like a fool for not having recognized your eyes immediately."

His eyes! Shawna thought. Aye, she should have recognized the eyes herself.

But she had not.

"The disguise was necessary," David said.

Indeed, Shawna thought.

Necessary.

Against all of them.

He had donned his disguise not just to watch her kin, she thought, but to watch her as well. Her anger grew.

She longed to fly at him and tear his fake whiskers off one by one. She struggled for control.

David had yet to glance her way.

"I left the castle to discover that James and Sloan had arrived. We heard gunshots and decided a show of force on horseback might serve us all well. It seemed that there was some fair firepower coming against you."

"Aye, that there was," Alistair said, surveying the three who had just arrived. "You all—know one another?" he said politely.

David grinned ruefully. "Aye, that we do, Alistair. Good Mr. McGregor here has been with me on my— journeys—I shall say. And I have known Sloan a very long time. He grew up in the same camp as my brother. Sloan, James—Alistair MacGinnis. And, of course..."

At last, he turned to Shawna. He'd been very aware of her presence, she was certain.

"And of course...Lady Shawna MacGinnis."

His voice seemed a combination of ice and fire as he said her name. His eyes fell on her in such a way that she felt as if she had been physically attacked.

Aye, it was true that he was so well costumed he had fooled even those who knew him best.

But something else had changed. Completely. He did not just seem angry. He seemed to loathe her. With an anger red-hot enough to kill one second, and cold enough to freeze the very air around them the next.

She was the one who had the right to be angry! She had been deceived.

But she smiled graciously at James McGregor, aware that he was the Dr. James McGregor who had helped David survive his captivity. She smiled equally graciously to Sloan Trelawny. "Indeed, it's a pleasure to meet you both. As Hawk has said, your timing is quite impeccable. I assure you, we're most grateful to have you among us."

"The pleasure is mine, Lady MacGinnis," Sloan Trelawny said, bowing his head to her, nodding in acknowledgment to Alistair. He was a very handsome man, white and Indian features combining to create an exceptionally arresting face, his collar-length hair dead straight and almost blue-black, his features especially well shaped and defined. Though it was obvious that he was quite tense and concerned about the situation, his quick smile was charming. His eyes, however, had a sharpness about them, and Shawna was certain that as an enemy, he would be quick and deadly.

"Aye, it's a pleasure to be here, except that we didna catch a one of them black-clad creatures. By God alive, what does go on here?" McGregor demanded, staring at David, then at Shawna.

David's eyes burned into her then as well.

Everyone, she realized, stared at her.

"What does go on? The mystery grows greater by the day," David said. "We've more than one enemy. There seem to be a number of people in those strange black cloaks seeking to commit murder. It's a very strange place, wouldn't you say—Lady MacGinnis?"

"It has become strange lately," she agreed. "In fact..." she began, then broke off, frowning, staring from Alistair to David.

"Alistair, you're not at all surprised to see that David Douglas is alive behind the deceptive brown wool of a friar's garb."

"We met in the mines," Alistair said.

"Oh? Recently?" Shawna inquired, staring at David.

He had chosen not to tell her much at all. Although he'd demanded her complete silence, he'd given nothing in return.

"Aye, recently," David said coldly.

Alistair stepped closer to Shawna and said in a reproachful whisper, "You kept a secret from the closest of your kin."

She ignored him. David was still staring at her coldly.

"Apparently, someone did not want you coming here," David said.

"You came to look for Sabrina. Have you found any trace of her?" Sloan asked, his dark eyes on Shawna.

Shawna gasped. In the midst of the gunfire and her shock regarding David's deception, she had forgotten all about Sabrina.

She spun around swiftly and hurried back into the McCloud vault. Sabrina.

Time could mean so much.

In many ways, the vault was a smaller version of the crypts within the castle, filled with shrouded bones and more modern coffins, and even drawers that were closed over with marble and mortar. Small openings lined the very top of the vault for ventilation for the living who visited the dead. Those openings allowed for just a trickle of fresh air and moonlight.

As she tore into the second room, barely lit by the moonlight, Shawna paused at first, aware only of the death that filled the room. Fear cast a clammy hand upon her. Dust lay heavy on the floor. Spiderwebs met and melded to keep the gray shadows of the vault as eerie as they might be.

Shawna swallowed hard and hurried through a maze of coffins upon the floor. She finally reached the far end of the vault's second room.

She stood dead still and let out a cry.

She had found Sabrina.

CHAPTER 20

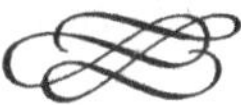

Bound hand and foot and gagged, Sabrina had been left lying on one of the burial shelves. Shawna's cry alerted the others. David was the first to reach her, slipping the gag, and carrying Sabrina quickly out of the mausoleum and into the moonlight. With his burden in bis arms, he knelt down just before the steps, the others gathering around him.

"Is she alive?" Sloan demanded hoarsely.

"My poor sister!" Skylar cried, cheeks damp with tears of hope. "Does she live? Is she injured?"

"Does she breathe?" Shawna whispered.

"Aye, she breathes, she lives, I can feel her heartbeat," David said. Sloan slipped a knife from a sheath at his calf to slice through the ropes that bound her hands and feet. Though she breathed, Sabrina's eyes remained closed.

"Sabrina? Sabrina, it's Skylar!" her sister said softly. "You're going to be all right now. We have you. No one is going to hurt you."

Sabrina's lashes fluttered. Her eyes, which looked unfocused, finally settled upon Shawna and opened wide with incredulity. "Shawna, you all have found me. Oh, thank God! I've been tied up in that wretched vault forever. I tried kicking the walls, shifting along the floor, screaming through that horrible gag...no one heard me! I'm so mad, I could scratch the eyes out of those terrible people. Oh, Shawna, now you will be in so much danger! They will come for you. They will come for you."

"Sabrina, who will come for me?" Shawna demanded.

Sabrina saw David then in his Brother Damian attire. She started to recoil from him, alarmed at the sight of the man who held her. "My god—"

"Sabrina, it's me, David."

"David!" she repeated, dazed. She seemed to lose her train of thought then. "They will come..."

"Sabrina, how did you get here? Who did this to you?" David demanded.

"I could really use some water!" she said. And her lashes fluttered and fell.

"Oh my god!" Skylar breathed, but Sloan was holding Sabrina's wrist, feeling her pulse. His eyes were focused very intently upon Sabrina, but he spoke reassuringly to Skylar, whom he seemed to regard with affection.

"She's all right, Skylar," he said. "As she said, she just needs some water and some food. You know your sister. She's going to be tearing mad and ready to fight as soon as she's moved her muscles a bit. She's going to be fine."

Shawna's gaze fell from Sloan as she became acutely aware of David staring at her again, for as she knelt by his side as he held Sabrina, she was but inches from his face. She met his eyes again and nearly recoiled at the searing emotion within them. She rose quickly to her feet, shaking both from Sabrina's strange graveyard warning and the look David had cast upon her.

David was rising. "We need to get her back to the castle. Hawk, I think it will be best if one of you bring her on a horse, as I intend to remain Brother Damian a while longer."

"Alistair," Shawna asked, "can you go to the village and bring Edwina?"

"We don't need Edwina," David said. "James—"

"Please! I want Edwina to see her," Shawna insisted. In his present mood, she was afraid he would refuse her.

"Fine, Alistair, if you will go for Edwina. Edwina," he explained for the benefit of the newcomers, hesitating only a minute, "is a healer. She'll have something to make Sabrina feel better right away."

"Aye, I can go for her right away," Alistair said.

Hawk was already mounted and reaching down to David. "I'll take Sabrina."

David gently handed Sabrina to him. "Skylar, come up behind me. She'll need you." Skylar did as directed.

James McGregor mounted his horse to follow behind Hawk. They rode quickly out of the cemetery toward the front entrance of the castle.

"I'll get going too, then," Alistair said.

"Take my horse," Sloan told Alistair.

Alistair nodded his agreement and mounted Sloan's horse. Sloan approached Alistair once he was mounted and said, "Perhaps you should take my gun as well."

"Perhaps I should," Alistair agreed, sliding the revolver offered to him into the saddle holster. "Thanks," Alistair said, nodding briefly, and nudging his horse into flight.

Sloan stared at the castle, then looked at David. "Naturally, David, I've quite a clear idea of what occurred in the past, since James McGregor had the whole of an ocean voyage to tell me about your days as convicts together. He worships the ground you walk on, by the by. Says you saved his life when a sadistic guard was about to beat him to death."

David shrugged. "Few men could watch such an injustice without becoming involved," he said.

"By God, David, it's indeed good to see you alive, but what is going on here? How did Sabrina end up in such trouble?"

"Perhaps my Lady MacGinnis could best answer that question."

Shawna stared at David, wondering what could have caused his furious mood toward her. She looked at Sloan. "Sabrina seems to have got caught up in whatever evil scheme is being carried out here. People dressed in hooded black cloaks are trying to kill other people, and that is all that I know. Perhaps David is much more aware of what is happening than I am. Especially since he himself is so very good at deceiving people."

"Perhaps we'd best hurry back to the castle," David said, "and learn what we can from Sabrina. Shawna, keep ahead of us, so we can watch your back."

Shawna stepped ahead of the men, walking quickly. Fog still misted near the ground, but the moon rode very high and clear as they made their way from the cemetery, stepping around old and new stones, tall ones, broken ones, and all manner of funerary art. The brick entry loomed before them and, just around the corner from it, the chapel entry into the castle, closed and gated unless the chapel was in use. The main gates remained far around the curve of the stone edifice.

"How is it that you've managed to come here?" David asked Sloan as they walked just slightly behind Shawna. "I understand that the situation in the Dakota Territory is far more grave than ever."

"Yes, it is that, and it grows worse, more and more of the whites determining that 'the only good Indian is a dead one.' And many of the commanders who favored crushing tactics during the war are making decisions in the West."

"Sherman?"

"Alive and well and ruthless as ever."

"But you remain in the cavalry?"

"I've taken a leave. I served through the war, and I've kept my commission since, and I've done what I can no matter what hotheaded politicians around me do or decree as policy. But now I believe I fight a losing battle. I have until January to return."

"Again, I say it's good to see you. I'm grateful, Sloan, that you have come. I think our numbers might matter greatly in this strange battle we're fighting here."

"A blood brother is a brother among the Sioux," Sloan said. "And if I recall, you were with us often enough against the Crow—and before that, during the war."

David nodded, moving closer to Shawna and brusquely slipping his arm around her waist. "We should move more quickly. We've no cover beyond the tombstones in the cemetery, and these cloaked figures seem to rise from sheer earth." His pace was brisk as he urged them along.

"Who are they? What are they, David?" Sloan asked.

"The villagers suggest the mysterious happenings here are caused by the witches of Craig Rock," David said quietly.

"The villagers are wrong. Edwina would never have hurt Sabrina in any way," Shawna insisted. "I would trust Edwina with my life far more quickly than I would trust your tavern drunks!" She met David's eyes in the moonlight. They remained so sharp, cold, and distant! His hold upon her felt like a grip of steel fingers. What had happened? She felt lost and betrayed. He had said that he'd loved her.

But he'd never really trusted her.

And now...

Something had happened that had made him angry with her all over again. What?

They reached the main entry to the castle and entered the great hall. Hawk awaited them near the door. "I've taken Sabrina to her room. Skylar is with her."

"Good," David said quietly. "Let's join them there."

Sabrina lay on the bed, her muddied gown replaced by a soft, angelic-looking nightdress. Her face had been bathed, her hair brushed. Skylar sat by Sabrina's side, and Sabrina was sipping warm soup from an oversize cup.

Shawna came around to the other side of the bed.

"Sabrina, how are you?" Shawna asked her.

"Incredibly angry—with those awful people and myself! I let them get me. I'm quite fine, Skylar needn't be fussing over me the way she is—I do have one hell of a headache. My bones ache. I'm in pain and—" she broke off, seeing Sloan where he stood next to Hawk and David. All the color that had come back into her face deserted her.

"Sloan!" she gasped.

"Yes, it's me," Sloan said.

Sabrina struggled for composure. "Major Trelawny, how in God's name are you here?"

"Ocean voyage," Sloan said briefly. "Which doesn't matter at all now. Sabrina, you need to tell us what happened,"

She didn't seem to hear him. She kept staring at him, remaining very pale.

"Sabrina?" Skylar said worriedly.

Sabrina forced her gaze from Sloan and looked at her sister. "They attacked me." She looked back to Sloan nervously. "I don't understand! How can you be here?"

After he explained, he added softly, "Sabrina, we need to know what happened to you."

She still stared at him, as if he were a ghost.

"Sabrina!" Shawna said. "Please, we need your help. People in those cloaks have attacked us several times now. They were shooting at us in the cemetery when we were searching for you. We need to see that 'they' don't come back for anyone. Who are 'they,' Sabrina?"

"The people in the cloaks," Sabrina repeated.

"Aye, but—"

Sabrina seemed to regain her wits. "Shawna, don't you think I'd say something if I knew who had done this? I was terrified and furious. They were going to kill me, I'm quite certain. It was terrible, waking up trussed like a hog in that awful vault...I'd like to see them hanged. But I didn't see anything at all. Except a white handkerchief coming at me and two—maybe three—people in cloaks."

"Where were you taken from?" David demanded.

Sabrina frowned. "I—I don't remember."

"From the castle?" David persisted.

Again, she caught sight of Sloan watching her. She focused her gaze on Shawna. "I—remember. I thought I heard a child crying. I followed the sound to the chapel—and then out the chapel door to the cemetery. That's—that's where they got me."

"Do you remember anything else at all?" David queried her gently.

Sabrina shook her head. "Maybe a few snatches of whispered conversation, but I'm not even sure it was real."

"What was said?" Shawna prompted her.

Sabrina arched a brow. "They said things like, 'Death will come for the innocents, the innocents feed the earth.' And..."

"What else?" Shawna prompted.

"I think that someone kept saying that I wasn't really who they wanted, but perhaps I would have to do. They—they wanted—you, Shawna. You have escaped death so far. This all sounds so ridiculous, but it seemed that one of them was saying that you have changed the destiny death requires, and the gods of the underworld will come for you."

"What nonsense!" Sloan said.

"It's what I heard!" Sabrina declared defensively.

"I didn't mean that you spoke nonsense, Sabrina," Sloan told her with a sigh of impatience. "This whole thing seems to be based on some pathetic, dangerous nonsense!"

"I agree," David murmured.

Someone was tapping on the door. Hawk opened it carefully. Edwina was there. She came hurrying in, an embroidered bag of her ointments and herbs at her side.

"Sabrina, lass. Thank God. You're all right."

She took Shawna's place beside Sabrina, touching her forehead, studying her intently.

"I'm really fine. This fuss isn't necessary."

"Everyone should be fussed over now and then," Edwina told her.

"Her wrists and ankles are chafed where she was tied," David said, the Irish lilt in his voice.

"I've ointments, Brother Damian. They'll heal her almost overnight," she promised.

Gawain and Alistair stood in the doorway. Gawain entered the room to come behind Edwina, silently setting a supporting hand upon her shoulder.

"Pour me a glass of water for her, please," Edwina said. Gawain did as she requested. Edwina added a vial of herbs from the bag to the water and bade Sabrina drink it. "It's a restorative," she assured Sabrina. "There's lemon rind, chamomile, and more of the like. It will help your aches and pains. This"—she produced a little jar—"is for your wrists and ankles." She stood, smiling at Sabrina. "You are a very strong young woman." She leaned close to Sabrina, speaking for her ears alone, except that from where she stood, Shawna heard her as well. "The sweet wee breed inside you fares well, you needn't fear."

Sabrina stared at her without blinking, and Edwina turned to the others. "The patient was healing fine without me, and I'll leave you all now to your private discussions," she said. "Gawain, will you offer me a sherry?"

"With the greatest pleasure!" Gawain assured her. "Brother Damian, will you join us?"

David seemed startled, at last taken by surprise himself. "Shortly, and I thank you for the invitation."

"I'm going to go have a drink. A huge one," Alistair said. He cleared his throat, "Hawk, your friend, Mr. McGregor, is downstairs. I'll see if he'd like a drink with me. A huge one."

Gawain, Alistair, and Edwina departed the room. David closed the door behind them.

"With Sabrina safe now, and nothing we can do about her kidnapping for the time, we've another bit of business to settle—Shawna," David said.

His voice again seemed laced with that underlying, barely leashed anger she had been hearing all night. A feeling of dread welled within her, but she couldn't begin to imagine what could cause such a rise of antagonism from him.

Even his brother seemed uncomfortable at the sound of his voice.

"Perhaps you two would like to find some privacy—"

"Nay, Hawk, this is a family affair we will discuss, and I can use your assistance—and eyesight—to assure me that I've not lost my mind."

"Perhaps I should join Alistair and James for a drink," Sloan suggested.

"Sloan, you knew my father as well as any man," David told him. "And as I said, it is a family affair. Blood brothers are the same to the Sioux. Naturally, Skylar, you are invited to stay as well."

"Well," Sabrina murmured, "it doesn't seem that I can leave."

"What in God's name—" Shawna started to demand.

"Indeed, what in God's name, my lady," he said furiously. "If you will all be so good as to allow me a moment's indulgence..."

They all stared blankly at him. David stepped out into the hall.

"Hawk, what is the matter with him now?" Shawna asked anxiously.

"Truly, Shawna, I don't know," Hawk said.

David returned then before anyone could say more, carrying the sleeping lad, Daniel. His eyes, when they touched Shawna's, were as cold as green ice.

Whatever he was going to say, she was suddenly glad of the others. She had never seen him quite like this, not even the night she had learned that he had returned.

"My lady, tell me now, you know no more about what happened the night of the Fire than what you have told me.

"What is this new accusation?" she demanded furiously. "I swear to you, there is nothing more—"

She broke off, her voice trailing away as he ignored her to take a hand and shift the ink-black curls from the neck of the sleeping youngster on the bed.

"Hawk, Sloan, if you please, take a look at this child for me?" David requested icily.

The two men walked curiously by Shawna.

Hawk and Sloan then both stared at David, startled.

"Damn you all!" Shawna cried. She had endured a great deal. Once upon a time, she had believed that she was a strong woman. But between the murderous cloaked men, Sabrina's kidnapping and rescue, and David's behavior, it was suddenly far too much. "Damn you all!" she repeated with soft vehemence. "What in God's name is it?"

"The boy is—" Hawk began.

"See," Sloan said gently, pointing to the hairline at the boy's nape where the hair grew in a peculiar pattern and a tiny half-moon of hair edged over that line in a small but distinct crescent shape.

"I don't know what you're saying," Shawna protested. "I've never seen such a mark. If it's a Douglas mark—David has no such mark."

Staring at her, Hawk lifted his thick black hair, twisting slightly so that she could see the crescent shape at his nape.

Skylar Douglas gasped, so stunned that indiscreet words tore from her lips. "Hawk, you told me that you'd never slept with Shawna!"

"Oh god!" Shawna breathed.

"And thank you, wife, for that vote of confidence!" Hawk returned, indignant and aggravated.

"The child is mine," David stated. "I've no such peculiar pattern of hair growth myself, but my father had it, and it often appears in the Douglas family." Staring at Danny in shock, Shawna suddenly felt the icy green fire of David's eyes burning into her again. "Lady MacGinnis knew nothing more of what happened that night, yet she bore my child and turned the babe over to the most wretched pair in all of Craig Rock to be raised among their brood!"

Indeed, the night had brought with it far too much.

Shawna was dimly aware of his murderous gaze, then no more. She fell to the floor in a dead faint.

Images whirled through her sleep. At first, she ran. Ran through wave after wave of thick, swirling ground fog. Cloaked figures chased her. Then they disappeared, and the images that haunted her were far worse, cutting through her like a knife.

She was in the small room she had taken at the Tudor-style tavern at Glasgow. She had left Craig Rock to be on her own, to decide how she would handle her life once her babe arrived.

The first pain hit her just at dawn. She refused to acknowledge it because it was more than a month too soon for the babe to arrive.

For hours, she had labored on her own. Then, miraculously, the midwife appeared.

And for hours more she had labored. The pain had been intense, and through it all, she had prayed for the child. To ease the pain, she fought again the constant battles in her mind. What to do? She didn't want to go back home because David had died there in the fire at the stables.

She carried the Douglas heir, and he was about to enter the world, but she'd never wed David Douglas, and in all the time that had passed since David had died, she hadn't decided whether to tell his father about the child. She didn't want him to think that she wanted anything from the Douglases, but by the same token, she didn't want to deny him David's child either.

Day turned into night.

In the end, it didn't matter. Because she'd gone into labor far too early.

Her pain was incredible, and still the babe didn't come. The midwife urged her to drink a painkilling brew, and she accepted it.

That was all she could remember until she awoke from a deep sleep to discover that it was daylight. The midwife told her that the child had been stillborn.

The gentle old woman told her, "Lass, there's no help for it, the wee bairn didna have the proper time for birthin', and there was nothing anyone could do."

Her poor wee bairn was dead. She fought against the exhaustion and pain that seized her. A misshapen bundle was placed in her arms, and she wept. She tried to look at it, but the midwife took it away again, telling her that the babe was a pile of deformed blood and bones.

All of David was now lost to her. In the end, in the only way that she could have done something for him, she had betrayed him. She had let his child die as well. She was disconsolate. Ready to die herself. But when she hadn't died, and her family had come...

Her child hadn't died! Her child was here. Danny, oh, aye, the boy looked like a MacGinnis, for he was a MacGinnis, her child, and some terrible, cruel prank had been played upon her by someone who had attempted to kill David and attempted to kill her.

And now...

David would kill her himself.

She opened her eyes, lost, disoriented. A fire crackled. She felt the clean smoothness of sheets beneath her. Her mouth was so dry.

She tried to focus, but she couldn't quite do so. She had been laid on a bed. Her purple riding habit loosened from her throat to her breast. She was in Sabrina Connor's bed, she realized, and Sabrina, looking very well in her anxiety regarding Shawna, was curled upon her knees at her side. Shawna's head was still spinning. The room seemed to lie in shadowy darkness, except for the two of them. She was grateful to be alone with Sabrina.

"Sabrina, it can't be, oh god..."

"Shush, it's all right..."

"Oh god, Sabrina—"

"It's all right, it's all right. I'm here. You're safe."

"Oh god!" she gasped, grasping Sabrina's sleeves. She had to get a grip upon herself, her emotions, but she couldn't. She felt hysteria rising within her.

"It can't be...it can't be. Oh, Sabrina, don't let terrible things happen to you. Tell everyone about your child. Oh! The father is an Indian, that's what Edwina meant, isn't it? 'A breed bairn.' Oh! Oh god, Sabrina, is it Hawk's babe?"

"What?" cried a voice from across the room.

It was Skylar.

With dismay, Shawna realized that she wasn't alone with Sabrina Connor. Sabrina stared down at her with stunned dismay as her sister, along with Hawk and Sloan, came forward to stand at the foot of the bed.

"Sweet Jesus, Hawk!" Skylar gasped.

Hawk's glance toward his wife was one of fury. "Skylar, what in God's name has come over you? I guarantee you that your sister's child is not mine!" Hawk sounded deeply offended.

"Of course not!" Sabrina gasped out, still staring down at Shawna.

"But, Sabrina," Skylar said quietly, "you didn't say a word to me. Are you—expecting a child?"

Sabrina hesitated, staring at Shawna.

"I thought we were alone!" Shawna mouthed softly. "I'm so sorry—"

"I know," Sabrina returned. "I doubt if it matters. David was in the tavern the day Edwina spoke to me about the babe. And they're all blood brothers," she added bitterly. "Especially now, he would have felt compelled to tell my brother-in-law eventually."

"Sabrina, I don't understand why you couldn't tell me," Skylar admonished softly. "And if the child is of blood, and it's not Hawk's—"

Sabrina tensed, not turning around, continuing to stare down at Shawna.

"Quite obviously," Sloan Trelawny drawled from the foot of the bed, "the child is mine."

"Oh god!" Skylar gasped. "Sloan, you needn't take responsibility if there's some mistake—"

"The child is mine," he repeated.

And it was true, Shawna knew. She saw it in Sabrina's eyes as she kept them glued to her own.

"Oh, Sabrina, I'm so, so sorry—" Shawna began again because there was another presence in the room, one she had so nearly forgotten...

David.

Whiskerless and clad in black denim pants and a black, full-sleeved cotton shirt, David came to stand by her side. He swept her up into his arms despite the wave of dread that filled her and her protesting hand upon his chest.

"It seems to me the time has come for private discussions," he said. "A little late, perhaps, since we've managed to give away the secrets of others and nearly destroy my brother's marriage."

"I asked for no audience—" Shawna began.

"I needed my brother and Sloan. For other than the lad's curious crescent-shaped hairline, he is all MacGinnis, and I had to make you realize the fact that he is a Douglas cannot be denied. But now...I think we should all fight our battles out alone. Sloan, Sabrina, Hawk, Skylar, forgive us, and excuse us."

She pushed against him as they exited the room and headed down the hallway and up the stairs for her tower abode. "Laird Douglas, I'm delighted that your intelligent, reasonable brother has met a kind and gentle lass and entered into what appears to be a tender and loving relationship, something with which you are entirely unfamiliar."

"Circumstances—lass."

"I'd not destroy his marriage, and I'd never purposely hurt Sabrina—"

"You'd only destroy the life of your own child to honor the MacGinnis name?"

"Nay!" she cried. "I didn't know, I swear to you, I didn't know."

"Do you deny that the boy is ours?"

"No...I don't know. It can't be—except that the lad is...oh god, where is he?" Shawna demanded.

"I've seen to him."

"You've seen to him? I must see him. David, you tell me that the child is mine, but you don't let me see him? David, tell me, where is—Danny?" she demanded in a pained whisper.

The expression on his handsome face was exceptionally hard. "Safe," he told her.

"Safe—where?"

He leaned toward her. "Safe—away from all who bear the name MacGinnis."

CHAPTER 21

Tears flooded Shawna's eyes. She willed them back, furiously blinking. They reached her tower room. He closed and bolted the door before setting her upon the foot of her bed.

Her child lived. All these years, she had been denied the babe. The crudest jest of all time had been played upon her, and now she was being asked to pay for the game!

"David, you don't understand. You had no right to take the boy!" she cried to him.

"You've had him for four years. You've not exactly given him great maternal care—"

Shawna leaped to her feet. "I didn't know! I still don't know, I can't believe...I—"

"You didn't know that you gave birth to a child?" he demanded hotly.

She shook her head. "I—"

"You ask me to believe that?" he demanded incredulously.

"Damn you, if Danny is our child, how could you take him away?" Shawna cried. She suddenly found herself up and running across the floor to him, slamming her fists against his chest.

He caught her wrists. She was sorry for her violence, sorry that she had touched him. His fingers wound around her upper arms, he lifted her, eyes burning into her, until he had retraced her path from the bed. He dropped her there, pinning her down as he leaned over her.

"You've no right to that child."

"Damn you, David, I didn't know!"

"How couldn't you know? You had to know that you were pregnant for a child to come so far!"

"I knew that I was expecting...aye! But I ran away to Glasgow to be away from everyone because I didn't know what had happened that night. And I didn't know what I was going to do after, I was just waiting for the babe...but he came early. I—I was in horrible pain, and the midwife gave me something to drink for it. When I came to, the midwife told me the babe had died. And she handed me a blood-soaked bundle, and she suggested that I look and...."

David suddenly pushed away from her, running his fingers raggedly through his hair. He walked away from her, then spun back to her.

"I told you to tell me everything! What more have you lied to me about?"

"I haven't lied to you!"

"Omitting the birth of a child is strangely akin to a lie, as I see it!"

Shawna eased up from the bed once again. "There was no reason to tell you, I tried...I tried to let you know that I certainly suffered from the consequences of that night, but then, it didn't make much sense to tell you that we'd had a child who had died without ever drawing breath."

"And when you saw Danny, it never occurred to you that he might be your own?"

"I was handed a dead baby!" Shawna cried. "I held what I thought was my own dead babe in my arms! The poor, misshapen soul was taken away, buried in the earth in a Glasgow kirk. I thought that Danny was a MacGinnis, aye, but I've three healthy young male cousins who have been known to tarry in the village."

He continued to stare at her, hard, implacable.

"God damn you, David, I didn't know!" she cried.

"Then who did?" he demanded.

"I—don't know."

"Who knew you were with child?" he shouted.

"They all—all my family."

"Who came to see you in Glasgow?"

She hesitated.

"Who?" he demanded.

"Alistair was the one who came most frequently. He was the one who finally convinced me to come home. But at one time or another, all of them came to see me."

"Who else from here?"

Shawna hesitated. She shook her head, lowering it. "No one. Just my uncles and cousins."

He came walking toward her then, clutching her shoulders, drawing her against him. "At least one of them, my love," he said to her furiously, "attempted to kill me. And, if what you say is true, made incredible arrangements to steal our child—to see it raised as a poverty-stricken ragamuffin to die in the mines! And you refuse to see it."

"Let me go, David. You've taken the child—"

"Damned right!"

"I'll never forgive you for what you're doing now."

"What betrayal do I choose never to forgive you for?" he demanded. He was shaking. Shaking even as he held her, his eyes glittering a liquid green torment. The warmth suddenly surrounding her was terrifying. She wanted to fight him. She leaned against him instead. "David, for the love of God! Can you honestly believe that I'd have ever allowed Danny to be with the Andersons if I had known?" she whispered. "David, you can't begin to imagine how hurt I was! I believed that my child, our child was dead. David..."

He was angry still. She knew that he was angry. But his fingers were suddenly moving in her hair.

"Shawna..."

She was in pain, she thought. Angry, hurt. And so tense that...

She wanted him. The passion of her anger seemed to be filling her blood, her limbs, her being. She gripped her fingers into his arms, trying to shake him, trying to make him listen to her, believe her.

"You have to understand!" she whispered with vehemence.

"Shawna!" he warned, but her force against him had upset them both. They fell back upon the softness of her tower bed, and she told him, "You are insufferable!"

"Aye," he queried.

"You need to let me go!"

"Aye!" he agreed.

His mouth fused with hers. He kissed her with a wild, emotional passion. His hands were everywhere as his mouth pinned hers. She dragged her fingers through his hair, raked his shoulders. Dimly, she was aware of a rending of fabric. Her purple riding habit was coming open in tatters. The ribbons of chemise and corset were torn. His mouth was against her bare flesh, and somehow, the blaze of fire between them that so awakened her body seemed to ease her soul. The play of his mouth against her breast sent a sudden spiral of lightning shafting through her, and she gasped, suddenly still, then suddenly trembling. Again, her fingers were in his hair. Her body arched and writhed to his. She felt him freeing himself from his trousers, felt the probe of his sex, and clung to him. Wanting him. Wanting him so badly.

Such passion burned like the great fire that had rendered the stables black ash and rubble, burned with a heat that could be sustained just so long. Wild, urgent, desperate, furious, it rose like a whipping wind, a storm surge.

Then was spent.

David's body strained like a bow, climaxing within her again and again, like waves against the shore. She dug her nails into his back, arching to each great thrust, then shuddering downward as the sweetness of satiation spilled atop her.

He fell to her side.

Shawna lay spent, her sense of bewilderment with herself strong. He had taken her child. And she wanted him still. Wanted to be held by him.

What were they doing to one another?

She wanted to curl away from him then as well. She wanted to tell him that she hated him, except she knew that she didn't really hate him. She hated the fact that she could no longer deny that someone she had loved and trusted all her life wanted her dead.

"Shawna?"

"I want you to leave me alone!" she whispered.

David was quiet a moment. Then he said, "Aye," and he pushed away, adjusting his clothing. "I'll leave you be, my lady, but don't play games. You're not so furious with me as you want to be. You can't bear to see the truth, and I have forced you to do so."

"Danny!" she whispered.

He leaned over her, touching her shoulder. "Shawna, the lad is safe, and that is what is important! Now I warn you, m'lady, don't leave this room! Your kin seek to kill you, and I'm afraid that I cannot let you die."

She rose as he walked away from her. "How can you! How dare you! You tell me that my child is returned, then take him from me. How dare you do this to me, then warn me—"

"I dare what I do, my lady, because five years ago I fell into your arms—and awoke a dead man. I dare because I have discovered that in all those years, I had a child. And that child was cast to the wolves."

"Damn you, you've got to believe me—"

"Shawna!" he said softly. "It's very difficult to believe what you never tried to tell me."

"David, you can't just lock me in here. I have to know what is happening for myself!" she cried. "I have to try—"

"You will stay here. I intend to find out just who is trying to kill us both!"

He turned from her and started for the door. She raced after him. "David, you can't just leave this way—"

"Indeed, I can."

And—as David Douglas, laird of Castle Rock—he departed the room. As the door slammed, Shawna jumped, and stared at it for a long moment, shivering.

She dragged the knit bedcover from the bed and swept it around her half-clad shoulders, then hurried back to the door, throwing it open.

David was gone.

But she hadn't been left unattended. James McGregor sat whittling in a chair at the doorway.

"How..." she began.

"Lady MacGinnis," he said, offering her his strange gamin grin. "Laird Douglas is gone, but y'may rest in peace if y'so desire."

"Rest in peace...they write that on gravestones!" she told him.

He reddened. "Begging your pardon, m'lady. What I meant was that I'd guard y'with me life."

"David has gone?"

"Aye, and ye'll not stop him this night, Lady. Trust me. I know him well."

"You'll protect me—and you'll not let me leave this room as well, I imagine?"

"M'lady, you do not want to leave your room. Evil is most assuredly afoot."

Indeed, she was a prisoner. David's prisoner. She nodded to the little man, stepped back in the room, and allowed the bedcover to fall from her shoulders. She ripped away what remained of her ruined clothing. For long moments she stood, shivering. Tears dripped down her cheeks, and she allowed herself the luxury of sobbing like a child.

But the tears only shook her so long, and she realized that she was standing naked in her bedroom, shaking. She donned a nightgown and a laced and ribboned robe, then went back to the hallway where James McGregor remained.

"Come in," she told him. "Come tell me just how well you know Laird Douglas. And if you know," she whispered, "for the love of God, please tell me where he's had Danny taken."

SABRINA FELT as if she were on fire.

Life was not fair in any way, shape, or form.

She had just come from a tomb, for God's sake. She deserved some reprieve. She needed peace and quiet, healing time. She needed to elude Sloan, but now, Shawna and David—having tossed Sabrina's world into chaos— had gone to fight their own battle, and Skylar and Hawk had deserted her as well.

The others had just left. Sabrina stared at the closed door, painfully aware that Sloan was behind her.

"How can you be here?" she whispered, leaning her forehead against the closed door.

He didn't reply to the question. "Sabrina, get back into bed before you fall down, will you. Please?" he added.

She didn't move. She should have. She felt his hands upon her shoulders. His grip seemed as hard as steel. There was no way to escape it.

Just as there had been no way to escape Sloan at the inn when she had inadvertently discovered his room while trying to hide from her stepfather, just as there had been no way out of playing the role that was to doom her to him tonight. It was all laughable, really. Upon just which occasion—out of two—had they managed to bring about her condition—the first time when she'd been so afraid, realizing far too late that she should have just told him the truth?

Or the second time, the following morning, when she had awakened, seduced? In no pain whatsoever, other than that of all but dying of humiliation.

"I'm all right."

"Indeed?" he queried, his voice husky at her earlobe. "It appears that you are trying to claw your way out of this room. The door opens freely enough, but there is really nowhere for you to go."

He suddenly swept her up into his arms.

"I can walk!" she cried in alarm, meeting his fathomless, dark mahogany gaze.

"You could fall."

"I won't."

"You could hurt yourself."

"But I won't."

"You could hurt our child."

"But—" Staring into his relentless gaze, she fell silent. They had already come back to the bed, and he set her down upon it, her back against the pillows plumped up at the headboard.

"Are you so terribly dismayed?" he asked her, sitting by her side. His hand lay upon the whiteness of the sheet, seeming very darkly bronzed. She felt a flush of fever within her. His fingers were very long. His hands were rough and calloused from the days he spent on horseback riding across the plains. But she knew their touch could be oddly gentle and rough...

"Dismayed?" she repeated in an incredulous whisper.

Was she so dismayed? In the endless hours in the tomb, she had prayed to live. Because of the child.

"Sabrina, we have to discuss this situation."

"Discuss the situation? Ah!" There was a bottle of brandy on her bedside table. "Major Trelawny, shall I pour you a drink? I think that I would like one myself—"

He caught her hand when she would have reached for the brandy bottle.

"Sabrina, you've just been rescued from vicious kidnappers who left you in a tomb and intended to kill you," he said.

"All the more reason I should have a drink!" she whispered.

She tried to free her hand from his to reach for the brandy bottle.

"Sabrina."

She bit into her lower lip, staring down at the white sheets. She slowly brought her eyes to his, feeling a rush of color flood her face. She looked to the door longingly again.

"Sabrina, you can't run away. I would think you'd realize," he said with a trace of humor, "since I am here, in a Scottish castle, that there is nowhere you can go where I cannot follow."

She stared into his eyes. "I really would like a drink."

"For courage?"

"I've plenty of courage."

"Reckless courage. No drink. Sabrina, you've taken Edwina's potion of herbs and such. You don't need brandy now."

She did—desperately. But she knew she wouldn't be able to get her hands on the brandy bottle.

"Right. I need—sleep?" she said hopefully.

He smiled. She wondered how he could become so arresting with that smile when at times, he looked so very...

Savage.

"Sloan, I—" She broke off. So much for courage. She pulled her hand from his and leaped from the bed. A mistake. She had moved too quickly. She only made it as far as the foot of the bed before she began to feel terribly dizzy.

"Oh god!" she breathed.

But he was there.

And she was not able to withhold a gasp when, once more, he swept her up into his arms. "No!" she whispered fervently, but he wasn't going to let her fall. He held her, and, as he stared down into her eyes, she could feel the warmth of his breath, the strength of his arms, and the inner fire of his determination.

"Why are you trying to run away from me?" he demanded.

"Why are you here?" she cried desperately in return.

"Well, I didn't know that I'd arrive to discover that you'd been kidnapped, so I can hardly say that I rushed across a raging sea to rescue you," he murmured. "I'm here because Hawk has been my friend all my life, and because James McGregor told me the extent of David's problems here. And I'm here because—" He broke off.

"Why?" she whispered.

"It doesn't matter right now. The child matters."

Her lashes fell again. "Look, Sloan, what happened was an accident. Sloan, please..."

"Put you down? You need only ask."

She found herself seated against the pillows on the bed once again.

"Go away?" she suggested softly.

"Not on your life."

"You said that I only need ask—"

"That was the wrong question."

"Sloan! You don't have to—"

"I don't have to what?" He reached out, lifting her chin to study her eyes.

She shook her head. "You don't have to be responsible."

"How do you ask someone not to be responsible for a life?" he demanded.

"Sloan, I don't need your help—"

"I'm not offering my help."

"No? I do need a drink!" Sabrina insisted.

"No," he said firmly.

"I'll not be told what to do—"

"You need to be told what to do. You think you're a cat with nine lives, but you've used up several that I know about already."

"Damn you, Sloan, will you please leave?"

"No."

"Then truly, I need a drink. Just a small brandy. Some doctors suggest that a small amount is actually good for women—women in the family way."

She reached for the snifter. He took it smoothly from her fingers. His eyes moved over her in a way that made her entire body seem to burn again. "Not that I didn't enjoy you when you had imbibed whiskey so heavily, but this doesn't seem the time...Alas, my dear, you need to learn to be careful with liquor. Too often your goal is to drown yourself in it."

"How can you be so wretched!"

Sloan's dark eyes grew very serious. "Drinking isn't good for expecting women. I've heard it from many wisewomen."

"What women? Sioux women?"

He arched a brow. "Yes," he said simply.

She looked down quickly at her hands. They were still trembling. This was all so absurd. She and Sloan had met under such awful, hostile circumstances.

And maybe she was just a little bit afraid. Afraid of the night she had been with him, afraid of his strength, afraid of the way he'd made her feel. And truthfully, mostly, she was afraid because he might be US Cavalry, but he was also Sioux, and he was very dangerous, and what he wanted, he would take. What was right, he would demand.

She closed her eyes, casting a hand against her forehead. "I really can't talk about this right now..."

His laughter infuriated her. She sat up, staring at him. "I shall throw something at you in a minute!" she cried, aggravated.

"You really do a wonderful Southern belle, but I can't begin to imagine you with the vapors, Sabrina."

"What vapors! I was cruelly kept a prisoner in a tomb."

He sobered. “Indeed, you were. You can’t seem to stay out of trouble.”

“I certainly didn’t ask for this trouble—”

“You did, if I remember your words correctly, go wandering off into a cemetery alone in the dead of night?”

The way he put it, she felt like a fool.

“I heard a child’s voice,” she reminded him with defensive anger.

“How encouraging. You’re going to make a wonderful mother.”

She looked down at her hands again. “Sloan, I want you to realize, you are not obligated in any way,” she told him, still looking at her hands and not meeting his eyes. “I don’t blame you for anything—”

“Blame me?” he queried, a brow arched very high. “Since you didn’t speak a word of truth the night we met, you most assuredly should not.”

Sabrina gritted her teeth, fighting the rise of her temper.

“You’re not obligated to me!”

“But you are obligated to me,” he told her very softly. “I know that you need sleep, and I intend for you to have it, after you’ve listened to what I have to say. You won’t be having my child without me, despite the fact that your journey here implies that you meant to disappear.”

“That’s not true—” she gasped. Was that what he believed?

“Nor, Sabrina, will I allow you to endanger your own life in any attempts to rid yourself of an infant with Sioux blood.”

She gasped, staring at him at last with incredulous anger. “I—I never suggested such a thing, you—bastard!” she breathed.

“In the white man’s eyes, that is probably exactly what I am, no matter my grandfather’s standing in the States. No matter, Sabrina, you may marry a bastard, but you’ll not have one.”

She broke off. She was shaking, completely unnerved by not just his appearance here, but the fact that...

He knew! Oh god, he knew. And she couldn’t deny what was happening to her, the life taking root inside of her, any longer.

She probably had wished at first that she might lose the child, and she was afraid of the fact that Sloan was Sioux. She had wished that until she had so nearly died herself, and then the life inside her had become everything. Yet she remained unnerved not just by what Sloan was, but who he was, the man who he was with the power both to infuriate her...and seduce her.

"Sloan, you don't have to marry me. I—I don't want to marry you."

"You intend to hand over the child to me?"

One look in the dark mahogany of his eyes, and she knew that he was in deadly earnest.

"No! You—can't take my child."

"My child."

She moistened her lips, thinking that she might try a new tactic. "You—you don't know that. You can't possibly—"

"Indeed, I know."

The heat in his words silenced her. He turned away, walking back to the door. Leaning against it, he slid down the length of it to take a seat upon the floor. He lowered his plumed slouch hat over his eyes.

"Sloan, what are you doing?" she asked frantically. "Please go away! I—won't marry you. I won't."

He lifted the brim of his hat, watching her. "You won't marry me? Or you won't marry a savage?" he asked her quietly.

"I—" she began and broke off. For her brother-in-law was a very unusual man, and he was married to her sister. She couldn't help how she felt toward the Indians in the West. She couldn't help the fear at the pit of her stomach. Sloan was one of them. Despite his charm, there was underlying fire with him. His exceptional good looks were...

Savage good looks. Good looks that seduced any number of women. He would always have a life she could never touch. He was amused by her, entertained by her. Frequently, she angered him. And he had wanted her...

But he would never love her.

"I—can't—" she began.

"Finish what you're trying to say."

"I—can't—"

"Marry a savage," he suggested.

Her cheeks flamed.

Only the visible tick of the pulse at his throat betrayed his anger. He spoke quietly to her. "Actually, our marriage isn't the primary focus at the moment."

"Then you'll—leave?"

He smiled, a curl of amusement in his lip. "I'm taking up position to guard you should any cloaked figures come your way."

"Oh!" she gasped, and she was amazed to realize that she would sleep, and feel safe, because he would be at her door.

"And I'm sorry, Sabrina, but circumstances being what they are, you will marry a savage. Me."

"Sloan, you can't make me marry you unless I want to," she whispered somewhat desperately.

He was silent a moment, then pulled his hat lower over his face.

"It seems, then, that I will have to make you want to," he said.

And despite herself, a feeling of heat seemed to sweep through her, and though she could sleep safely...

It seemed that she lay awake for hours before she did so, she was so very aware of his being very close...

FERGUS ANDERSON, filled, as was his custom, with plenty of whiskey, snored at his wife's side when he was suddenly and rudely awakened by the sound of his flimsy door breaking in. He groaned, thinking one of the boys had got drunk and forgotten that they did not lock the door.

He sat up in his sweaty nightshirt, stroking his grizzled chin, and he shouted out, "I'll beat the tar out of the lad who did such damage. I'll beat y'to within an inch of your scurvy life, that I—will."

He faltered in his speech, for he was suddenly aware of a massive presence filling his doorway. The chill November wind was blowing through the main room of his house and straight into the bedroom where he lay.

A man walked in.

Fergus gasped. "Nay, it canna' be!" he cried.

But it was.

"Da?"

His children were awakening. Mary and Hamell crawled out of their mats in the main room. His sons Daryl and Cedric did the same.

But though they came behind the towering dark man who had burst so violently into their home, they didn't attempt to touch him.

He was dressed all in black, and he looked like the devil. He wore a sword in a scabbard at his left side. Twin pistols sat in holsters at his hip.

The devil indeed.

He was spawn up from hell.

"Get your stinking carcass out of bed, Fergus Anderson."

"No!" Fergus gasped. "David Douglas—it cannot be."

"Laird Douglas it is, you lying, scurvy rot of humanity."

Fergus didn't move fast enough. His wife jumped up and shrieked, flying across the room to stand with her back glued to the wall as David Douglas wrenched Fergus from his bed by his nightshirt, dragging him to his feet and all but strangling him now.

"Me lads—" Fergus cried, seeking help from his sons.

"For once in your rotten life, Anderson, do something decent, and don't get your boys killed."

The lads, however, didn't seem to wish to be killed in any fight for their father's life and honor. They stood still, gaping.

"By all the Saints! It is you, Laird David!" Hamell said.

"Aye," David said, turning his attention back fully to Fergus. "There's only one thing I want from you, but I swear, if I don't get it, I'll leave your entrails draped across this room."

"Aye, aye, what—"

"The boy. Where did you get the boy, Danny?"

"Why, 'twas my daughter, Gena—"

"You lie!"

The sword was out, its point at Fergus's throat.

Gena let out a cry, racing forward. "The girl from the castle brought him to us. We were told that it must appear that he was one of ours and that it would be deeply appreciated if we were to keep the secret."

"What girl from the castle?" David demanded.

"The girl—woman—who has worked for Lady MacGinnis forever. The lady's maid. She brought the child, brought him while Lady MacGinnis was still away, and it seemed all of the place was in mourning. He came with gold coins, Laird Douglas," Fergus sputtered out at last. "And when he come so, we knew that we must keep the secret, as we were told. We knew who it was who really wanted the secret kept, of course."

"Who?"

Fergus, though terrified, was honestly puzzled. He cringed, very afraid that David Douglas's sword might well rend him in two at any minute. "Why—why, Lady Shawna, of course."

STRETCHED out in the master's chamber of the castle, arms folded behind his head, Hawk watched as his wife paced back and forth before the door. Though he had eaten fairly heartily of the fine venison stew Anne-Marie had brought on a tray from the kitchen, Skylar hadn't touched their food.

He watched another few minutes, then grew impatient. "Skylar, come to bed."

She kept pacing. He might have been no more than a bee buzzing on a spring day.

"Skylar! Quit that and come to bed."

She turned to him at last, silver eyes wide, blonde hair streaming brushed and beautiful down the length of her back.

"Hawk, your brother is in grave trouble—"

"And is seeing to things in his own way. Skylar, I would do anything for David, my god, I risked your life today, which I never intended, but what lies between him and Shawna now, I cannot solve. And you should quit bringing it up. I'm incensed each time I think of you assuming that I was spilling children about the world without a care."

Skylar flushed. "I didn't really think—"

"Then you spoke with careless haste."

She arched a brow, nearly replied, then thought better of it.

"So—is it my brother's fertility we're discussing here—or your sister's?"

"Well, she is my sister. Hawk, there is such friction between them!

What I can't fathom," she said, "is how it could have possibly happened."

Hawk patted the bedsheet. "Come on over. I'll show you."

"You know what I mean."

"Neither of us knows what happened. And for tonight, Sloan has asked to speak with Sabrina himself."

"We should be demanding to know—"

"Skylar, we need to be grateful tonight that Sabrina is alive and well and with us again!"

"Oh, sweet Jesus, yes, but this on top of the other—"

"Skylar, if Sabrina claims that she carried Sloan's child, and he denied it and all responsibility, I'd have to take a shotgun to a very good friend. He has denied nothing. She has denied nothing. He has said that he will marry her. What would you have me do?"

"Nothing."

"You want Sabrina to tell you what happened. Not how it happened, of course, you do know that. But you're eaten alive with curiosity to discover when and under just what circumstances."

"Aren't you?"

"No. I'm sure you'll tell me when you find out."

Skylar cast him a murderous glare and began pacing the floor once again.

"What about that precious little child? Hawk, you've a nephew! They have a little boy, Hawk, and they didn't even know it. And now your brother..."

"My brother what?"

"Has taken the child away."

"Skylar, there is some group within Craig Rock apparently trying to kill off the Douglases—and Shawna as well. That boy is the child of David Douglas, and if David were in truth dead, he would be Laird Douglas. And if his mother were to die, he would be laird of the MacGinnis holdings as well. He is only safe away from the castle."

"But where is he?"

"James McGregor saw to it that he was taken safely south."

"How can he be certain that the child is safe?"

Hawk arched a brow. "Do you doubt me again, my love?"

Skylar flushed. "Hawk—"

"The lad was taken to McGregor's mother."

"Oh!"

"Now, come to bed. We're all going to have to be alert tomorrow, even though I will cease to play at being Laird Douglas."

Skylar came to their bed, slipping between the covers. She sighed, laying her head upon the pillow and closing her eyes.

Hawk rose on an elbow, watching her. "It's your last night to sleep with a laird," he reminded her. "My brother will take back his wretched title come tomorrow. And then again, you did ask me how Sabrina might have come about being with child."

She opened her silver eyes to his. "I know how she did it. But you may feel free to refresh my memory."

Smiling, he did so.

And later, when he lay with his arm around her, holding her against his chest and trying again in his mind to solve the strange puzzles plaguing his brother's life, she suddenly snuggled more closely against him.

"Hawk? You know, we really do know how to do it."

"It what, my love?"

"What it is my sister has been about."

"Skylar, what—"

"I believe that our Douglas heir will arrive before the end of June."

"Skylar..." he began, then jerked up, bracing his arms around her to stare into her eyes. "Our..."

"Child, Hawk, child. We're going to have one ourselves."

He smiled slowly. "You're certain."

She nodded gravely. "I didn't particularly want to say anything to anyone else here—I didn't want to encourage anyone in the belief that there would be more Douglases, since it's dangerous enough around here not being an actual target."

"My love, that makes good sense. But you can share the secret with me."

She smiled. "I've done so. Are you happy?"

"Well, other than the fact that we are surrounded by danger, my brother is in grave difficulty, and my world in America is falling apart—yes. I am blissful."

"Oh, Hawk."

"I am blissful," he said softly. "For the core of my world is you. And now, you and our babe."

When David returned to the castle, he went straight to the great hall, heedless now of who might come upon him.

David, Laird Douglas, was back. He had learned what he could in disguise and as a dead man.

And now, it was time to take his rightful place. And to deal with those who had deceived him.

Shawna...

He poured a large tumbler of whiskey from a tray on the long table, then stood before the fire.

Shawna.

He slammed a fist against the stone of the mantel, seeking to rid himself of the visions of her face that plagued him. Her eyes, blue in the extreme, her hair, silken skeins of blue-black, entangling him, when he knew far better than to seek her, then to want her. Have her.

And every time he left her, he wanted her more.

He had believed her. He had believed her! But the fear inside him allowed him to doubt her. Damn Fergus Anderson!

He trembled, thinking of the boy. He had a son. Daniel. The boy was brave, resilient, intelligent. A handsome child. With the very strange Douglas hairline...

And his mother's eyes. And hair.

He'd believed in her again tonight. Her shock at being told that Danny was hers had seemed so very real. She had passed out quite cold. She had been deadweight in his arms.

Had she deceived him again? Even now, he didn't want to believe it. But Fergus, at sword's point, had spoken desperately. Shawna's maid had brought him the child, and according to Fergus, Shawna was the one who wanted the secret kept.

He inhaled deeply. He'd certainly not take Fergus Anderson's word over Shawna's. And come the morning, he meant to have a very long talk with Mary Jane.

Yet, still, perhaps...

God, he was tired.

And he had learned through great torment that love could weaken a man and make him vulnerable.

Even if he were to trust Shawna completely, she was still dragging him down dangerously every time he tried to find the truth. She kept trying to protect the MacGinnis family. He had to be firm with Shawna, cold if need be. Her loyalty to others could be their very death now. It was her maid—who had been with her and the MacGinnis clan for years—who had brought the child to Fergus. God! Shawna gave him so little of her faith, yet...

He was in love with sky blue eyes, silken hair, and a lithe form that awakened and renewed him, with a voice that was soft and sensual, stroking him like the gentle touch of a finger, with a promise...yet he could never quite capture the truth. It evaded him like a dark, winding trail.

She hadn't told him about having the bairn. If she had done so, he could rid himself of the doubts that tormented him now.

He heard a slight sound behind him and spun around, ready to draw a sword or pistol at a second's notice.

Alistair, tall, head high, a handsome young man. He was dressed in his own tartan, a variation of the Douglas pattern and colors, since the MacGinnises of Craig Rock were considered a Douglas of Craig Rock sept.

"Alistair," he said warily.

"Would you drink with me, David?" Alistair asked.

"Aye, that I will," David agreed carefully.

Alistair came forward, pouring himself a glass full of fiery whiskey from the decanter on the table. Alistair swallowed down all the whiskey, shuddered, and set his glass back down. He looked at David.

"I need to talk to you."

"And you seek courage to do so, so it seems."

"Aye, that's true."

"Talk to me, then, Alistair."

"I should have told you the truth—that truth which I know—when I came upon you and your brother in the tunnel."

"Any truth you have to tell me now, I'll be glad to hear."

Alistair hesitated only a moment longer. "Well, I was not surprised to discover that you weren't dead."

"Why was that?"

"Because," Alistair said, and he held his gaze steady with David's, "I've known since the morning that charred corpse was discovered it was not yours, and that somewhere, you were alive."

"How could you have known that?" David demanded.

"Because I was the one who switched your body with that of the convict. I was the one who carried Shawna from the stables before the flames could consume her, and I was the one who saw to it that the convict's body was charred beyond recognition before placing it there beside her.

"And I was the one who made sure that the convict, Collum MacDonald, was buried in the crypt below, in a coffin bearing your name."

CHAPTER 22

James McGregor sipped brandy, enjoying the comfort of the Queen Anne chair before the fire, his legs stretched out on the footstool before it. The flames warmed his face, and he offered Shawna a smile that managed to make his ugly little face somehow beautiful.

But though he'd accepted her invitation for a brandy, and though he sat so comfortably in the chair, he looked at her and said, "You know, Lady MacGinnis, I cannot tell you a thing. Not a single thing. It isn't my place."

Across from him, Shawna frowned. "Not even where he has had the wee lad taken?"

James leaned forward. "I swear, he's quite safe—will that help you?"

"'It will help. But what that tyrant has asked of you is quite cruel, you know."

James smiled, swirling his brandy in his glass. "The lad is healthy, well-tended, and in fine health."

"How do you know?"

He glanced at her, startled. "Why...I was a physician, my lady. In a different life. The lad is well, and your Sabrina will be fine as well. I could have tended her tonight, but you wanted your friend here."

"It was important to me. Edwina practices witchcraft, but she is not among these awful people. I know it."

"So, it's good that she came tonight," he agreed and shrugged. "I met Laird Douglas upon a ship that was taking us both away for a lifetime of servitude. I only escaped my fate because of Laird Douglas, and therefore, though I do not consider him a tyrant, I do his bidding and gladly."

"I don't know where my child is, so his bidding is wrong," Shawna said.

James leaned toward her, swirling his brandy, enjoying the amber color. "You cannot imagine how fine it seems to sit in comfort and drink something of such quality," he told her, and smiled.

"You are paying me no heed, Mr. McGregor."

"Ah, but I am. I have been quite anxious to meet you, of course. In the very first moment, when Laird Douglas awoke to find himself called a murderer, he thought that you had been killed. And I think that he would have torn out the throats of captain, mate, and crew—before dying himself, of course—if he had not quickly realized that you were alive and well—he was the dead man."

"So, he has spoken of me."

"Indeed."

"What he has said cannot have been kind."

"We lived together, my lady, in the cruelest of conditions. In London, good Queen Victoria has created a reign of chastity and propriety, but in her search for goodness, she overlooks the horror of the tenements, of the poor—and once a man is condemned, by fair means or foul, his fate is hell on earth. You are aware, I imagine, that David was taken aboard a ship and sent to hard labor camps. I have fought rigging with him in the fiercest storms. I have broken rock at his side. I have seen him do the labor for others to keep whips of sadistic guards off their backs—in fact, my lady, it was in fighting for me that he finally won our freedom. I was very nearly killed. I don't think that David intended to kill the guard. In the fighting, the guard's neck was broken. We freed ourselves and a number of the others and escaped. I tell you this just in case you don't understand what his past five years have been.

"You must bear in mind that obviously, over such an amount of time, a man would brood. And his anger would fester hard within his soul."

"But I'm not guilty of all that he thinks," Shawna protested. "Surely, he knows that now. I don't know exactly what he's told you, but I only meant to save my cousin—"

"Ah, well, lass, the best of intentions do not always serve us well!"

Shawna pulled up her legs, resting her chin upon her knees.

She knew what had happened, aye. David didn't speak much of it. Maybe there wasn't much to tell. He had served a convict's hard time. In chains. She understood that. She thought she understood that. But she couldn't know what it had been like for him, day after day, days becoming months, months becoming years.

All of that time.

Waiting to come back.

The thought of revenge a life force like air to breathe.

She shivered. She still wanted to see Danny. To hold him. To keep him safe. To make up for all the lost years.

She couldn't begin to imagine anything as cruel as what David was doing to her now. Telling her that her son lived and then taking him away. Maybe she couldn't clearly imagine or understand all that David had been through.

But he couldn't imagine or understand what it had been like for her. Awaking to find herself alive, yet next to a corpse she believed to be the man she had loved. Then discovering that she was going to have a child. The months of living, of dreaming, of waiting, planning, not knowing what to do, knowing only that the child would be some small precious memory of him...

The hours of labor only to be given a pathetically misshapen bundle that was dead.

Danny had been special from the time she had first seen him. Oh god, if she had only realized...

What had gone on in the past?

Would it ever matter? He'd wanted the boy taken away from anyone with the name MacGinnis. What did he intend? Surely, he could not mean to keep the child from her forever.

If they were to live long enough to have a forever.

How had the Andersons ever come into possession of her son?

She had to know. She leaped up suddenly. "I—have to go out."

McGregor arched a brow to her.

"I cannot let you go anywhere."

"But I must!" she exclaimed, staring at him. It was incredible. He would stop her. Whatever it took, he would stop her.

Unless she could devise a means of escape. She had to escape this room, no matter how rude or cruel a ruse she must devise.

"Why, you ugly, wretched little bastard!" she cried to him, wincing inwardly as she did so. He had been kind to her. No matter what David had said regarding her, he had been kind to her.

But she had no choice now. She had to get out—and demand the truth from the Andersons. Somewhere, there had to be a defense for her.

"Lady MacGinnis—"

"Oh, I don't expect you to understand!" she cried to him. "But I can't bear your presence a moment longer. Keep me prisoner—but get away from me while you obey your master's bidding."

James rose with dignity and walked across the room without a word. At the doorway, he paused. "Call him what you will, my lady. I would die for David Douglas, so if you plan on getting by me, you will have to kill me."

James exited her room. Shawna stared after him. "I'm so sorry!" she whispered.

She dressed quickly.

There was one benefit now to the fact that David had been slipping into and out of her room at night at will.

She wasn't exactly sure where the secret panel was.

But it existed.

And she was going to find it.

"I'D BEEN DULY CHASTISED," Alistair said, "and I was, you may believe me or not, wretchedly sorry for what I had done. I told Father that I should go straight to you, but he was uneasy. He wasn't certain that you would take matters into your own hands without going to the law. Anyway, my father knew you would have the contracts under which I had fraudulently managed to get myself paid in either your office or the master's chambers. All he needed was time. We needed to have you diverted. And actually..."

"Aye?" David said coldly.

Alistair stared at the fire. "I don't think that Shawna wanted to deceive you. But she was readily willing to lure you from your room."

"What you're telling me so far, I've basically deduced. How did I wind up on that ship?"

Alistair exhaled. "You were supposed to do no more than pass out in the stables. That was the family plan. I was the cause of it, but I wasn't even a part of it. I had gone down to the village of Wickshire to gamble and drink—and drown my sorrows. I was a black sheep then, you know. Blacker than ebony, as you can imagine. I had tarnished the name of the clan. Anyway, a group of constables was going through the village, looking for a fellow who'd escaped his guards and run north from Glasgow. He was bound for hard labor for the murder of a young lass—well, you know the history of the man. I gambled with a few of the constables and heard the time they were having searching for the fellow—he knew the Highlands, and they did not. When I left the tavern, I was attacked in the woods just beyond Castle Rock. The fellow was tough. He put up one hell of a fight. I was very nearly killed myself, but just when he was about to slit my throat, I wrenched my dirk from the sheath at my calf and caught him almost directly in the heart with my blade. Just at this same time, I saw the stables on fire. I came riding here as fast as I could. When I went into the stables, I found Shawna and you. One of the beams had crashed down on you."

"A beam? I was knocked out by a beam?"

"Wait—a beam wielded by a cloaked figure. You see, I got Shawna out first. Then, when I went back for you, that was when I first saw them."

"Saw who?"

Alistair shook his head.

"The figures," he said. "The cloaked figures. They hadn't seen me because they were concerned with burning down the whole of the stables, creating a massive blaze of it all. There were so many of them...I hid behind a haystack, and all I heard was one of them saying that it was fine, that the Douglas must die—if he came from the fire alive, they would kill him another way. I wasn't thinking clearly. I was terrified. And I'm not sure why I was quite so terrified. I had my share of fights. I fancy that I'd meet most any man in a fair situation...but there was something so determined and evil in their intent! There were far more of them than there were of me, and there was no one else about at all as yet—not my father, my uncle, my brother, or my cousin. I didn't stay. I set you over my horse and went running back into the woods. Then I ran into the constables, and..."

He hesitated. "I didn't think that I could be hanged for killing a murderer in the woods, but the entire stables were ablaze by then, and I didn't want it to appear that I might have been involved with what had happened there, and I didn't want to admit that I'd killed a man, and quite honestly, I was certain that you would be killed if the men in the stables discovered that you were still alive. The constables were looking for a living man, and I had you. The men at the stables wanted a corpse—and I had one of those as well. I gave you over to the constables. And I put the corpse in the stables. When it was burned beyond recognition, I dragged it next to the place where I had left my cousin." He hesitated again, staring at David. "Naturally, I was afraid for my own kin as well."

"In what way?" David queried.

"My father. My brother. I was afraid they might have been among the cloaked figures, and that, if you awoke safe and well in the morning, we'd have a great deal more to pay for than my petty thievery."

David, still leaning against the mantel, stared at Alistair incredulously.

"Well, then?" he queried.

"That's—it. That's my story," Alistair said.

David shook his head. "Are your father and brother involved with the figures in the cloaks?"

A pulse ticked at Alistair's throat. "I—don't believe so."

"You don't believe so?"

"I don't know," Alistair admitted. "But I don't believe so."

David didn't move. "What about the child?" he asked.

Alistair frowned. "What child?"

"Shawna's child. My child."

Alistair's frown deepened. "The babe died in Glasgow. I hadn't imagined that...frankly, I hadn't imagined that she would even have told you about the bairn...since it never drew breath."

David stared at Alistair, wondering just what in hell to believe.

Alistair's strange confession solved one part of the mystery and perhaps the strangest part. The fact that someone had wanted him dead—and yet he had been spirited away on a convict ship—made sense at last. But Danny was his child and Shawna's, and the mystery of how he had come to live, here, beneath the shadow of the castle that should have been his inheritance, still seemed to loom before him. Old Anderson had been terrified tonight. He had spoken what he believed to be the truth. The girl from the castle had brought them the child. They had known then that they needed to keep care of the boy.

Because of the Lady Shawna.

"David—sorry, Laird Douglas, isn't it?" Alistair said a bit wryly. "I don't suppose that you can forgive me any part in all this—it was my foolishness that started it all. But I had to tell you my truth, and naturally, I hope that you don't wish to skewer me through, slice my throat, and set my head out on gate spike for all to see."

David hesitated, a half grin forming on his lips. "I'm not sure what to think. You did save my life. You took me from the fire. And you saved Shawna's life as well."

"Aye, that's true. I was a wretchedly deceptive human being, but..."

"But not a murderer?" David suggested.

"No, not a murderer," Alistair said somberly.

David continued to watch him. "Shawna's bairn did not die," he said at last. "Daniel is our child, born from that night."

"Danny!" Alistair exclaimed. Then he started laughing. "My God, and Shawna accused me time and time again of fooling with poor sweet Gena Anderson! Why, the little wench! My god, I don't—"

Seeing David's piercing stare upon him, he sobered quickly. "I'm sorry. I just, I—my god!"

"So, you're convinced that Shawna didn't know the boy was hers?"

"Quite," Alistair said, frowning then. "She was in sorry shape when she lost her babe. I thought—I was actually afraid for a time there that she would take her own life. Except that she's stronger than that, of course, but you cannot imagine how disconsolate she was, you gone, and the babe...and I didn't dare tell her the truth about you at that point. What made you think that Shawna would allow her own child to go to the Andersons?" he inquired.

His tone was such that David felt a searing of guilt within himself.

Yet, even now, did he dare trust Alistair? Alistair had told him that he had acted partly out of fear of and for his own family.

"Anderson himself," he said quietly.

"Fergus Anderson said that Shawna brought him the babe?"

"Fergus said that Shawna's maid brought the boy to the Andersons."

"Mary Jane?"

"I imagine. Has Shawna taken another woman as a personal maid?"

Alistair shook his head. "No, we visited her, and perhaps Mary Jane even came to help her now and then, but basically, she stayed alone in Glasgow. When she came home, naturally, Mary Jane was her lady's maid once again."

David pushed away from the hearth and started for the stairs.

"David?" Alistair said.

David turned back. "Let's go!"

"Where?"

"I'm not waiting for morning. We're going to find Mary Jane."

"Oh god, of course!" Alistair breathed.

David turned, ready to start up the stairway again. Alistair was at his back.

And for a moment, it seemed to David that his spine crawled.

As he hurried on up the stairs with Alistair behind him, he remained alert.

And wary.

Damned wary.

SHAWNA HAD no intention of being a fool or being taken unaware. If she ventured out, she would be in danger. If she didn't venture out, she would never find the truth that she needed.

She was far from an expert, but she did know how to shoot, and she owned a pair of pearl-handled derringers that her father had given her years ago and which she had kept in good working order for that very reason.

She was sorry that David had made such a disaster of her purple riding habit—it would have stood her well now, the color being so dark and deep to match well with the night. But digging deeply enough had brought her to a mourning gown, high-necked and prim, yet a day gown in which it was easy to ride. In her black attire she would be ready to grab her guns and ease herself into the passage in the wall—once she found the way in.

She was so involved, tapping and pushing upon stonework and carpentry, when her door suddenly burst open.

She had stood near the balcony window. She quickly eased away from it as she saw that David had returned.

Towering in his black breeches, shirt, and boots, he filled the doorway. His green gaze flickered over her, taking in the black funeral gown. His lips curled in something of a taunting smile.

"The laird is not dead—haven't you heard yet, my lady?"

"What do you want?" she demanded.

"Many, many things. But in particular, at this moment, where is your maid?"

"My maid?" she repeated, astounded. Of all the questions she had expected from David, Mary Jane's whereabouts was not among them.

"Your maid, Shawna. Mary Jane. Where is she?"

"Sleeping, I imagine!"

"She's not."

"Then I—I don't know."

He walked into the room to where she stood, obviously trying very hard not to touch her. "Have you given her time off? Perhaps she has left conveniently now with your approval."

"I don't know what you're talking about."

"Are you certain?"

"Quite."

"Perhaps you're unaware that Mary Jane gave our son to the Andersons."

Shawna gasped. "She couldn't have—"

"Oh, but she did."

"How—"

"Fergus told me so, my lady."

"I don't believe it!" Mary Jane had served her loyally as long as she could remember! "David! You're going to take the word of that wretched drunkard?"

He stared at her for a very, very long moment. "Aye," he said. "That I am."

He turned and left her. He exited the room, closing the door behind him. Stunned, Shawna stared after him. He'd gone to the Andersons. He'd taken the step she had meant to take herself. And now...

Oh god! What else had Fergus said?

She ran for her door, throwing it open.

James McGregor stood there, arms crossed over his chest.

"'Tis a lovely dress, my lady," he said politely.

"Let me by, James."

"My lady—"

"He is just walking down the stairs. I can hear him!"

McGregor hesitated just a second, then let her by him. Shawna went tearing down the stairs herself.

David had reached the great hall. He was approaching the fire. She ran to him as if flying on wings of fury, slamming her hands against his back.

He whirled around, facing her. She locked her balled fists at her sides, staring at him.

"You belong on a convict ship!" she told him, tears stinging her eyes. "Lashed and whipped and torn to shreds."

She narrowed her eyes, wild with fear and fury and desperate frustration. He didn't say a word.

He didn't seem willing to take her word—against that of Fergus Anderson.

She could prove nothing!

"Is that quite all?" he inquired icily.

"Nay, nay, it is not!" she hissed, and before any good sense, reason, or self-preservation could leap forward to stop her, she slapped him across the cheek with all her strength.

He didn't move, didn't speak.

She stood dead still in horror herself.

Then gasped out a strangled cry because he lifted her, picking her up by her waist, throwing her over his shoulder. For a moment she perched there in shock. Afraid she would burst into tears any second, she pounded his back.

"You're an idiot! You're a fool! God has simply made you pay early for being such a complete ass—"

"Stop, Shawna!"

She stopped, but only to gasp for breath.

"Fool!" she repeated, pounding his back with her clenched fist. There had to be more that she could say, but she couldn't begin to express the fear and pain and frustration welling within her. "Fool!" she repeated more desperately.

He carried her so back up both stairways to her bedroom—past McGregor without a word.

He threw her down upon the bed without a word, started out, then turned back.

He noted her gown. Really noted it.

"You planned on going out."

She stood in silence.

"You call me fool. You planned on going out, when you seem to be target practice for someone every single time you make a move?"

"I—planned nothing."

"You're lying, and you know it well. Damn you, you will not get yourself killed."

"I will not be kept prisoner while you steal my child—"

"Don't play the injured party here, Shawna. And you know damned well that I'm right to keep that child safe now! Just as I am trying to keep you alive, though God knows why, since it seems you don't care in the least about being Danny's mother or anything else for that matter since you are so determined to risk death."

"You are as susceptible to a bullet as I am!"

"But I am much better with a gun and quite lethal with a sword."

"I'm not trying to risk death—"

"Why the black gown?"

"You destroyed the other, and since the room was a bit chill, I did not feel the urge to sit about in tatters. Damn you—you ruined the riding habit I wore. It is rags."

"By God, then, this one shall become confetti!"

He came at her then with such complete menace that she shrieked, attempting to fly from the bed and find some escape—the window seemed a fair choice, compared with the deadly gaze he had cast her way.

But he caught her long before she reached the window. Caught her arm, spun her around. His fingers caught hold of the very proper collar of her high-necked gown, and he ripped. "Stop!" she hissed, struggling, scratching, clawing, desperate to be free from him.

He had never been more determined, more ruthless, more relentless. With incredible purpose, he destroyed the gown, ripping with a vengeance. Choking, gasping, struggling, striking out, Shawna struggled in vain. Soon, it lay in absolute tatters at her feet.

His hands fell away from her.

She glared at her. He was looking only into her eyes. "You'll not leave this room!" he informed her with a quiet menace that was even more frightening in a strange way than the manner in which he had destroyed her clothing.

"Oh god!" she gasped out, once again spinning to run, when she realized he meant to reach for her again. "Nay, you will not touch me, you will not!" she cried.

But he did. Picking her up, he tossed her down upon the bed.

"Go to sleep. You're not leaving this room."

"I—" she protested, starting to rise.

He leaned over her. "Go to sleep!"

She lay dead still, her heart beating a thousand rounds a second, her lungs heaving for breath. "I—"

"This once, my lady, use some common sense. Not another word. I'm not leaving this room again tonight. Neither are you."

She swallowed hard, sinking back against the pillows, watching him very warily. She slipped beneath the covers.

Freezing.

She didn't think that she'd ever been so cold in all her life.

He turned away from her. Moving about the tower room, he doused the lights.

In the darkness and orange-gold shadows, he stood before the mantel, watching the flame. Shadow and light played over his features, the striking sculpture of his cheeks and brow, the set square of his chin. The light reflected against his eyes and played strangely upon his shirt, amplifying the supple ripple of muscle beneath it.

His face gave away nothing, none of his emotions, though it seemed he searched for something in the flames, while knowing that he could not find his answers there. Shawna shivered suddenly, remembering her earlier conversation with James McGregor.

Hard labor. He'd worked at hard labor. And the scar above his eye and other minute nicks and tears upon his body gave evidence to the fights he had fought through the years. If she had but lived his life, could she better understand his inability to trust her—especially when it did appear at every turn that she might have been involved more and more deeply with the happenings here?

He left the fire at last. She braced herself to remain still as he neared the bed.

He didn't touch her.

The fierce green flicker of his eyes upon her scalded her flesh, yet it seemed as well that he had no desire to touch her whatsoever.

He did not. He turned his back on her, sitting on the opposite side of the bed. He cast off his boots. Then he lay back upon the bed, hands folded behind his head.

Shawna lay silent for several long moments.

"I know nothing about Mary Jane. Nothing!"

"Curious that she is involved. And she is gone."

"If she is missing," Shawna insisted, "we should be searching for her!"

"She is missing by choice," he said flatly.

"How do you know that?"

"Her clothing is gone."

"She might have been forced from the castle, and her things might have been taken—"

"Shawna, stop."

She should have stopped, just as he suggested. But she couldn't.

She wrenched his pillow from beneath him, slamming it over his chest.

He moved like lightening. She was suddenly crushed against him. His arms were like the steel bars of a dungeon. She lay with her back flush against the cotton of his shirt and the denim of his breeches, her wrists held in a punishing grasp before her.

She could scarcely breathe.

And she scarcely dared to do so.

"I cannot believe this!" she whispered, tears stinging her eyes. Mary Jane! Who had pretended to be her friend as well as her servant! "Maybe it's not true. How could you so easily believe Fergus?"

"Because he told the truth."

"How can you believe that?"

"Because my sword was at his throat." He sighed with vast impatience. "Shawna! You cannot go on refusing to see that people close to you harmed you and mean you greater harm!"

She held very still for several moments, then said, "You're—crushing me."

His hold upon her eased. In fact, he moved away from her.

And she lay in bed with him, naked with him, and he did not touch her.

Their backs were now to one another.

And she wondered if it hadn't been much better when their anger ignited passion. The desperation of their sex seemed preferable to the chill that seemed to assail her from all over.

"David?'

"Damn it, Shawna, why didn't you tell me about having a child?"

She swallowed, moistening her lips. "You were too embittered over your own past for me to mention that losing a child had not been pleasant."

He didn't reply. He lay silent for so long that she thought he slept. Then she nearly jumped as he lashed out with, "Damn, my lady, do stop shaking!"

He suddenly pulled her hard against him.

She should protest. She should freeze for all eternity before allowing his touch in any way.

But she had been so cold. And he was warm. And though there was no tenderness in his touch, tonight, especially tonight, she did not want the cold.

"We should be looking for Mary Jane," she said.

He was silent for a moment.

"We will find Mary Jane tomorrow," he said.

"How can you be so certain?"

"Because it will be the Night of the Moon Maiden. I implore you, get some rest. And if you don't choose to, my god, allow me my sleep."

Shawna fell silent again. It plagued her now that she was lying in the arms of the man who had given her back her child—then stolen him from her again within minutes.

"David?"

"Oh god, what, Shawna?"

"When can I see Danny?"

He let out a very long sigh and rose then on an elbow at her side. He touched her lips with a finger and smiled slightly, and she realized that he wanted to trust her completely, believe in her completely...

She kept him from doing so. By refusing to believe that someone very close to her had nearly cost them both their lives.

"Soon," he promised her.

"How soon?"

"Hmm..." he mused. "Well, there's something I shall have you do tomorrow. A promise you will make to me at the Night of Moon Maiden. And when that's done, you will have Danny back."

"What promise?"

"You'll find out tomorrow."

"David—"

"Alistair pulled us both from the flames," he told her quietly then.

"What?"

"Alistair—"

"How can you know?" she inquired desperately. "Alistair wasn't even part of the plan, he—"

"He talked to me, Shawna. He told me."

"Oh god! Then he sold you to that convict ship! David, I know he meant you no harm! You can't—"

"I've no intention of slaying Alistair," David said with amusement. "He told me—and I believe—that he was convinced that I would be murdered if I didn't disappear. He'd been attacked by the escaped convict in the woods and killed the man in the fight. Alistair is no saint, but he is working hard at redeeming himself. Or so I believe. We'll find out tomorrow night, won't we?"

"The Night of the Moon Maiden," she said.

"And I beg you, go to sleep!"

She lay down, her head upon his chest. He had just said that he would bring Danny back to her, when she fulfilled a promise to him.

She would never sleep. Never.

For hours, she did remain awake. She didn't know if David slept or not.

Finally, however, she must have fallen asleep. She awoke to a scream so loud and high-pitched that it seemed to penetrate every nook and cranny of the huge castle.

"Sweet Jesus!" David gasped, bounding up.

He was still clad in his breeches, shirt, and stockings. He had only to pull on his boots. Shawna, leaping up as well, had a greater difficulty, seeking a gown and robe and slippers.

David was dressed and exiting the room. She eschewed the slippers and went tearing after him.

They raced down the stairs together, pausing at the landing to the great hall. As they stood there, Sloan Trelawny came silently behind them. Hawk, Skylar, and Sabrina nearly plowed into him.

Anne-Marie, her hand upon her heart, supported by Myer, stood before Gawain, Alistair, and Alaric at the hearth.

Anne-Marie spoke rapidly, gasping all the while, the words gushing from her lips. "I started bringing out the kegs with one of the lads...oh god! I say...by the Good Laird Jesus, I've never seen such a thing, never, in my days, so horrible...horrible...Oh god...it's him...his corpse...the poor, dead corpse of David Douglas. Black and charred, laid out, laid out, oh god, it was there when I brought the basket, I didn't realize... right on the Druid Stone, it was there—the corpse of David Douglas, laid out just like an ancient sacrifice."

"The corpse was on the Druid Stone?" Gawain repeated in astonishment. "Now, Anne-Marie, perhaps it was just some dirt, a prank by the village boys—"

"She's probably telling the truth, Father," Alistair said. "The corpse was stolen. Hawk and I found the coffin empty yesterday."

"You what?" Gawain inquired. "You found that the crypt had been broken into—and no one mentioned it to me?"

"Hawk is a Douglas, Father," Alistair reminded him.

"Aye, and we'll not have a Douglas grave dishonored, not while we are caretakers here!" Gawain said indignantly. "We'll have Master David reinterred immediately—"

"That won't be necessary," David interrupted, walking across the landing to address Gawain.

Gawain, startled, looked over to David, and watched as he approached him.

"As I live and breathe!" Gawain exclaimed. "David Douglas."

"Aye. And not dead yet," David said.

"David!" Alaric said, gaping as he stared at the man who should have been a ghost.

"Aye, 'tis me. Back. We should, however, see to it that the corpse is removed from the Druid Stone. I'd not have the Night of the Moon Maiden ruined for everyone."

A peculiar noise sounded.

It was a stuttering.

It was Anne-Marie.

David gently turned to her.

"'Tis most distressing that you should have found such a gruesome thing, Anne-Marie, and I'm sorry," David said.

Anne-Marie, her eyes very wide, let out another scream.

This one was rather a tiny shriek.

Then she passed out cold, falling flat with such deadweight against her husband that she brought Myer crashing down to the floor beneath her.

Alistair and Alaric bent quickly to help the struggling Myer.

Gawain stared at David, blue eyes cold and fierce upon him.

"By God, indeed, it is you. David Douglas. Laird Douglas. Sir, you must take care—a ghost is far more frightening than a corpse." His eyes remained hard upon David. What emotions he felt, he kept to himself. "David! Returned from the dead. Well. Welcome home, Laird Douglas. Welcome home."

CHAPTER 23

Shawna had no concept of how David planned to explain his sudden appearance. The entire household—Gawain, Lowell, Alaric, Aidan, Alistair, Hawk, Skylar, Sabrina, Sloan, James McGregor, Shawna, and David—sat down to breakfast together. And as they did so, David's story was a casual one.

"I imagine I must have stumbled into the woods from the stables on the night of the fire. Perhaps I was caught by some falling wood, I don't know. In truth, I know very little of that night. But I was no longer David Douglas."

"Amnesia?" Lowell inquired, curious and doubtful. "You had no idea of who you were, or what you were about?"

"Aye, I suppose it was amnesia. I was in the stables when the fire began—Shawna and I had gone there for business, as surely you are all aware," he said, his tone very dry, "but I know nothing more. I found myself on a ship with no real identity, drifting around the world."

"Whatever happened? How did you get to come back here?" Aidan demanded. There was excitement in his tone. He appeared to think that whatever had befallen David was surely the greatest adventure of a lifetime.

David shrugged, buttering one of Anne-Marie's finest scones and adding her homemade jam. “It had to do with another hit on the head —and I knew it was time to come back.”

It was amazing, Shawna thought. He was basically telling the truth.

“So, you came back home—with your friends?” Gawain asked suspiciously, nodding politely to James and Sloan.

“My good friends,” David replied simply.

“Friends from America,” Alaric commented, “and all arriving when your brother just happened to be here.”

“Alaric, life can be amazing.”

Alaric nodded. “Imagine, Father,” he said to Gawain, “we’d thought to see if Hawk might be interested in selling the Douglas holdings—seeing as how he spent most of his time in the States,” he explained to David.

“The property is certainly not for sale,” David said quietly.

Gawain cast his son Alaric an aggrieved glance, then turned his attention to David once again. “You look hale and hearty, lad. And it’s good to see you alive.”

“Thank you, MacGinnis.”

“Naturally, it’s a pity your father never knew,” Lowell told him.

“Indeed, it is that,” David said.

“Hawk, this rather changes your fortunes, doesn’t it? You came here Laird Douglas. You go home without a title,” Alaric said.

“I go home without a title, but with a brother returned from the dead. A fair trade, I think.”

“It’s quite amazing,” Gawain said, staring at David, shaking his head. “You were dead—you’ve suddenly reappeared. Just as your ‘corpse’ winds up on the Druid Stone.”

“Just after Sabrina was kidnapped,” Alaric murmured.

Shawna tensed, hoping no one else had heard what seemed like a tone of insinuation coming from her cousin. But David was no longer dead—and he was returned as laird of his castle. And there would be no insinuations cast in his direction to which he would not cast out a challenge.

“Do you imply something, Alaric?”

Alaric threw up his hands. “I imply nothing. I’m simply and

completely—stunned. And unnerved. Very strange events have been occurring in these parts lately."

"Like as not, it's the witches, and we should be doing something about the lot of them," Lowell said.

Shawna sighed. "Uncle Lowell, the Craig Rock witches are intelligent, gentle people who do nothing but practice freedom of religion. Edwina is the most kindly person—"

"That she is!" Gawain said angrily.

"Sabrina was found in the McCloud vault," Alaric said.

"We looked there because I was certain that anyone who was up to evil would try to blame what had happened on the witches if Sabrina was found."

"Perhaps," Aidan said slowly, looking around the table at all of them, "it's exactly the opposite. Perhaps Sabrina was taken by Edwina's people and kept prisoner in the McCloud vault so we'd think that she had to be innocent!"

"What?" Hawk said.

Aidan shrugged. "I realize you've just arrived, after a very long absence. And you know that the people can easily be swayed. But the mines themselves seem to come alive at times with tapping—some of the men claim they hear singing. A lot of people believe that the witches are up to evil deeds."

"Ah, 'tis the wind in the rock!" Lowell said impatiently.

"Then Sabrina was taken," Alaric said.

"And found in the graveyard last night," Gawain reminded them all.

"And that strange Brother Damian has been about," Aidan commented. Smiling, he shivered. "He rather unnerved me." He hesitated. "Perhaps he has something to do with it."

"Brother, my arse! He's probably one with the witches!" Lowell commented.

"Uncle Lowell!" Shawna protested.

Lowell snorted his impatience.

"Then," Aidan continued, "there's also the nasty matter of a rotted corpse placed on the Druid Stone."

"Ah, surely that was some prank by the village lads," Alistair murmured. "The sacrifice on the stone, and the like of it."

"It was hardly a prank," Hawk said. He cast a barely perceptible glance his brother's way, and Shawna found herself irritated to see how easily they communicated. They were manipulating the conversation, throwing out information now to see what might fall back their way. "Hardly a prank. Unless the village lads find it humorous to dress up in dark cloaks and shoot at people."

"Shoot at people!" Gawain exploded. "Nothing of this was said to me last night."

"Nothing of anything has been said to me," Lowell added, shaking his head sorrowfully.

"Would you mind explaining just what did happen when Sabrina was found?" Gawain demanded.

Hawk shrugged. "Shawna thought that we had searched everywhere—except for the vaults in the cemetery. The McCloud vault seemed an obvious place to Shawna to start, as she has said. But when we went to search for Sabrina, the place suddenly seemed alive with black-cloaked and cowled figures—firing at us."

"But no one was hit?" Aidan ascertained gravely. He stared at Shawna. "No one was hit? No one was hurt?"

"No," Shawna said.

"They were firing at my wife, Shawna, Sloan, and me. I hardly find that a prank."

"Creatures in cloaks and cowls!" Lowell muttered. He eyed his brother sternly. "Witches!"

"How convenient that Mr. McGregor and Mr. Trelawny and that Brother Damian were so close," Gawain said, ignoring his brother. He frowned then. "Laird Douglas—where were you?"

"Quite close behind them, actually," David said. He was giving a lot of explanations, Shawna thought, but apparently, an explanation for Brother Damian was not forthcoming.

Alistair, of course, knew that David himself dressed up as Brother Damian.

Could it be true that he had kept secrets as completely as she?

"Well, we've sent for the constable again," Gawain said, sounding tired. Then he smiled suddenly. "David, Laird Douglas! The fine thing about your being alive is that the responsibility for our troubles now lies with you!"

"Aye, that it does," David agreed.

"We need to announce to the village that David is alive and returned and will rule over the festivities for the Night of the Moon Maiden," Alaric said.

"I think that the villagers will know this morning that I have returned," David said.

"How is that?" Gawain asked.

"I paid a visit to Fergus Anderson last night."

"Well, Laird Douglas, that does not particularly compliment us as a family," Aidan said. "Why would you spend time with that ratty old drunkard—before letting us know that you were alive?"

David bit into a piece of bread before arching a brow and replying.

"Owing to a most curious dilemma—I found a lad within the castle bearing a most curious Douglas trait. And doing a wee bit of sleuthing I discovered that until recently, the old drunkard had been rearing that child. The child bears a striking resemblance to the MacGinnis family as well, but that Douglas trait is quite undeniable. The lad was, therefore, my son."

"Oh god!"

Anne-Marie, who had just been coming in with another tray, nearly dropped it, starting to fall.

Sloan was quick enough to catch her before she could hit the floor. And strong enough to keep her from doing so.

Alistair rescued the tray.

"David, y'are Laird Douglas, and that's a fact, but I've worked long and hard here, and I would like to know what game y'are playing, man." Gawain demanded angrily, standing and throwing his napkin down upon the table.

"No games," David said flatly, looking around the group, staring hard into each set of MacGinnis eyes. "You all knew that Shawna was going to have a child. And since none of us is pretending not to know Shawna's role in luring me from the castle the night of the fire, any imbecile would have known whose child she awaited."

Shawna felt her flesh burn. Her cheeks were afire.

"Well, of course, we knew," Aidan exploded. "But—"

"The wee bairn died!" Gawain grated out. "What cruel joke do you play upon us all?"

"The babe did not die," David said firmly.

"My brother does not play jokes," Hawk said warningly.

"The game, it seems, was played upon Shawna. But it is no matter now. I've taken the child."

"The Anderson child? Danny?" Lowell demanded, seemingly confused now by the turn of events.

"That would be the one," David said.

"Must we do this, here now—" Shawna gasped out.

"Aye, that we must!" David declared angrily.

"Have you gone daft?" Lowell demanded. "How could that lad be Shawna's—"

"At least I'll no longer be accused of the boy's begetting!" Aidan said.

"Nor I," Alaric mused.

"Amen," Alistair murmured.

"Y've determined that the lad is yours, when he's near on five years old, but now y'are back to your homeland, you sent the lad away?" Gawain demanded.

"For the time being."

Gawain stared at Shawna. "How did the boy come to be with the Andersons? Why did you tell us you had lost the child?"

Sweet Jesus, she could not believe it! Her own family was staring at her as if she might have done such a thing out of shame of bearing an illegitimate child.

"Because it was my belief the babe had died. I don't know what happened then, and I don't know how the boy came to be with the Andersons—from Glasgow here, alive and well. Fergus told David, however, that Mary Jane gave the lad over to the Andersons."

"Get her down here! Demand an explanation!" Gawain said.

"That can't be done," David told him.

"Why not?"

"Mary Jane has disappeared," David informed him.

"Disappeared?" Lowell said, outraged.

"The Saints preserve us, what in God's name is going on here?" Gawain bellowed.

"All mysteries here will be solved," David said firmly. "I will find out what is going on here. And anyone who has anything to tell me is certainly more than welcome to do so!" He stood and surveyed the faces around the table once again. "My son will come back to the castle —in time. For today it seems we have the business of the Moon Maiden at hand. And by tonight, by God, I will have explanations!"

Shawna discovered herself a prisoner in her bedroom once again for most of the day.

In the early afternoon, however—with James McGregor still dogging her heels—she went to the old turret room and dug through trunks with Sabrina and Skylar, costuming them as ladies from days gone by.

Skylar, sleek and beautiful with her long golden hair in a royal blue Napoleonic gown, swirled around. "This is lovely. Thank you so much."

"All of these things are quite beautiful," Sabrina said, sitting in a pile of silks and velvets from the same era. "I believe I will wear Empire fashion as well. What do most of the people wear?"

"Anything and everything," Shawna said. "Some of the lasses try to outdo one another dressing up as fairytale princesses. Some opt to dress as animals, some wear bizarre forest-type creations, even coming as fall foliage. It's usually great fun."

"Dressing up is fun," Skylar murmured, looking at Shawna, "except, of course, it means that you must be ever more careful. You'll not know whom to trust."

"I don't know whom to trust," Shawna said quietly, "when those about me are not wearing masks." She shook off the dread that seemed to be settling over her. "What is Hawk wearing?" she asked Skylar, trying to take her mind off the whirlwind of worry and fear and emotion that plagued it.

"He's undecided."

"Oh?"

"A Douglas tartan—or Sioux feathers."

"Oh!" Shawna laughed. More hesitantly, she asked Sabrina, "And... er...Major Trelawny?"

"Oh, there's no question," Sabrina muttered, straightening one of the garments on her lap. "He'll be in feathers." She must have realized the bitter sound of her tone. She smiled at Shawna. "What will you wear?"

Shawna offered her a wry smile in turn. "Again, there's no question. I will come in my MacGinnis colors."

"You'll wear Douglas," came a harsh, masculine voice.

Shawna jumped up. David was standing in the doorway, watching them. He came into the room, picking up an old dress, running his fingers over the fabric.

"I will wear MacGinnis colors," she said firmly.

"Lady MacGinnis, you've lived in the Douglas stronghold nearly five years now, taken charge of Douglas affairs. Tonight, you'll wear Douglas colors." He didn't wait for her agreement, perhaps knowing full well that she wouldn't give it. He would brook no argument. His mood was totally ruthless, as if he had completely lost patience. Yet the more tension that seemed to fill him, the less Shawna thought they might have any rational discussion on any matter.

He was cold to her and distant today. But he had told her that if she fulfilled a promise, she'd have Danny back after the Night of the Moon Maiden.

"The constable is downstairs," David continued. "He wants a word with us. Shawna, you'll need to explain how you knew where to look for Sabrina." He turned on his heels, leaving them. The women looked at one another, scrambled from their tasks, and hurried down the stairs.

Two hours later, the constable left. Shawna and David remained in the great hall alone.

Shawna was aggravated. David shrugged.

"What were you expecting?" he asked of her.

"He is the constable. I was expecting him to be more helpful."

"I've warned you before that we have to solve this ourselves. The constable thinks that we are harboring a community of witches, and they are all protecting one another. He's glad I'm alive—I thought that was quite decent of him. And he seemed heartily glad that Sabrina is found, alive and well."

"He hasn't taken much of this seriously at all."

David watched her carefully, replying slowly to her. "To the constable, my lady, it appears that I was merely knocked on the head and consequently lost from my home by regrettable accident—an untruth I am quite willing to encourage at this time."

"Why? Why don't you shout the truth, and force the constable to—"

"Someone tried to kill me, but my life was saved. The truth could endanger Alistair. Then, as to the sounds the miners hear, the constable is a steady, intelligent fellow. He doesn't believe in ghosts. Like your great-uncle, he believes that the wind whistles through the rocks. In his mind, Sabrina was surely taken as a lark. And the figures in the cemetery, shooting at us—" He paused and shrugged. "Well, to the constable, that just proves that allowing women to practice Wicca here is dangerous. Scotland was right to burn witches all those years."

Shawna groaned with impatience. "We've both known Edwina since we were children. She learned her herbal potions from her mother, and she and the other women practice earth healing, and a gentle way—"

"I'm telling you what the constable sees. He's quite impatient. We should turn in the witches for whatever crimes we can find that we can accuse them of legally."

"What about the body on the Druid Stone?"

"Definitely the prank of errant young men. Their fathers should discover them and see that they are all switched."

She stared at him, her blue gaze sharp, hard, and cold. "And what about Danny?"

He crossed his arms over his chest, returning her stare. "Ah, Danny. That's the most obvious—to the constable, of course. You were Lady MacGinnis. You couldn't bear the stigma of an illegitimate birth, and of course, since it appeared the father was quite dead, there was no way you would marry. You wouldn't do anything truly terrible to your own child—such as doing away with it. Bringing the babe back to Craig Rock to be raised locally—and then adopted into the castle—seemed a well-thought-out plan."

Shawna felt her anger seep into her. Dear God, it sounded as if that was exactly what David thought himself.

"David, you are being wretched."

"I'm telling you how the constable sees events, my lady," he informed her.

"And how Fergus Anderson sees them. Fergus has assuredly told you the truth."

"Mary Jane most definitely gave him the child," David said. He sounded tired then. Bone weary.

"And Mary Jane is gone."

"With all of her belongings."

"I still can't believe—"

He gripped her wrists. "Believe, Shawna. Believe because all these things have happened. Believe, because you lost more than four years of your child's life, just as I believe, because I lost nearly five years of my own."

He released her and turned away.

"It's growing dark. It's time to prepare for tonight."

"I'm wearing MacGinnis colors."

"Tonight, you'll wear Douglas."

"I'll not—"

"You will."

His eyes narrowed. "MacGinnis colors would make wonderful confetti."

"Since the world is aware that you are alive now, Laird Douglas, if you threaten me now, my cousins will be obliged to tear you apart!"

"Do you think so?" he queried. He crossed his arms over his chest. "Shall we risk battle within the house? Both Hawk and Sloan are experts with numerous weapons."

"You are a madman!" she assured him.

"A madman with a purpose." He reached out a hand to her. "You'll wear my colors, and you'll stay at my side. Throughout the night. Douglas plaid, my lady. Now. And if you think that you're going to stand against me, I promise I will make confetti of your family colors, I do so swear it."

"You truly are a tyrant."

"Remember that. Test me tonight, and you will spend the evening tied to the Druid Stone," he said, his eyes hard on hers as he held her wrist.

"You are so certain that something is going to happen tonight!" Shawna cried out. "What if—what if the night is uneventful, what if we learn nothing? Do we just go on, forever suspicious of one another?"

"Something will happen tonight."

"But if it doesn't...David, I want Danny back!" Shawna cried.

He swung on her. Suddenly he had her shoulders in a rugged grip as he stared down at her. "Don't you understand? I took him away because it's not safe for him here, Shawna! Damn it, it isn't safe."

"I want—my child!" she whispered.

"I have told you, after tonight, everything will be different."

She pulled away from his grasp.

"Excuse me, Laird Douglas, the night does draw near!"

Shawna escaped his touch. She hurried up the stairs, aware that Sloan lounged at the landing to the second floor—and James McGregor kept watch when she entered her tower room. She stared at him balefully, then slammed her way into the bedroom.

She came back out. "James, I'm quite sorry about last night."

"I know, m'lady. You wanted to wander on your own."

She frowned. "Aye. I am sorry."

"Apology accepted. And now, m'lady, don't be trying to shake me this evening, eh?"

"I shall be an angel. I promise."

She hurried back into her room. She had beautiful long woolen skirts in her own colors—and in the Douglas tartan. She hesitated, then swore, and dressed in a white laced blouse, the Douglas skirt, and her black vest and jacket.

Dusk was falling.

Already, out by the Druid Stones, bonfires had been lit. She heard the sounds of pipe-playing, laughter. She turned to exit the room and went still when she saw that David had come for her.

David, Laird Douglas.

He was kilted in his full dress tartan, black velvet jacket over his white cotton shirt, Douglas crest upon his chest.

"It's time," he told her.

She took his hand. His touch upon her still felt cold and hard.

"I should be wearing my own colors," she told him, as they went down the stairs.

"Soon you'll understand why you're clad this way," he told her.

"My mode of dress is going to help us find those who attempted to kill you?"

"Your mode of dress will serve as a warning that we stand together," he said.

The castle's great hall was already empty. Myer stood outside the main doors with horses for them. Though the Druid Stones were an easy walk from the castle, as laird of Castle Rock, David needed to arrive on horseback.

"Are you ready, my lady?" he inquired.

"For the night that we will meet our devils?" she inquired.

"Aye."

"How can you be so sure that someone will act?" she demanded.

"Because," he said, "we are a unique people. The Highlanders of Craig Rock. Traditions are ancient—and the moon is very full."

"We are Highlanders—not madmen!"

David stared up at the full moon, his features as striking as those of any ancient warrior.

"Aye, 'tis sure, we're not all madmen. But the moon has a powerful call, and the lore or legend is just as great. If we do have madmen among us, they will act. The moon will be as strong upon the blood in their veins as it is upon the tides in the sea. Shall we ride?"

Shawna stared at him, then nudged her horse.

And began to canter toward the Druid Stones.

Standing starkly white beneath the bright eerie light of the full moon.

CHAPTER 24

Violins and pipes played, men and women danced, ate, laughed, and played as they arrived at the Druid Stones. Tables were laden with wine and ale. Giant pits had been dug for meat to be roasted.

David overtook Shawna, riding a half-length ahead of her. A massive cheer went up as he appeared and as he greeted those who rushed forward to welcome him and wish him well. He dismounted from his horse and turned to help Shawna down from hers. Old friends embraced him. Village lasses blushed and curtsied, too, some brushing happy kisses upon his cheeks before hurrying away. Shawna realized that she had forgotten just how charming he could be, how gracious, and how the people of Craig Rock had loved him.

When they came to the flat stone where Anne-Marie had stumbled upon the corpse that morning, there was nothing but a lovely purple cloth and lanterns upon it. Excitement nearly crackled in the air. The arrival of the laird meant that the feast had truly begun.

David strode for the flat stone, keeping Shawna's hand locked in his own. The Reverend Massey waited there, ready to offer David a crown of flowers amid a great deal of cheering. He accepted his crown and turned and crowned Shawna with a second such tiara that had been made for the laird's chosen lady.

Shawna found her pleasure in the evening suddenly real. This was her home. She was a Highlander of Craig Rock through and through, and she loved the tradition of the night, the laughter, the dancing, the contests. She smiled at friends and saw Edwina, dressed beautifully as a sprite.

"To the people of Craig Rock!" David shouted, and the music stilled along with the dancing and shouting. The merrymakers, clad in all manner of costume from the beautiful to the bizarre—ladies, pirates, knights, animals, and mythical creatures—stopped to pay him heed. The night suddenly became so silent it was uncanny.

"My thanks that you are so gracious to welcome me back after such an awkward absence. I cannot tell you how pleased I am to be back with you, how grateful I am to be greeted warmly by so many dear old friends. And now, as laird of the festivities, I say—eat, drink, be merry!"

A cheer rose high on the air. Shawna, still close by David's side, noted that Hawk, Sloan, James, and her cousin Alistair seemed to be posted at the four corners of the Stones. As usual, she thought, the men had made plans.

About which they had neglected to inform the women.

"But there's more!" David continued. "As laird of Castle Rock, I am naturally free to choose my lady for the Night of the Moon Maiden. I've taken my lady, but I would do more. I invite you to join with me in a special feast this night. My wedding feast. I would like to take this occasion to invite you one and all to witness the joining of the Douglases and MacGinnises."

Stunned, Shawna stared at him. What was he doing? She felt a sudden, terrible pain in her heart. Marriage could not be part of a plan to catch criminals.

"I will not marry you!" she whispered. She did not need to speak so low. The cheers all around them were deafening. She tried to smile for the people who looked upon her with such affection, while desperately wondering what to do in the situation.

Mark Menzies was cheering delightedly. Edwina had clapped her hands to her cheeks with pleasure.

Anne-Marie was happily sobbing.

Even her own kin. She saw Gawain watching her, and she realized that Gawain had known what David intended. Oddly enough, it seemed, David had properly asked Gawain, as the oldest male MacGinnis, for her hand.

She tried to tug free from him.

She had loved him all her life. She had wanted to be Lady Douglas, his wife.

But not now, not this way. Not when he was so cold and distant, and it seemed that he didn't love her. She didn't want him to marry her just to protect her, or even for Danny's sake.

"I can't marry you—like this!"

"You must marry me. It's the promise I want from you," he told her.

It was blackmail!

He offered the crowd his most charming smile. "Gossip abounds in small villages, eh, my friends, and I'm quite certain that you've heard tales of a lad belonging to the laird of Castle Rock and the lady of Castle MacGinnis. Well, gossip stands true. The boy is ours. Heir to all that is mine. In honor of our son, we are delighted to make our relationship legal and proper."

Gasps sounded. So many of them, it was almost as if the crowd had inhaled and exhaled simultaneously.

Then there was silence.

The whispers began then along with the cheering and calls.

Whispers.

Speculation.

Some of the people had indeed surely heard that Danny was the lady's child. Some had doubted it. Some had believed.

Surely, all had gossiped.

And now David had made certain that everyone knew.

"Reverend Massey?" David said.

The reverend, looking completely pleased, smiled benignly at the two of them.

"Laird Douglas, m'lady, if you will?"

He stood before them and began to pray.

"I cannot do this!" Shawna whispered. "David!"

David ignored her.

Before Shawna managed to tell the reverend that though she loved David, she couldn't marry a man who completely mistrusted her, she found David dragging her down. She was on her knees, head bowed in prayer.

And she was praying, she discovered.

God, help me! What is right here, what do I do here? I cannot do this, or can I? I would do anything for Danny, but is it right to marry...

She glanced at David. His head was bowed. Dark and handsome, he appeared the sincere bridegroom, seeking the blessing of his maker as he entered into the holy sacrament of marriage.

Except that his eyes were actually open. And he was listening not just to the reverend, but to every word and whisper going on around them.

Yet he responded. When the Reverend Massey spoke to him, he responded. She watched him, amazed that he could appear to be so rapt in the proceedings when his attention was in fact for all those around him.

"Shawna?"

Her head jerked around as she looked at the Reverend Massey, curious as to what he wanted. "Aye?"

The Reverend Massey smiled, reaching out to her. "M'laird, m'lady, I now pronounce you man and wife."

Flowers flew, bagpipes screeched. She found herself drawn back to her feet and into David's arms.

He kissed her dutifully.

"Laird Douglas! Ye've been gone too long for so chaste a touch!" came a cry.

"Come now!" laughed someone. "Ye know what ye're about, ye've a child already, Laird Douglas."

Delighted laughter arose.

David responded, lifting a hand to those who tormented him. He swept Shawna nearly off her feet. His kiss was deep, passionate, blazing. So intimate those who had teased him cried out with hearty approval.

He released her, his eyes just above hers. And with her whole heart, she wondered what lay within them.

"Why did you do this?" she demanded. She ached to hear him say what he had told her before—he loved her. He had loved her forever.

"So that my son's mother need no longer be a MacGinnis," he replied, eyes dark upon hers.

"So you will bring Danny back?"

His grip upon her tightened. "Aye, as I'm able."

"You promised!" she reminded him, fighting his hold.

He arched a brow. "You've just promised to love, honor, and obey, my love."

"Indeed, well, you remember this! MacGinnis was my father's name. I will remain a MacGinnis until the day I die," she informed him.

"And I'm trying terribly hard to see that the day you die remains far in the future."

"This is a travesty."

"Nay, lady, this ends the travesty," he told her, and lifting her off her feet, he carried her to the throne chairs that had been prepared for them for the evening. "Friends, I give you Lady Douglas!" he announced.

The cheering began again.

And the windup of pipes screeched.

Well-wishers came forward.

"Ah, cousin!" she heard, and turned to see that Alistair was at her side. He was decked in his MacGinnis colors, not costumed. She was glad. She would easily recognize him.

"It's come about proper at last, eh?" He smiled. "I'm happy for you, cousin. Truly, I am."

"Thank you. Alistair?"

"Aye?"

"Why has he done this?"

Alistair's smile faded. "He is very afraid for you, I think. He wants everyone to know, it seems, that he is alive and well and healthy as an ox. His brother is alive and well—and healthy as an ox. And if something were to befall them both, he has left a child. Legal issue."

"This has to end!" she whispered. "Alistair, I can stand this no longer. Who would have done such a thing to me as to hire a midwife to switch my babe with a dead one? Who would have done such things to David? Who would try to kill him—"

She broke off.

Old Ioin Menzies had come up to her. He opened his arms, kissed both her cheeks.

"It's the witches, mind ye!" he said, and walked away.

A rise of shouting announced the caber throw. She suddenly felt David's fingers curl around her hand. She glanced at him sharply.

"My love, I am required to take part."

She followed at his side as they joined the men taking part. "Stay here with Skylar and Sabrina," David commanded, stepping onto the field.

The onlookers gathered around as the men took their turns throwing the massive log as far as they could.

"What is this?" Sabrina asked.

"The caber throw."

"They can't possibly throw that—log too far!"

"Aye, they do well enough!" Shawna assured her.

Despite the chill, many men stripped off their shirts and jackets, coming upon the field kilted only.

Shawna clapped as Gawain and Lowell took their places. Despite their ages, her great-uncles cut well-muscled and arresting figures—and their throws were among the best. A cry went up for the MacGinnises, and Shawna joined in with it.

The show was a good one, and it seemed that every man and woman of Craig Rock gathered around, close, shoving a bit to get closer still, yet laughing as they stepped upon one another, apologizing in good humor.

Especially those who were already drunk.

Shawna's cousins all joined in and showed admirably.

David took his turn last. Spitting upon his hands, rubbing them against his tartan, picking up his caber.

His throw was excellent, outdistancing Aidan's by at least a foot.

Despite herself, she felt a swell of pride as she watched David. His smile was so quick, so deep. His stance was so proud, his physique so well honed. She was, in truth, so much in love with him.

And she was his wife.

And no matter what the circumstances, it suddenly seemed quite wonderful.

The other contenders left the field of the caber throw. David stood alone in it, the undisputed winner.

As a roar of approval went up and the Douglas name was chanted, Hawk walked out to his brother's side. In a charming play between them, they challenged one another, and a contest was on between the two. Shawna found herself forgetting her bitterness and her fears and watching the play with as much laughter as anyone within the crowd.

"Shawna?"

She swung around. Alistair stood behind her. "Shawna, I need you to come with me."

"Why?"

"You've moved too far from the others in our party. We need to go back around the stones."

She saw what he was saying. The crowd had followed the action. There were still people near her, but she didn't recognize any of them. The crowd had parted her from Sabrina and Skylar.

She spun around, very uneasy. She didn't know a single soul close by. Those near her wore giant headdresses made of feathers, leaves, and fur. She stood among strangers, in the shadow of some of the larger stones.

"Shawna, come on!"

He was tugging upon her arm.

He was trying to lead her around the stones—into black shadows, in order to reach the crowd once again.

He stared at her with his blue MacGinnis eyes, and she thought of the times that she had trusted him.

And she was suddenly afraid. She jerked free from his hold upon her.

"I see Edwina. I'm going to get her," Shawna cried out.

In a panic, she whirled to escape him, pushing through the revelers. She hurried and looked back.

She didn't see Alistair. She leaned against a stone, closing her eyes, breathing hard.

How stupid. She shouldn't have run this way from Alistair. He had gone toward the bulk of the crowd.

She nearly shrieked aloud as she felt a tug on her shoulder. Her eyes flew open. A tall figure with a staff, dressed as Father Time, stood before her.

"Shawna, lass, are you alright?"

For a moment, her heart beat too quickly. Then she realized that Father Time was her great-uncle Lowell, re-costumed after his turn at the caber throw.

"I'm fine, Uncle."

He smiled broadly, then slipped an arm around her waist and kissed her cheek.

"Are ye happy, child?" he demanded.

"Aye, Uncle," she said carefully.

"It's good, when you think of the child."

"Aye," she said. His words had sounded somehow strange. As if he might have known something about Danny.

"Uncle Lowell, do you know something?"

"Eh? My ears are getting bad, lass. What did you say?"

"I said—"

"Too much noise here! Bleedin' pipes! And what a thing for a Scotsman to say, eh?"

"I said—"

"Come this way so I can hear what y'are a-sayin'."

He winced against the noise and motioned to her to follow him.

She did so.

They moved deeper into the field of the Druid Stones, returning to stand where her wedding had so recently taken place. Where the altar stone lay. Vacant now.

"Ah, Shawna, lass, it has become a strange world, eh?"

"Uncle Lowell, please, is there something you know about Danny—" she queried, breaking off abruptly.

She thought that she had seen a shadow. A cloaked figure, slipping from one Druid Stone to another.

"What's that?" she murmured.

He pulled her close against him. "What?" he demanded.

"A figure—one of the cloaked figures."

"Witches!" he whispered feverishly.

Shawna frowned. Looking across the slope of the hill where the play with the caber throw continued, she could clearly see Edwina standing with Sabrina and the women in her group of Wiccan healers.

"We need to get back, Uncle Lowell," she said uneasily. "But if you know something, if you can tell me something—"

"I can tell you something."

Shawna stared as the figure she had seen suddenly came around the stone nearest them. The figure allowed her cowl to fall back.

It was Mary Jane.

Shawna stared at her. "And I refused to believe that you might be guilty! You weren't even with me in Glasgow! How did you get your hands on my child?" Shawna demanded. "Uncle Lowell, get someone, we need help, we can't let her go."

"She won't be going anyplace," Lowell said strangely.

"Uncle—"

"Do her!" Mary Jane insisted. "Do her on the stone now."

"Nay, I cannot. She's Lady MacGinnis, there's a ceremony that must be—"

"The Druid Stone requires the sacrifice! And we might have had an innocent maid, if it hadn't been for this special MacGinnis blood of yours. And we might have had the child, with blood tenfold stronger!"

"Cease your chatter, woman!" Lowell demanded.

Shawna stared from Mary Jane to Lowell, incredulous. Then she realized that she must escape. Help was so close! Just beyond a few stones.

He had told her to stay near. At his side throughout the night. He had known that something would happen. The full moon would draw the blood of the lunatics just as it would the water of the loch. She had come to meet the devil—

Her own great-uncle. Her kin. Her blood.

Mary Jane lunged for her, sensing that she was ready to flee.

Shawna didn't hesitate. She wound her fingers into a fist and struck Mary Jane furiously in the jaw.

Mary Jane gasped in pain and fury. Shawna turned to run.

But Lowell was there.

She never got a chance to scream. A strange-smelling handkerchief was clapped over her face.

She started to struggle.

But she couldn't fight the drug.

She was out in seconds. Deadweight in her uncle's arms. Deadweight as he threw her down upon the Druid Stone. He quickly slipped his dirk from the sheath at his calf.

But a sudden rise of laughter stopped him.

He turned back to see that the caber throw had broken up. The revelers were returning here.

He wouldn't have the proper time.

Mary Jane came up behind. "She all but broke my jaw!" she cried softly. "Damn you, slit her throat! Have done with it."

"Nay, I need time."

"Time! You old fool! They are watching us! We'll lose her again! Just kill her."

"She's the MacGinnis," Lowell said.

"It doesn't matter! We'll sacrifice one of our own for the ceremony if need be. The Druid Stone demands a sacrifice, you've said so yourself. Kill her now!"

"Woman, we'll not!"

"Old fool, we will. The stone must have blood."

She wanted blood?

Lowell lifted his dirk, then plunged it downward.

Blood spilled over the altar stone.

The revelers were returning. Laughter and shouts were growing louder.

Lowell lifted his burden, disappeared behind a standing stone, and then began to run.

CHAPTER 25

"Where is she?" David demanded, returning to the spot not ten feet behind him where Shawna had stood just seconds before.

His brother and Sloan were quickly at his side.

"She's gone!" Sabrina cried.

"She can't be," Skylar protested.

"My God! She couldn't have gone far," Hawk said.

Alistair came rushing up. "David! I lost her. I was trying to get her to come back by Skylar and Sabrina. I've searched—"

"There!" Skylar shrieked suddenly. "By the altar!"

David looked. His heart grew heavy. Felt as if it was pierced by a thousand knives.

Something lay upon the altar.

David rushed through the crowd.

A body, covered in a dark cloak, dripping blood, lay upon the stone.

"No, God, no!"

David's voice was a fierce, sharp cry that rang to Heaven. He reached the altar, ripping away the cloak, then staring down with both amazement and relief.

It was not Shawna.

Mary Jane, her maid, lay upon the altar, the blood from the gash at her throat spilling upon the stone.

"It's not Shawna," he said. "Oh god, it's not Shawna! We've got to find her!" he cried. "We've got to find her quickly."

"It's the witches!" Old Ioin called out.

"Nay, it's not!" Edwina shouted furiously. "Yet it is someone who would have us take the blame for what is evil!" She spun to David. "Indeed, we must find her, quickly."

But the crowd had grown ugly. Bizarrely costumed men and women, masked and plumed, began to toss her between them.

"Witches! Witches! Witches!" began a chant.

David leaped upon the foot of the altar stone, firing his gun.

The chant was silenced.

Edwina was released.

"My wife has been taken. I will find her. And if I discover that any one of you knows what has happened here and does not aid me now, I will kill you with my bare hands. I promise."

"There!" Alistair shouted suddenly. "There, David, look! See! There are a number of them, hooded, cloaked figures, all but hidden in the darkness. Heading for the cliffs."

Indeed, there were a number of cloaked figures, huddled together, nothing more than a mass of shadow in the night, hurrying toward the cliffs by the loch.

And suddenly disappearing.

For a moment, he stared in disbelief. He had lived in the damned cliffs. He had made a lair in a cavern. He had explored the mines and the tunnels...

And he had apparently missed an entry.

Hawk suddenly rode up, leading his brother's horse. "David!"

David leaped atop his mount.

"Take me!" Edwina cried out to him.

He hesitated. Alistair and Sloan were alongside him now, on horseback also.

He reached down, catching Edwina's arm, bringing her up upon his horse. They began to race like the night wind for the cliffs.

Shawna awoke with a terrible pain searing her head. She remembered the scent, the feel, of the drug from before. She tried to lie very still, praying for the pain in her head to subside.

She started to shift position, then realized that she was freezing and very uncomfortable.

She was lying on stone.

The Druid Stone?

That couldn't be. The Druid Stone would be surrounded by people...

She tried to move.

She was tied fast to the stone.

She opened her eyes slowly and barely managed to contain the gasp that came to her lips.

She was in a small cavern in the caves, naked, and tied to a flat stone surface.

That much she realized fairly quickly, yet it all made little sense.

Then she saw more of her surroundings.

Before her, hung upon the cavern wall and looming hugely there, was a terrifying figure. The horns of a goat rested upon a cruelly leering mask of a man. The body of the figure had been made half-man, half-beast, with giant genitalia hanging in the appropriate place on the creature. Candles were lit all about the abomination.

She was not alone with it.

Cloaked figures were gathered around it, swaying back and forth.

She began to hear a low hum, a very strange chanting.

Oh god, oh god, where was she? The cliffs, aye, yes, where in the cliffs? How long had she been here?

She wanted to scream.

Scream and scream...

A shadow loomed over her. She closed her eyes to slits, desperate to see what was going on, terrified to do so.

Lowell.

Her great-uncle Lowell had brought her here.

Brought her here—with these creatures who had their own ceremony on the Night of the Moon Maiden. These were not the witches of Craig Rock because the witches were gentle, kind, honest women practicing an ancient belief and healing of the body and the soul.

This was something...different.

This was what the Church had feared for years, this was what had brought about the deaths of thousands of innocent people. This was some kind of hellish practice of the devil, and her great-uncle, it seemed, was high priest.

And now he was watching her.

He wanted her dead. Nay, worse. He apparently intended to kill her himself. Why? Oh god, why? It seemed that this was to be a very special ceremony. The blood of the MacGinnis female who had laid claim as head of the family was about to be shed in some hellish attempt at...

What?

To honor a prince of darkness?

Something was...touching her.

Damp, hot...slowing moving against her body.

Her eyes flew open. She could no longer keep them closed, for something was indeed brushing against her. She screamed, writhing, as she realized that a cloaked and cowled figure was painting her naked body with something red...

"Shush, shush!" She heard her great-uncle say, moving his fingers with a gentle touch upon her temple.

"You didn't drug her properly!" someone said. Did she recognize the voice? Aye, it was that of Fergus Anderson!

"Aye, she should be awake at the moment of the knife," someone else said.

"This isn't proper!"

Then she heard Lowell's voice, again.

Lowell. Her own great-uncle. Her own flesh and blood.

"I say what is and isn't here!" Lowell suddenly thundered, spinning around to accost anyone who would question his authority.

He turned back to Shawna. He smiled at her.

"Be still, child. You have to die."

"Why?" she demanded.

"It wasna right, lass, you being head of the family."

So that was it. His hatred had been brewing since her father's death.

Was it possible to reason with him?

"I'm not really head of the family now. I've married David Douglas."

"Aye, the ruddy bastard should have been dead. And instead, you've bred among them now, and the lad's been stolen away."

"You tried to kill David all those years ago."

"Aye, that I did. He was meant to die in the fire. Gawain was all consumed with worry about his lad Alistair, and it gave me great opportunity. You should have died in the fire as well."

"Why do I need to die?"

"You've no right to live, lass. But then..." He shrugged. "When one does murder in my way, lass, with my followers about it, it must be done the right way." He bent to whisper to her. "Ritual sacrifice, you know! A man can lose his followers if he is not careful."

"Don't talk to her, man!" Fergus cried.

"What does it matter?" Lowell asked.

"You promised a true celebration of the rites tonight, debauchery, and the like. If you'd take your time killing her, give her over to me and me boys—"

"Ach, shut up, Anderson!"

"'Tis not as if the lass is pure in any way—"

"Ye'll not touch her!" Lowell said. "She's here to die tonight."

"What will it matter if she dies a wee bit more tarnished?" Daryl Anderson cried out.

Shawna found herself closing her eyes, wincing, trying to close out other sounds in the room. There were men and women there. Those who were not in on the argument where she lay were over by the creature. Kissing it grotesquely, then turning to one another. She could hear grunts, laughter, and shrieks as the men and women groped one another in wild abandon.

How many? she wondered.

Perhaps ten or so...

Her great-uncle Lowell. Who else? Oh god, who else of her own kin would do this to her?

"We've little time, MacGinnis!" Fergus Anderson said angrily.

"We've all the time we need. They've not found this cavern in five years. They'll not find it now."

"I still say we get her fine ladyship then, before the knife plunges into her throat!" Fergus grumbled.

"Get away from her!" Lowell demanded. With a sweep of his cloak, he turned back to Shawna, blocking the others from her sight.

Lowell smiled, his face an obscure mask, and absurdly caricaturing her own. His eyes were so familiar. "Ah, Shawna! As to David Douglas. The ruddy bastard didn't die. No matter. He will."

"He will die...how many do you need to kill? Uncle Lowell, what are you doing, why are you doing this? I know that you're not practicing Wicca—"

He laughed. "The creatures of health and goodness and all the fine sciences of the earth? Nay, lass, I am not one of them."

"Then—"

He brought his lips close to her ear to whisper. "I've laughed so hard! For folks do not see the difference between those gentle practitioners of the earth and those of us who have seen and recognized the true power."

"True power?"

"Satan!" he thundered to her, looking around. Then he whispered once again. "Lucifer, the great laird of Darkness. Ah, but I find myself so well amused that we may play, rob, debauch, kill...and what strange things happen are laid at the doorstep of the Wiccans! Yet, of course, my means are twofold. I am high priest—and one by one, lass, I will manage to do away with all those who stand in my way."

"Uncle Lowell, you can't want to kill me."

"Ah, Shawna, there, lass, you are sorely mistaken. I always intended you for this night, but I wanted the other girl as well, for her innocence. Still, the laird of Darkness seeks a sacrifice such as yourself, a lusty young maid, as proved, and alas, the world is fully aware of your sins of the flesh—but you are beautiful and young. Your death will bring about power you cannot begin to imagine!"

"Uncle Lowell, you don't believe that for a moment."

"You are going to die."

"You're mad."

She, too, was mad, Shawna thought, feeling hysteria growing within her. What if a miracle occurred, and she convinced her uncle he shouldn't kill her? She was in a cave in the earth, surrounded by his followers. She didn't know how long she had been here, and she was terrified that she couldn't be helped. The caverns in the cliffs were endless. David's selkie's lair had been one such as this. These wretches had not stumbled upon David's lair.

And he had not stumbled upon theirs.

"Of course, I'd wanted the child as well for this night in particular," Lowell said.

Her heart quickened. "What child?"

"Now, Shawna, y'are no fool. Your child. Laird Douglas's bastard. A child is the best sacrifice to be had. A child of five, precisely, but when you brought the boy to the castle, I knew I dared wait no longer to take him. You should have all died. Eventually, I would have got to the others. Gawain might have expired of old age. Alistair has always been reckless. Alaric might have been a bit harder to kill. Ah, Shawna! Why do you think I let you live after the fire? To bear the child, so that I could nurture the boy to the right age, lass. I let you live all the time after because I wanted you to die with your son, the last of David Douglas and Shawna MacGinnis, their offspring, all together. The land should have been mine. All of it. Douglases never cared for it right. And as for MacGinnis property, I was the youngest son, but the strongest. When you create a cult such as this one, you accrue yourself followers who will do any deed for you. And eventually, you gain all that you want. But as for tonight, well, it will not be all I wanted. Douglas stole the boy from me. And as I said, an innocent maid is quite good, but you cost me young Sabrina as well. Yet what you have cost me can be repaid with your blood, my dear. I'd hoped to slay you at the stone—that would have been fitting. But you are the MacGinnis. And you must be slain properly. There was no time at the stone. But here...well, here, the ceremony will be far more complete."

She realized that Lowell had been a part of her life, and a part of the lives of every member of her family. They had loved him. He was one of them. But he'd meant to kill them all and claim both MacGinnis and Douglas land for his own. "They will be looking for me right now!"

"Perhaps. They'll never find you."

"They will know that you are a murderer, Uncle Lowell. They will all be searching for me, and you will not be among them."

"They will not notice that I am not running here and there with the others," he said.

"You cannot keep this up and survive!" she claimed.

His old face crinkled deeply for a moment. "You do not know the power of Satan, child. But soon, 'tis his bride in blood you will be this night!"

He swung around, his cloak swirling with him. He lifted his hand, and suddenly, the chanting stopped.

Even those who had argued with him began to sway. Now, they all waited.

With breathless anticipation.

The markings of Satan had been painted on her naked flesh in blood.

She was ready.

Lowell drew a wicked handled blade high to ripple silver in the glow of a half dozen torches and the myriad candles.

"Laird of Darkness, accept this sacrifice!" Lowell suddenly cried out.

Chanting began again. And Lowell started to walk around the altar where she lay.

Her mouth went dry with terror.

He was going to kill her.

Any moment now, any second, he would slay her. He had no more interest in hearing anything else that she might have to say, and he had nothing more to say to her.

She was surrounded by faceless, cloaked figures, and she was going to die.

Just when she had discovered that she'd had a child. Seized and stolen from her by these wretched, bloodthirsty lunatics. A child they might well have taken tonight for his innocent blood. A child Lowell had kept alive just for the right time to kill...

She had a child. A beautiful boy.

And she had...

A husband.

Oh god, David. He could be arrogant and aggravating, he could infuriate her to the greatest passion...

Trying to keep her alive.

She couldn't die. She couldn't die. She couldn't allow them to kill her!

And she would not do so.

She strained frantically against the ties that bound her, and she began to scream...

James McGregor had led a group of men into the mines. Hawk and Sloan had gone through the water to the lair David had discovered.

David chose the cliff tops himself, Alistair MacGinnis at his side, Edwina right behind him, while others followed closely in his wake.

"It's got to be something of an accessible entrance!" David called. "They entered so quickly."

"Sweet Jesus, I work at the wretched mines near every day of my life. The corridors, tunnels, crannies—are endless."

"It doesn't matter. We must find the entrance."

"We'll never find it!" Alistair claimed.

"We will find it! Be still!" Edwina commanded.

It couldn't be! David determined, *God, it couldn't be!* He knew where they had taken her, he was convinced he even knew who was involved in taking her—and he wasn't going to be able to find her.

He crawled desperately over rock, hesitated.

"Shawna!" he shouted.

Hopelessness filled him, pain, agony. He fought it. He had to find her. He'd search and search and search until he found her.

And pray that he did not find her too late.

He saw a crack in the stone and hurried toward it. It was a crack, and nothing more. In fury and frustration, he stood tall upon the rock, shouting her name again. "Shawna! Shawna! Shawna, for the love of mercy..."

His cry ricocheted and echoed off the rock. It rose into the night like the howl of a wolf beneath the full moon.

And amazingly, it was answered. Answered by the shriek that came to him faintly...

From the rock directly beneath him.

"Here!" he shouted suddenly. "She's right here! Goddamn, somewhere right here!"

"There, David, there's a shelf, an overlay!"

Edwina was right. There was an entrance right by them. It was there, the opening, behind an overlay of sheer rock. His sword in his hand, he tore through the opening.

Shawna twisted, shrieked, screamed, writhed, managing to break one of the ties that bound her ankles.

The creatures fell around her. Desperately, she kicked and struggled. Grunts, groans, and swearing sounded as she made contact with a number of jaws.

Her feet were held down.

Hands fell upon her naked shoulders.

She looked up.

Lowell stood there. Chanting. Chanting...faster, faster...faster.

The cloaked figures were dancing. Kissing the genitalia of their Goat God.

Lowell's voice rose to a terrible pitch. His arm jerked in an upward motion.

His dagger gleamed.

She shrieked and twisted wildly. The blade was falling.

Yet, just then, a body came dropping out of the darkness of the night, landing hard upon the cavern floor, then pitching atop hers, covering it, completely.

David. He lay atop her, guarding her flesh from the knife if it should fall.

With his own.

But he didn't intend to die. He had swiftly come upon her reaching out. His hands gripped Lowell's arm before it could descend to the stone with the blade.

The two men were locked in combat.

David went rolling from her, drawing Lowell down with him to fall on the other side of the altar.

Shawna screamed in panic once again. Another face appeared atop hers.

Alistair.

His eyes stared into hers.

Hers into his.

Alistair, another of her kin.

Oh god.

He had a knife.

She started to scream again.

"Hold still, Shawna, I've got to free you!"

She froze. He was working at her bonds.

"Still!" Alistair urged.

She held still. His blade slit the ropes that had held her. She was numb as he drew her body from the table, but he urged her to move, to hurry.

"Alistair—"

"Shawna, there's a lot of people here, move!"

She did so. He urged her back against a wall, and she saw that David had risen from the floor. His arm was soaked in blood, whose, she did not know. He backed away from the cloaked figures, motioning her and Alistair to keep behind him.

"Rush him!" someone cried.

And two brave souls did so, but David drew his sword and swung, and both of the cloaked figures were taken down in the one movement.

"Bloody bastards, can no one do anything right?" one of the figures shouted. Casting off his cloak, he came forward.

It was Fergus Anderson.

With a roar, he went flying toward David, his knife raised.

David sidestepped him.

Shawna turned away as David's sword plunged into the man's back.

The mood within the cavern suddenly changed.

"Escape!" a voice whispered, and madness ensued, all of the figures trying to reach the narrow entryway.

Then suddenly backing into the cavern once again.

Hawk Douglas and Sloan Trelawny had come. A figure moved against Sloan.

"Sloan!" Hawk warned.

Sloan drew a pistol with terrifying speed. One bullet was fired. The figure dropped.

No one moved.

Then one of the figures started to weep.

It was Gena Anderson, Shawna realized.

"We'll leave the rest of them to the law," David said quietly. "Come on, let's get out of here," he said.

He wrapped his black velvet jacket around Shawna. She tried to walk and stumbled. He picked her up and carried her from the cavern. She closed her eyes as they walked. She never wanted to see the Goat God, or her fallen uncle, again.

They came out into the chill of night. Clinging to David, Shawna looked up to the sky.

The moon was full and shimmering.

Naturally. It was the Night of the Moon Maiden. But it didn't matter.

Nothing mattered.

She was in David's arms. And she was his wife.

And the way that he was looking at her now...

She knew that he loved her.

That was all that she really knew, but it was enough. The huge orb of the moon began to fade. Darkness encroached, but she wasn't afraid.

She was in his arms.

She was safe.

And she was loved.

She'd been drugged more heavily than she had realized when lying in terror upon the stone altar in the cavern.

Hours later, she awoke in bed.

Her bed, in the master's chambers. She woke in a bit of a panic, trying to assure herself that she was no longer painted in blood.

She was not. She lay cleanly—and primly—in a white, high-necked, laced, and detailed nightgown.

And she was not alone.

David was by her side. David, Laird Douglas, still kilted, but cleaned, the blood gone from his arm and a white bandage around it.

His eyes were very green and dark and grave as they surveyed her, his hair fell just a bit mussed and rakish over his forehead. His features were at ease, very handsome, his mouth not at all pursed, his smile a full and sensual one as she opened her eyes and looked at him.

"Laird Douglas!" she said softly.

"Lady Douglas," he returned, and brushed her lips with a kiss.

Not a cold kiss.

Nor a mockingly passionate kiss.

A warm kiss. Tender. A leisurely kiss. Gentle. Given with lips that trembled ever so slightly.

Ohg od, it was so...provocative.

"David..." she murmured.

"Aye?"

Then she suddenly remembered that there remained things she didn't understand.

"David," she said anxiously, "truly, Alistair was no part of it—"

"Shawna, Aidan wasn't even a part of it. Sometime, long ago, your great-uncle's frustration at his place in the inheritance line sent him upon a very strange path. I'm not sure he was so much a Satanist himself as he was a man determined to seize some kind of power." David shrugged, then looked at her.

"My own great-uncle!" she breathed.

"But it's over, m'lady." He was silent a minute. "Shawna, I wanted revenge against the MacGinnises so badly, yet I hope you can believe that I'm truly sorry. I've spent some time with Aidan tonight—he is truly a wreck. Gawain is as astonished as anyone can be. The Andersons were in on Lowell's cult—as was your maid, Mary Jane. She—" He hesitated. "She's dead."

Shawna shivered. "She kept insisting that the Druid Stone needed a sacrifice. He wanted to kill me more slowly. He must have decided that if she wanted the stone to have a sacrifice, he'd let it happen."

"Maybe."

"What of Lowell?"

"I had to kill him, Shawna."

She sat up, throwing her arms around him tightly. "David, he meant to kill me, my own kin—"

"Shawna, Shawna, you can't think of it that way. He was sick, Shawna. Twisted. Your kin do love you. Gawain, Aidan, Alaric... Alistair."

She lay against his chest, shivering. It had all been so horrible, so far-reaching, and in the end, so completely terrifying.

Lowell had planned and plotted it all for truly evil designs.

Lowell was dead.

But David was alive.

"David?"

"Aye?"

"Are we really married?"

He drew back from her, offering her a strange half smile. "You do know the Reverend Massey?"

"Aye."

"And are we in the Douglas master's chambers, my love?"

"We are."

He hesitated just a second. She drew back. His green eyes were sparkling. His lashes lowered. He appeared to be having just a bit of trouble speaking.

"Do you wish to be married?"

She should tell him that in no way did she wish to be at the whim of such a tyrant for the rest of her life.

But she could not.

She knew that his anger and fear had been for them both. He had suffered very deeply. Trust had been difficult to come by. But he had believed in her, even if he hadn't always realized it. He had married her, and no matter what the circumstances, he would not have done so had he not wanted to do so.

She smiled.

"It's taken you that long to decide?"

"Umm..."

"Do you—forgive me?" he queried.

"For?"

"Well, for not being quite as open and honest as I might have been about my plans."

"I shall have to think about it. You kept a great deal from me."

"I did cover hill and vale to save your life."

"Indeed."

"So—do you forgive me?"

She smiled, trembling, leaning against the strong expanse of his chest once again.

"I am Lady Douglas?"

"You are. So do you forgive me?"

"Aye. Do you forgive me for seducing you that night five years ago?"

"You're admitting to seducing me."

"Perhaps."

"Then..."

"Aye. I admit to it."

He shrugged, leaning against her, his hands upon the delicate lace of her exceedingly prim gown.

"David?"

"Can you still say that you love me, Shawna?" he queried strangely.

Once again, she drew back, stilling his hand. "Aye. I love you, David Douglas. Man, beast, selkie, ghost—laird of all he surveys. I've loved you so long, David!"

"Aye, my love, through time, through death, we've sought one another so desperately. And now..."

"Now?"

"Now, we've a child. And one another. And life." He swept her into his arms, and his kiss was both slow and deep, filled with warmth, with passion. Tender, exciting.

"Aye, life..." he whispered against her lips.

Tears nearly flooded her eyes. Yet then he whispered, "It remains our wedding night, my lady. I will assuredly forgive you for luring me from domain and seducing me into sweet oblivion if only..."

"Aye?"

"If only you do so again. Well, my lady?"

Demurely, she cast her arms around him, replying with a gravity belied by the shimmer in her eyes. "Indeed, Laird Douglas. It seems only fair."

She kissed him...

And kissed him...

Yet suddenly, he drew back. “This is lovely, but...I did make a promise to you.”

“You did?”

“I said I was going to ask a promise of you in exchange for...wait just one moment.”

He left her. Shawna stared after him in disbelief as he opened the door and left the room. But a second later he returned to the room, Danny in his arms.

She let out a glad cry and leaped up to rush to her husband and her son.

And high over the castle, the full moon began to pale and the golden glow of a new day fell upon Craig Rock. A new day...

A new beginning.

A LOOK AT BOOK THREE

NO OTHER LOVE

***Dances with Wolves* meets *Outlander* in this breathtaking tale of enemies to lovers, forced marriage, and a love that defies two worlds in the untamed Dakota Territory.**

One desperate mistake in a frontier town changes everything. Fleeing her stepfather's murderous wrath, Sabrina Connor hides in a stranger's room—and pretends to be exactly what he thinks she is. But Sloan Trelawny, a half-Sioux scout with honor carved into his bones, doesn't make deals. When he discovers the truth and the consequences of their night together, he demands marriage. No negotiations. No escape.

Bound by vows neither wanted, Sabrina and Sloan return from Scotland to a Dakota Territory on the brink of war. Caught between Custer's cavalry and Sitting Bull's warriors, their forced marriage becomes a battleground of its own. She fears the world he comes from—a world she doesn't understand. He refuses to apologize for who he is. And neither can deny the fierce attraction that ignited between them, or the child that will tie them together forever.

But when violence erupts at Little Bighorn, and Sabrina is taken captive, Sloan must fight for the wife who never wanted him... and prove that some bonds are worth dying for.

One woman. One warrior. And a love forged in fire that neither war nor pride can destroy.

AVAILABLE MAY 2026

ABOUT THE AUTHOR

New York Times and *USA Today* bestselling author, Heather Graham, majored in theater arts at the University of South Florida. After a stint of several years in dinner theater, backup vocals, and bartending, she stayed home after the birth of her third child and began to write. Her first book was with Dell, and since then, she has written over two hundred novels and novellas including category, suspense, historical romance, vampire fiction, time travel, occult, sci-fi, young adult, and Christmas family fare.

She is pleased to have been published in approximately twenty-five languages. She has written over 200 novels and has 60 million books in print. Heather has been honored with awards from booksellers and writers' organizations for excellence in her work, and she is the proud to be a recipient of the Silver Bullet from Thriller Writers and was awarded the prestigious Thriller Master Award in 2016. She is also a recipient of the Lifetime Achievement Award from RWA. Heather has had books selected for the Doubleday Book Club and the Literary Guild, and has been quoted, interviewed, or featured in such publications as The Nation, Redbook, Mystery Book Club, People and USA Today and appeared on many newscasts including Today, Entertainment Tonight and local television.

Heather loves travel and anything that has to do with the water, and is a certified scuba diver. She also loves ballroom dancing. Each year she hosts a Vampire Ball and Dinner theater raising money for the Pediatric Aids Society and in 2006 she hosted the first Writers for New Orleans Workshop to benefit the stricken Gulf Region. She is also the founder of "The Slush Pile Players," presenting something that's "almost like entertainment" for various conferences and benefits. Married since high school graduation and the mother of five, her greatest love in life remains her family, but she also believes her career has been an incredible gift, and she is grateful every day to be doing something that she loves so very much for a living.

www.ingramcontent.com/pod-product-compliance
Lightning Source LLC
LaVergne TN
LVHW040214110826
845146LV00005B/1287

* 9 7 9 8 8 9 5 6 7 7 0 5 6 *